What happens when one good-and-angry man fights back is murder—and then some. . . .

ROADWORK

Bart Dawes is standing in the way of progress. A new highway extension is being built right over the laundry plant where he works—and right over his home. The house he has lived in for twenty years . . . where he has made love with his wife . . . played with his son. . . . But before the city paves over that part of Dawes' life, he's got one more party to throw—and it'll be a blast. . . .

WORKS BY STEPHEN KING

NOVELS

Carrie
'Salem's Lot
The Shining
The Stand
The Dead Zone
Firestarter
Cujo
THE DARK TOWER I:
The Gunslinger
Christine
Pet Sematary
Cycle of the Werewolf
The Talisman
(with Peter Straub)
It
The Eyes of the Dragon
Misery
The Tommyknockers
THE DARK TOWER II:
*The Drawing
of the Three*
THE DARK TOWER III:
The Waste Lands

The Dark Half
Needful Things
Gerald's Game
Dolores Claiborne
Insomnia
Rose Madder
Desperation
The Green Mile
THE DARK TOWER IV:
Wizard and Glass
Bag of Bones
The Girl Who Loved Tom
Gordon
Dreamcatcher
Black House
(with Peter Straub)
From a Buick 8
THE DARK TOWER V:
Wolves of the Calla
THE DARK TOWER VI:
Song of Susannah
THE DARK TOWER VII:
The Dark Tower

AS RICHARD BACHMAN

Rage
The Long Walk
Roadwork
The Running Man
Thinner
The Regulators

COLLECTIONS

Night Shift
Different Seasons
Skeleton Crew
Four Past Midnight
Nightmares and
Dreamscapes
Hearts in Atlantis
Everything's Eventual

NONFICTION

Danse Macabre
On Writing

SCREENPLAYS

Creepshow
Cat's Eye
Silver Bullet
Maximum Overdrive
Pet Sematary
Golden Years
Sleepwalkers
The Stand
The Shining
Rose Red
Storm of the Century

ROADWORK

Stephen King

writing as Richard Bachman

With an Introduction by the author,
"The Importance of Being Bachman"

A SIGNET BOOK

SIGNET
Published by New American Library, a division of
Penguin Group (USA) Inc., 375 Hudson Street, New York, New York 10014, USA
Penguin Group (Canada), 10 Alcorn Avenue, Toronto,
Ontario M4V 3B2, Canada (a division of Pearson Penguin Canada Inc.)
Penguin Books Ltd., 80 Strand, London WC2R 0RL, England
Penguin Ireland, 25 St. Stephen's Green, Dublin 2, Ireland (a division of Penguin
Books Ltd.)
Penguin Group (Australia), 250 Camberwell Road, Camberwell, Victoria 3124,
Australia (a division of Pearson Australia Group Pty. Ltd.)
Penguin Books India Pvt. Ltd., 11 Community Centre, Panchsheel Park, New Delhi -
110 017, India
Penguin Group (NZ), Cnr Airborne and Rosedale Roads, Albany, Auckland 1310,
New Zealand (a division of Pearson New Zealand Ltd.)
Penguin Books (South Africa) (Pty.) Ltd., 24 Sturdee Avenue, Rosebank,
Johannesburg 2196, South Africa

Penguin Books Ltd., Registered Offices: 80 Strand, London WC2R 0RL, England

Roadwork was first published in a Signet edition under the name Richard Bachman, and
later appeared in NAL hardcover and Plume trade paperback omnibus editions titled
The Bachman Books under the name Stephen King. "The Importance of Being Bachman"
appeared in slightly different form in the 1996 Plume edition of *The Bachman Books*.

First Printing, March 1981
First Printing (King Introduction), June 1999
20 19 18 17 16 15 14 13 12

Copyright © Richard Bachman, 1981
Introduction copyright © Stephen King, 1996
All rights reserved

 REGISTERED TRADEMARK—MARCA REGISTRADA

Printed in the United States of America

The Importance of Being Bachman

by Stephen King

This is my second introduction to the so-called Bachman Books—a phrase which has come to mean (in my mind, at least) the first few novels published with the Richard Bachman name, the ones which appeared as unheralded paperback originals under the Signet imprint. My first introduction wasn't very good; to me it reads like a textbook case of author obfuscation. But that is not surprising. When it was written, Bachman's alter ego (me, in other words) wasn't in what I'd call a contemplative or analytical mood; I was, in fact, feeling robbed. Bachman was never created as a short-term alias; he was supposed to be there for the long haul, and when my name came out in connection with his, I was surprised, upset, and pissed off. That's not a state conducive to good essay-writing. This time I may do a little better.

Probably the most important thing I can say about Richard Bachman is that *he became real*. Not entirely, of course (he said with a nervous smile); I am not writing this in a delusive state. Except . . . well . . . maybe I am. Delusion is, after all, something writers of fiction try to encourage in their readers, at least during the time that the book or story is open before them, and the writer is hardly immune from this state of . . . what shall I call it? How does "directed delusion" sound?

At any rate, Richard Bachman began his career not as a delusion but as a sheltered place where I could publish a few early works which I felt readers might like. Then he began to grow and come alive, as the creatures of a writer's imagination so frequently do. I began to imagine his life as a dairy farmer . . . his wife, the beautiful Claudia Inez Bachman . . . his solitary New Hampshire mornings, spent milking the cows, getting in the wood, and thinking about his stories . . . his evenings spent writing, always with a glass of whiskey beside his Olivetti typewriter. I once knew a writer who would say his current story or novel was "putting on weight" if it was going well. In much the same way, my pen-name began to put on weight.

Then, when his cover was blown, Richard Bachman died. I made light of this in the few interviews I felt required to give on the subject, saying that he'd died of cancer of the pseudonym, but it was actually shock that killed him: the realization that sometimes people just won't let you alone. To put it in more fulsome (but not at all inaccurate) terms, Bachman was the vampire side of my existence, killed by the sunlight of disclosure. My feelings about all this were confused enough (and *fertile* enough) to bring on a book (a Stephen King book, that is), *The Dark Half*. It was about a writer whose pseudonym, George Stark, actually comes to life. It's a novel my wife has always detested, perhaps because, for Thad Beaumont, the dream of being a writer overwhelms the reality of being a man; for Thad, delusive thinking overtakes rationality completely, with horrific consequences.

I didn't have that problem, though. Really. I put Bachman aside, and although I was sorry that he had to die, I would be lying if I didn't say I felt some relief as well.

The books in this omnibus were written by a young man who was angry, energetic, and deeply infatuated with the art and craft of writing. They weren't written as Bachman books per se (Bachman hadn't been invented yet, after all), but in a Bachman state of mind: low rage, sexual frustration, crazy good humor, and simmering despair. Ben Richards, the scrawny, pretubercular protagonist of *The Running Man* (he is about as far from the Arnold Schwarzenegger character in the movie as you can get), crashes his hijacked plane into the Network Games skyscraper, killing himself but taking hundreds (maybe thousands) of Free-Vee executives with him; this is the Richard Bachman version of a happy ending. The conclusions of the other Bachman novels are even more grim. Stephen King has always understood that the good guys don't always win (see *Cujo*, *Pet Sematary*, and—perhaps—*Christine*), but he has also understood that mostly they do. Every day, in real life, the good guys win. Mostly these victories go unheralded (MAN ARRIVES HOME SAFE FROM WORK YET AGAIN wouldn't sell many papers), but they are nonetheless real for all that . . . and fiction should reflect reality.

And yet . . .

In the first draft of *The Dark Half*, I had Thad Beaumont quote Donald E. Westlake, a very funny writer who has penned a series of very grim crime novels under the name Richard Stark. Once asked to explain the dichotomy between Westlake and Stark, the writer in question said, "I write Westlake stories on sunny days. When it rains, I'm Stark." I don't think that made it into the final version of *The Dark Half*, but I have always loved it (and *related* to it, as it has become fashionable to say). Bachman—a fictional creation who became more real to me with each published book which bore his byline—was a rainy-day sort of guy if ever there was one.

The good folks mostly win, courage usually triumphs over fear, the family dog hardly ever contracts rabies; these are things I knew at twenty-five, and things I still know now, at the age of 25 × 2. But I know something else as well: there's a place in most of us where the rain is pretty much constant, the shadows are always long, and the woods are full of monsters. It is good to have a voice in which the terrors of such a place can be articulated and its geography partially described, without denying the sunshine and clarity that fill so much of our ordinary lives.

In *Thinner*, Bachman spoke for the first time on his own—it was the only one of the early Bachman novels that had his name on the first draft instead of mine—and it struck me as really unfair that, just as he was starting to talk with his own voice, he should have been mistaken for me. And a mistake was just what it felt like, because by then Bachman had become a kind of id for me; he said the things I couldn't, and the thought of him out there on his New Hampshire dairy farm—not a best-selling writer who gets his name in some stupid *Forbes* list of entertainers too rich for their own good or his face on the *Today* show or doing cameos in movies—quietly writing his books gave him permission to think in ways I could not think and speak in ways I could not speak. And then these new stories came out saying "Bachman is really King," and there was no one—not even me—to defend the dead man, or to point out the obvious: that King was also really Bachman, at least some of the time.

Unfair I thought then and unfair I think now, but sometimes life bites you a little, that's all. I determined to put Bachman out of my thoughts and my life, and so I did, for a number of years. Then, while I was writing a novel (a *Stephen King* novel) called *Desperation*, Richard Bachman suddenly appeared in my life again.

I was working on a Wang dedicated word processor at that time; it looked like a visiphone in an old Flash Gordon serial. This was paired with a marginally more state-of-the-art laser printer, and from time to time, when an idea occurred to me, I would write down a phrase or a putative title on a scrap of paper and Scotch-tape it to the side of the printer. As I neared the three-quarter mark on *Desperation*, I had a scrap with a single word printed on it: REGULATORS. I had had a great idea for a novel, something that had to do with toys, guns, TV, and suburbia. I didn't know if I would ever write it—lots of those "printer notes" never came to anything—but it was certainly cool to think about.

Then, one rainy day (a Richard Stark sort of day), as I was pulling into my driveway, I had an idea. I don't know where it came from; it was totally unconnected to any of the trivia tumbling through my head at the time. The idea was to take the characters from *Desperation* and put them into *The Regulators*. In some cases, I thought, they could play the same people; in others, they would change; in neither case would they do the same things or react in the same ways, because the different stories would dictate different courses of action. It would be, I thought, like the members of a repertory company acting in two different plays.

Then an even more exciting idea struck me. If I could use the rep company concept with the *characters*, I could use it with the plot itself as well—I could stack a good many of the *Desperation* elements in a brand-new configuration, and create a kind of mirror world. I knew even before setting out that plenty of critics would call this twinning a stunt . . . and they would not be wrong, exactly. But, I thought, it could be a good stunt. Maybe even an illuminating stunt, one which showcased the muscularity and versatility of story, its all but limitless ability to adapt a few basic elements into endlessly pleasing variations, its prankish charm.

But the two books couldn't *sound* exactly the same, and they couldn't *mean* the same, any more than an Edward Albee play and one by William Inge can sound and mean the same, even if they are performed on successive nights by the same company of actors. How could I possibly create a different voice?

At first I thought I couldn't, and that it would be best to consign the idea to the Rube Goldberg bin I keep in the bottom of my mind—the one marked INTERESTING BUT UNWORKABLE CONTRAPTIONS. Then it occurred to me that I had had the answer all along: Richard Bachman could write *The Regulators*. His voice sounded superficially the same as mine, but underneath there was a world of difference—all the difference between sunshine and rain, let us say. And his view of people was always different from mine, simultaneously funnier and more cold-hearted (Bart Dawes in *Roadwork*, my favorite of the early Bachman books, is an excellent example).

Of course Bachman was dead, I had announced that myself, but death is actually a minor problem for a novelist—just ask Paul Sheldon, who brought Misery Chastain back for Annie Wilkes, or Arthur Conan Doyle, who brought Sherlock Holmes back from Reichenbach Falls when fans all over the British Empire clamored for him. I didn't actually bring Richard Bachman back from the dead, anyway; I just visualized a box of neglected manuscripts in his basement, with *The Regulators* on top. Then I transcribed the book Bachman had already written.

That transcription was a little tougher . . . but it was also immensely exhilarating. It was wonderful to hear Bachman's voice again, and what I had hoped might happen *did* happen: a book rolled out that was a kind of fraternal twin to the one I had written under my own name (and the two books were quite literally written back-to-back, the King book finished on one day and the Bachman book commenced on the very next). They were no more alike than King and Bachman themselves. *Desperation* is about God; *The Regulators* is about TV. I guess that makes them both about higher powers, but very different ones just the same.

The importance of being Bachman was always the importance of finding a good voice and a valid point of view that were a little different from my own. Not *really* different; I am not schizo enough to believe that. But I do believe that there are tricks all of us use to change our perspectives and our perceptions—to see ourselves new by dressing up in different clothes and doing our hair in different styles—and that such tricks can be very useful, a way of revitalizing and refreshing old strategies for living life, observing life, and creating art. None of these comments are intended to suggest that I have done anything great in the Bachman books, and they are surely not made as arguments for artistic merit. But I love what I do too much to want to go stale if I can help it. Bachman has been one way in which I have tried to refresh my craft, and to keep from being too comfy and well-padded.

These early books show some progression of the Bachman *persona*, I hope, and I hope they also show the essence of that *persona*. Dark-toned, despairing even when he is laughing (despairing *most* when he's laughing, in fact), Richard Bachman isn't a fellow I'd want to be all the time, even if he *were* still alive . . . but it's good to have that option, that window on the world, polarized though it may be. Still, as the reader works his or her way through these stories, he/she may discover that Dick Bachman has one thing in common with Thad Beaumont's alter ego, George Stark: he's not a very nice guy.

And I wonder if there are any other good manuscripts, at or near completion, in that box found by the widowed Mrs. Bachman in the cellar of her New Hampshire farmhouse.

Sometimes I wonder about that *a lot*.

—Stephen King

Lovell, Maine
April 16, 1996

ROADWORK

In memory of Charlotte Littlefield.
Proverbs 31:10–28.

Prologue

I don't know why. You don't know why.
Most likely God don't know why, either.
It's just Government business, that's all.
  —Man-in-the-street interview
    concerning Viet Nam, circa 1967

But Viet Nam was over and the country was getting on.

On this hot August afternoon in 1972, the WHLM Newsmobile was parked near Westgate at the end of the Route 784 expressway. There was a small crowd around a bunting-covered podium that had been hurriedly tossed together; the bunting was thin flesh on a skeleton of naked planks. Behind it, at the top of a grassy embankment, were the highway tollbooths. In front of it, open, marshy land stretched toward the suburban hem of the city's outskirts.

A young reporter named Dave Albert was doing a series of man-on-the-street interviews while he and his co-workers waited for the mayor and the governor to arrive for the ground-breaking ceremony.

He held the microphone toward an elderly man wearing tinted spectacles.

"Well," the elderly man said, looking tremulously into the camera, "I think it's a great thing for the city. We've needed this a long time. It's . . . a great thing for the city." He swallowed, aware that his mind was broadcasting echoes of itself, helpless to stop, hypnotized by the grinding, Cyclopean eye of posterity. "Great," he added limply.

"Thank you, sir. Thank you very much."

"Do you think they'll use it? On the news tonight?"

Albert flashed a professional, meaningless smile. "Hard to tell, sir. There's a good chance."

His sound man pointed up to the tollgate turnaround, where the governor's Chrysler Imperial had just pulled up, winking and gleaming like a chrome-inlaid eight ball in the summer sunshine. Albert nodded back, held up a single finger. He and the cameraman approached a guy in a white shirt with rolled-up sleeves. The guy was looking moodily at the podium.

"Would you mind stating your opinion of all this, Mr. . . . ?"

"Dawes. No, I don't mind." His voice was low, pleasant.

"Speed," the cameraman murmured.

The man in the white shirt said, still pleasantly, "I think it's a piece of shit."

The cameraman grimaced. Albert nodded, looking at the man in the white shirt reproachfully, and then made cutting gestures with the first two fingers of his right hand.

The elderly gentleman was looking at this tableau with real horror. Above, up by the tollbooths, the governor was getting out of his Imperial. His green tie was resplendent in the sun.

The man in the white shirt said politely: "Will that be on the six or eleven o'clock news?"

"Ho-ho, fella, you're a riot," Albert said sourly, and walked away to catch the governor. The cameraman trailed after him. The man in the white shirt watched the governor as he came carefully down the grassy slope.

Albert met the man in the white shirt again seventeen months later, but since neither of them remembered that they had met before, it might as well have been the first time.

Part One

NOVEMBER

Late last night the rain was knocking on my window
I moved across the darkened room and in the lampglow
I thought I saw down in the street
The spirit of the century
Telling us that we're all standing on the border.
                                              —Al Stewart

November 20, 1973

He kept doing things without letting himself think about them. Safer that way. It was like having a circuit breaker in his head, and it thumped into place every time part of him tried to ask: *But why are you doing this?* Part of his mind would go dark. Hey Georgie, who turned out the lights? Whoops, I did. Something screwy in the wiring, I guess. Just a sec. Reset the switch. The lights go back on. But the thought is gone. Everything is fine. Let us continue, Freddy—where were we?

He was walking to the bus stop when he saw the sign that said:

AMMO HARVEY'S GUN SHOP AMMO
Remington Winchester Colt Smith & Wesson
HUNTERS WELCOME

It was snowing a little out of a gray sky. It was the first snow of the year and it landed on the pavement like white splotches of baking soda, then melted. He saw a little boy in a red knitted cap go by with his mouth open and his tongue out to catch a flake. It's just going to melt, Freddy, he thought at the kid, but the kid went on anyway, with his head cocked back at the sky.

He stopped in front of Harvey's Gun Shop, hesitating. There was a rack of late edition newspapers outside the door, and the headline said:

SHAKY CEASE-FIRE HOLDS

Below that, on the rack, was a smudged white sign
that said:

PLEASE PAY FOR YOUR PAPER!
THIS IS AN HONOR RACK, DEALER MUST PAY
FOR ALL PAPERS

It was warm inside. The shop was long but not very
wide. There was only a single aisle. Inside the door
on the left was a glass case filled with boxes of ammunition. He recognized the .22 cartridges immediately,
because he'd had a .22 single-shot rifle as a boy in
Connecticut. He had wanted that rifle for three years
and when he finally got it he couldn't think of anything to do with it. He shot at cans for a while, then
shot a blue jay. The jay hadn't been a clean kill. It
sat in the snow surrounded by a pink blood stain, its
beak slowly opening and closing. After that he had
put the rifle up on hooks and it had stayed there for
three years until he sold it to a kid up the street for
nine dollars and a carton of funny books.

The other ammunition was less familiar. Thirty-
thirty, thirty-ought-six, and some that looked like
scale-model howitzer shells. What animals do you kill
with those? he wondered. Tigers? Dinosaurs? Still it
fascinated him, sitting there inside the glass case like
penny candy in a stationery store.

The clerk or proprietor was talking to a fat man in
green pants and a green fatigue shirt. The shirt had
flap pockets. They were talking about a pistol that was
lying on top of another glass case, dismembered. The
fat man thumbed back the slide and they both peered
into the oiled chamber. The fat man said something
and the clerk or proprietor laughed.

"Autos always jam? You got that from your father,
Mac. Admit it."

"Harry, you're full of bullshit up to your eyebrows."

You're full of it, Fred, he thought. Right up to your eyebrows. You know it, Fred?

Fred said he knew it.

On the right was a glass case that ran the length of the shop. It was full of rifles on pegs. He was able to pick out the double-barreled shotguns, but everything else was a mystery to him. Yet some people—the two at the far counter, for example—had mastered this world as easily as he had mastered general accounting in college.

He walked further into the store and looked into a case filled with pistols. He saw some air guns, a few .22's, a .38 with a wood-grip handle, .45's, and a gun he recognized as a .44 Magnum, the gun Dirty Harry had carried in that movie. He had heard Ron Stone and Vinnie Mason talking about that movie at the laundry, and Vinnie had said: They'd never let a cop carry a gun like that in the city. You can blow a hole in a man a mile away with one of those.

The fat man, Mac, and the clerk or proprietor, Harry (as in Dirty Harry), had the gun back together.

"You give me a call when you get that Menschler in," Mac said.

"I will . . . but your prejudice against autos is irrational," Harry said. (He decided Harry must be the proprietor—a clerk would never call a customer irrational.) "Have you got to have the Cobra next week?"

"I'd like it," Mac said.

"I don't promise."

"You never do . . . but you're the best goddam gunsmith in the city, and you know it."

"Of course I do."

Mac patted the gun on top of the glass case and turned to go. Mac bumped into him—*Watch it, Mac. Smile when you do that*—and then went on to the door. The paper was tucked under Mac's arm, and he could read:

SHAKY CEA

Harry turned to him, still smiling and shaking his head. "Can I help you?"

"I hope so. But I warn you in advance, I know nothing about guns."

Harry shrugged. "There's a law you should? Is it for someone else? For Christmas?"

"Yes, that's just right," he said, seizing on it. "I've got this cousin—Nick, his name is. Nick Adams. He lives in Michigan and he's got yea guns. You know. Loves to hunt, but it's more than that. It's sort of a, well, a—"

"Hobby?" Harry asked, smiling.

"Yes, that's it." He had been about to say *fetish*. His eyes dropped to the cash register, where an aged bumper sticker was pasted on. The bumper sticker said:

IF GUNS ARE OUTLAWED, ONLY OUTLAWS
WILL HAVE GUNS

He smiled at Harry and said, "That's very true, you know."

"Sure it is," Harry said. "This cousin of yours . . ."

"Well, it's kind of a one-upmanship type of thing. He knows how much I like boating and I'll be damned if he didn't up and give me an Evinrude sixty-horsepower motor last Christmas. He sent it by REA express. I gave him a hunting jacket. I felt sort of like a horse's ass."

Harry nodded sympathetically.

"Well, I got a letter from him about six weeks ago, and he sounds just like a kid with a free pass to the circus. It seems that he and about six buddies chipped in together and bought themselves a trip to this place in Mexico, sort of like a free-fire zone—"

"A no-limit hunting preserve?"

"Yeah, that's it." He chuckled a little. "You shoot as much as you want. They stock it, you know. Deer, antelope, bear, bison. Everything."

"Was it Boca Rio?"

"I really don't remember. I think the name was longer than that."

Harry's eyes had gone slightly dreamy. "That guy that just left and myself and two others went to Boca Rio in 1965. I shot a zebra. A goddam zebra! I got it mounted in my game room at home. That was the best time I ever had in my life, bar none. I envy your cousin."

"Well, I talked it over with my wife," he said, "and she said go ahead. We had a very good year at the laundry. I work at the Blue Ribbon Laundry over in Western."

"Yes, I know where that is."

He felt that he could go on talking to Harry all day, for the rest of the year, embroidering the truth and the lies into a beautiful, gleaming tapestry. Let the world go by. Fuck the gas shortage and the high price of beef and the shaky ceasefire. Let there be talk of cousins that never were, right, Fred? Right on, Georgie.

"We got the Central Hospital account this year, as well as the mental institution, and also three new motels."

"Is the Quality Motor Court on Franklin Avenue one of yours?"

"Yes, it is."

"I've stayed there a couple of times," Harry said. "The sheets were always very clean. Funny, you never think about who washes the sheets when you stay at a motel."

"Well, we had a good year. And so I thought, maybe I can get Nick a rifle and a pistol. I know he's always wanted a .44 Magnum, I've heard him mention that one—"

Harry brought the Magnum up and laid it carefully on top of the glass case. He picked it up. He liked the heft of it. It felt like business.

He put it back down on the glass case.

"The chambering on that—" Harry began.

He laughed and held up a hand. "Don't sell me. I'm sold. An ignoramus always sells himself. How much ammunition should I get with that?"

Harry shrugged. "Get him ten boxes, why don't you? He can always get more. The price on that gun is two-eighty-nine plus tax, but I'm going to give it to you for two-eighty, ammo thrown in. How's that?"

"Super," he said, meaning it. And then, because something more seemed required, he added: "It's a handsome piece."

"If it's Boca Rio, he'll put it to good use."

"Now the rifle—"

"What does he have?"

He shrugged and spread his hands. "I'm sorry. I really don't know. Two or three shotguns, and something he calls an auto-loader—"

"Remington?" Harry asked him so quickly that he felt afraid; it was as if he had been walking in waist-deep water that had suddenly shelved off.

"I think it was. I could be wrong."

"Remington makes the best," Harry said, and nodded, putting him at ease again. "How high do you want to go?"

"Well, I'll be honest with you. The motor probably cost him four hundred. I'd like to go at least five. Six hundred tops."

"You and this cousin really get along, don't you?"

"We grew up together," he said sincerely. "I think I'd give my right arm to Nick, if he wanted it."

"Well, let me show you something," Harry said. He picked a key out of the bundle on his ring and went to one of the glass cabinets. He opened it, climbed up on a stool, and brought down a long, heavy rifle with an inlaid stock. "This may be a little higher than you want to go, but it's a beautiful gun." Harry handed it to him.

"What is it?"

"That's a four-sixty Weatherbee. Shoots heavier ammunition than I've got here in the place right now.

I'd have to order however many rounds you wanted from Chicago. Take about a week. It's a perfectly weighted gun. The muzzle energy on that baby is over eight thousand pounds . . . like hitting something with an airport limousine. If you hit a buck in the head with it, you'd have to take the tail for a trophy."

"I don't know," he said, sounding dubious even though he had decided he wanted the rifle. "I know Nick wants trophies. That's part of—"

"Sure it is," Harry said, taking the Weatherbee and chambering it. The hole looked big enough to put a carrier pigeon in. "Nobody goes to Boca Rio for meat. So your cousin gutshoots. With this piece, you don't have to worry about tracking the goddam animal for twelve miles through the high country, the animal suffering the whole time, not to mention you missing dinner. This baby will spread his insides over twenty feet."

"How much?"

"Well, I'll tell you. I can't move it in town. Who wants a freaking anti-tank gun when there's nothing to go after anymore but pheasant? And if you put them on the table, it tastes like you're eating exhaust fumes. It retails for nine-fifty, wholesales for six-thirty. I'd let you have it for seven hundred."

"That comes to . . . almost a thousand bucks."

"We give a ten percent discount on orders over three hundred dollars. That brings it back to nine." He shrugged. "You give that gun to your cousin, I guarantee he hasn't got one. If he does, I'll buy it back for seven-fifty. I'll put that in writing, that's how sure I am."

"No kidding?"

"Absolutely. Absolutely. Of course, if it's too steep, it's too steep. We can look at some other guns. But if he's a real nut on the subject, I don't have anything else he might not have two of."

"I see." He put a thoughtful expression on his face. "Have you got a telephone?"

"Sure, in the back.. Want to call your wife and talk it over?"

"I think I better."

"Sure. Come on."

Harry led him into a cluttered back room. There was a bench and a scarred wooden table littered with gun guts, springs, cleaning fluid, pamphlets, and labeled bottles with lead slugs in them.

"There's the phone," Harry said.

He sat down, picked up the phone, and dialed while Harry went back to get the Magnum and put it in the box.

"Thank you for calling the WDST Weatherphone," the bright, recorded voice said. "This afternoon, snow flurries developing into light snow late this evening—"

"Hi, Mary?" he said. "Listen, I'm in this place called Harvey's Gun Shop. Yeah, about Nicky. I got the pistol we talked about, no problem. There was one right in the showcase. Then the guy showed me this rifle—"

"—clearing by tomorrow afternoon. Lows tonight will be in the thirties, tomorrow in the mid to upper forties. Chance of precipitation tonight—"

"—so what do you think I should do?" Harry was standing in the doorway behind him; he could see the shadow.

"Yeah," he said. "I know that."

"Thank you for dialing the WDST Weatherphone, and be sure to watch Newsplus-Sixty with Bob Reynolds each weekday evening at six o'clock for a weather update. Good-bye."

"You're not kidding, I *know* it's a lot."

"Thank you for calling the WDST Weatherphone. This afternoon, snow flurries developing into—"

"You sure, honey?"

"Chance of precipitation tonight eighty percent, tomorrow—"

"Well, okay." He turned on the bench, grinned at Harry, and made a circle with his right thumb and forefinger. "He's a nice guy. Said he'd guarantee me Nick didn't have one."

"—by tomorrow afternoon. Lows tonight—"

"I love you too, Mare. Bye." He hung up. Jesus, Freddy, that was neat. It was, George. It was.

He got up. "She says go if I say okay. I do."

Harry smiled. "What are you going to do if he sends you a Thunderbird?"

He smiled back. "Return it unopened."

As they walked back out Harry asked, "Check or charge?"

"American Express, if it's okay."

"Good as gold."

He got his card out. On the back, written on the special strip, it said:

BARTON GEORGE DAWES

"You're sure the shells will come in time for me to ship everything to Fred?"

Harry looked up from the credit blank. "Fred?"

His smile expanded. "Nick is Fred and Fred is Nick," he said. "Nicholas Frederic Adams. It's kind of a joke about the name. From when we were kids."

"Oh." He smiled politely as people do when the joke is in and they are out. "You want to sign here?"

He signed.

Harry took another book out from under the counter, a heavy one with a steel chain punched through the upper left corner, near the binding. "And your name and address here for the federals."

He felt his fingers tighten on the pen. "Sure," he said. "Look at me, I never bought a gun in my life and I'm mad." He wrote his name and address in the book:

Barton George Dawes 1241 Crestallen Street West

"They're into everything," he said.

"This is nothing to what they'd like to do," Harry said.

"I know. You know what I heard on the news the other day? They want a law that says a guy riding on a motorcycle has to wear a mouth protector. A *mouth* protector, for God's sake. Now is it the government's business if a man wants to chance wrecking his bridgework?"

"Not in my book it isn't," Harry said, putting his book under the counter.

"Or look at that highway extension they're building over in Western. Some snot-nose surveyor says 'It's going through here' and the state sends out a bunch of letters and the letters say, 'Sorry, we're putting the 784 extension through here. You've got a year to find a new house.'"

"It's a goddam shame."

"Yes, it is. What does 'eminent domain' mean to someone who's lived in the frigging house for twenty years? Made love to their wife there and brought their kid up there and come home to there from trips? That's just something from a law book that they made up so they can crook you better."

Watch it, watch it. But the circuit breaker was a little slow and some of it got through.

"You okay?" Harry asked.

"Yeah. I had one of those submarine sandwiches for lunch, I should know better. They give me gas like hell."

"Try one of these," Harry said, and took a roll of pills from his breast pocket. Written on the outside was:

ROLAIDS

"Thanks," he said. He took one off the top and popped it into his mouth, never minding the bit of lint on it. Look at me, I'm in a TV commercial. Consumes forty-seven times its own weight in excess stomach acid.

"They always do the trick for me," Harry said.

"About the shells—"

"Sure. A week. No more than two. I'll get you seventy rounds."

"Well, why don't you keep these guns right here? Tag them with my name or something. I guess I'm silly, but I really don't want them in the house. That's silly, isn't it?"

"To each his own," Harry said equably.

"Okay. Let me write down my office number. When those bullets come in—"

"Cartridges," Harry interrupted. "Cartridges or shells."

"Cartridges," he said, smiling. "When they come in, give me a ring. I'll pick the guns up and make arrangements about shipping them. REA will ship guns, won't they?"

"Sure. Your cousin will have to sign for them on the other end, that's all."

He wrote his name on one of Harry's business cards. The card said:

Harold Swinnerton   849-6330

HARVEY'S GUN SHOP
Ammunition   Antique Guns

"Say," he said. "If you're Harold, who's Harvey?"

"Harvey was my brother. He died eight years ago."

"I'm sorry."

"We all were. He came down here one day, opened up, cleared the cash register, and then dropped dead of a heart attack. One of the sweetest men you'd ever want to meet. He could bring down a deer at two hundred yards."

He reached over the counter and they shook.

"I'll call," Harry promised.

"Take good care."

He went out into the snow again, past SHAKY CEASE-FIRE HOLDS. It was coming down a little harder now, and his gloves were home.

What were you doing in there, George?

Thump, the circuit breaker.

By the time he got to the bus stop, it might have been an incident he had read about somewhere. No more.

Crestallen Street West was a long, downward-curving street that had enjoyed a fair view of the park and an excellent view of the river until progress had intervened in the shape of a high-rise housing development. It had gone up on Westfield Avenue two years before and had blocked most of the view.

Number 1241 was a split-level ranch house with a one-car garage beside it. There was a long front yard, now barren and waiting for snow—real snow—to cover it. The driveway was asphalt, freshly hot-topped the previous spring.

He went inside and heard the TV, the new Zenith cabinet model they had gotten in the summer. There was a motorized antenna on the roof which he had put up himself. She had not wanted that, because of what was supposed to happen, but he had insisted. If it could be mounted, he had reasoned, it could be dismounted when they moved. Bart, don't be silly. It's just extra expense . . . just extra work for you. But he had outlasted her, and finally she said she would "humor" him. That's what she said on the rare occasions when he cared enough about something to force it through the sticky molasses of her arguments. All right, Bart. This time I'll "humor" you.

At the moment she was watching Merv Griffin chat with a celebrity. The celebrity was Lorne Greene, who was talking about his new police series, *Griff*. Lorne was telling Merv how much he loved doing the show. Soon a black singer (a negress songstress, he thought) who no one had ever heard of would come on and sing a song. "I Left My Heart in San Francisco," perhaps.

"Hi, Mary," he called.

"Hi, Bart."

Mail on the table. He flipped through it. A letter to Mary from her slightly psycho sister in Baltimore. A Gulf credit card bill—thirty-eight dollars. A checking account statement: 49 debits, 9 credits, $954.47 balance. A good thing he had used American Express at the gun shop.

"The coffee's hot," Mary called. "Or did you want a drink?"

"Drink," he said. "I'll get it."

Three other pieces of mail: An overdue notice from the library. *Facing the Lions,* by Tom Wicker. Wicker had spoken to a Rotary luncheon a month ago, and he was the best speaker they'd had in years.

A personal note from Stephan Ordner, one of the managerial bigwigs in Amroco, the corporation that now owned the Blue Ribbon almost outright. Ordner wanted him to drop by and discuss the Waterford deal—would Friday be okay, or was he planning to be away for Thanksgiving? If so, give a call. If not, bring Mary. Carla always enjoyed the chance to see Mary and blah-blah and bullshit-bullshit, etc., *et al.*

And another letter from the highway department.

He stood looking down at it for a long time in the gray afternoon light that fell through the windows, and then put all the mail on the sideboard. He made himself a scotch-rocks and took it into the living room.

Merv was still chatting with Lorne. The color on the new Zenith was more than good; it was nearly occult. He thought, if our ICBM's are as good as our color TV, there's going to be a hell of a big bang someday. Lorne's hair was silver, the most impossible shade of silver conceivable. *Boy, I'll snatch you bald-headed,* he thought, and chuckled. It had been one of his mother's favorite sayings. He could not say why the image of Lorne Greene bald-headed was so amusing. A light attack of belated hysteria over the gun shop episode, maybe.

Mary looked up, a smile on her lips. "A funny?"

"Nothing," he said. "Just my thinks."

He sat down beside her and pecked her cheek. She was a tall woman, thirty-eight now, and at that crisis of looks where early prettiness is deciding what to be in middle age. Her skin was very good, her breasts small and not apt to sag much. She ate a lot, but her conveyor-belt metabolism kept her slim. She would not be apt to tremble at the thought of wearing a bathing suit on a public beach ten years from now, no matter how the gods decided to dispose of the rest of her case. It made him conscious of his own slight bay window. Hell, Freddy, every executive has a bay window. It's a success symbol, like a Delta 88. That's right, George. Watch the old ticker and the cancer-sticks and you'll see eighty yet.

"How did it go today?" she asked.

"Good."

"Did you get out to the new plant in Waterford?"

"Not today."

He hadn't been out to Waterford since late October. Ordner knew it—a little bird must have told him—and hence the note. The site of the new plant was a vacated textile mill, and the smart mick realtor handling the deal kept calling him. We have to close this thing out, the smart mick realtor kept telling him. You people aren't the only ones over in Westside with your fingers in the crack. I'm going as fast as I can, he told the smart mick realtor. You'll have to be patient.

"What about the place in Crescent?" she asked him. "The brick house."

"It's out of our reach," he said. "They're asking forty-eight thousand."

"For that place?" she asked indignantly. "High-way robbery!"

"It sure is." He took a deep swallow of his drink. "What did old Bea from Baltimore have to say?"

"The usual. She's into consciousness-raising group hydrotherapy now. Isn't that a sketch? Bart—"

"It sure is," he said quickly.

"Bart, we've got to get moving on this. January twentieth is coming, and we'll be out in the street."

"I'm going as fast as I can," he said. "We just have to be patient."

"That little Colonial on Union Street—"

"—is sold," he finished, and drained his drink.

"Well that's what I mean," she said, exasperated. "That would have been perfectly fine for the two of us. With the money the city's allowing us for this house and lot, we could have been ahead."

"I didn't like it."

"You don't seem to like very much these days," she said with surprising bitterness. "He didn't like it," she told the TV. The negress songstress was on now, singing "Alfie."

"Mary, I'm doing all I can."

She turned and looked at him earnestly. "Bart, I know how you feel about this house—"

"No you don't," he said. "Not at all."

November 21, 1973

A light skim of snow had fallen over the world during the night, and when the bus doors chuffed open and he stepped onto the sidewalk, he could see the tracks of the people who had been there before him. He walked down Fir Street from the corner, hearing the bus pull away behind him with its tiger purr. Then Johnny Walker passed him, headed out for his second pickup of the morning. Johnny waved from the cab of his blue and white laundry van, and he waved back. It was a little after eight o'clock.

The laundry began its day at seven when Ron Stone, the foreman, and Dave Radner, who ran the wash-

room, got there and ran up the pressure on the boiler.
The shirt girls punched in at seven-thirty, and the girls
who ran the speed ironer came in at eight. He hated
the downstairs of the laundry where the brute work
went on, where the exploitation went on, but for some
perverse reason the men and women who worked
there liked him. They called him by his first name.
And with a few exceptions, he liked them.

He went in through the driver's loading entrance
and threaded through the baskets of sheets from last
night that the ironer hadn't run yet. Each basket was
covered tightly with plastic to keep the dust off. Down
front, Ron Stone was tightening the drive belt on the
old Milnor single-pocket while Dave and his helper, a
college dropout named Steve Pollack, were loading
the industrial Washex machines with motel sheets.

"Bart!" Ron Stone greeted him. He bellowed everything; thirty years of talking to people over the com-
bined noises of dryers, ironers, shirt presses, and
washers on extract had built the bellow into his system. "This son of a bitch Milnor keeps seizing up. The
program's so far over to bleach now that Dave has to
run it on manual. And the extract keeps cutting out."

"We've got the Kilgallon order," he soothed. "Two
more months— "

"In the Waterford plant?"

"Sure," he said, a little giddy.

"Two more months and I'll be ready for the nut-
hatch," Stone said darkly. "And switching over . . .
it's gonna be worse than a Polish army parade."

"The orders will back up, I guess."

"Back up! We won't get dug out for three months.
Then it'll be summer."

He nodded, not wanting to go on with it. "What
are you running first?"

"Holiday Inn."

"Get a hundred pounds of towels in with every load.
You know how they scream for towels."

"Yeah, they scream for everything."

"How much you got?"

"They marked in six hundred pounds. Mostly from the Shriners. Most of them stayed over Monday. Cummyest sheets I ever seen. Some of em'd stand on end."

He nodded toward the new kid, Pollack. "How's he working out?" The Blue Ribbon had a fast turnover in washroom helpers. Dave worked them hard and Ron's bellowing made them nervous, then resentful.

"Okay so far," Stone said. "Do you remember the last one?"

He remembered. The kid had lasted three hours.

"Yeah, I remember. What was his name?"

Ron Stone's brow grew thundery. "I don't remember. Baker? Barker? Something like that. I saw him at the Stop and Shop last Friday, handing out leaflets about a lettuce boycott or something. That's something, isn't it? A fellow can't hold a job, so he goes out telling everyone how fucking lousy it is that America can't be like Russia. That breaks my heart."

"You'll run Howard Johnson next?"

Stone looked wounded. "We always run it first thing."

"By nine?"

"Bet your ass."

Dave waved to him, and he waved back. He went upstairs, through dry-cleaning, through accounting, and into his office. He sat down behind his desk in his swivel chair and pulled everything out of the IN box to read. On his desk was a plaque that said:

THINK!
It May Be A New Experience

He didn't care much for that sign but he kept it on his desk because Mary had given it to him—when? Five years back? He sighed. The salesmen that came through thought it was funny. They laughed like hell. But then if you showed a salesman a picture of starving kids or Hitler copulating with the Virgin Mary, he would laugh like hell.

Vinnie Mason, the little bird who had undoubtedly been chirruping in Steve Ordner's ear, had a sign on his desk that said:

THIMK

Now what kind of sense did that make, THIMK? Not even a salesman would laugh at that, right, Fred? Right, George—kee-rect. There were heavy diesel rumblings outside, and he swiveled his chair around to look. The highway people were getting ready to start another day. A long flatbed with two bulldozers on top of it was going by the laundry, followed by an impatient line of cars.

From the third floor, over dry-cleaning, you could watch the progress of the construction. It cut across the Western business and residential sections like a long brown incision, an operation scar poulticed with mud. It was already across Guilder Street, and it had buried the park on Hebner Avenue where he used to take Charlie when he was small . . . no more than a baby, really. What was the name of the park? He didn't know. Just the Hebner Avenue Park I guess, Fred. There was a Little League ball park and a bunch of teeter-totters and a duck pond with a little house in the middle of it. In the summertime, the roof of the little house was always covered with bird shit. There had been swings, too. Charlie got his first swing experience in the Hebner Avenue Park. What do you think of that, Freddy old kid old sock? Scared him at first and he cried and then he liked it and when it was time to go home he cried because I took him off. Wet his pants all over the car seat coming home. Was that really fourteen years ago?

Another truck went by, carrying a payloader.

The Garson Block had been demolished about four months ago; that was three or four blocks west of

Hebner Avenue. A couple of office buildings full of loan companies and a bank or two, the rest dentists and chiropractors and foot doctors. That didn't matter so much, but Christ it had hurt to see the old Grand Theater go. He had seen some of his favorite movies there, in the early fifties. *Dial M for Murder,* with Ray Milland. *The Day the Earth Stood Still,* with Michael Rennie. That one had been on TV just the other night and he had meant to watch it and then fell asleep right in front of the fucking TV and never woke up until the national anthem. He had spilled a drink on the rug and Mary had had a bird over that, too.

The Grand, though—that had really been something. Now they had these new-breed movie theaters out in the suburbs, crackerjack little buildings in the middle of four miles of parking lot. Cinema I, Cinema II, Cinema III, Screening Room, Cinema MCMXLVII. He had taken Mary to one out in Waterford to see *The Godfather* and the tickets were $2.50 a crack and inside it looked like a fucking bowling alley. No balcony. But the Grand had had a marble floor in the lobby and a balcony and an ancient, lovely, grease-clotted popcorn machine where a big box cost a dime. The character who tore your ticket (which had cost you sixty cents) wore a red uniform, like a doorman, and he was at least six hundred. And he always croaked the same thing. "Hopeya enjoy da show." Inside, the auditorium was huge and dark and filled with the smell of dusty velvet. When you sat down you didn't crack your knees on the seat in front of you. And there was a huge cut-glass chandelier overhead. You never wanted to sit under it, because if it ever fell on you they'd have to scrape you up with a putty knife. The Grand was—

He looked at his wristwatch guiltily. Almost forty minutes had gone by. Christ, that was bad news. He had just lost forty minutes, and he hadn't even been *thinking* that much. Just about the park and the Grand Theater.

Is there something wrong with you, Georgie?

There might be, Fred. I guess maybe there might be.

He wiped his fingers across his cheek under his eye and saw by the wetness on them that he had been crying.

He went downstairs to talk to Peter, who was in charge of deliveries. The laundry was in full swing now, the ironer thumping and hissing as the first of the Howard Johnson sheets were fed into its rollers, the washers grinding and making the floor vibrate, the shirt presses going *hissss-shuh!* as Ethel and Rhonda whipped them through.

Peter told him the universal had gone on number four's truck and did he want to look at it before they sent it out to the shop? He said he didn't. He asked Peter if Holiday Inn had gone out yet. Peter said it was being loaded, but the silly ass who ran the place had already called twice about his towels.

He nodded and went back upstairs to look for Vinnie Mason, but Phyllis said Vinnie and Tom Granger had gone out to that new German restaurant to dicker about tablecloths.

"Will you have Vinnie stop in when he gets back?"

"I will, Mr. Dawes. Mr. Ordner called and wanted to know if you'd call him back."

"Thanks, Phyllis."

He went back into the office, got the new things that had collected in the IN box and began to shuffle through them.

A salesman wanted to call about a new industrial bleach, Yello-Go. Where do they come up with the names, he wondered, and put it aside for Ron Stone. Ron loved to inflict Dave with new products, especially if he could wangle a free five hundred pounds of the product for test runs.

A letter of thanks from the United Fund. He put it aside to tack on the announcement board downstairs by the punch-clock.

A circular for office furniture in Executive Pine. Into the wastebasket.

A circular for a Phone-Mate that would broadcast a message and record incoming calls when you were out, up to thirty seconds. *I'm not here, stupid. Buzz off.* Into the wastebasket.

A letter from a lady who had sent the laundry six of her husband's shirts and had gotten them back with the collars burned. He put it aside for later action with a sigh. Ethel had been drinking her lunch again.

A water-test package from the university. He put it aside to go over with Ron and Tom Granger after lunch.

A circular from some insurance company with Art Linkletter telling you how you could get eighty thousand dollars and all you had to do for it was die. Into the wastebasket.

A letter from the smart mick realtor who was peddling the Waterford plant, saying there was a shoe company that was very interested in it, the Thom McAn shoe company no less, no small cheese, and reminding him that the Blue Ribbon's ninety-day option to buy ran out on November 26. *Beware, puny laundry executive. The hour draweth nigh.* Into the wastebasket.

Another salesman for Ron, this one peddling a cleaner with the larcenous name of Swipe. He put it with Yello-Go.

He was turning to the window again when the intercom buzzed. Vinnie was back from the German restaurant.

"Send him in."

Vinnie came right in. He was a tall young man of twenty-five with an olive complexion. His dark hair was combed into its usual elaborately careless tumble. He was wearing a dark red sport coat and dark brown pants. A bow tie. Very rakish, don't you think, Fred? I do, George, I do.

"How are you, Bart?" Vinnie asked.

"Fine," he said. "What's the story on that German restaurant?"

Vinnie laughed. "You should have been there. That old kraut just about fell on his knees he was so happy to see us. We're really going to murder Universal when we get settled into the new plant, Bart. They hadn't even sent a circular, let alone their rep. That kraut, I think he thought he was going to get stuck washing those tablecloths out in the kitchen. But he's got a place there you wouldn't believe. Real beer hall stuff. He's going to murder the competition. The aroma . . . God!" He flapped his hands to indicate the aroma and took a box of cigarettes from the inside pocket of his sport coat. "I'm going to take Sharon there when he gets rolling. Ten percent discount."

In a weird kind of overlay he heard Harry the gun shop proprietor saying: *We give a ten percent discount on orders over three hundred.*

My God, he thought. Did I buy those guns yesterday? Did I really?

That room in his mind went dark.

Hey, Georgie, what are you—

"What's the size of the order?" he asked. His voice was a little thick and he cleared his throat.

"Four to six hundred tablecloths a week once he gets rolling. Plus napkins. All genuine linen. He wants them done in Ivory Snow. I said that was no problem."

He was taking a cigarette out of the box now, doing it slowly, so he could read the label. There was something he could really come to dislike about Vinnie Mason: his dipshit cigarettes. The label on the box said:

PLAYER'S NAVY CUT
CIGARETTES
MEDIUM

Now who in God's world except Vinnie would smoke Player's Navy Cut? Or King Sano? Or English

Ovals? Or Marvels or Murads or Twists? If someone put out a brand called Shit-on-a-Stick or Black Lung, Vinnie would smoke them.

"I did tell him we might have to give him two-day service until we get switched over," Vinnie said, giving him a last loving flash of the box as he put it away. "When we go up to Waterford."

"That's what I wanted to talk to you about," he said. Shall I blast him, Fred? Sure. Blow him out of the water, George.

"Really?" He snapped a light to his cigarette with a slim gold Zippo and raised his eyebrows through the smoke like a British character actor.

"I had a note from Steve Ordner yesterday. He wants me to drop over Friday evening for a little talk about the Waterford plant."

"Oh?"

"This morning I had a phone call from Steve Ordner while I was down talking to Peter Wasserman. Mr. Ordner wants me to call him back. That sounds like he's awfully anxious to know something, doesn't it?"

"I guess it does," Vinnie said, flashing his number 2 smile—*Track wet, proceed with caution.*

"What I want to know is who made Steve Ordner so all-at-once fucking anxious. That's what I want to know."

"Well—"

"Come on, Vinnie. Let's not play coy chambermaid. It's ten o'clock and I've got to talk to Ordner, I've got to talk to Ron Stone, I've got to talk to Ethel Gibbs about burnt shirt collars. Have you been picking my nose while I wasn't looking?"

"Well, Sharon and I were over to St—to Mr. Ordner's house Sunday night for dinner—"

"And you just happened to mention that Bart Dawes has been laying back on Waterford while the 784 extension gets closer and closer, is that it?"

"Bart!" Vinnie protested. "It was all perfectly friendly. It was very—"

"I'm sure it was. So was his little note inviting me to court. I imagine our little phone call will be perfectly friendly, too. That's not the point. The point is that he invited you and your wife to dinner in hopes that you'd run off at the mouth and he had no cause to be disappointed."

"Bart—"

He leveled his finger at Vinnie. "You listen to me, Vinnie. If you drop any more shit like this for me to walk in, you'll be looking for a new job. Count on it."

Vinnie was shocked. The cigarette was all but forgotten between his fingers.

"Vinnie, let me tell you something," he said, dropping his voice back to normal. "I know that a young guy like you has listened to six thousand lectures on how old guys like me tore up the world when they were your age. But you earned this one."

Vinnie opened his mouth to protest.

"I don't think you slipped the knife into me," he said, holding up a hand to forestall Vinnie's protest. "If I thought that, I would have had a pink for you when you walked in here. I just think you were dumb. You got in that great big house and had three drinks before dinner and then a soup course and a salad with Thousand Island dressing and then surf and turf for the main course and it was all served by a maid in a black uniform and Carla was doing her lady-of-the-manor bit—but not being the least bit condescending—and there was a strawberry tort or blueberry buckle with whipped cream for dessert and then a couple of coffee brandies or Tia Maria and you just spilled your guts. Is that about how it went?"

"Something like that," Vinnie whispered. His expression was three parts shame and two parts bullish hate.

"He started off by asking how Bart was. You said Bart was fine. He said Bart was a damned good man, but wouldn't it be nice if he could pick his feet up a little on that Waterford deal. You said, it sure would.

He said, By the way, how's that going. You said, Well it really isn't my department and he said, Don't tell me, Vincent, you know what's going on. And you said, All I know is that Bart hasn't closed the deal yet. I heard that the Thom McAn people are interested in the site but maybe that's just a rumor. Then he said, Well I'm sure Bart knows what he's doing and you said, Yeah, sure and then you had another coffee brandy and he asked you if you thought the Mustangs would make the play-offs and then you and Sharon were going home and you know when you'll be out there again, Vinnie?"

Vinnie didn't say anything.

"You'll be out there when Steve Ordner needs another snitch. That's when."

"I'm sorry," Vinnie said sulkily. He started to get up.

"I'm not through."

Vinnie sat down again and looked into the corner of the room with smoldering eyes.

"I was doing your job twelve years ago, do you know that? Twelve years, that probably seems like a long time to you. To me, I hardly know where the fuck the time went. But I remember the job well enough to know you like it. And that you do a good job. That reorganization in dry-cleaning, with the new numbering system . . . that was a masterpiece."

Vinnie was staring at him, bewildered.

"I started in the laundry twenty years ago," he said. "In 1953, I was twenty years old. My wife and I were just married. I'd finished two years of business administration and Mary and I were going to wait, but we were using the interruption method, you see. We were going to town and somebody slammed the door downstairs and startled me right into an orgasm. She got pregnant out of it. So whenever I get feeling smart these days I just remind myself that one slammed door is responsible for me being where I am today. It's humbling. In those days there was no slick abortion law. When you got a girl pregnant, you married her or you ran out on her. End of options. I married her and took the first job I could get, which was here. Washroom helper, exactly the same job that Pollack kid is doing downstairs right this minute. Everything was manual in those days, and everything had to be pulled wet out of the washers and extracted in a big Stonington wringer that held five hundred pounds of wet flatwork. If you loaded it wrong, it would take your fucking foot off. Mary lost the baby in her seventh month and the doctor said she'd never have another one. I did the helper's job for three years, and my average take-home for fifty-five hours was fifty-five dollars. Then Ralph Albertson, who was the boss of the washroom in those days, got in a little fender-bender accident and died of a heart attack in the street while he and the other guy were exchanging insurance companies. He was a fine man. The whole laundry shut down the day of his funeral. After he was decently buried, I went to Ray Tarkington and asked for his job. I was pretty sure I'd get it. I knew everything about how to wash, because Ralph had shown me.

"This was a family business in those days, Vinnie. Ray and his dad, Don Tarkington, ran it. Don got it from his father, who started the Blue Ribbon in 1926. It was a non-union shop and I suppose the labor people would say all three of the Tarkingtons were paternalistic exploiters of the uneducated working man and woman. And they were. But when Betty Keeson slipped on the wet floor and broke her arm, the Tarkingtons paid the hospital bill and there was ten bucks a week for food until she could come back. And every Christmas they put on a big dinner out in the marking-in room—the best chicken pies you ever ate, and cranberry jelly and rolls and your choice of chocolate or mince pudding for dessert. Don and Ray gave every woman a pair of earrings for Christmas and every man a brand-new tie. I've still got my nine ties in the closet at home. When Don Tarkington died in 1959, I wore one of them to his funeral. It was out of style and Mary gave me holy hell, but I wore it anyway. The place was dark and the hours were long and the work was drudgery, but the people cared about you. If the extractor broke down, Don and Ray would be right down there with the rest of us, the sleeves of their white shirts rolled up, wringing out those sheets by hand. That's what a family business was, Vinnie. Something like that.

"So when Ralph died and Ray Tarkington said he'd already hired a guy from outside to run the washroom, I couldn't understand what in hell was going on. And Ray says, My father and I want you to go back to college. And I say, Great, on what? Bus tokens? And he hands me a cashier's check for two thousand dollars. I looked at it and couldn't believe what I was seeing. I say, What is this? And he says, It's not enough, but it'll get your tuition, your room, and your books. For the rest you work your summers here, okay? And I say, is there a way to thank you? And he says, yeah, three ways. First, repay the loan. Second, repay the interest. Third, bring what you learn back to the Blue Ribbon. I took the check home and showed Mary and she cried. Put her hands right over her face and cried."

Vinnie was looking at him now with frank amazement.

"So in 1955 I went back to school and I got a degree in 1957. I went back to the laundry and Ray put me to work as boss of the drivers. Ninety dollars a week. When I paid the first installment on the loan, I asked Ray what the interest was going to run. He says, One percent. I said, *What?* He says, You heard me. Don't you have something to do? So I say, Yeah I think I better go downtown and get a doctor up here to examine your head. Ray laughs like hell and tells me to get the fuck out of his office. I got the last of that money repaid in 1960, and do you know what, Vinnie? Ray gave me a watch. This watch."

He shot his cuff and showed Vinnie the Bulova watch with its gold expansion band.

"He called it a deferred graduation present. Twenty dollars interest is what I paid on my education, and that son of a bitch turns around and gives me an eighty-buck watch. Engraved on the back it says: *Best from Don & Ray, The Blue Ribbon Laundry.* Don was already a year in his grave then.

"In 1963 Ray put me on your job, keeping an eye on dry-cleaning, opening new accounts, and running the laundromat branches—only in those days there were just five instead of eleven. I stayed with that until 1967, and then Ray put me in this job here. Then, four years ago, he had to sell. You know about that, the way the bastards put the squeeze on him. It turned him into an old man. So now we're part of a corporation with two dozen other irons in the fire—fast food, Ponderosa golf, those three eyesore discount department stores, the gas stations, all that shit. And Steve Ordner's nothing but a glorified foreman. There's a board of directors somewhere in Chicago or Gary that spends maybe fifteen minutes a week on the Blue Ribbon operation. They don't give a shit about running a laundry. They don't *know* shit about it. They know how to read a cost accountant's report, that's what they know. The cost accountant says, Listen. They're extending 784 through Westside and the Blue Ribbon is standing right in the way, along with half the residential district. And the directors say, Oh, is that right? How much are they allowing us on the property? And that's it. Christ, if Don and Ray Tarkington were alive, they'd have those cheap highway department fucks in court with so many restraining orders on their heads that they wouldn't get out from under until the year 2000. They'd go after them with a good sharp stick. Maybe they were a couple of buck-running paternalistic bastards, but they had a sense of *place*, Vinnie. You don't get that out of a cost accountant's report. If they were alive and someone told them that the highway commission was going to bury the laundry in eight lanes of composition hot-top, you would have heard the scream all the way down to city hall."

"But they're dead," Vinnie said.

"Yeah, they're dead, all right." His mind suddenly felt flabby and unstrung, like an amateur's guitar. Whatever he had needed to say to Vinnie had been lost in a welter of embarrassing personal stuff. Look at him, Freddy, he doesn't know what I'm talking about. He doesn't have a clue. "Thank God they're not here to see this."

Vinnie didn't say anything.

He gathered himself with an effort. "What I'm trying to say, Vinnie, is that there are two groups involved here. Them and us. We're laundry people. That's our business. They're cost accountant people. That's *their* business. They send down orders from on high, and we have to follow them. But that's *all* we have to do. Do you understand?"

"Sure, Bart," Vinnie said, but he could see that Vinnie didn't understand at all. He wasn't sure he did himself.

"Okay," he said. "I'll speak to Ordner. But just for your information, Vinnie, the Waterford plant is as good as ours. I'm closing the deal next Tuesday."

Vinnie grinned, relieved. "Jesus, that's great."

"Yes. Everything's under control."

As Vinnie was leaving, he called after him: "You tell me how that German restaurant is, okay?"

Vinnie Mason tossed him his number 1 grin, bright and full of teeth, all systems go. "I sure will, Bart."

Then Vinnie was gone and he was looking at the closed door. I made a mess of that, Fred. I didn't think you did so badly, George. Maybe you lost the handle at the end, but it's only in books that people say everything right the first time. No, I frigged up. He went out of here thinking Barton Dawes has lost a few cards out of his deck. God help him he's right. George, I have to ask you something, man to man. No, don't shut me off. Why did you buy those guns, George? Why did you do that?

Thump, the circuit breaker.

He went down on the floor, gave Ron Stone the salesmen's folders, and when he walked away Ron was bawling for Dave to come over and look at this stuff, might be something in it. Dave rolled his eyes. There was something in it, all right. It was known as work.

He went upstairs and called Ordner's office, hoping Ordner would be out drinking lunch. No breaks today. The secretary put him right through.

"Bart!" Steve Ordner said. "Always good to talk with you."

"Same here. I was talking to Vinnie Mason a little earlier, and he seemed to think you might be a little worried about the Waterford plant."

"Good God, no. Although I did think, maybe Friday night, we could lay out a few things—"

"Yeah, I called mainly to say Mary can't make it."

"Oh?"

"A virus. She doesn't dare go five seconds from the nearest john."

"Say, I'm sorry to hear that."

Cram it, you cheap dick.

"The doctor gave her some pills and she seems to be feeling better. But she might be, you know, catching."

"What time can you make it, Bart? Eight?"

"Yeah, eight's fine."

That's right, screw up the Friday Night Movie, *prick. What else is new?*

"How is the Waterford business progressing, Bart?"

"That's something we'd better talk about in person, Steve."

"That's fine." Another pause. "Carla sends her best. And tell Mary that both Carla and I . . ."

Sure. Yeah. Blah, blah, blah.

November 22, 1973

He woke up with a jerk that knocked the pillow onto the floor, afraid he might have screamed. But Mary was still sleeping in the other bed, a silent mound. The digital clock on the bureau said:

4:23 A.M.

It clicked into the next minute. Old Bea from Baltimore, the one who was into consciousness-raising hydrotherapy, had given it to them last Christmas. He didn't mind the clock, but he had never been able to get used to the click when the numbers changed. 4:23 *click*, 4:24 *click,* a person could go nuts.

He went down to the bathroom, turned on the light, and urinated. It made his heart thump heavily in his chest. Lately when he urinated his heart thumped like a fucking bass drum. Are you trying to tell me something, God?

He went back to bed and lay down, but sleep didn't come for a long time. He had thrashed around while he slept, and the bed had been remolded into enemy territory. He couldn't get it right again. His arms and legs also seemed to have forgotten which way they arranged themselves when he slept.

The dream was easy enough to figure out. No sweat there, Fred. A person could work that circuit breaker trick easy enough when he was awake; he could go on coloring in some picture piece by piece and pretending he couldn't see the whole thing. You could bury the big picture under the floor of your mind. But there was a trapdoor. When you were asleep, some-

times it banged open and something crawled up out
of the darkness. *Click.*

4:42 A.M.

In the dream he had been at Pierce Beach with
Charlie (funny, when he had given Vinnie Mason that
little thumb-nail autobiography he had forgotten to
mention Charlie—isn't that funny, Fred? No, I don't
think it's too funny, George. Neither do I, Fred. But
it's late. Or early. Or something.).

He and Charlie were on that long white beach and
it was a fine day for the beach—bright blue sky and
the sun beaming down like the face on one of those
idiotic smiley-smile buttons. People on bright blankets
and under umbrellas of many different hues, little kids
dibbling around the water's edge with plastic pails. A
lifeguard on his whitewashed tower, his skin as brown
as a boot, the crotch of his white Latex swim trunks
bulging, as if penis and testicle size were somehow a
job prerequisite and he wanted everyone in the area
to know they were not being let down. Someone's
transistor radio blaring rock and roll and even now he
could remember the tune:

But I love that dirty water,
Owww, Boston, you're my home.

Two girls walking by in bikinis, safe and sane inside
beautiful screwable bodies, never for you but for boy-
friends nobody ever saw, their toes kicking up tiny
fans of sand.

Only it was funny, Fred, because the tide was coming and there was no tide at Pierce Beach because the
nearest ocean was nine hundred miles away.

He and Charlie were making a sand castle. But they
had started too near the water and the incoming waves
kept coming closer and closer.

We have to build it farther back, Dad, Charlie said,

but he was stubborn and kept building. When the tide brought the water up to the first wall, he dug a moat with his fingers, spreading the wet sand like a woman's vagina. The water kept coming.

Goddam it! He yelled at the water.

He rebuilt the wall. A wave knocked it down. People started to scream about something. Others were running. The lifeguard's whistle blew like a silver arrow. He didn't look up. He had to save the castle. But the water kept coming, lapping his ankles, slurping a turret, a roof, the back of the castle, all of it. The last wave withdrew, showing only bland sand, smooth and flat and brown and shining.

There were more screams. Someone was crying. He looked up and saw the lifeguard was giving Charlie mouth-to-mouth. Charlie was wet and white except for his lips and eyelids, which were blue. His chest was not rising and falling. The lifeguard stopped trying. He looked up. He was smiling.

He was out over his head, the lifeguard was saying through his smile. *Isn't it time you went?*

He screamed: *Charlie!* and that was when he had wakened, afraid he might really have screamed.

He lay in the darkness for a long time, listening to the digital clock click, and tried not to think of the dream. At last he got up to get a glass of milk in the kitchen, and it was not until he saw the turkey thawing on a plate on the counter that he remembered it was Thanksgiving and today the laundry was closed. He drank his milk standing up, looking thoughtfully at the plucked body. The color of its skin was the same as the color of his son's skin in his dream. But Charlie hadn't drowned, of course.

When he got back into bed, Mary muttered something interrogative, thick and indecipherable with sleep.

"Nothing," he said. "Go to sleep."

She muttered something else.

"Okay," he said in the darkness.

She slept.

Click.

It was five o'clock, five in the morning. When he finally dozed off, dawn had come into the bedroom like a thief. His last thought was of the Thanksgiving turkey, sitting on the kitchen counter below the glare of the cold fluorescent overhead, dead meat waiting thoughtlessly to be devoured.

November 23, 1973

He drove their two-year-old LTD into Stephan Ord-ner's driveway at five minutes of eight and parked it behind Ordner's bottle-green Delta 88. The house was a rambling fieldstone, discreetly drawn back from Henreid Drive and partially hidden behind a high privet that was now skeletal in the smoky butt end of autumn. He had been here before, and knew it quite well. Downstairs was a massive rock-lined fireplace, and more modest ones in the bedrooms upstairs. They all worked. In the basement there was a Brunswick billiard table, a movie screen for home movies, a KLH sound system that Ordner had converted to quad the year before. Photos from Ordner's college basketball days dotted the walls—he stood six foot five and still kept in shape. Ordner had to duck his head going through doorways, and he suspected that Ordner was proud of it. Maybe he had had the doorways lowered so he could duck through them. The dining room table was a slab of polished oak, nine feet long. A wormy-oak highboy complemented it, gleaming richly through six or eight coats of varnish. A tall china cabinet at the other end of the room; it stood—oh, about six foot five, wouldn't you say, Fred? Yes, just about that. Out back there was a sunken barbecue pit almost big enough to broil an uncut dinosaur, and a putting green. No kidney-shaped pool. Kidney-shaped pools

were considered jejune these days. Strictly for the Ra-
worshiping Southern California middle-classers. The
Ordners had no children, but they supported a Korean
kid, a South Vietnamese kid, and were putting a
Ugandan through engineering school so he could go
back home and build hydroelectric dams. They were
Democrats, and had been Democrats for Nixon.

His feet whispered up the walk and he rang the bell.
The maid opened the door.

"Mr. Dawes," he said.

"Of course, sir. I'll just take your coat. Mr. Ordner
is in the study."

"Thank you."

He gave her his topcoat and walked down the hall
past the kitchen and the dining room. Just a peek at
the big table and the Stephan Ordner Memorial Highboy. The rug on the floor ended and he walked down
a hallway floored with white-and-black waxed linoleum checks. His feet clicked.

He reached the study door and Ordner opened it
just as he was reaching for the knob, as he had known
Ordner would.

"Bart!" Ordner said. They shook hands. Ordner
was wearing a brown cord jacket with patched elbows,
olive slacks, and Burgundy slippers. No tie.

"Hi, Steve. How's finance?"

Ordner groaned theatrically. "Terrible. Have you
looked at the stock market page lately?" He ushered
him in and closed the door behind him. The walls
were lined with books. To the left there was a small
fireplace with an electric log. In the center, a large
desk with some papers on it. He knew there was an
IBM Selectric buried in that desk someplace; if you
pressed the right button it would pop out on top like
a sleek-black torpedo.

"The bottom's falling out," he said.

Ordner grimaced. "That's putting it mildly. You can
hand it to Nixon, Bart. He finds a use for everything.
When they shot the domino theory to hell over in

Southeast Asia, he just took it and put it to work on the American economy. Worked lousy over there. Works great over here. What are you drinking?"

"Scotch-rocks would be fine."

"Got it right here."

He went to a fold-out cabinet, produced a fifth of scotch which returned only pocket change from your ten when purchased in a cut-rate liquor store, and splashed it over two ice cubes in a pony glass. He gave it to him and said, "Let's sit down."

They sat in wing chairs drawn up by the electric fire. He thought: *If I tossed my drink in there, I could blow that fucking thing to blazes.* He almost did it, too.

"Carla couldn't be here either," Ordner said. "One of her groups is sponsoring a fashion show. Proceeds to go to some teenage coffeehouse down in Norton."

"The fashion show is down there?"

Ordner looked startled. "In *Norton*? Hell no. Over in Russell. I wouldn't let Carla down in the Landing Strip with two bodyguards and a police dog. There's a priest . . . Drake, I think his name is. Drinks a lot, but those little pick'ninnies love him. He's sort of a liaison. Street priest."

"Oh."

"Yes."

They looked into the fire for a minute. He knocked back half of his scotch.

"The question of the Waterford plant came up at the last board meeting," Ordner said. "Middle of November. I had to admit my pants were a little loose on the matter. I was given . . . uh, a mandate to find out just what the situation is. No reflection on your management, Bart—"

"None taken," he said, and knocked back some more scotch. There was nothing left in there now but a few blots of alcohol trapped between the ice cubes and the glass. "It's always a pleasure when our jobs coincide, Steve."

Ordner looked pleased. "So what's the story? Vin Mason was telling me the deal wasn't closed."

"Vinnie Mason has got a dead short somewhere between his foot and his mouth."

"Then it's closed?"

"Closing. I expect to sign us into Waterford next Friday, unless something comes up."

"I was given to understand that the realtor made you a fairly reasonable offer, which you turned down."

He looked at Ordner, got up, and freshened the blots. "You didn't get that from Vinnie Mason."

"No."

He returned to the wing-back chair and the electric fire. "I don't suppose you'd care to tell me where you did get it?"

Ordner spread his hands. "It's business, Bart. When I hear something, I have to check into it—even if all my personal and professional knowledge of a man indicates that the something must be off-whack. It's nasty, but that's no reason to piss it around."

Freddy, nobody knew about the turn-down except the real estate guy and me. Old Mr. Just Business did a little personal checking, looks like. But that's no reason to piss it around, right? Right, George. Should I blow him out of the water, Freddy? Better be cool, George. And I'd slow down on the firewater.

"The figure I turned down was four-fifty," he said. "Just for the record, is that what you heard?"

"That's about it."

"And that sounded reasonable to you."

"Well," Ordner said, crossing his legs, "actually, it did. The city assessed the old plant at six-twenty, and the boiler can go right across town. Of course, there isn't quite as much room for expansion, but the boys uptown say that since the main plant had already reached pretty much optimum size, there was no need for the extra room. It looked to me as if we might at least break even, perhaps turn a profit . . . although

that wasn't the main consideration. We've got to locate, Bart. And damn quick."

"Maybe you heard something else."

Ordner recrossed his legs and sighed. "Actually, I
did. I heard that you turned down four-fifty and then
Thom McAn came along and offered five."

"A bid the realtor can't accept, in good faith."

"Not yet, but our option to buy runs out on Tuesday. You know that."

"Yes, I do. Steve, let me make three or four points,
okay?"

"Be my guest."

"First, Waterford is going to put us three miles away
from our industrial contracts—that's an average.
That's going to send our operating overhead way up.
All the motels are out by the Interstate. Worse than
that, our service is going to be slower. Holiday Inn
and Hojo are on our backs now when we're fifteen
minutes late with the towels. What's it going to be
like when the trucks have to fight their way through
three miles of crosstown traffic?"

Ordner was shaking his head. "Bart, they're *extending* the Interstate. That's why we're moving, remember? Our boys say there will be no time lost in
deliveries. It may even go quicker, using the extension.
And they also say the motel corporations have already
bought up good land in Waterford and Russell, near
what will be the new interchange. We're going to improve our position by going into Waterford, not
worsen it."

I stubbed my toe, Freddy. He's looking at me like
I've lost all my marbles. Right, George. Kee-rect.

He smiled. "Okay. Point taken. But those other motels won't be up for a year, maybe two. And if this
energy business is as bad as it looks—"

Ordner said flatly: "That's a policy decision, Bart.
We're just a couple of foot soldiers. We carry out the
orders." It seemed to him that there was a dart of
reproach there.

"Okay. But I wanted my own view on record."

"Good. It is. But you don't make policy, Bart. I want that perfectly clear. If the gasoline supplies dry up and all the motels fall flat, we'll take it on the ear, along with everyone else. In the meantime, we'd better let the boys upstairs worry about that and do our jobs."

I've been rebuked, Fred. That you have, George.

"All right. Here's the rest. I estimate it will take two hundred and fifty thousand dollars for renovations before the Waterford plant ever turns out a clean sheet."

"What?" Ordner set his drink down hard.

Aha, Freddy. Hit a bare nerve there.

"The walls are full of dry rot. The masonry on the east and north sides has mostly crumbled away to powder. And the floors are so bad that the first heavy-duty washer we put in there is going to end up in the basement."

"That's firm? That two-fifty figure?"

"Firm. We're going to need a new outside stack. New flooring, downstairs and up. And it's going to take five electricians two weeks to take care of that end. The place is only wired for two-forty-volt circuits and we have to have five-fifty loads. And since we're going to be at the far end of all the city utility conduits, I can promise you our power and water bills are going to go up twenty percent. The power increases we can live with, but I don't have to tell you what a twenty percent water-cost increase means to a laundry."

Ordner was looking at him now, shocked.

"Never mind what I said about the utility increase. That comes under operating overhead, not renovations. So where was I? The place has to be rewired for five-fifty. We're going to need a good burglar alarm and closed circuit TV. New insulation. New roofing. Oh yeah, and a drainage system. Over on Fir Street we're up on high ground, but Douglas Street sits at the bottom of a natural basin. The drainage system alone will cost anywhere from forty to seventy thousand dollars to put in."

"Christ, how come Tom Granger hasn't told me any of this?"

"He didn't go with me to inspect the place."

"Why not?"

"Because I told him to stay at the plant."

"You did *what*?"

"That was the day the furnace went out," he said patiently. "We had orders piling up and no hot water. Tom had to stay. He's the only one in the place that can talk to that furnace."

"Well Christ, Bart, couldn't you have taken him down another day?"

He knocked back the rest of his drink. "I didn't see the point."

"You didn't see the—" Ordner couldn't finish. He set his glass down and shook his head, like a man who has been punched. "Bart, do you know what it's going to mean if your estimate is wrong and we lose that plant? It's going to mean your *job*, that's what it's going to mean. My God, do you want to end up carrying your ass home to Mary in a basket? Is that what you want?"

You wouldn't understand, he thought, because you'd never make a move unless you were covered six ways and had three other fall guys lined up. That's the way you end up with four hundred thousand in stocks and funds, a Delta 88, and a typewriter that pops out of a desk at you like some silly jack-in-the-box. You stupid fuckstick, I could con you for the next ten years. I just might do it, too.

He grinned into Ordner's drawn face. "That's my last point, Steve. That's why I'm not worried."

"What do you mean?"

Joyously, he lied:

"Thom McAn had already notified the realtor that they're not interested in the plant. They had their guys out to look at it and they hollered holy hell. So what you've got is my word that the place is shit at four-fifty. What you've also got is a ninety-day option that runs out on Tuesday. What you've *also* got is a smart mick realtor named Monohan, who had been bluffing our pants off. It almost worked."

"What are you suggesting?"

"I'm suggesting we let the option run out. That we stand pat until next Thursday or so. You talk to your boys in cost and accounting about that twenty percent utility hike. I'll talk to Monohan. When I get through with him, he'll be down on his knees for two hundred thousand."

"Bart, are you sure?"

"Sure I am," he said, and smiled tightly. "I wouldn't be sticking out my neck if I thought somebody was going to cut it off."

George, what are you doing???

Shut up, shut up, don't bother me now.

"What we've got here," he said, "is a smart-ass realtor with no buyer. We can afford to take our time. Every day we keep him swinging in the wind is another day the price goes down when we do buy."

"All right," Ordner said slowly. "But let's have one thing clear, Bart. If we fail to exercise our option and then somebody else *does* go in there, I'd have to shoot you out of the saddle. Nothing—"

"I know," he said, suddenly tired. "Nothing personal."

"Bart, are you sure you haven't picked up Mary's bug? You look a little punk tonight."

You look a little punk yourself, asshole.

"I'll be fine when we get this settled. It's been a strain."

"Sure it has." Ordner arranged his face in sympathetic lines. "I'd almost forgotten . . . your house is right in the line of fire, too."

"Yes."

"You've found another place?"

"Well, we've got our eye on two. I wouldn't be surprised if I closed the laundry deal and my personal deal on the same day."

Ordner grinned. "It may be the first time in your life you've wheeled and dealed three hundred thousand to half a million dollars between sunrise and sunset."

"Yes, it's going to be quite a day."

On the way home Freddy kept trying to talk to him—scream at him, really—and he had to keep yanking the circuit breaker. He was just pulling onto Crestallen Street West when it burnt out with a smell of frying synapses and overloaded axons. All the questions spilled through and he jammed both feet down on the power brake. The LTD screeched to a halt in the middle of the street, and he was thrown against his seat belt hard enough to lock it and force a grunt up from his stomach.

When he had control of himself, he let the car creep over to the curb. He turned off the motor, killed the lights, unbuckled his seat belt, and sat trembling with his hands on the steering wheel.

From where he sat, the street curved gently, the streetlights making a graceful fish hook of light. It was a pretty street. Most of the houses which now lined it had been built in the postwar period 1946–1958, but somehow, miraculously, it had escaped the Fifties Crackerbox Syndrome, and the diseases that went with it: crumbling foundation, balding lawn, toy proliferation, premature aging of cars, flaking paint, plastic storm windows.

He knew his neighbors—why not? He and Mary had been on Crestallen Street almost fourteen years now. That was a long time. The Upslingers in the house above them; their boy Kenny delivered the morning paper. The Langs across the street; the Hobarts two houses down (Linda Hobart had baby-sat for Charlie, and now she was a doctoral student at City College); the Stauffers; Hank Albert, whose wife had died of emphysema four years ago; the Darbys' and just four houses up from where he was parked and shaking in his car, the Quinns. And a dozen other families that he and Mary had a nodding acquaintance with—mostly the ones with small children.

A nice street, Fred. A nice neighborhood. Oh, I know how the intellectuals sneer at suburbia—it's not as romantic as the rat-infested tenements or the hale-and-hearty back-to-the-land stuff. There are no great museums in suburbia, no great forests, no great challenges.

But there had been good times. I know what you're thinking, Fred. Good times, what are good times? There's no great joy in good times, no great sorrow, no great nothing. Just blah. Backyard barbecues in the summer dusk, everybody a little high but nobody getting really drunk or really ugly. Car pools we got up to go see the Mustangs play. The fucking Musties, who couldn't even beat the Pats the year the Pats were 1–12. Having people in to dinner or going out. Playing golf over at the Westside course or taking the wives to Ponderosa Pines and driving those little go-karts. Remember the time Bill Stauffer drove his right through that board fence and into some guy's swimming pool? Yeah, I remember that, George, we all laughed like hell. But George—

So bring on the bulldozers, right, Fred? Let's bury all of that. There'll be another suburb pretty quick, over in Waterford, where there was nothing but a bunch of vacant lots until this year. The March of Time. Progress in Review. Billion Dollar Babies. So what is it when you go over there to look? A bunch of saltine boxes painted different colors. Plastic pipes that are going to freeze every winter. Plastic wood. Plastic everything. Because Moe at the Highway Commission told Joe down at Joe's Construction, and Sue who works at the front desk at Joe's told Lou at Lou's Construction and pretty soon the big Waterford land boom is on and the developments are going up in the vacant lots, and also the high rises, the condominiums.

You get a house on Lilac Lane, which intersects Spain Lane going north and Dain Lane going south. You can pick Elm Street, Oak Street, Cypress Street, White Pine Blister Street. Each house has a full bathroom downstairs, a half-bathroom upstairs, and a fake chimney on the east side. And if you come home drunk you can't even find your own fucking house.

But George—

Shut up, Fred, I'm talking. And where are your neighbors? Maybe they weren't so much, those neighbors, but you knew who they were. You knew who you could borrow a cup of sugar from when you were tapped out. Where are they? Tony and Alicia Lang are in Minnesota because he requested a transfer to a new territory and got it. The Hobarts've moved out to Northside. Hank Albert has got a place in Waterford, true, but when he came back from signing the papers he looked like a man wearing a happy mask. I could see his eyes, Freddy. He looked like somebody who had just had his legs cut off and was trying to fool everybody that he was looking forward to the new plastic ones because they wouldn't get scabs if he happened to bang them against a door. So we move, and where are we? What are we? Just two strangers sitting in a house that's sitting in the middle of a lot more strangers' houses. That's what we are. The March of Time, Freddy. That's what it is. Forty waiting for fifty waiting for sixty. Waiting for a nice hospital bed and a nice nurse to stick a nice catheter inside you. Freddy, forty is the end of being young. Well, actually thirty's the end of being young, forty is where you stop fooling yourself. I don't want to grow old in a strange place.

He was crying again, sitting in his cold dark car and crying like a baby.

George, it's more than the highway, more than the move. I know what's wrong with you.

Shut up, Fred. I warn you.

But Fred wouldn't shut up and that was bad. If he

couldn't control Fred anymore, how would he ever get any peace?

It's Charlie, isn't it, George? You don't want to bury him a second time.

"It's Charlie," he said aloud, his voice thick and strange with tears. "And it's me. I can't. I really can't . . ."

He hung his head over and let the tears come, his face screwed up and his fists plastered into his eyes like any little kid you ever saw who lost his candy-nickle out the hole in his pants.

When he finally drove on, he was husked out. He felt dry. Hollow, but dry. Perfectly calm. He could even look at the dark houses on both sides of the street where people had already moved out with no tremor.

We're living in a graveyard now, he thought. Mary and I, in a graveyard. Just like Richard Boone in *I Bury the Living*. The lights were on at the Arlins', but they were leaving on the fifth of December. And the Hobarts had moved last weekend. Empty houses.

Driving up the asphalt of his own driveway (Mary was upstairs; he could see the mild glow of her reading lamp) he suddenly found himself thinking of something Tom Granger had said a couple of weeks before. He would talk to Tom about that. On Monday.

November 25, 1973

He was watching the Mustangs-Chargers game on the color TV and drinking his private drink, Southern Comfort and Seven-Up. It was his private drink because people laughed when he drank it in public. The Chargers were ahead 27–3 in the third quarter. Rucker had been intercepted three times. Great game, huh, Fred? It sure is, George. I don't see how you stand the tension.

Mary was asleep upstairs. It had warmed up over the weekend, and now it was drizzling outside. He felt sleepy himself. He was three drinks along.

There was a time-out, and a commercial came on. The commercial was Bud Wilkenson telling about how this energy crisis was a real bitch and everybody should insulate their attics and also make sure that the fireplace flue was closed when you weren't toasting marshmallows or burning witches or something. The logo of the company presenting the commercial came on at the end; the logo showed a happy tiger peeking at you over a sign that said:

EXXON

He thought that everyone should have known the evil days were coming when Esso changed its name to Exxon. Esso slipped comfortably out of the mouth like the sound of a man relaxing in a hammock. Exxon sounded like the name of a warlord from the planet Yurir.

"Exxon demands that all puny Earthlings throw down their weapons," he said. "Off the pig, puny Earthmen." He snickered and made himself another drink. He didn't even have to get up; the Southern Comfort, a forty-eight-ounce bottle of Seven-Up, and a plastic bowl of ice were all sitting on a small round table by his chair.

Back to the game. The Chargers punted. Hugh Fednach, the Mustangs' deep man, collected the football and ran it out to the Mustangs' 31. Then, behind the steely-eyed generalship of Hank Rucker, who might have seen the Heisman trophy once in a newsreel, the Mustangs mounted a six-yard drive. Gene Voreman punted. Andy Cocker of the Chargers returned the ball to the Mustangs' 46. And so it goes, as Kurt Von-

negut had so shrewdly pointed out. He had read all
of Kurt Vonnegut's books. He liked them mostly because they were funny. On the news last week it had
been reported that the school board of a town called
Drake, North Dakota, had burned yea copies of Vonnegut's novel *Slaughterhouse Five*, which was about
the Dresden fire bombing. When you thought about
it, there was a funny connection there.

Fred, why don't those highway department fuck-
sticks go build the 784 extension through Drake? I bet
they'd love it. George, that's a fine idea. Why don't
you write *The Blade* about that? Fuck you, Fred.

The Chargers scored, making it 34–3. Some cheer-
leaders pranced around on the Astroturf and shook
their asses. He fell into a semidoze, and when Fred
began to get at him, he couldn't shake him off.

George, since you don't seem to know what you're
doing, let me tell you. Let me spell it out for you, old
buddy. *(Get off my back, Fred.)* First, the option on
the Waterford plant is going to run out. That will happen at midnight on Tuesday. On Wednesday, Thom
McAn is going to close their deal with that slavering
little piece of St. Patrick's Day shit, Patrick J. Monohan. On Wednesday afternoon or Thursday morning,
a big sign that says *SOLD!* is going up. If anyone
from the laundry sees it, maybe you can postpone the
inevitable by saying: Sure. Sold to us. But if Ordner
checks, you're dead. Probably he won't. But *(Freddy,
leave me alone)* on Friday a new sign will go up. That
sign will say:

SITE OF OUR NEW WATERFORD PLANT
THOM MCAN SHOES
Here We Grow Again!!!

On Monday, bright and early, you are going to lose
your job. Yes, the way I see it, you'll be unemployed
before your ten o'clock coffee break. Then you can
come home and tell Mary. I don't know when that

will be. The bus ride only takes fifteen minutes, so conceivably you *could* end twenty years of marriage and twenty years of gainful employment in just about half an hour. But after you tell Mary, comes the explanation scene. You could put it off by getting drunk, but sooner or later—

Fred, shut your goddam mouth.

—sooner or later, you're going to have to explain just how you lost your job. You'll just have to fess up. Well, Mary, the highway department is going to rip down the Fir Street plant in a month or so, and I kind of neglected to get us a new one. I kept thinking that this whole 784 extension business was some kind of nightmare I was going to wake up from. Yes, Mary, yes, I located us a new plant—Waterford, that's right, you *capish*—but somehow I couldn't go through with it. How much is it going to cost Amroco? Oh, I'd say a million or a million-five, depending on how long it takes them to find a new plant location and how much business they lose for good.

I'm warning you, Fred.

Or you could tell her what no one knows better than you, George. That the profit margin on the Blue Ribbon has gotten so thin that the cost accountants might just throw up their hands and say, Let's ditch the whole thing, guys. We'll just take the city's money and buy a penny arcade down in Norton or a nice little pitch 'n' putt out in Russell or Crescent. There's too much potential red ink in this after the sugar that son of a bitch Dawes poured into our gas tank. You could tell her that.

Oh, go to hell.

But that's just the first movie, and this is a double feature, isn't it? Part two comes when you tell Mary there isn't any house to go to and there isn't going to be any house. And how are you going to explain that?

I'm not doing anything.

That's right. You're just some guy who fell asleep in his rowboat. But come Tuesday midnight, your boat is going over the falls, George. For Christ's sweet sake, go see Monohan on Monday and make him an unhappy man. Sign on the dotted line. You'll be in trouble anyway, with all those lies you told Ordner Friday night. But you can bail yourself out of that. God knows you've bailed yourself out of trouble before this.

Let me alone. I'm almost asleep.

It's Charlie, isn't it. This is a way of committing suicide. But it's not fair to Mary, George. It's not fair to anybody. You're—

He sat bolt upright, spilling his drink on the rug. "No one except maybe me."

Then what about the guns, George? What about the guns?

Trembling, he picked up his glass and made another drink.

November 26, 1973

He was having lunch with Tom Granger at Nicky's, a diner three blocks over from the laundry. They were sitting in a booth, drinking bottles of beer and waiting for their meals to come. There was a jukebox, and it was playing "Good-bye Yellow Brick Road," by Elton John.

Tom was talking about the Mustangs–Chargers game, which the Chargers had won 37–6. Tom was in love with all the city's sports teams, and their losses sent him into frenzies. Someday, he thought as he listened to Tom castigate the whole Mustangs' roster man by man, Tom Granger will cut off one of his ears with a laundry pin and send it to the general manager. A crazy man would send it to the coach, who would laugh and pin it to the locker room bulletin board, but Tom would send it to the general manager, who would brood over it.

The food came, brought by a waitress in a white nylon pants suit. He estimated her age at three hundred, possibly three hundred and four. Ditto weight. A small card over her left breast said:

GAYLE
Thanks For Your Patronage
Nicky's Diner

Tom had a slice of roast beef that was floating belly up in a plateful of gravy. He had ordered two cheeseburgers, rare, with an order of French fries. He knew the cheeseburgers would be well done. He had eaten at Nicky's before. The 784 extension was going to miss Nicky's by half a block.

They ate. Tom finished his tirade about yesterday's game and asked him about the Waterford plant and his meeting with Ordner.

"I'm going to sign on Thursday or Friday," he said.

"Thought the options ran out on Tuesday."

He went through his story about how Thom McAn had decided they didn't want the Waterford plant. It was no fun lying to Tom Granger. He had known Tom for seventeen years. He wasn't terribly bright. There was no challenge in lying to Tom.

"Oh," Tom said when he had finished, and the subject was closed. He forked roast beef into his mouth and grimaced. "Why do we eat here? The food is lousy here. Even the coffee is. My *wife* makes better coffee."

"I don't know," he said, slipping into the opening. "But do you remember when that new Italian place opened up? We took Mary and Verna."

"Yeah, in August. Verna still raves about that ricotta stuff . . . no, rigatoni. That's what they call it. Rigatoni."

"And that guy sat down next to us? That big fat guy?"

"Big, fat . . ." Tom chewed, trying to remember. He shook his head.

"You said he was a crook."

"Ohhhhh." His eyes opened wide. He pushed his plate away and lit a Herbert Tareyton and dropped the dead match into his plate, where it floated on the gravy. "Yeah, that's right. Sally Magliore."

"Was that his name?"

"Yeah, that's right. Big guy with thick glasses. Nine chins. Salvatore Magliore. Sounds like the specialty in an Italian whorehouse, don't it? Sally One-Eye, they used to call him, on account of he had a cataract on one eye. He had it removed at the Mayo Clinic three or four years ago . . . the cataract, not the eye. Yeah, he's a big crook."

"What's he in?"

"What are they all in?" Tom asked, tapping his cigarette ash into his plate. "Dope, girls, gambling, crooked investments, sharking. And murdering other crooks. Did you see that in the paper? Just last week. They found some guy in the trunk of his car behind a filling station. Shot six times in the head and his throat cut. That's really ridiculous. Why would anyone want to cut a guy's throat after they just shot him six times in the head? Organized crime, that's what Sally One-Eye's in."

"Does he have a legitimate business?"

"Yeah, I think he does. Out on the Landing Strip, beyond Norton. He sells cars. Magliore's Guaranteed Okay Used Cars. A body in every trunk." Tom laughed and tapped more ashes into his plate. Gayle came back and asked them if they wanted more coffee. They both ordered more.

"I got those cotter pins today for the boiler door," Tom said. "They remind me of my dork."

"Is that right?"

"Yeah, you should see those sons of bitches. Nine inches long and three through the middle."

"Did you mention my dork?" he asked, and they both laughed and talked shop until it was time to go back to work.

He got off the bus that afternoon at Barker Street and went into Duncan's, which was a quiet neighborhood bar. He ordered a beer and listened to Duncan bitch for a little while about the Mustangs–Chargers game. A man came up from the back and told Duncan that the Bowl-a-Score machine wasn't working right. Duncan went back to look at it, and he sipped his beer and looked at the TV. There was a soaper on, and two women were talking in slow, apocalyptic tones about a man named Hank. Hank was coming home from college, and one of the women had just found out that Hank was her son, the result of a disastrous experiment that had occurred after her high school prom twenty years ago.

Freddy tried to say something, and George shut him right up. The circuit breaker was in fine working order. Had been all day.

That's right, you fucking schizo! Fred yelled, and then George sat on him. Go peddle your papers, Freddy. You're persona non grata around here.

"Of course I'm not going to tell him," said one of the women on the tube. "How do you expect me to tell him that?"

"Just . . . tell him," said the other woman.

"Why should I tell him? Why should I knock his whole life out of orbit over something that happened twenty years ago?"

"Are you going to lie to him?"

"I'm not going to tell him anything."

"You *have* to tell him."

"Sharon, I can't afford to tell him."

"If you don't tell him, Betty, I'll tell him myself."

"That fucking machine is all fucked to shit," Duncan said, coming back. "That's been a pain in the ass ever since they put it in. Now what have I got to do? Call the fucking Automatic Industries Company. Wait twenty minutes until some dipshit secretary connects me with the right line. Listen to some guy tell me that they're pretty busy but they'll try to send a guy out Wednesday. *Wednesday!* Then some guy with his brains between the cheeks of his ass will show up on Friday, drink four bucks' worth of free beer, fix whatever's wrong and probably rig something else to break in two weeks, and tell me I shouldn't let the guys throw the weights so hard. I used to have pinball machines. That was good. Those machines hardly ever fucked up. But this is progress. If I'm still here in 1980, they'll take out the Bowl-a-Score and put in an Automatic Blow-Job. You want another beer?"

"Sure," he said.

Duncan went to draw it. He put fifty cents on the bar and walked back to the phone booth beside the broken Bowl-a-Score.

He found what he was looking for in the yellow pages under *Automobiles, New and Used.* The listing there said: MAGLIORE'S USED CARS, Rt. 16, Norton 892-4576.

Route 16 became Venner Avenue as you went farther into Norton. Venner Avenue was also known as the Landing Strip, where you could get all the things the yellow pages didn't advertise.

He put a dime in the phone and dialed Magliore's Used Cars. The phone was picked up on the second ring, and a male voice said: "Magliore's Used Cars."

"This is Dawes," he said. "Barton Dawes. Can I talk to Mr. Magliore?"

"Sal's busy. But I'll be glad to help you if I can. Pete Mansey."

"No, it has to be Mr. Magliore, Mr. Mansey. It's about those two Eldorados."

"You got a bum steer," Mansey said. "We're not taking any big cars in trade the rest of the year, on account of this energy business. Nobody's buying them. So—"

"*I'm* buying," he said.

"What's that"

"Two Eldorados. One 1970, one 1972. One gold, one cream. I spoke to Mr. Magliore about them last week. It's a business deal."

"Oh yeah, right. He really isn't here now, Mr. Dawes. To tell you the truth, he's in Chicago. He's not getting in until eleven o'clock tonight."

Outside, Duncan was hanging a sign on the Bowl-a-Score. The sign said:

OUT OF ORDER

"Well he be in tomorrow?"

"Yeah, sure will. Was this a trade deal?"

"No, straight buy."

"One of the specials?"

He hesitated a moment, then said: "Yes, that's right. Would four o'clock be okay?"

"Sure, fine."

"Thanks, Mr. Mansey."

"I'll tell him you called."

"You do that," he said, and hung up carefully. His palms were sweating.

Merv Griffin was chatting with celebrities when he got home. There was nothing in the mail; that was a relief. He went into the living room.

Mary was sipping a hot rum concoction in a teacup. There was a box of Kleenex beside her and the room smelled of Vicks.

"Are you all right?" he asked her.

"Don'd kiss be," she said, and her voice had a distant foghorning quality. "I cabe downd with sobe-thing."

"Poor kid." He kissed her forehead.

"I hade do ask you, Bard, bud would you ged the

groceries tonighd? I was goig with Meg Carder, bud I had to call her ad beg off."

"Sure. Are you running a fever?"

"Dno. Well, baybe a liddle."

"Want me to make an appointment with Fontaine for you?"

"Dno. I will toborrow if I don'd feel bedder."

"You're really stuffy."

"Yes. The Vicks helbed for a while, bud dow—" She shrugged and smiled wanly. "I soud like Dodald Duck."

He hesitated a moment and then said, "I'll be home a little bit late tomorrow night."

"Oh?"

"I'm going out to Northside to look at a house. It seems like a good one. Six rooms. A little backyard. Not too far from the Hobarts."

Freddy said quite clearly: *Why, you dirty low-life son of a bitch.*

Mary brightened. "That's woderful! Cad I go look with you?"

"Better not, with that cold."

"I'll buddle ub."

"Next time," he said firmly.

"Ogay." She looked at him. "Thang God you're finally boving on this," she said. "I was worried."

"Don't worry."

"I wodn't."

She took a sip of the hot rum drink and snuggled against him. He could hear her breath snuffling in and out. Merv Griffin was chatting with James Brolin about his new movie, *Westworld.* Soon to be showing at barbershops all over the country.

After a while Mary got up and put TV dinners in the oven. He got up, switched the TV over to reruns of "F Troop" and tried not to listen to Freddy. After a while, though, Freddy changed his tune.

*   *   *

Do you remember how you got the first TV, Georgie?

He smiled a little, looking not at Forrest Tucker but right through him. I do, Fred. I surely do.

They had come home one evening, about two years after they were married, from the Upshaws, where they had been watching "Your Hit Parade" and "Dan Fortune," and Mary had asked him if he didn't think Donna Upshaw had seemed a little . . . well, off. Now, sitting here, he could remember Mary, slim and oddly, fetchingly taller in a pair of white sandals she had gotten to celebrate summer. She had been wearing white shorts, too; her legs looked long and coltish, as if they really might go all the way up to her chin. In truth, he hadn't been very interested in whether or not Donna Upshaw had seemed a little off; he had been interested in divesting Mary of those tight shorts. That had been where his interest lay—not to put too fine a point on it.

"Maybe she's getting a little tired of serving Spanish peanuts to half the neighborhood just because they're the only people on the street with a TV," he said.

He supposed he had seen the little frown line between her eyes—the one that always meant Mary was cooking something up, but by then they were halfway upstairs, his hand was roaming down over the seat of those shorts—what little seat there was—and it wasn't until later, until after, that she said:

"How much would a table model cost us, Bart?"

Half asleep, he had answered, "Well, I guess we could get a Motorola for twenty-eight, maybe thirty bucks. But the Philco—"

"Not a radio. A TV."

He sat up, turned on the lamp, and looked at her. She was lying there naked, the sheet down around her hips, and although she was smiling at him, he thought she was serious. It was Mary's I-dare-you grin.

"Mary, we can't afford a TV."

"How much for a table model? A GE or a Philco or something?"

"New?"

"New?"

He considered the question, watching the play of lamplight across the lovely round curves of her breasts. She had been so much slimmer then (although she's hardly a fatty now, George, he reproached himself; never said she was, Freddy my boy), so much more alive somehow. Even her hair had crackled out its own message: *alive, awake, aware* . . .

"Around seven hundred and fifty dollars," he said, thinking that would douse the grin . . . but it hadn't.

"Well, look," she said, sitting up Indian-fashion in bed, her legs crossed under the sheet.

"I am," he said, grinning.

"Not at *that.*" But she laughed, and a flush had spread prettily down her cheeks to her neck (although she hadn't pulled the sheet up, he remembered).

"What's on your mind?"

"Why do men want a TV?" she asked. "To watch all the sports on the weekends. And why do women want one? Those soap operas in the afternoon. You can listen while you iron or put your feet up if your work's done. Now suppose we each found something to do—something that *pays*—during that time we'd otherwise just be sitting around . . ."

"Reading a book, or maybe even making love?" he suggested.

"We always find time for *that,*" she said, and laughed, and blushed, and her eyes were dark in the lamplight and it threw a warm, semicircular shadow between her breasts, and he knew then that he was going to give in to her, he would have promised her a fifteen-hundred-dollar Zenith console model if she would just let him make love to her again, and at the thought he felt himself stiffening, felt the snake turning to stone, as Mary had once said when she'd had a little too much to drink at the Ridpaths' New Year's

Eve party (and now, eighteen years later, he felt the snake turning to stone again—over a memory).

"Well, all right," he said. "I'm going to moonlight weekends and you're going to moonlight afternoons. But what, dear Mary, Oh-not-so-Virgin Mary, are we going to do?"

She pounced on him, giggling, her breasts a soft weight on his stomach (flat-enough in those days, Freddy, not a sign of a bay window). "That's the trick of it!" she said. "What's today? June eighteenth?"

"That's right."

"Well, you do your weekend things, and on December eighteenth we'll put our money together—"

"—and buy a toaster," he said, grinning.

"—and get that TV," she said solemnly. "I'm sure we can do it, Bart." Then the giggles broke out again. "But the fun part'll be that we won't tell each other what we're up to until after."

"Just as long as I don't see a red light over the door when I come home from work tomorrow," he said, capitulating.

She grabbed him, got on top of him, started to tickle. The tickling turned to caresses.

"Bring it to me," she whispered against his neck, and gripped him with gentle yet excruciating pressure, guiding him and squeezing him at the same time. "Put it in me, Bart."

And later, in the dark again, hands crossed behind his head, he said: "We don't tell each other, right?"

"Nope."

"Mary, what brought this on? What I said about Donna Upshaw not wanting to serve Spanish peanuts to half the neighborhood?"

There were no giggles in her voice when she replied. Her voice was flat, austere, and just a little frightening: a faint taste of winter in the warm June air of their third-floor walkup apartment. "I don't like to freeload, Bart. And I won't. Ever."

For a week and a half he had turned her quirky

little proposal over in his mind, wondering just what in the hell he was suppose to do to bring in his half of the seven hundred and fifty dollars (and probably more like three-quarters of it, the way it'll turn out, he thought) on the next twenty or so weekends. He was a little old to be mowing lawns for quarters. And Mary had gotten a look—a smug sort of look—that gave him the idea that she had either landed something or was landing something. Better get on your track shoes, Bart, he thought, and had to laugh out loud at himself.

Pretty fine days, weren't they, Freddy? he asked himself now as Forrest Tucker and "F Troop" gave way to a cereal commercial where an animated rabbit preached that "Trix are for kids." They were, Georgie. They were fucking *great* days.

One day he had been unlocking his car after work, and he had happened to look at the big industrial smokestack behind dry-cleaning, and it came to him.

He had put the keys back in his pocket and went in to talk to Don Tarkington. Don leaned back in his chair, looked at him from under shaggy eyebrows that were even then turning white (as were the hairs which bushed out of his ears and curled from his nostrils), hands steepled on his chest.

"Paint the stack," Don said.

He nodded.

"Weekends."

He nodded again.

"Flat fee—three hundred dollars."

And again.

"You're crazy."

He burst out laughing.

Don smiled a little. "You got a dope habit, Bart?"

"No," he said. "But I've got a little thing on with Mary."

"A bet?" The shaggy eyebrows went up half a mile.

"More gentlemanly than that. A wager, I guess you'd call it. Anyway, Don, the stack needs the paint, and I need the three hundred dollars. What do you say? A painting contractor would charge you four and a quarter."

"You checked."

"I checked."

"You crazy bastard," Don said, and burst out laughing. "You'll probably kill yourself."

"Yeah, I probably will," he said, and began laughing himself (and here, eighteen years later, as the Trix rabbit gave way to the evening news, he sat grinning like a fool).

And that was how, one weekend after the Fourth of July, he found himself on a shaky scaffolding eighty feet in the air, a paintbrush in his hand and his ass wagging in the wind. Once a sudden afternoon thunderstorm had come up, snapped one of the ropes which held up the scaffolding as easily as you might snap a piece of twine holding a package, and he almost did fall. The safety rope around his waist had held and he had lowered himself to the roof, heart thudding like a drum, sure that no power on earth would get him back up there—not for a lousy table-model TV. But he had gone back. Not for the TV, but for Mary. For the look of the lamplight on her small, uptilted breasts, for the dare-you grin on her lips and in her eyes—her dark eyes which could sometimes turn so light or darken even more, into summer thunderheads.

By early September he had finished the stack; it stood cleanly white against the sky, a chalk mark on a blueboard, slim and bright. He looked at it with some pride as he scrubbed his spattered forearms with paint thinner.

Don Tarkington paid him by check. "Not a bad job," was his only comment, "considering the jackass that did it."

He picked up another fifty dollars paneling the walls of Henry Chalmers' new family room—in those days, Henry had been the plant foreman—and painting Ralph Tremont's aging Chris-Craft. When December

18 rolled around, he and Mary sat down at their small dining room table like adversary but oddly friendly gunslingers, and he put three hundred and ninety dollars in cash in front of her—he had banked the money and there had been some interest.

She put four hundred and sixteen dollars with it. She took it from her apron pocket. It made a much bigger wad than his, because most of it was ones and fives.

He gasped at it and then said, "What the Christ did you *do*, Mary?"

Smiling, she said: "I made twenty-six dresses, hemmed up forty-nine dresses, hemmed down sixty-four dresses; I made thirty-one skirts; I crocheted three samplers; I hooked four rugs, one of latch-hook style; I made five sweaters, two afghans and one complete set of table linen; I embroidered sixty-three handkerchiefs; twelve sets of towels and twelve sets of pillowcases, and I can see all the monograms in my sleep."

Laughing, she held out her hands, and for the first time he really noticed the thick pads of calluses on the tips of the fingers, like the calluses a guitar player eventually builds up.

"Oh Christ, Mary," he said, his voice hoarse. "Christ, look at your hands."

"My hands are fine," she said, and her eyes darkened and danced. "And you looked very cute up there on the smokestack, Bart. I thought once I'd buy a slingshot and see if I couldn't hit you in the butt—"

Roaring, he had jumped up and chased her through the living room and into the bedroom. Where we spent the rest of the afternoon, as I recall it, Freddy old man.

They discovered that they not only had enough for a table model TV, but that for another forty dollars they actually could have a console model. RCA had jumped the model year, the proprietor of John's TV downtown told them (John's was already buried under the 784 extension of course, long gone, along with the Grand and everything else), and was going for broke. He would be happy to let them have it, and for just ten dollars a week—

"No," Mary said.

John looked pained. "Lady, it's only four weeks. You're hardly signing your life away on easy credit terms."

"Just a minute," Mary said, and led him outside into the pre-Christmas cold where carols tangled in each other up and down the street.

"Mary," he said, "he's right. It's not as if—"

"The first thing we buy on credit ought to be our own house, Bart," she said. That faint line appeared between her eyes. "Now listen—"

They went back inside. "Will you hold it for us?" he asked John.

"I guess so—for a while. But this is my busy season, Mr. Dawes. How long?"

"Just over the weekend," he said. "I'll be in Monday night."

They had spent that weekend in the country, bundled up against the cold and the snow which threatened but did not fall. They drove slowly up and down back roads, giggling like kids, a six-pack on the seat for him and a bottle of wine for Mary, and they saved the beer bottles and picked up more, bags of beer bottles, bags of soda bottles, each one of the small ones worth two cents, the big ones worth a nickle. It had been one hell of a weekend, Bart thought now— Mary's hair had been long, flowing out behind her over that imitation-leather coat of hers, the color flaming in her cheeks. He could see her now, walking up a ditch filled with fallen autumn leaves, kicking through them with her boots, producing a noise like a steady low forest fire . . . then the click of a bottle and she raised it up in triumph, waggled it at him from across the road, grinning like a kid.

They don't have returnable bottles anymore, either,

Georgie. The gospel these days is no deposit, no return. Use it up and throw it out.

That Monday, after work, they had turned in thirty-one dollars' worth of bottles, visiting four different supermarkets to spread the wealth around. They had arrived at John's ten minutes before the store closed.

"I'm nine bucks short," he told John.

John wrote PAID across the bill of sale that had been taped to the RCA console. "Merry Christmas, Mr. Dawes," he said. "Let me get my dolly and I'll help you out with it."

They got it home, and an excited Dick Keller from the first floor helped him carry it up, and that night they had watched TV until the national anthem had come on the last operating channel and then they had made love in front of the test pattern, both of them with raging headaches from eyestrain.

TV had rarely looked so good since.

Mary came in and saw him looking at the TV, his empty scotch-rocks glass in his hand.

"Your dinner's ready, Bart," she said. "You want it in here?"

He looked at her, wondering exactly when he had seen the dare-you grin on her lips for the last time . . . exactly when the little line between her eyes had begun to be there all the time, like a wrinkle, a scar, a tattoo proclaiming age.

You wonder about some things, he thought, that you'd never in God's world want to know. Now why the hell is that?

"Bart?"

"Let's eat in the dining room," he said. He got up and snapped the TV off.

"All right."

They sat down. He looked at the meal in the aluminum tray. Six little compartments, and something that looked pressed in each one. The meat had gravy on it. It was his impression that the meats in TV dinners *always* had gravy on them. TV dinnermeat would look naked without gravy, he thought, and then he remembered his thought about Lorne Greene for absolutely no reason at all: *Boy, I'll snatch you bald-headed.*

It didn't amuse him this time. Somehow it scared him.

"What were you sbiling about in the living roob, Bart?" Mary asked. Her eyes were red from her cold, and her nose had a chapped, raw look.

"I don't remember," he said, and for the moment he thought: *I'll just scream now, I think. For lost things. For your grin, Mary. Pardon me while I just throw back my head and scream for the grin that's never there on your face anymore. Okay?*

"You looked very habby," she said.

Against his will—it was a secret thing, and tonight he felt he needed his secret things, tonight his feelings felt as raw as Mary's nose looked—against his will he said: "I was thinking of the time we went out picking up bottles to finish paying for that TV. The RCA console."

"Oh, that," Mary said, and then sneezed into her hankie over her TV dinner.

He ran into Jack Hobart at the Stop 'n' Shop. Jack's cart was full of frozen foods, heat-and-serve canned products, and a lot of beer.

"Jack!" he said. "What are you doing way over here?"

Jack smiled a little. "I haven't got used to the other store yet, so . . . I thought . . ."

"Where's Ellen?"

"She had to fly back to Cleveland," he said. "Her mother died."

"Jesus, I'm sorry Jack. Wasn't that sudden?"

Shoppers were moving all around them under the cold overhead lights. Muzak came down from hidden speakers, old standards that you could never quite recognize. A woman with a full cart passed them, dragging a screaming three-year-old in a blue parka with snot on the sleeves.

"Yeah, it was," Jack Hobart said. He smiled meaninglessly and looked down into his cart. There was a large yellow bag there that said:

KITTY-PAN KITTY LITTER
Use It, Throw It Away!
Sanitary!

"Yeah, it was. She'd been feeling punk, thank you, but she thought it might have been a, you know, sort of leftover from change of life. It was cancer. They opened her up, took a look, and sewed her right back up. Three weeks later she was dead. Hell of a hard thing for Ellen. I mean, she's only twenty years younger."

"Yeah," he said.

"So she's out in Cleveland for a little while."

"Yeah."

"Yeah."

They looked at each other and grinned shamefacedly over the fact of death.

"How is it?" he asked. "Out there in Northside?"

"Well, I'll tell you the truth, Bart. Nobody seems very friendly."

"No?"

"You know Ellen works down at the bank?"

"Yeah, sure."

"Well, a lot of the girls used to have a car pool—I used to let Ellen have the car every Thursday. That was her part. There's a pool out in Northside into the city, but all the women who use it are part of some club that Ellen can't join unless she's been there at least a year."

"That sounds pretty damn close to discrimination, Jack."

"Fuck them," Jack said angrily. "Ellen wouldn't join their goddam club if they crawled up the street on their hands and knees. I got her her own car. A used Buick. She loves it. Should have done it two years ago."

"How's the house?"

"It's fine," Jack said, and sighed. "The electricity's high, though. You should see our bill. That's no good for people with a kid in college."

They shuffled. Now that Jack's anger had passed, the shamefaced grin was back on his face. He realized that Jack was almost pathetically glad to see someone from the neighborhood and was prolonging the moment. He had a sudden vision of Jack knocking around in the new house, the sound from the TV filling the rooms with phantom company, his wife a thousand miles away seeing her mother into the ground.

"Listen, why don't you come back to the house?" he asked. "We'll have a couple of six-packs and listen to Howard Cosell explain everything that's wrong with the NFL."

"Hey, that'd be great."

"Just let me call Mary after we check out."

He called Mary and Mary said okay. She said she would put some frozen pastries in the oven and then go to bed so she wouldn't give Jack her cold.

"How does he like it out there?" she asked.

"Okay, I guess. Mare, Ellen's mother died. She's out in Cleveland for the funeral. Cancer."

"Oh, *no*."

"So I thought Jack might like the company, you know—"

"Sure, of course." She paused. "Did you tell hib we bight be neighbors before log?"

"No," he said. "I didn't tell him that."

"You ought to. It bight cheer hib ub."

"Sure. Good-bye, Mary."

"Bye."

"Take some aspirin before you go to bed."

"I will."

"Bye."

"Bye, George." She hung up.

He looked at the phone, chilled. She only called him that when she was very pleased with him. Fred-and-George had been Charlie's game originally.

He and Jack Hobart went home and watched the game. They drank a lot of beer. But it wasn't so good.

When Jack was getting into his car to go home at quarter past twelve, he looked up bleakly and said: "That goddam highway. That's what fucked up the works."

"It sure did." He thought Jack looked old, and it scared him. Jack was about his age.

"You keep in touch, Bart."

"I will."

They grinned hollowly at each other, a little drunk, a little sick. He watched Jack's car until its taillights had disappeared down the long, curving hill.

November 27, 1973

He was a little hung-over and a little sleepy from staying up so late. The sound of the laundry washers kicking onto the extract cycle seemed loud in his ears, and the steady *thump-hiss* of the shirt presses and the ironer made him want to wince.

Freddy was worse. Freddy was playing the very devil today.

Listen, Fred was saying. This is your last chance, my boy. You've still got all afternoon to get over to Monohan's office. If you let it wait until five o'clock, it's going to be too late.

The option doesn't run out until midnight.

Sure it doesn't. But right after work Monohan is going to feel a pressing need to go see some relatives. In Alaska. For him it means the difference between a forty-five-thousand-dollar commission and fifty thousand dollars—the price of a new car. For that kind of money you don't need a pocket calculator. For that kind of money you might discover relatives in the sewer system under Bombay.

But it didn't matter. It had gone too far. He had let the machine run without him too long. He was hypnotized by the coming explosion, almost lusted for it. His belly groaned in its own juices.

He spent most of the afternoon in the washroom, watching Ron Stone and Dave run test loads with one of the new laundry products. It was loud in the washroom. The noise hurt his tender head, but it kept him from hearing his thoughts.

After work he got his car out of the parking lot—Mary had been glad to let him have it for the day since he was seeing about their new house—and drove through downtown and through Norton.

In Norton, blacks stood around on street corners and outside bars. Restaurants advertised different kinds of soul food. Children hopped and danced on chalked sidewalk grids. He saw a pimpmobile—a huge pink Eldorado Cadillac—pull up in front of an anonymous brownstone apartment building. The man who got out was a Wilt Chamberlain-size black in a white planter's hat and a white ice cream suit with pearl buttons and black platform shoes with huge gold buckles on the sides. He carried a malacca stick with a large ivory ball on the top. He walked slowly, majestically, around to the hood of the car, where a set of caribou antlers were mounted. A tiny silver spoon hung on a silver chain around his neck and winked in the thin autumn sun. He watched the man in the rearview mirror as the children ran to him for sweets.

Nine blocks later the tenements thinned to ragged, open fields that were still soft and marshy. Oily water stood between hummocks in puddles, their surfaces flat, deadly rainbows. On the left, near the horizon, he could see a plane landing at the city's airport.

He was now on Route 16, traveling past the exurban sprawl between the city and the city limits. He passed

McDonald's. Shakey's, Nino's Steak Pit. He passed a
Dairy Freez and the Noddy-Time Motel, both closed for
the season. He passed the Norton Drive-In, where the
marquee said:

> FRI—SAT—SUN
>
> RESTLESS WIVES
> SOME CAME RUNNING   RATED X
> EIGHT-BALL

He passed a bowling alley and a driving range that
was closed for the season. Gas stations—two of them
with signs that said:

> SORRY, NO GAS

It was still four days until they got their gasoline
allotments for December. He couldn't find it in himself to feel sorry for the country as a whole as it went
into this science-fiction-style crisis—the country had
been pigging petroleum for too long to warrant his
sympathy—but he could feel sorry for the little men
with their peckers caught in the swing of a big door.

A mile farther on he came to Magliore's Used Cars.
He didn't know what he had expected, but he felt
disappointed. It looked like a cut-rate, fly-by-night operation. Cars were lined up on the lot facing the road
under looped lines of flapping banners—red, yellow,
blue, green—that had been tied between light standards that would shine down on the product at night.
Prices and slogans soaped on the windshields:

> $795
> RUNS GOOD!

and

> $550
> GOOD TRANSPORTATION!

and on a dusty old Valiant with flat tires and a
cracked windshield:

$75

MECHANIX SPECIAL!

A salesman wearing a gray-green topcoat was nodding
and smiling noncommittally as a young kid in a red silk
jacket talked to him. They were standing by a blue Mustang with cancer of the rocker panels. The kid said
something vehement and thumped the driver's side door
with the flat of his hand. Rust flaked off in a small
flurry. The salesman shrugged and went on smiling. The
Mustang just sat there and got a little older.

There was a combination office and garage in the
center of the lot. He parked and got out of his car.
There was a lift in the garage, and an old Dodge with
giant fins was up on it. A mechanic walked out from
under, holding a muffler in both grease-gloved hands
like a chalice.

"Say, you can't park there, mister. That's in the
right-of-way."

"Where should I park?"

"Take it around back if you're goin in the office."

He drove the LTD around to the back, creeping
carefully down the narrow way between the corru-
gated metal side of the garage and a row of cars. He
parked behind the garage and got out. The wind,
strong and cutting, made him wince. The heater had
disarmed his face and he had to squint his eyes to
keep them from tearing.

There was an automobile junkyard back here. It
stretched for acres, amazing the eye. Most of the cars
had been gutted of parts and now they sat on their
wheel rims or axles like the victims of some awful
plague who were too contagious to even be dragged
to the dead-pit. Grilles with empty headlight sockets
gazed at him raptly.

He walked back out front. The mechanic was installing the muffler. An open bottle of Coke was balanced on a pile of tires to his right.

He called to the mechanic: "Is Mr. Magliore in?" Talking to mechanics always made him feel like an asshole. He had gotten his first car twenty-four years ago, and talking to mechanics still made him feel like a pimply teenager.

The mechanic looked over his shoulder and kept working his socket wrench. "Yeah, him and Mansey. Both in the office."

"Thanks."

"Sure."

He went into the office. The walls were imitation pine, the floor muddy squares of red and white linoleum. There were two old chairs with a pile of tattered magazines between them—*Outdoor Life, Field and Stream, True Argosy.* No one was sitting in the chairs. There was one door, probably leading to an inner office, and on the left side, a little cubicle like a theater box office. A woman was sitting in there, working an adding machine. A yellow pencil was poked into her hair. A pair of harlequin glasses hung against her scant bosom, held by a rhinestone chain. He walked over to her, nervous now. He wet his lips before he spoke.

"Excuse me."

She looked up. "Yes?"

He had a crazy impulse to say: *I'm here to see Sally One-Eye, bitch. Shake your tail.*

Instead, he said: "I have an appointment with Mr. Magliore."

"You do?" She looked at him warily for a moment and then riffled through some slips on the table beside the adding machine. She pulled one out. "Your name is Dawes? Barton Dawes?"

"That's right."

"Go right in." She stretched her lips at him and began to peck at the adding machine again.

He was very nervous. Surely they knew he had

conned them. They were running some kind of midnight auto sales here, that much had been obvious from the way Mansey had spoken to him yesterday. And they knew he knew. Maybe it would be better to go right out the door, drive like hell to Monohan's office, and maybe catch him before he left for Alaska or Timbuktu or wherever he would be leaving for.

Finally, Freddy said. The man shows some sense.

He walked over to the door in spite of Freddy, opened it, and stepped into the inner office. There were two men. The one behind the desk was fat and wearing heavy glasses. The other was razor thin and dressed in a salmon-pink sports coat that made him think of Vinnie. He was bending over the desk. They were looking at a J.C. Whitney catalogue.

They looked up at him. Magliore smiled from behind his desk. The glasses made his eyes appear faded and enormous, like the yolks of poached eggs.

"Mr. Dawes?"

"That's right."

"Glad you could drop by. Want to shut the door?"

"Okay."

He shut it. When he turned back, Magliore was no longer smiling. Neither was Mansey. They were just looking at him, and the room temperature seemed to have gone down twenty degrees.

"Okay," Magliore said. "What is this shit?"

"I wanted to talk to you."

"I talk for free. But not to shitbirds like you. You call up Pete and give him a line of crap about two Eldorados." He pronounced it "Eldoraydos." "You talk to me, mister. You tell me what your act is."

Standing by the door, he said: "I heard maybe you sold things."

"Yeah, that's right. Cars. I sell cars."

"No," he said. "Other stuff. Stuff like . . ." He looked around at the fake-pine-paneled walls. God knew how many agencies were bugging this place. "Just stuff," he finished, and the words came out on crutches.

"You mean stuff like dope and whores ('hoors') and off-track betting? Or did you want to buy a hitter to knock off your wife or your boss?" Magliore saw him wince and laughed harshly. "That's not too bad, mister, not bad at all for a shitbird. That's the big 'What if this place is bugged' act, right? That's number one at the police academy, am I right?"

"Look, I'm not a—"

"Shut up," Mansey said. He was holding the J.C. Whitney catalogue in his hands. His fingernails were manicured. He had never seen manicured nails exactly like that except on TV commercials where the announcer had to hold a bottle of aspirin or something. "If Sal wants you to talk, he'll tell you to talk."

He blinked and shut his mouth. This was like a bad dream.

"You guys get dumber every day," Magliore said. "That's all right. I like to deal with dummies. I'm *used* to dealing with dummies. I'm good at it. Now. Not that you don't know it, but this office is as clean as a whistle. We wash it every week. I got a cigar box full of bugs at home. Contact mikes, button mikes, pressure mikes, Sony tape recorders no bigger than your hand. They don't even try that much anymore. Now they send shitbirds like you."

He heard himself say: "I'm not a shitbird."

An expression of exaggerated surprise spread across Magliore's face. He turned to Mansey. "Did you hear that? He said he wasn't a shitbird."

"Yeah, I heard that," Mansey said.

"Does he look like a shitbird to you?"

"Yeah, he does," Mansey said.

"Even talks like a shitbird, doesn't he?"

"Yeah."

"So if you're not a shitbird," Magliore said, turning back to him, "what are you?"

"I'm—" he began, not sure of just what to say. What *was* he? Fred, where are you when I need you?

"Come on, come on," Magliore said. "State Police?

City? IRS? FBI? He look like prime Effa Bee Eye to you, Pete?''

"Yeah," Pete said.

"Not even the city police would send out a shitbird like you, mister. You must be Effa Bee Eye or a private detective. Which is it?"

He began to feel angry.

"Throw him out, Pete," Magliore said, losing interest. Mansey started forward, still holding the J.C. Whitney catalogue.

"You stupid dork!" He suddenly yelled at Magliore. "You probably see policemen under your bed, you're so stupid! You probably think they're home screwing your wife when you're here!"

Magliore looked at him, magnified eyes widening. Mansey froze, a look of unbelief on his face.

"Dork?" Magliore said, turning the word over in his mouth the way a carpenter will turn a tool he doesn't know over in his hands. "Did he call me a dork?"

He was stunned by what he had said.

"I'll take him around back," Mansey said, starting forward again.

"Hold it," Magliore breathed. He looked at him with honest curiosity. "Did you call me a dork?"

"I'm not a cop," he said. "I'm not a crook, either. I'm just a guy that heard you sold stuff to people who had the money to buy it. Well, I've got the money. I didn't know you had to say the secret word or have a Captain Midnight decoder ring or all that silly shit. Yes, I called you a dork. I'm sorry I did if it will stop this man from beating me up. I'm . . ." He wet his lips and could think of no way to continue. Magliore and Mansey were looking at him with fascination, as if he had just turned into a Greek marble statue before their very eyes.

"Dork," Magliore breathed. "Frisk this guy, Pete."

Pete's hands slapped his shoulders and he turned around.

"Put your hands on the wall," Mansey said, his

mouth beside his ear. He smelled like Listerine. "Feet out behind you. Just like on the cop shows."

"I don't watch the cop shows," he said, but he knew what Mansey meant, and he put himself in the frisk position. Mansey ran his hands up his legs, patted his crotch with all the impersonality of a doctor, slipped a hand into his belt, ran his hands up his sides, slipped a finger under his collar.

"Clean," Mansey said.

"Turn around, you," Magliore said.

He turned around. Magliore was still regarding him with fascination.

"Come here."

He walked over.

Magliore tapped the glass top of his desk. Under the glass there were several snapshots: A dark woman who was grinning into the camera with sunglasses pushed back on top of her wiry hair; olive-skinned kids splashing in a pool; Magliore himself walking along the beach in a black bathing suit, looking like King Farouk, a large collie at his heel.

"Dump out," he said.

"Huh?"

"Everything in your pockets. Dump it out."

He thought of protesting, then thought of Mansey, who was hovering just behind his left shoulder. He dumped out.

From his topcoat pockets, the stubs of the tickets from the last movie he and Mary had gone to. Something with a lot of singing in it, he couldn't remember the name.

He took off his topcoat. From his suit coat, a Zippo lighter with his initials—BGD—engraved on it. A package of flints. A single Phillies Cheroot. A tin of Phillips milk of magnesia tablets. A receipt from A&S Tires, the place that had put on his snow tires. Mansey looked at it and said with some satisfaction: "Christ you got burned."

He took off his jacket. Nothing in his shirt breast

pocket but a ball of lint. From the right front pocket of his pants he produced his car keys and forty cents in change, mostly in nickles. For some reason he had never been able to fathom, nickles seemed to gravitate to him. There was never a dime for the parking meter; only nickles, which wouldn't fit. He put his wallet on the glass-topped desk with the rest of his things.

Magliore picked up the wallet and looked at the faded monogram on it—Mary had given it to him on their anniversary four years ago.

"What's the *G* for?" Magliore asked.

"George."

He opened the wallet and dealt the contents out in front of him like a solitaire hand.

Forty-three dollars in twenties and ones.

Credit cards: Shell, Sunoco, Arco, Grant's, Sears, Carey's Department Store, American Express.

Driver's license. Social Security. A blood donor card, type A-positive. Library card. A plastic flip-folder. A photostated birth certificate card. Several old receipted bills, some of them falling apart along the fold seams from age. Stamped checking account deposit slips, some of them going back to June.

"What's the matter with you?" Magliore asked irritably. "Don't you ever clean out your wallet? You load a wallet up like this and carry it around for a year, that wallet's hurting."

He shrugged. "I hate to throw things away." He was thinking that it was strange, how Magliore calling him a shitbird had made him angry, but Magliore criticizing his wallet didn't bother him at all.

Magliore opened the flip-folder, which was filled with snapshots. The top one was of Mary, her eyes crossed, her tongue popped out at the camera. An old picture. She had been slimmer then.

"This your wife?"

"Yeah."

"Bet she's pretty when there ain't a camera stuck in her face."

He flipped up another one and smiled.

"Your little boy? I got one about that age. Can he hit a baseball? Whacko! I guess he can."

"That was my son, yes. He's dead now."

"Too bad. Accident?"

"Brain tumor."

Magliore nodded and looked at the other pictures. Fingernail clippings of a life: The house on Crestallen Street West, he and Tom Granger standing in the laundry washroom, a picture of him at the podium of the launderers' convention the year it had been held in the city (he had introduced the keynote speaker), a backyard barbecue with him standing by the grill in a chef's hat and an apron that said: DAD'S COOKIN', MOM'S LOOKIN'.

Magliore put the flip-folder down, bundled the credit cards into a pile, and gave them to Mansey. "Have them photocopied," he said. "And take one of those deposit slips. His wife keeps the checkbook under lock and key, just like mine." Magliore laughed.

Mansey looked at him skeptically. "Are you going to do business with this shitbird?"

"Don't call him a shitbird and maybe he won't call me a dork again." He uttered a wheezy laugh that ended with unsettling suddenness. "You just mind your business, Petie. Don't tell me mine."

Mansey laughed, but exited in a modified stalk.

Magliore looked at him when the door was closed. He chuckled. He shook his head. "Dork," he said. "By God, I thought I'd been called everything."

"Why is he going to photocopy my credit cards?"

"We have part of a computer. No one owns all of it. People use it on a time-sharing basis. If a person knows the right codes, that person can tap into the memory banks of over fifty corporations that have city business. So I'm going to check on you. If you're a cop, we'll find out. If those credit cards are fake, we'll find out. If they're real but not yours, we'll find that out, too. But you got me convinced. I think you're straight. Dork." He shook his head and laughed. "Was yesterday Monday? Mister, you're lucky you didn't call me a dork on Monday."

"Can I tell you what I want to buy now?"

"You could, and if you were a cop with six recorders on you, you still couldn't touch me. It's called entrapment. But I don't want to hear it now. You come back tomorrow, same time, same station, and I'll tell you if I want to hear it. Even if you're straight, I may not sell you anything. You know why?"

"Why?"

Magliore laughed. "Because I think you're a fruitcake. Driving on three wheels. Flying on instruments."

"Why? Because I called you a name?"

"No," Magliore said. "Because you remind me of something that happened to me when I was a kid about my son's age. There was a dog that lived in the neighborhood where I grew up. Hell's Kitchen, in New York. This was before the Second World War, in the Depression. And this guy named Piazzi had a black mongrel bitch named Andrea, but everybody just called her Mr. Piazzi's dog. He kept her chained up all the time, but that dog never got mean, not until this one hot day in August. It might have been 1937. She jumped a kid that came up to pet her and put him in the hospital for a month. Thirty-seven stitches in his neck. But I knew it was going to happen. That dog was out in the hot sun all day, every day, all summer long. In the middle of June it stopped wagging its tail when kids came up to pet it. Then it started to roll its eyes. By the end of July it would growl way back in its throat when some kid patted it. When it started doing that, I stopped patting Mr. Piazzi's dog. And the guys said, Wassa matta, Sally? You chickenshit? And I said, No, I ain't chickenshit but I ain't stupid, either. That dog's gone mean. And they all said, Up your ass, Mr. Piazzi's dog don't bite, she never bit nobody, she wouldn't bite a baby that stuck its head down her throat. And I said, You go on and pat her, there's no law that says you can't pat a dog, but I ain't gonna. And so they all go around saying, Sally's chickenshit, Sally's a girl, Sally wants his mama to walk him past Mr. Piazzi's dog. You know how kids are."

"I know," he said. Mansey had come back in with his credit cards and was standing by the door, listening.

"And one of the kids who was yelling the loudest was the kid who finally got it. Luigi Bronticelli, his name was. A good Jew like me, you know?" Magliore laughed. "He went up to pat Mr. Piazzi's dog one day in August when it was hot enough to fry an egg on the sidewalk, and he ain't talked above a whisper since that day. He's got a barbershop in Manhattan, and they call him Whispering Gee."

Magliore smiled at him.

"You remind me of Mr. Piazzi's dog. You ain't growling yet, but if someone was to pat you, you'd roll your eyes. And you stopped wagging your tail a long time ago. Pete, give this man his things."

Mansey gave him the bundle.

"You come back tomorrow and we'll talk some more," Magliore said. He watched him putting things back into his wallet. "And you really ought to clean that mess out. You're racking that wallet all to shit."

"Maybe I will," he said.

"Pete, show this man out to his car."

"Sure."

He had the door open and was stepping out when Magliore called after him: "You know what they did to Mr. Piazzi's dog, mister? They took her to the pound and gassed her."

After supper, while John Chancellor was telling about how the reduced speed limit on the Jersey Turnpike had probably been responsible for fewer accidents, Mary asked him about the house.

"Termites," he said.

Her face fell like an express elevator. "Oh. No good, huh?"

"Well, I'm going out again tomorrow. If Tom Granger knows a good exterminator, I'll take the guy out with me. Get an expert opinion. Maybe it isn't as bad as it looks."

"I hope it isn't. A backyard and all . . ." She trailed off wistfully.

Oh, you're a prince, Freddy said suddenly. A veritable prince. How come you're so good to your wife, George? Was it a natural talent or did you take lessons?

"Shut up," he said.

Mary looked around, startled. "What?"

"Oh . . . Chancellor," he said. "I get so sick of gloom and doom from John Chancellor and Walter Cronkite and the rest of them."

"You shouldn't hate the messenger because of the message," she said, and looked at John Chancellor with doubtful, troubled eyes.

"I suppose so," he said, and thought. *You bastard, Freddy.*

Freddy told him not to hate the messenger for the message.

They watched the news in silence for a while. A commercial for a cold medicine came on—two men whose heads had been turned into blocks of snot. When one of them took the cold pill, the gray-green cube that had been encasing his head fell off in large lumps.

"Your cold sounds better tonight," he said.

"It is. Bart, what's the realtor's name?"

"Monohan," he said automatically.

"No, not the man that's selling you the plant. The one that's selling the house."

"Olsen," he said promptly, picking the name out of an internal litter bag.

The news came on again. There was a report on

David Ben-Gurion, who was about to join Harry Truman in that great Secretariat in the sky.

"How does Jack like it out there?" she asked presently.

He was going to tell her Jack didn't like it at all and heard himself saying, "Okay, I guess."

John Chancellor closed out with a humorous item about flying saucers over Ohio.

He went to bed at half past ten and must have had the bad dream almost at once—when he woke up the digital clock said:

11:22 P.M.

In the dream he had been standing on a corner in Norton—the corner of Venner and Rice Street. He had been standing right under the street sign. Down the street, in front of a candy store, a pink pimpmobile with caribou antlers mounted on the hood had just pulled up. Kids began to run toward it from stoops and porches.

Across the street, a large black dog was chained to the railing of a leaning brick tenement. A little boy was approaching it confidently.

He tried to cry out: *Don't pet that dog! Go get your candy!* But the words wouldn't come out. As if in slow motion, the pimp in the white suit and planter's hat turned to look. His hands were full of candy. The children who had crowded around him turned to look. All the children around the pimp were black, but the little boy approaching the dog was white.

The dog struck, catapulting up from its haunches like a blunt arrow. The boy screamed and staggered backward, hands to his throat. When he turned around, the blood was streaming through his fingers. It was Charlie.

That was when he had wakened.

The dreams. The goddam *dreams*.

His son had been dead three years.

November 28, 1973

It was snowing when he got up, but it had almost stopped by the time he got to the laundry. Tom Granger came running out of the plant in his shirt-sleeves, his breath making short, stiff plumes in the cold air. He knew from the expression on Tom's face that it was going to be a crummy day.

"We've got trouble, Bart."

"Bad?"

"Bad enough. Johnny Walker had an accident on his way back from Holiday Inn with his first load. Guy in a Pontiac skidded through a red light on Deakman and hit him dead center. *Kapow.*" He paused and looked aimlessly back toward the loading doors. There was no one there. "The cops said Johnny was in a bad way."

"Holy Christ."

"I got out there fifteen or twenty minutes after it happened. You know the intersection—"

"Yeah, yeah, it's a bitch."

Tom shook his head. "If it wasn't so fucking awful you'd have to laugh. It looks like somebody threw a bomb at a washerwoman. There's Holiday Inn sheets and towels everywhere. Some people were stealing them, the fucking ghouls, can you believe what people will do? And the truck . . . Bart, there's nothing left from the driver's side door up. Just junk. Johnny got thrown."

"Is he at Central?"

"No, St. Mary's. Johnny's a Catholic, didn't you know that?"

"You want to drive over with me?"

"I better not. Ron's hollering for pressure on the

boiler." He shrugged, embarrassed. "You know Ron. The show must go on."

"All right."

He got back into his car and drove out toward St. Mary's Hospital. Jesus Christ, of all the people for it to happen to. Johnny Walker was the only person left at the laundry besides himself who had been working at the Blue Ribbon in 1953—Johnny, in fact, went back to 1946. The thought lodged in his throat like an omen. He knew from reading the papers that the 784 extension was going to make the dangerous Deakman intersection pretty much obsolete.

His name wasn't Johnny at all, not really. He was Corey Everett Walker—he had seen it on enough time cards to know that. But he had been known as Johnny even twenty years ago. His wife had died in 1956 on a vacation trip in Vermont. Since then he had lived with his brother, who drove a sanitation truck for the city. There were dozens of workers at the Blue Ribbon who called Ron "Stoneballs" behind his back, but Johnny had been the only one to use it to his face and get away with it.

He thought: If Johnny dies, I'm the oldest employee the laundry has got. Held over for a twentieth record-breaking year. Isn't that a sketch, Fred?

Fred didn't think so.

Johnny's brother was sitting in the waiting room of the emergency wing, a tall man with Johnny's features and high complexion, dressed in olive work clothes and a black cloth jacket. He was twirling an olive-colored cap between his knees and looking at the floor. He glanced up at the sound of footsteps.

"You from the laundry?" he asked.

"Yes. You're . . ." He didn't expect the name to come to him, but it did. "Arnie, right?"

"Yeah, Arnie Walker." He shook his head slowly. "I dunno, Mr. . . . ?"

"Dawes."

"I dunno, Mr. Dawes. I seen him in one of those examinin rooms. He looked pretty banged up. He ain't a kid anymore. He looked bad."

"I'm very sorry," he said.

"That's a bad corner. It wasn't the other guy's fault. He just skidded in the snow. I don't blame the guy. They say he broke his nose but that was all. It's funny the way those things work out, you know it?"

"Yes."

"I remember one time when I was driving a big rig for Hemingway, this was in the early sixties, and I was on the Indiana Toll Road and I saw—"

The outer door banged open and a priest came in. He stamped snow from his boots and then hurried up the corridor, almost running. Arnie Walker saw him, and his eyes widened and took on the glazed look of shock. He made a whining, gasping noise in his throat and tried to stand up. He put an arm around Arnie's shoulders and restrained him.

"Jesus!" Arnie cried. "He had his pyx, did you see it? He's gonna give him the last rites . . . maybe he's dead, already. *Johnny*—"

There were other people in the waiting room: a teen-age kid with a broken arm, an elderly woman with an elastic bandage around one leg, a man with his thumb wrapped in a giant dressing. They looked up at Arnie and then down, self-consciously, at their magazines.

"Take it easy," he said meaninglessly.

"Let me go," Arnie said. "I got to go see."

"Listen—"

"Let me go!"

He let him go. Arnie Walker went around the corner and out of sight, the way the priest had gone. He sat in the plastic contour seat for a moment, wondering what to do. He looked at the floor, which was covered with black, slushy tracks. He looked at the nurses' station, where a woman was covering a switchboard. He looked out the window and saw that the snow had stopped.

There was a sobbing scream from up the corridor, where the examining rooms were.

Everybody looked up, and the same half-sick expression was on every face.

Another scream, followed by a harsh, braying cry of grief.

Everyone looked back at their magazines. The kid with the broken arm swallowed audibly, producing a small click in the silence.

He got up and went out quickly, not looking back.

At the laundry everyone on the floor came over, and Ron Stone didn't stop them.

I don't know, he told them. I never found out if he was alive or dead. You'll hear. I just don't know.

He fled upstairs, feeling weird and disconnected.

"Do you know how Johnny is, Mr. Dawes?" Phyllis asked him. He noticed for the first time that Phyllis, jaunty blue-rinsed hair notwithstanding, was looking old.

"He's bad," he said. "The priest came to give him the last rites."

"Oh, what a dirty shame. And so close to Christmas."

"Did someone go out to Deakman to pick up his load?"

She looked at him a little reproachfully. "Tom sent out Harry Jones. He brought it in five minutes ago."

"Good," he said, but it wasn't good. It was bad. He thought of going down to the washroom and dumping enough Hexlite into the washers to disintegrate all of it—when the extract ended and Pollack opened the machines there would be nothing but a pile of gray fluff. *That* would be good.

Phyllis had said something and he hadn't heard.

"What? I'm sorry."

"I said that Mr. Ordner called. He wants you to call back right away. And a fellow named Harold Swinnerton. He said the cartridges had come in."

"Harold—?" And then he remembered. Harvey's

Gun Shop. Only Harvey, like Marley, was as dead as a doornail. "Yes, right."

He went into his office and closed the door. The sign on his desk still said:

THINK!
It May Be A New Experience

He took it off the desk and dropped it into the wastebasket. *Clunk.*

He sat behind his desk, took everything out of the IN basket and threw it into the wastebasket without looking at it. He paused and looked around the office. The walls were wood-paneled. On the left were two framed degrees: one from college, one from the Laundry Institute, where he had gone during the summers of 1969 and 1970. Behind the desk was a large blow-up of himself shaking hands with Ray Tarkington in the Blue Ribbon parking lot just after it had been hot-topped. He and Ray were smiling. The laundry stood in the background, three trucks backed into the loading bay. The smokestack still looked very white.

He had been in this office since 1967, over six years. Since before Woodstock, before Kent State, before the assassination of Robert Kennedy and Martin Luther King, since before Nixon. Years of his life had been spent between these four walls. Millions of breaths, millions of heartbeats. He looked around, seeing if he felt anything. He felt faintly sad. That was all.

He cleaned out his desk, throwing away personal papers and his personal account books. He wrote his resignation on the back of a printed wash formula and slipped it into a laundry pay envelope. He left the impersonal things—the paper clips, the Scotch tape, the big book of checks, the pile of blank time cards held together with rubber bands.

He got up, took the two degrees off the wall, and threw them into the wastebasket. The glass covering the Laundry Institute diploma shattered. The squares where the degrees had hung all these years were a little brighter than the rest of the wall, and that was all.

The phone rang and he picked it up, thinking it would be Ordner. But it was Ron Stone, calling from downstairs.

"Bart?"

"Yeah."

"Johnny passed away a half hour ago. I guess he never really had a chance."

"I'm very sorry. I want to shut it down the rest of the day, Ron."

Ron sighed. "That's best, I guess. But won't you catch hell from the big bosses?"

"I don't work for the big bosses anymore. I just wrote my resignation." There. It was out. That made it real.

A dead beat of silence on the other end. He could hear the washers and the steady thumping hiss of the ironer. The mangler, they called it, on account of what would happen to you if you ever got caught in it.

"I must have heard you wrong," Ron said finally. "I thought you said—"

"I said it, Ron. I'm through. It's been a pleasure working with you and Tom and even Vinnie, when he could keep his mouth shut. But it's over."

"Hey, listen, Bart. Take it easy. I know this has got you upset— "

"It's not over Johnny," he said, not knowing if it was true or not. Maybe he still would have made an effort to save himself, to save the life that had existed under a protective dome of routine for the last twenty years. But when the priest had walked quickly past them down the hall, almost running, to the place where Johnny lay dying or dead, and when Arnie Walker had made that funny whining noise high up in his throat, he had given up. Like driving a car in a skid, or fooling yourself that you were driving, and then just taking your hands off the wheel and putting them over your eyes.

"It's not over Johnny," he repeated.

"Well, listen . . . listen . . ." Ron sounded very upset.

"Look, I'll talk to you later, Ron," he said, not knowing if he would or not. "Go on, have them punch out."

"Okay. Okay, but—"

He hung up gently.

He took the phone book out of the drawer and looked in the yellow pages under GUNS. He dialed Harvey's Gun Shop.

"Hello, Harvey's."

"This is Barton Dawes," he said.

"Oh, right. Those shells came in late yesterday afternoon. I told you I'd have them in plenty of time for Christmas. Two hundred rounds."

"Good. Listen, I'm going to be awfully busy this afternoon. Are you open tonight?"

"Open nights until nine right up to Christmas."

"Okay. I'll try to get in around eight. If not, tomorrow afternoon for sure."

"Good enough. Listen, did you find out if it was Boca Rio?"

"Boca . . ." Oh, yes, Boca Rio, where his cousin Nick Adams would soon be hunting. "Boca Rio. Yeah, I think it was."

"Jesus, I envy him. That was the best time I ever had in my life."

"Shaky cease-fire holds," he said. A sudden image came to him of Johnny Walker's head mounted over Stephan Ordner's electric log fireplace, with a small polished bronze plaque beneath, saying:

HOMO LAUNDROMAT
November 28, 1973
Bagged on the corner of Deakman

"What was that?" Harry Swinnerton asked, puzzled.

"I said, I envy him too," he said, and closed his

eyes. A wave of nausea raced through him. *I'm crack-ing up,* he thought. *This is called cracking up.*

"Oh. Well, I'll see you, then."

"Sure. Thanks again, Mr. Swinnerton."

He hung up, opened his eyes, and looked around his denuded office again. He flicked the button on the intercom.

"Phyllis?"

"Yes, Mr. Dawes?"

"Johnny died. We're going to shut it down."

"I saw people leaving and thought he must have." Phyllis sounded as if she might have been crying.

"See if you can get Mr. Ordner on the phone before you go, will you?"

"Surely."

He swiveled around in his chair and looked out the window. A road grader, bright orange, was lumbering by with chains on its oversize wheels, lashing at the road. This is their fault, Freddy. All their fault. I was doing okay until those guys down at City Hall decided to rip up my life. I was doing fine, right, Freddy?

Freddy?

Fred?

The phone rang and he picked it up. "Dawes."

"You've gone crazy," Steve Ordner said flatly. "Right out of your mind."

"What do you mean?"

"I mean that I personally called Mr. Monohan this morning at nine-thirty. The McAn people signed the papers on the Waterford plant at nine o'clock. Now what the fuck happened, Barton?"

"I think we'd better discuss that in person."

"So do I. And I think you ought to know that you're going to have to do some fast talking if you want to save your job."

"Stop playing games with me, Steve."

"What?"

"You've got no intention of keeping me on, not even as the sweeper. I've written my resignation already. It's sealed up, but I can quote it from memory. 'I quit. Signed, Barton George Dawes.' "

"But why?" He sounded physically wounded. But he wasn't whining like Arnie Walker. He doubted if Steve Ordner had done any whining since his eleventh birthday. Whining was the last resort of lesser men.

"Two o'clock?" he asked.

"Two is fine."

"Good-bye, Steve."

"Bart—"

He hung up and looked blankly at the wall. After a while, Phyllis poked her head in, looking tired and nervous and bewildered beneath her smart Older Person hairdo. Seeing her boss sitting quietly in his denuded office did nothing to improve her state of mind.

"Mr. Dawes, should I go? I'd be glad to stay, if—"

"No, go on, Phyllis. Go home."

She seemed to be struggling to say something else, and he turned around and looked out the window, hoping to spare them both embarrassment. After a moment, the door snicked closed, very softly.

Downstairs, the boiler whined and died. Motors began to start up in the parking lot.

He sat in his empty office in the empty laundry until it was time to go and see Ordner. He was saying good-byes.

Ordner's office was downtown, in one of the new highrise office buildings that the energy crisis might soon make obsolete. Seventy stories high, all glass, inefficient to heat in winter, a horror to cool in summer. Amroco's offices were on the fifty-fourth floor.

He parked his car in the basement parking lot, took the escalator up to lobby level, went through a revolving door, and found the right bank of elevators. He rode up with a black woman who had a large Afro. She was wearing a jumper and was holding a steno notebook.

"I like your Afro," he said abruptly, for no reason.

She looked at him coolly and said nothing. Nothing at all.

The reception room of Stephan Ordner's office was furnished with free-form chairs and a redheaded secretary who sat beneath a reproduction of Van Gogh's "Sunflowers." There was an oyster-colored shag rug on the floor. Indirect lighting. Indirect Muzak, piping Mantovani.

The redhead smiled at him. She was wearing a black jumper, and her hair was bound with a hank of gold yarn. "Mr. Dawes?"

"Yes."

"Go right in, please."

He opened the door and went right in. Ordner was writing something at his desk, which was topped with an impressive slab of Lucite. Behind him, a huge window gave on a western view of the city. He looked up and put his pen down. "Hello, Bart," he said quietly.

"Hello."

"Sit down."

"Is this going to take that long?"

Ordner looked at him fixedly. "I'd like to slap you," he said. "Do you know that? I'd like to slap you all the way around this office. Not hit you or beat you up. Just slap you."

"I know that," he said, and did.

"I don't think you have any idea of what you threw away," Ordner said. "I suppose the McAn people got to you. I hope they paid you a lot. Because I had you personally earmarked for an executive vice-presidency in this corporation. That would have paid thirty-five thousand a year to start. I hope they paid you more than that."

"They didn't pay me a cent."

"Is that the truth?"

"Yes."

"Then why, Bart? Why in the name of God?"

"Why should I tell you, Steve?" He took the chair

he was supposed to take, the supplicant's chair, on the other side of the big, Lucite-topped desk.

For a moment Ordner seemed to be at a loss. He shook his head the way a fighter will when he has been tagged, but not seriously.

"Because you're my employee. How's that for a start?"

"Not good enough."

"What does that mean?"

"Steve, I was Ray Tarkington's employee. He was a real person. You might not have cared for him, but you had to admit he was real. Sometimes when you were talking to him he broke wind or burped or picked dead skin out of his ear. He had real problems. Sometimes I was one of them. Once, when I made a bad decision about billing a motel out in Crager Plaza, he threw me against a door. You're not like him. The Blue Ribbon is Tinkertoys to you, Steve. You don't care about me. You care about your own upward mobility. So don't give me that employee shit. Don't pretend you stuck your cock in my mouth and I bit it."

If Ordner's face was a facade, there was no crack in it. His features continued to register modulated distress, no more. "Do you really believe that?" Ordner asked.

"Yes. You only give a damn about the Blue Ribbon as it affects your status in the corporation. So let's cut the shit. Here." He slid his resignation across the Lucite top of the desk.

Ordner gave his head another little shake. "And what about the people you've hurt, Bart? The little people. Everything else aside, you were in a position of importance." He seemed to taste the phrase. "What about the people at the laundry who are going to lose their jobs because there's no new plant to switch to?"

He laughed harshly and said: "You cheap son of a bitch. You're too fucking high to see down, aren't you?"

Ordner colored. He said carefully: "You better explain that, Bart."

"Every single wage earner at the laundry, from Tom

Granger on down to Pollack in the washroom, has unemployment insurance. It's theirs. They *pay* for it. If you're having trouble with that concept, think of it as a business deduction. Like a four-drink lunch at Benjamin's."

Stung, Ordner said, "That's welfare money and you know it."

He reiterated: "You cheap son of a bitch."

Ordner's hands came together and formed a double fist. They clenched together like the hands of a child that has been taught to say the Lord's Prayer by his bed. "You're overstepping yourself, Bart."

"No, I'm not. You called me here. You asked me to explain. What did you want to hear me say? I'm sorry, I screwed up, I'll make restitution? I can't say that. I'm not sorry. I'm not going to make restitution. And if I screwed up, that's between me and Mary. And she'll never even know, not for sure. Are you going to tell me I hurt the corporation? I don't think even you are capable of such a lie. After a corporation gets to a certain size, nothing can hurt it. It gets to be an act of God. When things are good it makes a huge profit, and when times are bad it just makes a profit, and when things go to hell it takes a tax deduction. Now you *know* that."

Ordner said carefully: "What about your own future? What about Mary's?"

"You don't care about that. It's just a lever you think you might be able to use. Let me ask you something, Steve. Is this going to hurt you? Is it going to cut into your salary? Into your yearly dividend? Into your retirement fund?"

Ordner shook his head. "Go on home, Bart. You're not yourself."

"Why? Because I'm talking about you and not just about bucks?"

"You're disturbed, Bart."

"You don't know," he said, standing up and planting his fists on the Lucite top of Ordner's desk.

"You're mad at me but you don't know why. Someone told you that if a situation like this ever came up you should be mad. But you don't know why."

Ordner repeated carefully. "You're disturbed."

"You're damn right I am. What are you?"

"Go home, Bart."

"No, but I'll leave you alone and that's what you want. Just answer one question. For one second stop being the corporation man and answer one question for me. Do you care about this? Does any of it mean a damn to you?"

Ordner looked at him for what seemed a long time. The city was spread out behind him like a kingdom of towers, wrapped in grayness and mist. He said: "No."

"All right," he said softly. He looked at Ordner without animosity. "I didn't do it to screw you. Or the corporation."

"Then why? I answered your question. You answer mine. You could have signed on the Waterford plant. After that it would have been someone else's worry. Why didn't you?"

He said: "I can't explain. I listened to myself. But people talk a different language inside. It sounds like the worst kind of shit if you try to talk about it. But it was the right thing."

Ordner looked at him unflinchingly. "And Mary?"

He was silent.

"Go home, Bart," Ordner said.

"What do you want, Steve?"

Ordner shook his head impatiently. "We're done, Bart. If you want to have an encounter session with someone, go to a bar."

"What do you want from me?"

"Only for you to get out of here and go home."

"What do you want from life, then? Where are you hooked into things?"

"Go home, Bart."

"*Answer me!* What do you *want*?" He looked at Ordner nakedly.

Ordner answered quietly, "I want what everyone wants. Go home, Bart."

He left without looking back. And he never went there again.

When he got to Magliore's Used Cars, it was snowing hard and most of the cars he passed had their headlights on. His windshield wipers beat a steady back-and-forth tune, and beyond their sweep snow that had been defrosted into slush ran down the Saf-T-Glass like tears.

He parked in back and walked around to the office. Before he went in, he looked at his ghostly reflection in the plate glass and scrubbed a thin pink film from his lips. The encounter with Ordner had upset him more than he would have believed. He had picked up a bottle of Pepto-Bismol in a drugstore and had chugged half of it on the way out here. Probably won't shit for a week, Fred. But Freddy wasn't at home. Maybe he had gone to visit Monohan's relatives in Bombay.

The woman behind the adding machine gave him a strange speculative smile and waved him in.

Magliore was alone. He was reading *The Wall Street Journal,* and when he came in, Magliore threw it across the desk and into the wastebasket. It landed with a rattling thump.

"It's going right to fucking *hell,*" Magliore said, as if continuing an interior dialogue that had started some time ago. "All these stockbrokers are old women, just like Paul Harvey says. Will the president resign? Will he? Won't he? Will he? Is GE going to go bankrupt with the energy shortage? It gives me a pain in the ass."

"Yeah," he said, but not sure of what he was agreeing to. He felt uneasy, and he wasn't totally sure Magliore remembered who he was. What should he say? *I'm the guy who called you a dork, remember?* Christ, that was no way to start.

"Snowing harder, ain't it?"

"Yes, it is."

"I hate the snow. My brother, he goes to Puerto Rico November first every year, stays until April fifteenth. He owns forty percent of a hotel there. Says he has to look after his investment. Shit. He wouldn't know how to look after his own ass if you gave him a roll of Charmin. What do you want?"

"Huh?" He jumped a little, and felt guilty.

"You came to me to get something. How can I get it for you if I don't know what it is?"

When it was put with such abrupt baldness, he found it hard to speak. The word for what he wanted seemed to have too many corners to come out of his mouth. He remembered something he had done as a kid and smiled a little.

"What's funny?" Magliore asked with sharp pleasantness. "With business the way it is, I could use a joke."

"Once, when I was a kid, I put a yo-yo in my mouth," he said.

"That's funny?"

"No, I couldn't get it out. *That's* funny. My mother took me to the doctor and he got it out. He pinched my ass and when I opened my mouth to yell, he just yanked it out."

"I ain't going to pinch your ass," Magliore said. "What do you want, Dawes?"

"Explosives," he said.

Magliore looked at him. He rolled his eyes. He started to say something and slapped one of his hanging jowls instead. "Explosives."

"Yes."

"I knew this guy was a fruiter," Magliore told himself. "I told Pete when you left, 'There goes a guy looking for an accident to happen.' That's what I told him."

He said nothing. Talk of accidents made him think of Johnny Walker.

"Okay, okay, I'll bite. What do you want explosives for? You going to blow up the Egyptian Trade Exposition? You going to skyjack an airplane? Or maybe just blow your mother-in-law to hell?"

"I wouldn't waste explosives on her," he said stiffly, and that made them both laugh, but it didn't break the tension.

"So what is it? Who have you got a hardon against?"

He said: "I don't have a hardon against anyone. If I wanted to kill somebody, I'd buy a gun." Then he remembered he *had* bought a gun, had bought *two* guns, and his Pepto-Bismol-drugged stomach began to roll again.

"So why do you need explosives?"

"I want to blow up a road."

Magliore looked at him with measured incredulity. All his emotions seemed larger than life; it was as if he had adopted his character to fit the magnifying properties of his glasses. "You want to blow up a road? What road?"

"It hasn't been built yet." He was beginning to get a sort of perverse pleasure from this. And of course, it was postponing the inevitable confrontation with Mary.

"So you want to blow up a road that hasn't been built. I had you wrong, mister. You're not a fruitcake. You're a psycho. Can you make sense?"

Picking his words carefully, he said: "They're building a road that's known as the 784 extension. When it's done, the state turnpike will go right through the city. For certain reasons I don't want to go into—because I can't—that road has wrecked twenty years of my life. It's—"

"Because they're gonna knock down the laundry where you work, and your house?"

"How did you know that?"

"I told you I was gonna check you. Did you think I was kidding? I even knew you were gonna lose your job. Maybe before you did."

"No, I knew that a month ago," he said, not thinking about what he was saying.

"And how are you going to do it? Were you planning to just drive past the construction, lighting fuses with your cigar and throwing bundles of dynamite out of your car window?"

"No. Whenever there's a holiday, they leave all their machines at the site. I want to blow them all up. And all three of the new overpasses. I want to blow them up, too."

Magliore goggled at him. He goggled for a long time. Then he threw back his head and laughed. His belly shook and his belt buckle heaved up and down like a chip of wood riding a heavy swell. His laughter was full and hearty and rich. He laughed until tears splurted out of his eyes and then he produced a huge comic-opera handkerchief from some inner pocket and wiped them. He stood watching Magliore laugh and was suddenly very sure that this fat man with the thick glasses was going to sell him the explosives. He watched Magliore with a slight smile on his face. He didn't mind the laughter. Today laughter sounded good.

"Man, you're crazy, all right," Magliore said when his laughter had subsided to chuckles and hitchings. "I wish Pete could have been here to hear this. He's never gonna believe it. Yesterday you call me a d-dork and t-today . . . t-t-today . . ." And he was off again, roaring his laughter, mopping his eyes with his handkerchief.

When his mirth had subsided again, he asked, "How were you gonna finance this little venture, Mr. Dawes? Now that you're no longer gainfully employed?"

That was a funny way to put it. *No longer gainfully employed*. When you said it that way, it really sounded true. He was out of a job. All of this was not a dream.

"I cashed in my life insurance last month," he said. "I'd been paying on a ten-thousand-dollar policy for ten years. I've got about three thousand dollars."

"You've really been planning this for that long?"

"No," he said honestly. "When I cashed the policy in, I wasn't sure what I wanted it for."

"In those days you were still keeping your options open, right? You thought you might burn the road, or machine-gun it to death, or strangle it, or—"

"No. I just didn't know what I was going to do. Now I know."

"Well count me out."

"What?" He blinked at Magliore, honestly stunned. This wasn't in the script. Magliore was supposed to give him a hard time, in a fatherly sort of way. Then sell him the explosive. Magliore was supposed to offer a disclaimer, something like: *If you get caught, I'll deny I ever heard of you.*

"What did you say?"

"I said no. N-o. That spells no." He leaned forward. All the good humor had gone out of his eyes. They were flat and suddenly small in spite of the magnification the glasses caused. They were not the eyes of a jolly Neapolitan Santa Claus at all.

"Listen," he said to Magliore. "If I get caught, I'll deny I ever heard of you. I'll never mention your name."

"The fuck you would. You'd spill your fucking guts and cop an insanity plea. I'd go up for life."

"No, listen—"

"*You* listen," Magliore said. "You're funny up to a point. That point has been got to. I said no, I meant no. No guns, no explosive, no dynamite, no nothing. Because why? Because you're a fruitcake and I'm a businessman. Somebody told you I could 'get' things. I can get them, all right. I've gotten lots of things for lots of people. I've also gotten a few things for myself. In 1946, I got a two-to-five bit for carrying a concealed weapon. Did ten months. In 1952 I got a conspiracy rap, which I beat. In 1955, I got a tax-evasion rap, which I also beat. In 1959 I got a receiving-stolen-property rap which I didn't beat. I did eighteen months in Castleton, but the guy who talked to the grand jury got life in a hole in the ground. Since 1959 I been up three times, case dismissed twice, rap beat once. They'd like to get me again because one more good one and I'm in for twenty years, no time off for good behavior. A man in my condition, the only part of him that comes out after twenty years is his kidneys, which they give to some Norton nigger in the welfare ward. This is some game to you. Crazy, but a game. It's no game to me. You think you're telling the truth when you say you'd keep your mouth shut. But you're lying. Not to me, to *you*. So the answer is flat no." He threw up his hands. "If it had been broads, Jesus, I woulda given you two free just for that floor show you put on yesterday. But I ain't going for any of this."

"All right," he said. His stomach felt worse than ever. He felt like he was going to throw up.

"This place is clean," Magliore said, "and I know it's clean. Furthermore, I know *you're* clean, although God knows you're not going to be if you go on like this. But I'll you something. About two years ago, this nigger came to me and said he wanted explosives. He wasn't going to blow up something harmless like a road. He was going to blow up a fucking federal courthouse."

Don't tell me any more, he was thinking. I'm going to puke, I think. His stomach felt full of feathers, all of them tickling at once.

"I sold him the goop," Magliore said. "Some of this, some of that. We dickered. He talked to his guys, I talked to my guys. Money changed hands. A lot of money. The goop changed hands. They caught the guy and two of his buddies before they could hurt anyone, thank God. But I never lost a minute's sleep worrying was he going to spill his guts to the cops or the county prosecutor or the Effa Bee Eye. You know why? Because he was with a whole *bunch* of fruitcakes, nigger fruitcakes, and they're the worst kind, and a *bunch* of fruitcakes is a different proposition altogether. A single nut like you, he doesn't give a shit. He burns out like a lightbulb. But if there are thirty guys and three of them get caught, they just zip up their lips and put things on the back burner."

"All right," he said again. His eyes felt small and hot.

"Listen," Magliore said, a little more quietly. "Three thousand bucks wouldn't buy you what you want, anyway. This is like the black market, you know what I mean?—no pun intended. It would take three or four times that to buy the goop you need."

He said nothing. He couldn't leave until Magliore dismissed him. This was like a nightmare, only it wasn't. He had to keep telling himself that he wouldn't do something stupid in Magliore's presence, like trying to pinch himself awake.

"Dawes?"

"What?"

"It wouldn't do any good anyway. Don't you know that? You can blow up a person or you can blow up a natural landmark or you can destroy a piece of beautiful art, like that crazy shit that took a hammer to the Pietà, may his dink rot off. But you can't blow up buildings or roads or anything like that. It's what all these crazy niggers don't understand. If you blow up a federal courthouse, the feds build two to take its place—one to replace the blown-up one and one just to rack up each and every black ass that gets busted through the front door. If you go around killing cops, they hire six cops for every one you killed—and every one of the new cops is on the prod for dark meat. You can't win, Dawes. White or black. If you get in the way of that road, they'll plow you under along with your house and your job."

"I have to go now," he heard himself say thickly.

"Yeah, you look bad. You need to get this out of your system. I can get you an old whore if you want her. Old and stupid. You can beat the shit out of her,

if you want to. Get rid of the poison. I sort of like
you, and—"

He ran. He ran blindly, out the door and through
the main office and out into the snow. He stood there
shivering, drawing in great white freezing gulps of the
snowy air. He was suddenly sure that Magliore would
come out after him, collar him, take him back into the
office, and talk to him until the end of time. When
Gabriel trumpeted in the Apocalypse, Sally One-Eye
would still be patiently explaining the invulnerability
of all systems everywhere and urging the old whore
on him.

When he got home the snow was almost six inches
deep. The plows had been by and he had to drive the
LTD through a crusted drift of snow to get in the
driveway. The LTD made it no sweat. It was a good
heavy car.

The house was dark. When he opened the door and
stepped in, stamping snow off on the mat, it was also
silent. Merv Griffin was not chatting with the
celebrities.

"Mary?" He called. There was no answer. *"Mary?"*

He was willing to think she wasn't home until he
heard her crying in the living room. He took off his
topcoat and hung it on its hanger in the closet. There
was a small box on the floor under the hanger. The
box was empty. Mary put it there every winter, to
catch drips. He had sometimes wondered: Who cares
about drips in a closet? Now the answer came to him,
perfect in its simplicity. Mary cared. That's who.

He went into the living room. She was sitting on
the couch in front of the blank Zenith TV, crying. She
wasn't using a handkerchief. Her hands were at her
sides. She had always been a private weeper, going
into the upstairs bedroom to do it, or if it surprised
her, hiding her face in her hands or a handkerchief.
Seeing her this way made her face seem naked and

obscene, the face of a plane crash victim. It twisted his heart.

"Mary," he said softly.

She went on crying, not looking at him. He sat down beside her.

"Mary," he said. "It's not as bad as that. Nothing is." But he wondered.

"It's the end of everything," she said, and the words came out splintered by her crying. Oddly, the beauty she had not achieved for good or lost for good was in her face now, shining. In this moment of the final smash, she was a lovely woman.

"Who told you?"

"Everybody told me!" She cried. She still wouldn't look at him, but one hand came up and made a twisting, beating movement against the air before falling against the leg of her slacks. "Tom Granger called. Then Ron Stone's *wife* called. Then Vincent Mason called. They wanted to know what was wrong with you. And I didn't *know*! I didn't know anything *was* wrong!"

"Mary," he said, and tried to take her hand. She snatched it away as if he might be catching.

"Are you punishing me?" she asked, and finally looked at him. "Is that what you're doing? Punishing me?"

"No," he said urgently. "Oh Mary, no." He wanted to cry now, but that would be wrong. That would be very wrong.

"Because I gave you a dead baby and then a baby with a built-in self-destruct? Do you think I murdered your son? Is that why?"

"Mary, he was *our* son—"

"He was yours!" she screamed at him.

"Don't, Mary. Don't." He tried to hold her and she fought away from him.

"Don't you touch me."

They looked at each other, stunned, as if they had discovered for the first time that there was more to them than they had ever dreamed of—vast white spaces on some interior map.

"Mary, I can't help what I did. Please believe that." But it could have been a lie. Nonetheless, he plunged on: "If it had something to do with Charlie, it did. I've done some things I don't understand. I . . . I cashed in my life insurance policy in October. That was the first thing, the first *real* thing, but things had been happening in my mind long before that. But it was easier to do things than to talk about them. Can you understand that? Can you try?"

"What's going to happen to me, Barton? I don't know anything but being your wife. What's going to happen to me?"

"I don't know."

"It's like you raped me," she said, and began to cry again.

"Mary, please don't do that anymore. Don't . . . try not to do that anymore."

"When you were doing all those *things,* didn't you ever think of me? Didn't you ever think that I *depend* on you?"

He couldn't answer. In a strange, disconnected way it was like talking to Magliore again. It was as if Magliore had beaten him home and put on a girdle and Mary's clothes and a Mary mask. What next? The offer of the old whore?

She stood. "I'm going upstairs. I'm going to lie down."

"Mary—" She did not cut him off, but he discovered there were no words to follow that first.

She left the room and he heard her footsteps going upstairs. After that he heard the creak of her bed as she lay down on it. After that he heard her crying again. He got up and turned on the TV and jacked the volume so he wouldn't be able to hear it. On the TV, Merv Griffin was chatting with celebrities.

Part Two

DECEMBER

Ah, love, let us be true
To one another! for the world, which seems
To lie before us like a land of dreams,
So various, so beautiful, so new,
Hath really neither joy, nor love, nor light,
Nor certitude, nor peace, nor help for pain;
And we are here as on a darkling plain
Swept with confused armies of struggle and flight,
Where ignorant armies clash by night.
                                    —MATTHEW ARNOLD
                                        "Dover Beach"

December 5, 1973

He was drinking his private drink, Southern Comfort and Seven-Up, and watching some TV program he didn't know the name of. The hero of the program was either a plainclothes cop or a private detective, and some guy had hit him over the head. This had made the plainclothes cop (or private detective) decide that he was getting close to something. Before he had a chance to say what, there was a commercial for Gravy Train. The man in the commercial was saying that Gravy Train, when mixed with warm water, made its own gravy. He asked the audience if it didn't look just like beef stew. To Barton George Dawes it looked just like a loose bowel movement that somebody had done in a red dog dish. The program came back on. The private eye (or plainclothes police detective) was questioning a black bartender who had a police record. The bartender said *dig*. The bartender said *flake off*. The bartender said *dude*. He was a very hip bartender, all right, but Barton George Dawes thought that the private cop (or plainclothes investigator) had his number.

He was quite drunk, and he was watching television in his shorts and nothing else. The house was hot. He had turned the thermostat to seventy-eight degrees and had left it there ever since Mary left. What energy crisis? Fuck you, Dick. Also the horse you rode in on. Fuck Checkers, too. When he got on the turnpike, he drove at seventy, giving the finger to motorists who honked at him to slow down. The president's consumer expert, some woman who looked as if she might have been a child star in the 1930s before passing time had turned her into a political hermaphrodite, had been on a public-service program two nights ago, talking about the ways!! You & I!! could save electricity around the house. Her name was Virginia Knauer, and she was very big on different ways YOU & I could save energy, because this thing was a real bitch and we were all in it together. When the program was over he had gone into the kitchen and turned on the electric blender. Mrs. Knauer had said that blenders were the second-biggest small appliance energy wasters. He had let the blender run on all night and when he got up the next morning—yesterday morning—the motor had burned out. The greatest electricity waster, Mrs. Knauer had said, were those little electric space heaters. He didn't have an electric space heater, but he had toyed with the idea of getting one so he could run it day and night until it burned up. Possibly, if he was drunk and passed out, it would burn him up, too. That would be the end of the whole silly self-pitying mess.

He poured himself another drink and fell to musing over the old TV programs, the ones they had been running when he and Mary were still practically newlyweds and a brand new RCA console model TV— your ordinary, garden-variety RCA console model black-and-white TV—was something to boggle over. There had been "The Jack Benny Program" and "Amos 'n Andy," those original jiveass niggers. There was "Dragnet," the original "Dragnet" with Ben Alexander for Joe Friday's partner instead of that new guy, Harry somebody. There had been "Highway Patrol," with Broderick Crawford growling ten-four into his mike and everybody driving around in Buicks that still had portholes on the side. "Your Show of Shows." "Your Hit Parade," with Gisele MacKenzie singing things like "Green Door" and "Stranger in Paradise." Rock and roll had killed that one. Or, how about the quiz shows, how about them? "Tic-Tac-Dough" and "Twenty-One" every Monday night, starring Jack Barry. People going into isolation booths and putting

UN-style earphones on their heads to hear fucking incredible questions they had already been briefed on. "The $64,000 Question," with Hal March. Contestants staggering offstage with their arms full of reference books. "Dotto," with Jack Narz. And Saturday morning programs like "Annie Oakley," who was always saving her kid brother Tag from some Christless mess. He had always wondered if that kid was really her bastard. There was "Rin-Tin-Tin," who operated out of Fort Apache. "Sergeant Preston," who operated out of the Yukon—sort of a roving assignment, you might say. "Range Rider," with Jock Mahoney. "Wild Bill Hickok," with Guy Madison and Andy Devine as Jingles. Mary would say Bart, if people knew you watched all that stuff, they'd think you were feeble. Honestly, a man your age! And he had always replied, I want to be able to talk to my kids, kid. Except there had never been any kids, not really. The first one had been nothing but a dead mess—what was that old joke about putting wheels on miscarriages?—and the second had been Charlie, who it was best not to think of. I'll be seeing you in my dreams, Charlie. Every night it seemed he and his son got together in one dream or another. Barton George Dawes and Charles Frederick Dawes, reunited by the wonders of the subconscious mind. And here we are, folks, back in Disney World's newest head trip, Self-Pity Land, where you can take a gondola ride down The Canal of Tears, visit the Museum of Old Snapshots, and go for a ride in The Wonderful NostalgiaMobile, driven by Fred MacMurray. The last stop on your tour is this wonderful replica of Crestallen Street West. It's right here inside this giant Southern Comfort bottle, preserved for all time. That's right, madam, just duck your head as you walk into the neck. It'll widen out soon. And this is the home of Barton George Dawes, the last living resident of Crestallen Street West. Look right in the window here—just a second, sonny, I'll boost you up. That's George all right, sitting in front of his

Zenith color TV in his stupid boxer shorts, having a drink and crying. Crying? Of course he's crying. What else would he be doing in Self-Pity Land? He cries all the time. The flow of his tears is regulated by our WORLD-FAMOUS TEAM OF ENGINEERS. On Mondays he just mists a little, because that's a slow night. The rest of the week he cries a lot more. On the weekend he goes into overdrive, and on Christmas we may float him right away. I admit he's a little disgusting, but nonetheless, he's one of Self-Pity Land's most popular inhabitants, right up there with our recreation of King Kong atop the Empire State Building. He—

He threw his drink at the television.

He missed by quite a bit. The glass hit the wall, fell to the floor, and shattered. He burst into fresh tears.

Crying, he thought: Look at me, look at me, Jesus you're disgusting. You're such a fucking mess it's beyond belief. You spoiled your whole life and Mary's too and you sit here joking about it, you fucking waste. Jesus, Jesus, Jesus—

He was halfway to the telephone before he could stop himself. The night before, drunk and crying, he had called Mary and begged her to come back. He had begged until she began to cry and hung up on him. It made him squirm and grin to think of it, that he had done such a Godawful embarrassing thing.

He went on to the kitchen, got the dustpan and the whiskbroom, and went back to the living room. He shut off the TV and swept up the glass. He took it into the kitchen, weaving slightly, and dumped it into the trash. Then he stood there, wondering what to do next.

He could hear the insectile buzz of the refrigerator and it frightened him. He went to bed. And dreamed.

December 6, 1973

It was half past three and he was slamming up the turnpike toward home, doing seventy. The day was clear and hard and bright, the temperature in the low thirties. Every day since Mary had left he went for a long ride on the turnpike—in a way, it had become his surrogate work. It soothed him. When the road was unrolling in front of him, its edges clearly marked by the low early winter snowbanks, on either side, he was without thought and at peace. Sometimes he sang along with the radio in a lusty, bellowing voice. Often on these trips he thought he should just keep going, letting way lead on to way, getting gas on the credit card. He would drive south and not stop until he ran out of roads or out of land. Could you drive all the way to the tip of South America? He didn't know.

But he always came back. He would get off the turnpike, eat hamburgers and French fries in some pickup restaurant, and then drive into the city, arriving at sunset or just past.

He always drove down Stanton Street, parked, and got out to look at whatever progress the 784 extension had made during the day. The construction company had mounted a special platform for rubberneckers—mostly old men and shoppers with an extra minute—and during the day it was always full. They lined up along the railing like clay ducks in a shooting gallery, the cold vapor pluming from their mouths, gawking at the bulldozers and graders and the surveyors with their sextants and tripods. He could cheerfully have shot all of them.

But at night, with the temperatures down in the 20's, with sunset a bitter orange line in the west and thousands of stars already pricking coldly through the firmament overhead, he could measure the road's progress alone and undisturbed. The moments he spent there were becoming very important to him—he suspected that in an obscure way, the moments spent on the observation platform were recharging him, keeping him tied to a world of at least half-sanity. In those moments before the evening's long plunge into drunkenness had begun, before the inevitable urge to call Mary struck, before he began the evening's activities in Self-Pity Land—he was totally himself, coldly and blinkingly sober. He would curl his hands over the iron pipe and stare down at the construction until his fingers became as unfeeling as the iron itself and it became impossible to tell where the world of himself—the world of human things—ended and the outside world of tractors and cranes and observation platforms began. In those moments there was no need to blubber or pick over the rickrack of the past that jumbled his memory. In those moments he felt his *self* pulsing warmly in the cold indifference of the early-winter evening, a real person, perhaps still whole.

Now, whipping up the turnpike at seventy, still forty miles away from the Westgate tollbooths, he saw a figure standing in the breakdown lane just past exit 16, muffled up in a CPO coat and wearing a black knitted watchcap. The figure was holding up a sign that said (amazingly, in all this snow): LAS VEGAS. And underneath that, defiantly: OR BUST!

He slammed on the power brake and felt the seat belt strain a groove in his middle with the swift deceleration, a little exhilarated by the Richard Petty sound of his own squealing tires. He pulled over about twenty yards beyond the figure. It tucked its sign under its arm and ran toward him. Something about the way the figure was running told him the hitchhiker was a girl.

The passenger door opened and she got in.

"Hey, thanks."

"Sure." He glanced in the rearview mirror and

pulled out, accelerating back to seventy. The road un-rolled in front of him again. "A long way to Vegas."

"It sure is." She smiled at him, the stock smile for people that told her it was a long way to Vegas, and pulled off her gloves. "Do you mind if I smoke?"

"No, go ahead."

She pulled out a box of Marlboros. "Like one?"

"No, thanks."

She stuck a cigarette in her mouth, took a box of kitchen matches from her CPO pocket, lit her smoke, took a huge drag and chuffed it out, fogging part of the windshield, put Marlboros and matches away, loosened the dark blue scarf around her neck and said: "I appreciate the ride. It's cold out there."

"Were you waiting long?"

"About an hour. The last guy was drunk. Man, I was glad to get out."

He nodded. "I'll take you to the end of the turnpike."

"End?" She looked at him. "You're going all the way to Chicago?"

"What? Oh, no." He named his city.

"But the turnpike goes through there." She pulled a Sunoco road map, dog-earned from much thumbing, from her other coat pocket. "The map *says* so."

"Unfold it and look again."

She did so.

"What color is the part of the turnpike we're on now?"

"Green."

"What color is the part going through the city?"

"Dotted green. It's . . . oh, Christ! It's under *construction!*"

"That's right. The world-famous 784 extension. Girl, you'll never get to Las Vegas if you don't read the key to your map."

She bent over it, her nose almost touching the paper. Her skin was clear, perhaps normally milky, but now the cold had brought a bloom to her cheeks and forehead. The tip of her nose was red, and a small drop of water hung beside her left nostril. Her hair was clipped short, and not very well. A home job. A pretty chestnut color. Too bad to cut it, worse to cut it badly. What was that Christmas story by O. Henry? "The Gift of the Magi." Who did you buy a watch chain for, little wanderer?

"The solid green picks up at a place called Landy," she said. "How far is that from where this part ends?"

"About thirty miles."

"Oh *Christ*."

She puzzled over the map some more. Exit 15 flashed by.

"What's the bypass road?" she asked finally. "It just looks like a snarl to me."

"Route 7's best," he said. "It's at the last exit, the one they call Westgate." He hesitated. "But you'd do better to just hang it up for the night. There's a Holiday Inn. We won't get there until almost dark, and you don't want to try hitching up Route 7 after dark."

"Why not?" she asked, looking over at him. Her eyes were green and disconcerting; an eye color you read about occasionally but rarely see.

"It's a city bypass road," he said, taking charge of the passing lane and roaring past a whole line of vehicles doing fifty. Several of them honked at him angrily. "Four lanes with a little bitty concrete divider between them. Two lanes west toward Landy, two lanes east into the city. Lots of shopping centers and hamburger stands and bowling alleys and all that. Everybody is going in short hops. No one wants to stop."

"Yeah." She sighed. "Is there a bus to Landy?"

"There used to be a city bus, but it went bankrupt. I guess there must be a Greyhound—"

"Oh, fuck it." She squidged the map back together and stuffed it into her pocket. She stared at the road, looking put out and worried.

"Can't afford a motel room?"

"Mister, I've got thirteen bucks. I couldn't rent a doghouse."

"You can stay at my house if you want," he said.

"Yeah, and maybe you better let me out right here."

"Never mind. I withdraw the offer."

"Besides, what would your wife think?" She looked pointedly at the wedding ring on his finger. It was a look that suggested she thought he might also hang around school play yards after the monitor had gone home for the day.

"My wife and I are separated."

"Recently?"

"Yes. As of December first."

"And now you've got all these hang-ups that you could use some help with," she said. There was contempt in her voice but it was an old contempt, not aimed specifically at him. "Especially some help from a young chick."

"I don't want to lay anybody," he said truthfully. "I don't even think I could get it up." He realized he had just used two terms that he had never used before a woman in his life, but it seemed all right. Not good or bad but all right, like discussing the weather.

"Is that supposed to be a challenge?" she asked. She drew deeply on her cigarette and exhaled more smoke.

"No," he said. "I suppose it sounds like a line if you're looking for lines. I suppose a girl on her own has to be looking for them all the time."

"This must be part three," she said. There was still mild contempt and hostility in her tone, but now it was cut with a certain tired amusement. "How did a nice girl like you get in a car like this?"

"Oh, to hell with it," he said. "You're impossible."

"That's right, I am." She snuffed her cigarette in his ashtray and then wrinkled her nose. "Look at this. Full of candy wrappers and cellophane and every other kind of shit. Why don't you get a litterbag?"

"Because I don't smoke. If you had just called ahead and said, Barton old boy, I intend to be hitching the turnpike today so give me a ride, would you? And by the way, clear the shit out of your ashtray because I intend to smoke—then I would have emptied it. Why don't you just throw it out the window?"

She was smiling. "You have a nice sense of irony."

"It's my sad life."

"Do you know how long it takes filter tips to biodegrade? Two hundred years, that's how long. By that time your grandchildren will be dead."

He shrugged. "You don't mind me breathing in your used carcinogens, screwing up the cilia in my lungs, but you don't want to throw a filter tip out into the turnpike. Okay."

"What's that supposed to mean?"

"Nothing."

"Listen, do you want to let me out? Is that it?"

"No," he said. "Why don't we just talk about something neutral? The state of the dollar. The state of the Union. The state of Arkansas."

"I think I'd rather catch a little nap if you don't mind. It looks like I'm going to be up most of the night."

"Fine."

She tilted the watchcap over her eyes, folded her arms, and became still. After a few moments her breathing deepened to long strokes. He looked at her in short snatches, shoplifting an image of her. She was wearing blue jeans, tight, faded, thin. They molded her legs closely enough to let him know that she wasn't wearing a second pair or longhandles. They were long legs, folded under the dashboard for comfort, and they were probably blushing lobster red now, itching like hell. He started to ask her if her legs itched, and then thought how it would sound. The thought of her hitchhiking all night on Route 7, either getting rides in short hops or not getting rides at all, made him feel uncomfortable. Night, thin pants, temperatures in the

20's. Well, it was her business. If she got cold enough, she could go in someplace and warm up. No problem.

They passed exits 14 and 13. He stopped looking at her and concentrated on his driving. The speedometer needle stayed pegged at seventy, and he stayed in the passing lane. More cars honked at him. As they passed exit 12, a man in a station wagon which bore a KEEP IT AT 50 bumper sticker honked three times and blipped his lights indignantly. He gave the station wagon the finger.

With her eyes still closed she said: "You're going too fast. That's why they're honking."

"I know why they're doing it."

"But you don't care."

"No."

"Just another concerned citizen," she intoned, "doing his part to rid America of the energy squeeze."

"I don't give a tin weasel about the energy squeeze."

"So say we; so say we all."

"I used to drive at fifty-five on the turnpike. No more, no less. That's where my car got the best mileage. Now I'm protesting the Trained Dog Ethic. Surely you read about it in your sociology courses? Or am I wrong? I took it for granted you were a college kid."

She sat up. "I was a sociology major for a while. Well, sort of. But I never heard of the Trained Dog Ethic."

"That's because I made it up."

"Oh. April Fool." Disgust. She slid back down in the seat and tilted the watchcap over her eyes again.

"The Trained Dog Ethic, first advanced by Barton George Dawes in late 1973, fully explains such mysteries as the monetary crisis, inflation, the Viet Nam war, and the current energy crisis. Let us take the energy crisis as an example. The American people are the trained dogs, trained in this case to love oil-guzzling toys. Cars, snowmobiles, large boats, dune buggies, motorcycles, minicycles, campers, and many, many more. In the years 1973 to 1980 we will be trained to hate energy toys. The American people love to be trained. Training makes them wag their tails. Use energy. Don't use energy. Go pee on the newspaper. I don't object to saving energy, I object to training."

He found himself thinking of Mr. Piazzi's dog, who had first stopped wagging his tail, had then started rolling his eyes, and had then ripped out Luigi Bronticelli's throat.

"Like Pavlov's dogs," he said. "They were trained to salivate at the sound of a bell. We've been trained to salivate when somebody shows us a Bombardier Skidoo with overdrive or a Zenith color TV with a motorized antenna. I have one of those at my house. The TV has a Space Command gadget. You can sit in your chair and change the channels, hike the volume or lower it, turn it on or off. I stuck the gadget in my mouth once and pushed the on button and the TV came right on. The signal went right through my brain and still did the job. Technology is wonderful."

"You're crazy," she said.

"I guess so." They passed exit 11.

"I think I'll go to sleep. Tell me when we get to the end."

"Okay."

She folded her arms and closed her eyes again.

They passed exit 10.

"It isn't the Trained Dog Ethic I object to anyway," he said. "It's the fact that the masters are mental, moral, and spiritual idiots."

"You're trying to soothe your conscience with a lot of rhetoric," she said with her eyes still closed. "Why don't you just slow down to fifty? You'll feel better."

"I will not feel better." And he spat it out so vehemently that she sat up and looked at him.

"Are you all right?"

"I'm fine," he said. "I lost my wife and my job because either the world has gone crazy or I have.

Then I pick up a hitchhiker—a nineteen-year-old kid for Chrissake, the kind that's supposed to take it for granted that the world's gone crazy—and she tells me it's me, the world is doing just fine. Not much oil, but other than that, just fine."

"I'm twenty-one."

"Good for you," he said bitterly. "If the world's so sane, what's a kid like you doing hitchhiking to Las Vegas in the middle of winter? Planning to spend the whole night hitchhiking along Route 7 and probably getting frostbite in your legs because you're not wearing anything under those pants?"

"I am so wearing something underneath! What do you think I *am*?"

"I think you're *stupid*!" he roared at her. "You're going to freeze your *ass* off!"

"And then you won't be able to get a piece of it, right?" she inquired sweetly.

"Oh boy," he muttered. "Oh boy."

They roared past a sedan moving at fifty. The sedan beeped at him. *"Eat it!"* He yelled. *"Raw!"*

"I think you better let me off right now," she said quietly.

"Never mind," he said. "I'm not going to crash us up. Go to sleep."

She looked at him distrustfully for a long second, then folded her arms and closed her eyes. They went past exit 9.

They passed exit 2 at five after four. The shadows stretching across the road had taken on the peculiar blue cast that is the sole property of winter shadows. Venus was already in the east. The traffic had thickened as they approached the city.

He glanced over toward her and saw she was sitting up, looking out at the hurrying, indifferent automobiles. The car directly in front of them had a Christmas tree lashed to its roof rack. The girl's green eyes were very wide, and for a moment he fell into them and saw out of them in the perfect empathy that comes to human beings at mercifully infrequent intervals. He saw that all the cars were going to someplace where it was warm, someplace where there was business to transact or friends to greet or a loom of family life to pick up and stitch upon. He saw their indifference to strangers. He understood in a brief, cold instant of comprehension what Thomas Carlyle called the great dead locomotive of the world, rushing on and on.

"We're almost there?" she asked.

"Fifteen minutes."

"Listen, if I was hard on you—"

"No, I was hard on you. Listen, I've got nothing in particular to do. I'll take you around to Landy."

"No—"

"Or I'll stick you in the Holiday Inn for the night. No strings attached. Merry Christmas and all that."

"Are you really separated from your wife?"

"Yes."

"And so recently?"

"Yes."

"Has she got your kids?"

"We have no kids." They were coming up on the tollbooths. Their green go-lights twinkled indifferently in the early twilight.

"Take me home with you, then."

"I don't have to do that. I mean, you don't have to—"

"I'd just as soon be with somebody tonight," she said. "And I don't like to hitchhike at night. It's scary."

He slid up to a tollbooth and rolled down his window, letting in cold air. He gave the toll taker his card and a dollar ninety. He pulled out slowly. They passed a reflectorized sign that said:

THANK YOU FOR DRIVING SAFELY!

"All right," he said cautiously. He knew he was

probably wrong to keep trying to reassure her—probably achieving just the opposite effect—but he couldn't seem to help it. "Listen, it's just that the house is very lonely by myself. We can have supper, and then maybe watch TV and eat popcorn. You can have the upstairs bedroom and I'll—"

She laughed a little and he glanced at her as they went around the cloverleaf. But she was hard to see now, a little indistinct. She could have been something he dreamed. The idea bothered him.

"Listen," she said. "I better tell you this right now. That drunk I was riding with? I spent the night with him. He was going on to Stilson, where you picked me up. That was his price."

He paused for the red light at the foot of the cloverleaf.

"My roommate told me it would be like that, but I didn't believe her. I wasn't going to fuck my way across the country, not me." She looked at him fleetingly, but he still couldn't read her face in the gloom. "But it's not people *making* you. It's being so disconnected from everything, like spacewalking. When you come into a big city and think of all the people in there, you want to cry. I don't know why, but you do. It gets so you'd spend the night picking some guy's bleeding pimples just to hear him breathe and talk."

"I don't care who you've been sleeping with," he said and pulled out into traffic. Automatically he turned onto Grand Street, heading for home past the 784 construction.

"This salesman," she said. "He's been married fourteen years. He kept saying that while he was humping me. Fourteen years, Sharon, he keeps saying, fourteen years, fourteen years. He came in about fourteen seconds." She uttered a short bark of laughter, rueful and sad.

"Is that your name? Sharon?"

"No. I guess that was his wife's name."

He pulled over to the curb.

"What are you doing?" she asked, instantly distrustful.

"Nothing much," he said. "This is part of going home. Get out, if you want. I'll show you something."

They got out and walked over to the observation platform, now deserted. He laid his bare hands on the cold iron pipe of the railing and looked down. They had been undercoating today, he saw. The last three working days they had put down gravel. Now undercoat. Deserted equipment—trucks and bulldozers and yellow backhoes—stood silently about in the shades of evening like a museum exhibit of dinosaurs. Here we have the vegetarian stegosaurus, the flesh-eating triceratops, the fearsome earth-munching diesel shovel. *Bon appétit.*

"What do you think of it?" he asked her.

"Am I supposed to think something?" She was fencing, trying to figure this out.

"You must think something," he said.

She shrugged. "It's roadwork, so what? They're building a road in a city I'll probably never be in again. What am I supposed to think? It's ugly."

"Ugly," he echoed, relieved.

"I grew up in Portland, Maine," she said. "We lived in a big apartment building and they put this shopping center up across the street—"

"Did they tear anything down to make it?"

"Huh?"

"Did they—"

"Oh. No, it was just a vacant lot with a big field behind it. I was just six or seven. I thought they were going to go on digging and ripping and plowing forever. And all I could think . . . it's funny . . . all I could think was the poor old earth, it's like they're giving it an enema and they never asked if it wanted one or if there was something wrong. I had some kind of an intestinal infection that year, and I was the block expert on enemas."

"Oh," he said.

"We went over one Sunday when they weren't working and it was a lot like this, very quiet, like a corpse that died in bed. They had part of the foundations laid, and there were all of these yellow metal things sticking out of the cement—"

"Core rods."

"Whatever. And there was lots of pipe and bundles of wire covered with clear plastic wrap and there was a lot of raw dirt around. Funny to think of it that way, whoever heard of cooked dirt, but that's how it looked. Just raw. We played hide-and-go-seek around the place and my mother came over and got us and gave me and my sister hell for it. She said little kids can get into bad trouble around construction. My little sister was only four and she cried her head off. Funny to remember all that. Can we get back in the car now? I'm cold."

"Sure," he said, and they did.

As they drove on she said: "I never thought they'd have anything out of that place but a mess. Then pretty soon the shopping center was all there. I can remember the day they hot-topped the parking lot. And a few days after that some men came with a little push-wagon and made all the yellow parking lines. Then they had a big party and some hot-shit cut a ribbon and everybody started using it and it was just like they never built it. The name of the big department store was Mammoth Mart, and my mom used to go there a lot. Sometimes when Angie and I were with her I'd think of all those orange rods sticking through the cement down in the basement. It was like a secret thought."

He nodded. He knew about secret thoughts.

"What does it mean to you?" she asked.

"I'm still trying to figure that out," he said.

He was going to make TV dinners, but she looked in the freezer and saw the roast and said she'd fix it if he didn't mind waiting for it to cook.

"Sure," he said. "I didn't know how long to cook it or even what temperature."

"Do you miss your wife?"

"Like hell."

"Because you don't know how to cook the roast?" she asked, and he didn't answer that. She baked potatoes and cooked frozen corn. They ate in the breakfast nook and she ate four thick slices of the roast, two potatoes, and two helpings of corn.

"I haven't eaten like that in a year," she said, lighting a cigarette and looking into her empty plate. "I'll probably heave my guts."

"What have you been eating?"

"Animal crackers."

"What?"

"Animal crackers."

"I thought that's what you said."

"They're cheap," she said. "And they fill you up. They've got a lot of nutrients and stuff, too. It says so right on the box."

"Nutrients my ass. You're getting zits, girl. You're too old for those. Come here."

He led her into the dining room and opened Mary's china cupboard. He took out a silver serving dish and pulled a thick pile of paper money out of it. Her eyes widened.

"Who'd you off, mister?"

"I offed my insurance policy. Here. Here's two hundred bucks. Eat on it."

But she didn't touch the money. "You're nuts," she said. "What do you think I'm going to do to you for two hundred dollars?"

"Nothing."

She laughed.

"All right." He put the money on the sideboard and put the silver serving dish back into the cupboard. "If you don't take it with you in the morning, I'll flush it down the john." But he didn't think he would.

She looked into his face. "You know, I think you would."

He said nothing.

"We'll see," she said. "In the morning."

"In the morning," he echoed.

He was watching "To Tell the Truth" on the television. Two of the contestants were lying about being the world's champion female bronc rider, and one was telling the truth. The panel, which included Soupy Sales, Bill Cullen, Arlene Dahl, and Kitty Carlisle, had to guess which one was telling the truth. Garry Moore, television's only three-hundred-year-old game show host, smiled and cracked jokes and dinged a bell when each panelist's time was up.

The girl was looking out the window. "Hey," she said. "Who lives on this street, anyway? All the houses look dark."

"Me and the Dankmans," he said. "And the Dankmans are moving out January fifth."

"Why?"

"The road," he said. "Would you like a drink?"

"What do you mean, the road?"

"It's coming through here," he said. "This house is going to be somewhere in the middle of the median strip, as near as I can figure."

"That's why you showed me the construction?"

"I guess so. I used to work for a laundry about two miles from here. The Blue Ribbon. It's going through there, too."

"That's why you lost your job? Because the laundry was closing?"

"Not exactly. I was supposed to sign an option on a new plant in a suburb called Waterford and I didn't do it."

"Why not?"

"I couldn't bear to," he said simply. "You want a drink?"

"You don't have to get me drunk," she said.

"Oh, Christ," he said, rolling his eyes. "Your mind runs on just one track, doesn't it?"

There was a moment of uncomfortable silence.

"Screwdrivers are about the only drinks I like. Do you have vodka and orange juice?"

"Yes."

"No pot, I guess."

"No, I've never used it."

He went out into the kitchen and made her a screwdriver. He mixed himself a Comfort and Seven-Up and took them back into the living room. She was playing with the Space Command gadget, and the TV switched from channel to channel, displaying its seven-thirty wares: "To Tell the Truth," snow, "What's My Line," "I Dream of Jeannie," "Gilligan's Island," snow, "I Love Lucy," snow, snow, Julia Child making something with avocados that looked a little like dog whoop, "The New Price Is Right," snow, and then back to Garry Moore, who was daring the panel to discover which of the three contestants was the real author of a book about what it was like to be lost for a month in the forests of Saskatchewan.

He gave her her drink.

"Did you eat beetles, number two?" Kitty Carlisle asked.

"What's the matter with you people?" the girl asked. "No 'Star Trek.' Are you heathens?"

"They run it at four o'clock on channel eight," he said.

"Do you watch it?"

"Sometimes. My wife always watches Merv Griffin."

"I didn't see any beetles," number two said. "If I'd seen any, I would have eaten them." The audience laughed heartily.

"Why did she move out? You don't have to tell me if you don't want to." She looked at him warily, as if the price of his confession might be tiresomely high.

"The same reason I got fired off my job," he said, sitting down.

"Because you didn't buy that plant?"

"No. Because I didn't buy a new house."

"I voted for number two," Soupy Sales said, "because he looks like he'd eat a beetle if he saw one." The audience laughed heartily.

"Didn't . . . wow. Oh, wow." She looked at him over her drink without blinking. The expression in her eyes seemed to be a mixture of awe, admiration, and terror. "Where are you going to go?"

"I don't know."

"You're not working?"

"No."

"What do you do all day?"

"I ride on the turnpike."

"And watch TV at night?"

"And drink. Sometimes I make popcorn. I'm going to make popcorn later on tonight."

"I don't eat popcorn."

"Then I'll eat it."

She punched the off button on the Space Command gadget (he sometimes thought of it as a "module" because today you were encouraged to think of everything that zapped on and off as a module) and the picture on the Zenith twinkled down to a bright dot and then winked out.

"Let me see if I've got this straight," she said. "You threw your wife and your job down the drain—"

"But not necessarily in that order."

"Whatever. You threw them away over this road. Is that right?"

He looked at the blank TV uncomfortably. Even though he rarely followed what was happening on it very closely, it made him uncomfortable to have it off. "I don't know if it is or not," he said. "You can't always understand something just because you did it."

"Was it a protest?"

"I don't *know*. If you're protesting something, it's because you think something else would be better. All those people protested the war because they thought peace would be better. People protest drug laws because they think other drug laws would be fairer or more fun or less harm or . . . I don't know. Why don't you turn the TV on?"

"In a minute." He noticed again how green her eyes were, intent, catlike. "Is it because you hate the road? The technological society it represents? The dehumanizing effect of—"

"No," he said. It was so difficult to be honest, and he wondered why he was even bothering when a lie would end the discussion so much more quickly and neatly. She was like the rest of the kids, like Vinnie, like the people who thought education was truth: she wanted propaganda, complete with charts, not an answer. "I've seen them building roads and buildings all my life. I never even thought about it, except it was a pain in the ass to use a detour or have to cross the street because the sidewalk was ripped up or the construction company was using a wrecking ball."

"But when it hit home . . . to *your* house and your job, you said no."

"I said no all right." But he wasn't sure what he had said no to. Or had he said yes? Yes, finally yes to some destructive impulse that had been part of him all along, as much a built-in self-destruct mechanism as Charlie's tumor? He found himself wishing Freddy would come around. Freddy could tell her what she wanted to hear. But Fred had been playing it cool.

"You're either crazy or really remarkable," she said.

"People are only remarkable in books," he said. "Let's have the TV."

She turned it on. He let her pick the show.

"What are you drinking?"

It was quarter of nine. He was tipsy, but not as

drunk as he would have been by now alone. He was making popcorn in the kitchen. He liked to watch it pop in the tempered glass popper, rising and rising like snow that had sprung up from the ground rather than come down from the sky.

"Southern Comfort and Seven-Up," he said.

"What?"

He chuckled, embarrassed.

"Can I try one?" She showed him her empty glass and grinned. It was the first completely unselfconscious expression she had shown him since he had picked her up. "You make a lousy screwdriver."

"I know," he said. "Comfort and Seven-Up is my private drink. In public I stick to scotch. Hate scotch."

The popcorn was done, and he poured it into a large plastic bowl.

"Can I have one?"

"Sure."

He mixed her a Comfort and Seven-Up, then poured a melted stick of butter over the popcorn.

"That's going to put a lot of cholesterol in your bloodstream," she said, leaning in the doorway between the kitchen and the dining room. She sipped her drink. "Hey, I *like* this."

"Sure you do. Keep it a secret and you'll always be one up."

He salted the popcorn.

"That cholesterol clogs up your heart," she said. "The passageways for the blood get smaller and smaller and then one day . . . *graaag!*" She clutched dramatically at her bosom and spilled some of her drink on her sweater.

"I metabolize it all away," he told her, and went through the doorway. He brushed her breast (primly bra-ed, by the feel) on the way by. It felt a way Mary's breast hadn't felt in years. It was maybe not such a good way to think.

She ate most of the popcorn.

* * *

She started to yawn during the eleven o'clock news, which was mostly about the energy crisis and the White House tapes.

"Go on upstairs," he said. "Go to bed."

She gave him a look.

He said, "We're going to get along good if you stop looking like somebody goosed you every time the word 'bed' comes up. The primary purpose of the Great American Bed is sleeping, not intercoursing."

That made her smile.

"You don't even want to turn down the sheets?"

"You're a big girl."

She looked at him calmly. "You can come up with me if you want," she said. "I decided that an hour ago."

"No . . . but you don't have any idea how attractive the invitation is. I've only slept with three women in my entire life, and the first two were so long ago I can hardly remember them. Before I was married."

"Are you kidding?"

"Not at all."

"Listen, it wouldn't be just because you gave me a ride or let me sleep over or anything like that. Or the money you offered."

"It's good of you to say that," he said, and got up. "You better go up now."

But she didn't follow his suit. "You ought to know why you're not doing it."

"I should?"

"Yes. If you do things and can't explain them—like you said—that might be okay because they still get done. But if you decide not to, you ought to know why."

"All right," he said. He nodded toward the dining room, where the money still lay in the silver dish. "It's the money. You're too young to be off whoring."

"I won't take it," she said promptly.

"I know you won't. That's why *I* won't. I want you to take it."

"Because everybody isn't as nice as you?"

"That's right." He looked at her challengingly.

She shook her head in an exasperated way and stood up. "All right. But you're a bourgeois, you know that?"

"Yes."

She came over and kissed him on the mouth. It was exciting. He could smell her, and the smell was nice. He was almost instantly hard.

"Go on," he said.

"If you reconsider during the night—"

"I won't." He watched her go to the stairs, her feet bare. "Hey?"

She turned, her eyebrows raised.

"What's your name?"

"Olivia, if it matters. Stupid, isn't it? Like Olivia De Havilland."

"No, it's okay. I like it. Night, Olivia."

"Night."

She went up. He heard the light click on, the way he had always heard it when Mary went up before him. If he listened closely, he might be able to hear the quietly maddening sound of her sweater against her skin as she pulled it over her head, or the snap of the catch that held her jeans nipped in to her waist . . .

Using the Space Command module, he turned on the TV.

His penis was still fully erect, uncomfortable. It bulged against the crotch of his pants, what Mary had sometimes called the rock of ages and sometimes the snake-that-turned-to-stone in their younger days, when bed was nothing but another playground sport. He pulled at the folds of his underwear and when it didn't go down, he stood up. After a while the erection wilted and he sat down again.

When the news was over, a movie came on—John Agar in *Brain from Planet Arous*. He fell asleep sitting in front of the TV with the Space Command module still clasped loosely in one hand. A few minutes later there was a stirring beneath the fly of his pants as his erection returned, stealthily, like a murderer revisiting the scene of an ancient crime.

December 7, 1973

But he did go to her in the night.

The dream of Mr. Piazzi's dog came to him, and this time he knew the boy approaching the dog was Charlie before the bitch struck. That made it worse and when Mr. Piazzi's dog lunged, he struggled up from sleep like a man clawing his way out of a shallow, sandy grave.

He clawed at the air, not awake but not asleep either, and he lost his sense of balance on the couch, where he had finally curled up. He tottered miserably on the edge of balance for a moment, disoriented, terrified for his dead son who died over and over again in his dreams.

He fell onto the floor, banging his head and hurting his shoulder, and came awake enough to know he was in his own living room and that the dream was over. The reality was miserable, but not actively terrifying.

What was he doing? A sort of gestalt reality of what he had done to his life came to him, a hideous overview. He had ripped it right down the middle, like a cheap piece of cloth. Nothing was right anymore. He was hurting. He could taste stale Southern Comfort in the back of his throat, and he burped up some acid-tasting sour stuff and swallowed it back.

He began to shiver and seized his knees in a futile effort to stop it. In the night everything was strange. What was he doing, sitting on the floor of his living room and holding his knees and shaking like an old drunk in an alley? Or like a catatonic, a fucking psycho, that was more like it. Was that it? Was he a psycho? Nothing sort of funny and whimsical like a fruitcake or a dork or a rubber crutch but an out-and-out psycho? The thought dumped him into fresh terror. Had he gone to a hoodlum in an effort to get explosives? Was he really hiding two guns out in the garage, one of them big enough to kill an elephant? A little whining noise came out of his throat and he got up tentatively, his bones creaking like those of a very old man.

He went up the stairs without allowing himself to think, and stepped into his bedroom. "Olivia?" he whispered. This was preposterous, like an old-time Rudolph Valentino movie. "Are you awake?"

"Yes," she said. She didn't even sound sleepy. "The clock was keeping me awake. That digital clock. It kept going *click*. I pulled the plug."

"That's all right," he said. It was a ludicrous thing to say. "I had a bad dream."

The sound of covers being thrown back. "Come on. Get in with me."

"I—"

"*Will* you shut up?"

He got in with her. She was naked. They made love. Then slept.

In the morning, the temperature was only 10 degrees. She asked him if he got a newspaper.

"We used to," he said. "Kenny Upslinger delivered it. His family moved to Iowa."

"Iowa, yet," she said, and turned on the radio. A man was giving the weather. Clear and cold.

"Would you like a fried egg?"

"Two, if you've got them."

"Sure. Listen, about last night—"

"Never mind last night. I came. That's very rare for me. I enjoyed it."

He felt a certain sneaking pride, maybe what she

had wanted him to feel. He fried the eggs. Two for her, two for him. Toast and coffee. She drank three cups with cream and sugar.

"So what are you going to do?" she asked him when they had both finished.

"Take you out to the highway," he said promptly.

She made an impatient gesture. "Not that. About your *life*."

He grinned. "That sounds serious."

"Not for me," she said. "For you."

"I haven't thought about it," he said. "You know, before"—he accented the word *before* slightly to indicate all of his life and all of its parts he had sailed off the edge of the world—"before the ax fell, I think I must have felt the way some condemned man feels in the death house. Nothing seemed real. It seemed I was living in a glass dream that would go on and on. Now everything seems real. Last night . . . that was very real."

"I'm glad," she said, and she looked glad. "But what will you do now?"

"I really don't know."

She said: "I think that's sad."

"Is it?" he asked. It was a real question.

They were in the car again, driving Route 7 toward Landy. The traffic near the city was stop and go. People were on their way to work. When they passed the construction on the 784 extension, the day's operation was already cranking up. Men in yellow hi-impact plastic construction hats and green rubber boots were climbing into their machines, frozen breath pluming from their mouths. The engine of one of the orange city payloaders cranked, cranked, kicked over with a coughing mortar-explosion sound, cranked again, then roared into a choppy idle. The driver gunned it in irregular bursts like the sound of warfare.

"From up here they look like little boys playing trucks in a sandpile," she said.

Outside the city, traffic smoothed out. She had taken the two hundred dollars with neither embarrassment nor reluctance—with no special eagerness, either. She had slit a small section of the CPO coat's lining, had put the bills inside, and had then sewed the slit back up with a needle and some blue thread from Mary's sewing box. She had refused his offer of a ride to the bus station, saying the money would last longer if she went on hitching.

"So what's a nice girl like you doing in a car like this?" he asked.

"Humh?" She looked at him, bumped out of her own thoughts.

He smiled. "Why you? Why Las Vegas? You're living in the margins same as me. Give me some background."

She shrugged. "There isn't much. I was going to college at the University of New Hampshire, in Durham. That's near Portsmouth. I was a junior this year. Living off campus. With a guy. We got into a heavy drug thing."

"You mean like heroin?"

She laughed merrily. "No, I've never known anyone who did heroin. Us nice middle-class druggies stick to the hallucinogens. Lysergic acid. Mescaline. Peyote a couple of times, STP a couple of times. Chemicals. I did sixteen or eighteen trips between September and November."

"What's it like?" he asked.

"Do you mean, did I have any 'bad trips'?"

"No, I didn't mean that at all," he said defensively.

"There were some bad trips, but they all had good parts. And a lot of the good trips had bad parts. Once I decided I had leukemia. That was scary. But mostly they were just strange. I never saw God. I never wanted to commit suicide. I never tried to kill anyone."

She thought that over for a minute. "Everybody has hyped the shit out of those chemicals. The straights, people like Art Linkletter, say they'll kill you. The freaks say they'll open all the doors you need to open. Like you can find a tunnel into the middle of yourself, as if your soul was like the treasure in an H. Rider Haggard novel. Have you ever read him?"

"I read *She* when I was a kid. Didn't he write that?"

"Yes. Do you think your soul is like an emerald in the middle of an idol's forehead?"

"I never thought about it."

"I don't think so," she said. "I'll tell you the best and the worst that ever happened to me on chemicals. The best was topping out in the apartment one time and watching the wallpaper. There were all these little round dots on the wallpaper and they turned into snow for me. I sat in the living room and watched a snowstorm on the wall for better than an hour. And after a while, I saw this little girl trudging through the snow. She had a kerchief on her head, a very rough material like burlap, and she was holding it like this—" She made a fist under her chin. "I decided she was going home, and bang! I saw a whole street in there, all covered with snow. She went up the street and then up a walk and into a house. That was the best. Sitting in the apartment and watching wallovision. Except Jeff called it headovision."

"Was Jeff the guy you were living with?"

"Yes. The worst trip was one time I decided to plunge out the sink. I didn't know why. You get funny ideas sometimes when you're tripping, except they seem perfectly normal. It seemed like I *had* to plunge the sink. So I got the plunger and did it . . . and all this *shit* came out of the drain. I still don't know how much of it was real shit and how much was head shit. Coffee grounds. An old piece of shirt. Great big hunks of congealed grease. Red stuff that looked like blood. And then the hand. Some guy's hand."

"A what?"

"A *hand*. I called to Jeff and said, Hey, somebody put somebody down the drain. But he had taken off someplace and I was alone. I plunged like hell and finally got the forearm out. The hand was lying on the porcelain, all spotted with coffee grounds, and there was the forearm, going right down the drain. I went into the living room for a minute to see if Jeff had come back, and when I went into the kitchen again, the arm and the hand was gone. It sort of worried me. Sometimes I dream about it."

"That's crazy," he said, slowing down as they crossed a bridge that was under construction.

"Chemicals make you crazy," she said. "Sometimes that's a good thing. Mostly it isn't. Anyway, we were into this heavy drug thing. Have you ever seen one of those drawings of what an atom looks like, with the protons and neutrons and electrons going around?"

"Yes."

"Well, it was like our apartment was the nucleus and all the people who drifted in and out were the protons and electrons. People coming and going, drifting in and out, all disconnected, like in *Manhattan Transfer.*"

"I haven't read that one."

"You ought to. Jeff always said Dos Passos was the original gonzo journalist. Freaky book. Anyway, some nights we'd be sitting around watching TV with the sound shut off and a record on the stereo, everyone stoned, people balling in the bedroom, maybe, and you wouldn't even know who the fuck everyone *was*. You know what I mean?"

Thinking of some of the parties he had wandered drunkenly through, as bemused as Alice in Wonderland, he said that he did.

"So one night there was a Bob Hope special on. And everybody was sitting around all smoked up, laughing like hell at all those old one-liners, all those same stock expressions, all that good-natured kidding of the power-crazies in Washington. Just sitting around the tube like all the mommies and daddies back home and I thought well, that's what we went through View Nam for, so Bob Hope could close the generation gap. It's just a question of how you're getting high."

"But you were too pure for all that."

"Pure? No, that wasn't it. But I started to think of the last fifteen years or so like some kind of grotesque Monopoly game. Francis Gary Powers gets shot down in his U-2. Lose one turn. Niggers dispersed by fire hoses in Selma. Go directly to jail. Freedom riders shotgunned in Mississippi, marches, rallies, Lester Maddox with his ax handle, Kennedy getting blown up in Dallas, Viet Nam, more marches, Kent State, student strikes, women's liberation, and all for what? So a bunch of heads can sit around stoned in a crummy apartment watching Bob Hope? Fuck that. So I decided to split."

"What about Jeff?"

She shrugged. "He has a scholarship. He's doing good. He says he's going to come out next summer, but I won't look for him until I see him." There was a peculiar disillusioned expression on her face that probably felt like hardy forbearance on the inside.

"Do you miss him?"

"Every night."

"Why Vegas? Do you know someone out there?"

"No."

"It seems like a funny place for an idealist."

"Is that what you think I am?" She laughed and lit a cigarette. "Maybe. But I don't think an ideal needs any particular setting. I want to see that city. It's so different from the rest of the country that it must be good. But I'm not going to gamble. I'm just going to get a job."

"Then what?"

She blew out smoke and shrugged. They were passing a sign that said:

LANDY 5 MILES

"Try to get something together," she said. "I'm not going to put any dope in my head for a long time and I'm going to quit these." She gestured her cigarette in the air, and it made an accidental circle, as if it knew a different truth. "I'm going to stop pretending my life hasn't started yet. It has. It's twenty percent over. I've drunk the cream."

"Look. There's the turnpike entrance."

He pulled over to the side.

"What about you, man? What are you going to do?"

Carefully, he said: "See what develops. Keep my options open."

She said: "You're not in such hot shape. If you don't mind me saying so."

"No, I don't mind."

"Here. Take this." She was holding out a small aluminum packet between the first and second fingers of her right hand.

He took it and looked at it. The foil caught the bright morning sun and heliographed darts of light at his eyes. "What is it?"

"Product four synthetic mescaline. The heaviest, cleanest chemical ever made." She hesitated. "Maybe you should just flush it down the john when you get home. It might fuck you up worse than you are. But it might help. I've heard of it."

"Have you ever seen it?"

She smiled bitterly. "No."

"Will you do something for me? If you can?"

"If I can."

"Call me on Christmas day."

"Why?"

"You're like a book I haven't finished. I want to know how a little more of it comes out. Make it a collect call. Here, I'll write down the number."

He was fumbling a pen out of his pocket when she said, "No."

He looked at her, puzzled and hurt. "No?"

"I can get the number from directory assistance if I need it. But maybe it would be best not to."

"Why?"

"I don't know. I like you, but it's like someone put a hurtin' on you. I can't explain. It's like you were going to do something really bonkers."

"You think I'm a fruitcake," he heard himself say. "Well, fuck you."

She got out of the car stiffly. He leaned over. "Olivia—"

"Maybe that's not my name."

"Maybe it is. Please call."

"Be careful with that stuff," she said, pointing at the little aluminum packet. "You're space walking, too."

"Good-bye. Be careful."

"Careful, what's that?" The bitter smile again. "Good-bye, Mr. Dawes. Thanks. You're good in bed, do you mind me saying that? You are. Good-bye."

She slammed the door closed, crossed Route 7, and stood at the base of the turnpike entrance ramp. He watched her show a thumb to a couple of cars. Neither of them stopped. Then the road was clear and he U-turned, honking once. In the rearview mirror he saw a small facsimile of her wave.

Silly twit, he thought, stuffed full of every strange conceit in the world. Still, when he put his hand out to turn on the radio, the fingers trembled.

He drove back to the city, got on the turnpike, and drove two hundred miles at seventy. Once he almost threw the small aluminum packet out the window. Once he almost took the pill inside. At last he just put it in his coat pocket.

When he got home he felt washed out, empty of emotion. The 784 extension had progressed during the day; in a couple of weeks the laundry would be ready for the wrecking ball. They had already taken out the heavy equipment. Tom Granger had told him about

that in an odd, stilted phone conversation three nights
ago. When they leveled it he would spend the day
watching. He would even pack a bag lunch.

There was a letter for Mary from her brother in
Jacksonville. He didn't know about the split, then. He
put it aside absently with some other mail for Mary
that he kept forgetting to forward.

He put a TV dinner in the oven and thought about
making himself a drink. He decided not to. He wanted
to think about his sexual encounter with the girl the
night before, relish it, explore its nuances. A few
drinks and it would take on the unnatural, fevered
color of a bad sex movie—*Restless Coeds, ID Required*—and he didn't want to think of her like that.

But it wouldn't come, not the way he wanted it. He
couldn't remember the precise tight feel of her breasts
or the secret taste of her nipples. He knew that the
actual friction of intercourse had been more pleasur-
able with her than with Mary. Olivia had been a snug-
ger fit, and once his penis had popped out of her
vagina with an audible sound, like the pop of a cham-
pagne cork. But he couldn't really say what the pleasure had been. Instead of being able to feel it, he
wanted to masturbate. The desire disgusted him. Furthermore, his disgust disgusted him. She wasn't holy,
he assured himself as he sat down to eat his TV dinner. Just a tramp on the bum. To Las Vegas, yet. He
found himself wishing that he could view the whole
incident with Magliore's jaundiced eye, and that disgusted him most of all.

Later that night he got drunk in spite of all his
good intentions, and around ten o'clock the familiar
maudlin urge to call Mary rose up in him. He mastur-
bated instead, in front of the TV, and came to climax
while an announcer was showing incontrovertibly that
Anacin hit and held the highest pain-relief level of
any brand.

December 8, 1973

He didn't go riding Saturday. He wandered uselessly
around the house, putting off the thing that had to be
done. At last he called the home of his in-laws. Lester
and Jean Calloway, Mary's parents, were both nearing
their seventies. On his previous calls, Jean (whom
Charlie had always called "Mamma Jean") had answered the telephone, her voice freezing to ice chips
when she realized who was on the line. To her, and
to Lester also, undoubtedly, he was like some animal
that had run amok and bitten her daughter. Now the
animal kept calling up, obviously drunk, whining for
their girl to come back so he could bite her again.

He heard Mary herself answer, "Hello?" with
enough relief so he could talk normally.

"Me, Mary."

"Oh, Bart. How are you?" Impossible to read her
voice.

"Fair."

"How are the Southern Comfort supplies holding
out?"

"Mary, I'm not drinking."

"Is that a victory?" She sounded cold, and he felt
a touch of panic, mostly that his judgment had been
impossibly bad. Could someone he had known so long
and whom he thought he knew so well be slipping
away so easily?

"I guess it is," he said lamely.

"I understand the laundry had to close down," she
said.

"Probably just temporary." He had the weird sensa-
tion that he was riding in an elevator, conversing uncomfortably with someone who regarded him as a
bore.

"That isn't what Tom Granger's wife said." There, accusation at last. Accusation was better than nothing.

"Tom won't have any problem. The competition uptown has been after him for years. The Brite-Kleen people."

He thought she sighed. "Why did you call, Bart?"

"I think we ought to get together," he said carefully. "We have to talk this over, Mary."

"Do you mean a divorce?" She said it calmly enough, but he thought it was her voice in which he sensed panic now.

"Do you want one?"

"I don't know *what* I want." Her calm fractured and she sounded angry and scared. "I thought everything was fine. I was happy and I thought you were. Now, all at once, that's all changed."

"You thought everything was fine," he replied. He was suddenly furious with her. "You must have been pretty stupid if you thought that. Did you think I kicked away my job for a practical joke, like a high school senior throwing a cherry bomb into a toilet?"

"Then what is it, Bart? What happened?"

His anger collapsed like a rotten yellow snowbank and he found that there were tears beneath. He fought them grimly, feeling betrayed. This wasn't supposed to happen sober. When you were sober you should be able to keep fucking control of yourself. But here he was, wanting to spill out everything and sob on her lap like a kid with a busted skate and a skinned knee. But he couldn't tell her what was wrong because he didn't precisely know and crying without knowing was too much like it's-time-for-the-loony-bin stuff.

"I don't know," he said finally.

"Charlie?"

Helplessly, he said: "If that was part of it, how could you be so blind to the rest of it?"

"I miss him too, Bart. Still. Every day."

Resentment again. *You've got a funny way of showing it, then.*

"This is no good," he said finally. Tears were tricking down his cheeks but he had kept them out of his voice. *Gentlemen, I think we've got it licked,* he thought, and almost cackled. "Not over the phone, I called to suggest lunch on Monday. Handy Andy's."

"All right. What time?"

"It doesn't matter. I can get off work." The joke fell to the floor and died bloodlessly there.

"One o'clock?" she asked.

"Sure. I'll get us a table."

"Reserve one. Don't just get there at eleven and start drinking."

"I won't," he said humbly, knowing he probably would.

There was a pause. There seemed nothing else to say. Faintly, almost lost in the hum of the open wire, ghostly other voices discussed ghostly other things. Then she said something that surprised him totally.

"Bart, you need to see a psychiatrist."

"I need a what?"

"Psychiatrist. I know how that sounds, just coming out flat. But I want you to know that whatever we decide, I won't come back and live with you unless you agree."

"Good-bye, Mary," he said slowly. "I'll see you on Monday."

"Bart, you need help I can't give."

Carefully, inserting the knife as well as he could over two miles of blind wire, he said: "I knew that anyway. Good-bye, Mary."

He hung up before he could hear the result and caught himself feeling glad. Game, set, and match. He threw a plastic milk pitcher across the room and caught himself feeling glad that he hadn't thrown something breakable. He opened the cupboard over the sink, yanked out the first two glasses his hands came to, and threw them on the floor. They shattered.

Baby, you fucking baby! he screamed at himself.

Why don't you just hold your fucking breath until you turn fucking BLUE?

He slammed his right fist against the wall to shut out the voice and cried out at the pain. He held his wounded right in his left and stood in the middle of the floor, trembling. When he had himself under control he got a dustpan and the broom and swept the mess up, feeling scared and sullen and hung over.

December 9, 1973

He got on the turnpike, drove a hundred and fifty miles, and then drove back. He didn't dare drive any farther. It was the first gasless Sunday and all the turnpike pit stops were closed. And he didn't want to walk. See? He told himself. This is how they get shitbirds like you, Georgie.

Fred? Is that really you? To what do I owe the honor of this visit, Freddy?

Fuck off, buddy.

On the way home he heard this public service ad on the radio:

"So you're worried about the gasoline shortage and you want to make sure that you and your family aren't caught short this winter. So now you're on your way to your neighborhood gas station with a dozen five-gallon cans. But if you're really worried about your family, you better turn around and go back home. Improper storage of gasoline is dangerous. It's also illegal, but never mind that for a minute. Consider this: When gasoline fumes mix with the air, they become explosive. And one gallon of gas has the explosive potential of twelve sticks of dynamite. Think about that before you fill those cans. And then think about your family. You see—we want you to live.

"This has been a public service announcement from WLDM. The Music People remind you to leave gasoline storage to the people who are equipped to do it properly."

He turned off the radio, slowed down to fifty, and pulled back into the cruising lane. "Twelve sticks of dynamite," he said. "Man, that's amazing."

If he had looked into the rearview mirror, he would have seen that he was grinning.

December 10, 1973

He got to Handy Andy's at just past eleven-thirty and the headwaiter gave him a table beside the stylized batwings that led to the lounge—not a good table, but one of the few empties left as the place filled up for lunch. Handy Andy's specialized in steaks, chops, and something called the Andyburger, which looked a little like a chef's salad stuck between a huge sesame seed roll with a toothpick to hold the whole contraption together. Like all big city restaurants within executive walking distance, it went through indefinable cycles of inness and outness. Two months ago he could have come in here at noon and had his pick of tables—three months hence he might be able to do the same. To him, it had always been one of life's minor mysteries, like the incidents in the books of Charles Fort, or the instinct that always brought the swallows back to Capistrano.

He looked around quickly as he sat down, afraid he would see Vinnie Mason or Steve Ordner or some other laundry executive. But the place was stuffed with strangers. To his left, a young man was trying to persuade his girl that they could afford three days in Sun Valley this February. The rest of the room's conversation was just soft babble—soothing.

"A drink, sir?" The waiter was at his elbow.

"Scotch-rocks, please," he said.

"Very good, sir," the waiter said.

He made the first one last until noon, killed two more by twelve-thirty, and then, just mulishly, he ordered a double. He was just draining it dry when he saw Mary walk in and pause in the door between the foyer and the dining room, looking for him. Heads turned to look at her and he thought: *Mary, you ought to thank me—you're beautiful.* He raised his right hand and waved.

She raised her hand in return greeting and came to his table. She was wearing a knee-length wool dress, soft patterned gray. Her hair was braided in a single thick cable that hung down to her shoulder blades, a way he could not recall having seen her wear it (and maybe worn that way for just that reason). It made her look youthful, and he had a sudden guilty flash of Olivia, working beneath him on the bed he and Mary had shared so often.

"Hello, Bart," she said.

"Hi. You look awful pretty."

"Thanks."

"Do you want a drink?"

"No . . . just an Andyburger. How long have you been here?"

"Oh, not long."

The lunch crowd had thinned, and his waiter appeared almost at once. "Would you like to order now, sir?"

"Yes. Two Andyburgers. Milk for the lady. Another double for myself." He glanced at Mary, but her face showed nothing. That was bad. If she had spoken, he would have canceled the double. He hoped he wouldn't have to go to the bathroom, because he wasn't sure he could walk straight. That would be a wonderful tidbit to carry back to the old folks at home. Carry me back to Ol' Virginnie. He almost giggled.

"Well, you're not drunk, but you're on your way," she said, and unfolded her napkin on her lap.

"That's pretty good," he said. "Did you rehearse it?"

"Bart, let's not fight."

"No," he agreed.

She toyed with her water glass; he picked at his coaster.

"Well?" she said finally.

"Well what?"

"You seemed to have something in mind when you called. Now that you're full of Dutch courage, what is it?"

"Your cold is better," he said idiotically, and tore a hole in his coaster without meaning to. He couldn't tell her what was on the top of his mind: how she seemed to have changed, how she seemed suddenly sophisticated and dangerous, like a cruising secretary who has bartered for a later lunch hour and who would refuse any offer of a drink unless it came from a man inside a four-hundred-dollar suit. And who could tell just by glancing at the cut of the fabric.

"Bart, what are we going to do?"

"I'll see a psychiatrist if you want me to," he said, lowering his voice.

"When?"

"Pretty soon."

"You can make an appointment this afternoon if you want to."

"I don't know any shr—any."

"There's the Yellow Pages."

"That seems like a half-assed sort of way to pick a brainpeeker."

She only looked at him and he looked away, uncomfortable.

"You're angry with me, aren't you?" she asked.

"Yeah, well, I'm not working. Fifty dollars an hour seems sort of high for an unemployed fellow."

"What do you think I'm living on?" she asked sharply. "My folks' charity. And as you'll recall, they're both retired."

"As I recall, your father's got enough shares in SOI and Beechcraft to keep the three of you on easy street well into the next century."

"Bart, that's not so." She sounded startled and hurt.

"Bull*shit* it's not. They were in Jamaica last winter, Miami the year before that, at the Fountainbleau no less, and Honolulu the year before *that*. Nobody does that on a retired engineer's salary. So don't give me that poorbox routine, Mary—"

"Stop it, Bart. The green's showing."

"Not to mention a Cadillac Gran DeVille and a Bonneville station wagon. Not bad. Which one do they use when they go to pick up their food stamps?"

"Stop it!" she hissed at him, her lips drawn back a bit from her small white teeth, her fingers gripping the edge of the table.

"Sorry," he muttered.

"Lunch is coming."

The temperature between them cooled a little as the waiter set their Andyburgers and French fries before them, added minuscule dishes of green peas and baby onions, then retired. They ate without speaking for a while, both concentrating on not drooling down their chins or in their laps. I wonder how many marriages the Andyburger has saved? he wondered. Simply by its one providential attribute—when you're eating one you have to shut up.

She put hers down half-eaten, blotted her mouth with her napkin, and said, "They're as good as I remember. Bart, do you have any sensible idea at all about what to do?"

"Of course I do," he said, stung. But he didn't know what his idea was. If he'd gotten in another double, he might have.

"Do you want a divorce?"

"No," he said. Something positive seemed to be called for.

"Do you want me to come back?"

"Do you want to?"

"I don't know," she said. "Shall I tell you something, Bart? I'm worried about myself for the first time in twenty years. I'm *fending* for myself." She started to take a bite of her Andyburger, then set it down again. "Did you know I almost didn't marry you? Had that thought ever crossed your mind?"

The surprise on his face seemed to satisfy her.

"I didn't think it had. I was pregnant, so of course I wanted to marry you. But part of me didn't. Something kept whispering that it would be the worst mistake of my life. So I roasted myself over a slow fire for three days, throwing up every morning when I woke up, hating *you* for that, thinking this, that, and the other. Run away. Get an abortion. Have the baby and put it up for adoption. Have the baby and keep it. But I finally decided to do the sensible thing. The sensible thing." She laughed. "And then lost the baby anyway."

"Yes, you did," he muttered, wishing the conversation would turn from this. It was too much like opening a closet and stepping into puke.

"But I was happy with you, Bart."

"Were you?" he asked automatically. He found he wanted to get away. This wasn't working. Not for him anyway.

"Yes. But something happens to a woman in marriage that doesn't happen to a man. Do you remember when you were a child how you never worried about your parents? You just expected them to be there and they were, same as the food and the heat and the clothes."

"I guess so. Sure."

"And I went and got my silly self pregnant. And for three days a whole new world opened up around me." She was leaning forward, her eyes glowing and anxious, and he realized with dawning shock that this recitation was *important* to her, that it was more than getting together with her childless friends or deciding which pair of slacks to buy in Banberry's or guessing which celebrities Merv would be chatting with at four-thirty. This was *important* to her, and had she really gone through twenty years of marriage with only this one important thought? *Had* she? She had almost said as much. Twenty years, my God. He felt suddenly sick to his stomach. He liked the image of her picking up the empty bottle and waving it at him gleefully from her side of the road so much better.

"I saw myself as an independent person," she was saying. "An independent person with no one to explain myself to or subordinate myself to. No one around to try and change me, because I knew I *could* be changed. I was always weak that way. But also no one to fall back on when I was sick or scared or maybe broke. So I did the sensible thing. Like my mother and *her* mother. Like my friends. I was tired of being a bridesmaid and trying to catch the bouquet. So I said yes, which was what you expected and things went on. There were no worries, and when the baby died and when Charlie died there was you. And you were always good to me. I know that, I appreciate that. But it was a sealed environment. I stopped thinking. I thought I was thinking, but I wasn't. And now it hurts to think. It *hurts.*" She looked at him with bright resentment for a minute, and then it faded. "So I'm asking you to think for me, Bart. What do we do now?"

"I'm going to get a job," he lied.

"A job."

"And see a psychiatrist. Mary, things are going to be fine. Honest. I was a little off the beam, but I'm going to get back on. I'm—"

"Do you want me to come home?"

"In a couple of weeks, sure. I just have to get things together a little and—"

"Home? What am I talking about? They're going to tear it down. What am I talking about, home? Jesus," she groaned, "what a mess. Why did you have to drag me into such a shitty mess?"

He couldn't stand her this way. She wasn't like Mary, not at all. "Maybe they won't," he said, taking her hand across the table. "Maybe they won't tear it down, Mary, they might change their minds, if I go and talk to them, explain the situation, they might just—"

She jerked her hand away. She was looking at him, horrified.

"Bart," she whispered.

"What—" He broke off, uncertain. What had he been saying? What could he possibly have been saying to make her look so awful?

"You *know* they're going to tear it down. You knew it a long time ago. And we're sitting here, going around and around—"

"No, we're not," he said. "We're not. Really. We're not. We . . . we . . . ." But what *were* they doing? He felt unreal.

"Bart, I think I better go now."

"I'm going to get a job—"

"I'll talk to you." She got up hastily, her thigh bumping the edge of the table, making the silverware gossip.

"The psychiatrist, Mary, I promise—"

"Mamma wanted me to go to the store—"

"Then go on!" he shouted at her, and heads turned. "Get out of here, you bitch! You had the best of me and what have I got? A house the city's going to rip down. Get out of my *sight*!"

She fled. The room was horribly quiet for what seemed like eternity. Then the talk picked up again. He looked down at his dripping half-eaten hamburger, trembling, afraid he was going to vomit. When he knew he was not, he paid the check and left without looking around.

December 12, 1973

He made out a Christmas list the night before (drunk) and was now downtown filling an abridged version. The completed list had been staggering—over a hundred and twenty names, including every relative near and distant that he and Mary had between them, a great many friends and acquaintances, and at the bottom—God save the queen—Steve Ordner, his wife, and their for Chrissakes *maid*.

He had pruned most of the names from the list, chuckling bemusedly over some of them, and now strolled slowly past windows filled with Christmas goodies, all to be given in the name of that long-ago Dutch thief who used to slide down people's chimneys and steal everything they owned. One gloved hand patted a five-hundred-dollar roll of ten-dollar bills in his pocket.

He was living on the insurance money, and the first thousand dollars of it had melted away with amazing speed. He estimated that he would be broke by the middle of March at this rate, possibly sooner, but found the thought didn't bother him at all. The thought of where he might be or what he might be doing in March was as incomprehensible as calculus.

He went into a jewelry store and bought a beaten-silver owl pin for Mary. The owl had coldly flashing diamond chips for eyes. It cost one hundred and fifty dollars, plus tax. The saleslady was effusive. She was sure his wife was going to love it. He smiled. There goes three appointments with Dr. Psycho, Freddy. What do you think about that?

Freddy wasn't talking.

He went into a large department store and took an

escalator up to the toy department, which was dominated by a huge electric train display—green plastic
hills honey-combed with tunnels, plastic train stations,
overpasses, underpasses, switching points, and a Lio-
nel locomotive that bustled through all of it, puffing
ribbons of synthetic smoke from its stack and hauling
a long line of freight cars—B&O, SOO LINE, GREAT
NORTHERN, GREAT WESTERN, WARNER BROTHERS
(WARNER BROTHERS??), DIAMOND INTERNATIONAL,
SOUTHERN PACIFIC. Young boys and their fathers were
standing by the wooden picket fence that surrounded
the display, and he felt a warm surge of love for them
that was untainted by envy. He felt he could have
gone to them, told them of his love for them, his
thankfulness for them and the season. He would also
have urged them to be careful.

He wandered down an aisle of dolls, and picked one
up for each of his three nieces: Chatty Cathy for Tina,
Maisie the Acrobat for Cindy, and a Barbie for Sylvia,
who was eleven now. In the next aisle he got a GI
Joe for Bill, and after some deliberation, a chess set
for Andy. Andy was twelve, an object of some worry
in the family. Old Bea from Baltimore had confided
in Mary that she kept finding stiff places on Andy's
sheets. Could it be possible? So early? Mary had told
Bea that children were getting more precocious every
year. Bea said she supposed it was all the milk they
drank, and vitamins, but she *did* wish Andy liked team
sports more. Or summer camp. Or horseback riding.
Or anything.

Never mind, Andy, he thought, tucking the chess
set under his arm. You practice knight's gambits and
queen to rook-4 and beat off under the table if you
want to.

There was a huge Santa Claus throne at the front
of the toy department. The throne was empty, and
a sign was propped on an easel in front of it. The
sign said:

SANTA IS HAVING LUNCH AT OUR FAMOUS
"MID-TOWN GRILL"

Why Not Join Him?

There was a young man in a denim jacket and jeans
looking at the throne, his arms full of packages, and
when the young man turned around, he saw it was
Vinnie Mason.

"Vinnie!" he said.

Vinnie smiled and colored a little, as if he had been
caught doing something a bit nasty. "Hello, Bart," he
said, and walked over. There was no embarrassment
over shaking hands; their arms were too full of packages.

"Christmas shopping a little?" he asked Vinnie.

"Yeah." He chuckled. "I brought Sharon and Bobbie—that's my daughter Roberta—over to look on
Saturday. Bobbie's three now. We wanted to get her
picture taken with Santa Claus. You know they do
that on Saturdays. Just a buck. But she wouldn't do
it. Cried her head off. Sharon was a little upset."

"Well, it's a strange man with a big beard. The little
ones get scared sometimes. Maybe she'll go to him
next year."

"Maybe." Vinnie smiled briefly.

He smiled back, thinking it was much easier with
Vinnie now. He wanted to tell Vinnie not to hate his
guts too much. He wanted to tell Vinnie he was sorry
if he had fucked up Vinnie's life. "So what are you
doing these days, Vinnie?"

Vinnie absolutely beamed. "You won't believe this,
it's so good. I'm managing a movie theater. And by
next summer I'll be handling three more."

"Media Associates?" It was one of the corporation's companies.

"That's right. We're part of the Cinemate Releasing
chain. They send in all the movies . . . proven box-
office stuff. But I'm handling the Westfall Cinema
completely."

"They're going to add on?"

"Yeah, Cinema II and III by next summer. And the Beacon Drive-In, I'll be handling that, too."

He hesitated. "Vinnie, you tell me if I'm stepping out of line, but if this Cinemate outfit picks the films and books them, then what exactly do you do?"

"Well, handle the money, of course. And order stuff, that's very important. Did you know that the candy stand *alone* can almost pay for one night's film rental if it's handled efficiently? Then there's maintenance and—" He swelled visibly, "and hiring and firing. It's going to keep me busy. Sharon likes it because she's a big movie freak, especially Paul Newman and Clint Eastwood. I like it because all of a sudden I jumped from nine thousand to eleven thousand-five."

He looked at Vinnie dully for a moment, wondering if he should speak. This was Ordner's prize, then. Good doggie. Here's the bone.

"Get out of it, Vinnie," he said. "Get out of it just as quick as you can."

"What, Bart?" Vinnie's brow wrinkled in honest puzzlement.

"Do you know what the word 'gofer' means, Vinnie?"

"Gopher? Sure. It's a little animal that digs holes—"

"No, gofer. G-O-F-E-R."

"I guess I don't know that one, Bart. Is it Jewish?"

"No, it's white-collar. It's a person who does errands. A glorified office boy. Gofer coffee, gofer Danish, gofer a walk around the block, sonny. Gofer."

"What are you talking about, Bart? I mean—"

"I mean that Steve Ordner kicked your special case around with the other members of the board—the ones who matter, anyway—and said, Listen, fellas, we've got to do something about Vincent Mason, and it's a delicate sort of case. He warned us that Bart Dawes was riding a rubber bike, and even though Mason didn't swing quite enough weight to enable us to stop Dawes before he screwed up the waterworks, we owe this Mason something. But of course we can't give him too much responsibility. And do you know why, Vinnie?"

Vinnie was looking at him resentfully. "I know I don't have to eat your shit anymore, Bart. I know that."

He looked at Vinnie earnestly. "I'm not trying to shit you. What you do doesn't mean anything to me anymore. But Chrissakes, Vinnie, you're a young man. I don't want to see him fuck you over this way. The job you've got is a short-term plum, a long-term lemon. The toughest decision you're going to have is when to reorder Buttercup containers and Milky Ways. And Ordner's going to see that it stays that way as long as you're with the corporation."

The Christmas spirit, if that was what it had been, curdled in Vinnie's eyes. He was clutching his packages tightly enough to make the wrappings crackle, and his eyes were gray with resentment. Picture of a young man who steps out his door whistling, ready for the evening's heavy date, only to see all four tires on his new sports car have been slashed. *And he's not listening. I could play him tapes and he still wouldn't believe it.*

"As it turned out, you did the responsible thing," he went on. "I don't know what people are saying about me now—"

"They're saying you're crazy, Bart," Vinnie said in a thin, hostile voice.

"That word's as good as any. So you were right. But you were wrong, too. You spilled your guts. They don't give positions of responsibility to people who spill their guts, not even when they were right to do it, not even when the corporation suffers because of their silence. Those guys on the fortieth floor, Vinnie, they're like doctors. And they don't like loose talk any more than doctors like an intern that goes around blowing off about a doctor who muffed an operation because he had too many cocktails at lunch."

"You're really determined to mess up my life, aren't

you?" Vinnie asked. "But I don't work for you any-more, Bart. Go waste your poison on someone else."

Santa Claus was coming back, a huge bag slung over one shoulder, bellowing wild laughter and trailing small children like parti-colored exhaust.

"Vinnie, Vinnie, don't be blind. They're sugar-coating the pill. Sure you're making eleven-five this year and next year when you pick up the other theaters, they'll buck you up to maybe fourteen thousand. And there you'll be twelve years from now, when you can't buy a lousy Coke for thirty cents. Gofer that new carpet-ing, gofer that consignment of theater seats, gofer those reels of film that got sent across town by mis-take. Do you want to be doing that shit when you're forty, Vinnie, with nothing to look forward to but a gold watch?"

"Better than what you're doing." Vinnie turned away abruptly, almost bumping Santa, who said some-thing that sounded suspiciously like *watch where the fuck you're going*.

He went after Vinnie. Something about the set ex-pression on Vinnie's face convinced him he was get-ting through, despite the defensive emplacements. God, God, he thought. Let it be.

"Leave me alone, Bart. Get lost."

"Get out of it," he repeated. "If you wait even until next summer it may be too late. Jobs are going to be tighter than a virgin's chastity belt if this energy crisis goes into high gear, Vinnie. This may be your last chance. It—"

Vinnie wheeled around. "I'm telling you for the last time, Bart."

"You're flushing your future right down the john, Vinnie. Life's too short for that. What are you going to tell your daughter when— "

Vinnie punched him in the eye. A bolt of white pain flashed up into his head and he staggered backward, arms flying out. The kids who had been following

Santa scattered as his packages—dolls, GI Joe, chess set—went flying. He hit a rack of toy telephones, which sprayed across the floor. Somewhere a little girl screamed like a hurt animal and he thought *Don't cry, darling, it's just dumb old George falling down, I do it frequently around the house these days* and someone else—jolly old Santa, maybe—was cursing and yelling for the store detective. Then he was on the floor amid the toy telephones, which all came equipped with battery-powered tape loops, and one of them was saying over and over in his ear: "Do you want to go to the circus? Do you want to go to the circus? Do you . . ."

December 17, 1973

The shrilling of the telephone brought him out of a thin, uneasy afternoon sleep. He had been dreaming that a young scientist had discovered that, by changing the atomic composition of peanuts just a little, America could produce unlimited quantities of low-polluting gasoline. It seemed to make everything all right, personally and nationally, and the tone of the dream was one of burgeoning jubilation. The phone was a sinister counterpoint that grew and grew until the dream split open and let in an unwelcome reality.

He got up from the couch, went to the phone, and fumbled it to his ear. His eye didn't hurt anymore, but in the hall mirror he could see that it was still colorful.

"Hello?"

"Hi, Bart. Tom."

"Yeah, Tom. How are you?"

"Fine. Listen, Bart. I thought you'd want to know. They're demolishing the Blue Ribbon tomorrow."

His eyes snapped wide. "Tomorrow? It can't be tomorrow. They . . . hell, it's almost Christmas!"

"That's why."

"But they're not up to it yet."

"It's the only industrial building left in the way," Tom said. "They're going to raze it before they knock off for Christmas."

"Are you sure?"

"Yes. They had a news feature on that morning program. 'City Day.' "

"Are you going to be there?"

"Yeah," Tom said. "Too much of my life went by inside that pile for me to be able to stay away."

"Then I guess I'll see you there."

"I guess you will."

He hesitated. "Listen, Tom. I want to apologize. I don't think they're going to reopen the Blue Ribbon, in Waterford or anyplace else. If I screwed you up royally—"

"No, I'm not hurting. I'm up at Brite-Kleen, doing maintenance. Shorter hours, better pay. I guess I found the rose in the shitheap."

"How is it?"

Tom sighed across the wire. "Not so good," he said. "But I'm past fifty now. It's hard to change. It would have been the same in Waterford."

"Tom, about what I did—"

"I don't want to hear about it, Bart." Tom sounded uncomfortable. "That's between you and Mary. Really."

"Okay."

"Uh . . . you getting along good?"

"Sure. I've got a couple of things on the line."

"I'm glad to hear that." Tom paused so long that the silence on the line became thick, and he was about to thank him for calling and hang up when Tom added: "Steve Ordner called up about you. Called me right up at my house."

"Is that so? When?"

"Last week. He's pissed like a bear at you, Bart. He kept asking if any of us had any idea you had been sandbagging the Waterford plant. But it was more than that. He was asking all sorts of other things."

"Like what?"

"Like did you ever take stuff home, office supplies and stuff like that. Did you ever draw from petty cash without putting in a voucher. Or get your laundry done on the company clock. He even asked me if you had any kind of kickback deal going with the motels."

"That son of a bitch," he said wonderingly.

"Like I say, he's hunting around for a nice raw cob to stick up your pump, Bart. I think he'd like to find a criminal charge he could get you on."

"He can't. It's all in the family. And the family's broken up now."

"It broke up a long time ago," Tom said evenly. "When Ray Tarkington died. I don't know anyone who's pissed off at you but Ordner. Those guys downtown . . . it's just dollars and cents to them. They don't know nothing about the laundry business and they don't care to know."

He could think of nothing to say.

"Well . . ." Tom sighed. "I thought you ought to know. And I s'pose you heard about Johnny Walker's brother."

"Arnie? No, what about him?"

"Killed himself."

"What?"

Tom sounded as if he might be sucking back spit through his upper plate. "Ran a hose from the exhaust pipe of his car into the back window and shut everything up. The newsboy found him."

"Holy God," he whispered. He thought of Arnie Walker sitting in the hospital waiting room chair and shivered, as if a goose had walked over his grave. "That's awful."

"Yeah . . ." That sucking noise again. "Listen, I'll be seeing you, Bart."

"Sure. Thanks for calling."

"Glad to do it. Bye."

He hung up slowly, still thinking of Arnie Walker and that funny, whining gasp Arnie had made when the priest hurried in.

Jesus, he had his pyx, did you see it?

"Oh, that's too bad," he said to the empty room, and the words fell dead as he uttered them and he went into the kitchen to fix himself a drink.

Suicide.

The word had a hissing trapped sound, like a snake squirming through a small crevice. It slipped between the tongue and the roof of the mouth like a convict on the lam.

Suicide.

His hand trembled as he poured Southern Comfort, and the neck of the bottle chattered against the rim of the glass. Why did he do that, Freddy? They were just a couple of old farts who roomed together. Jesus Christ, why would *anybody* do that?

But he thought he knew why.

December 18-19, 1973

He got to the laundry around eight in the morning and they didn't start to tear it down until nine, but even at eight there was quite a gallery on hand, standing in the cold with their hands thrust into their coat pockets and frozen breath pluming from their mouths like comic strip balloons—Tom Granger, Ron Stone, Ethel Diment, the shirt girl who usually got tipsy on her lunch break and then burned the hell out of unsuspecting shirt collars all afternoon, Gracie Floyd and her cousin Maureen, both of whom had worked on the ironer, and ten or fifteen others.

The highway department had put out yellow sawhorses and smudge pots and large orange-and-black signs that said:

DETOUR

The signs would route traffic around the block. The sidewalk that fronted the laundry had been closed off, too.

Tom Granger tipped a finger at him but didn't come over. The others from the laundry glanced at him curiously and then put their heads together.

A paranoid's dream, Freddy. Who'll be the first to trot over and scream *j'accuse* in my face?

But Fred wasn't talking.

Around quarter of nine a new '74 Toyota Corolla pulled up, the ten-day plate still taped in the rear window, and Vinnie Mason got out, resplendent and a little self-conscious in a new camel's hair overcoat and leather gloves. Vinnie shot him a sour glance that would have bent steel nails out of plumb and then walked over to where Ron Stone was standing with Dave and Pollack.

At ten minutes of nine they brought a crane up the street, the wrecking ball dangling from the top of the gantry like some disembodied Ethiopian teat. The crane was rolling very slowly on its ten chest-high wheels, and the steady, crackling roar of its exhaust beat into the silvery chill of the morning like an artisan's hammer shaping a sculpture of unknown import.

A man in a yellow hard hat directed it up over the curb and through the parking lot, and he could see the man high up in the cab changing gears and clutching with one blocklike foot. Brown smoke pumped from the crane's overhead stack.

A weird, diaphanous feeling had been haunting him ever since he had parked the station wagon three blocks over and walked here, a simile that wouldn't quite connect. Now, watching the crane halt at the base of the long brick plant, just to the left of what

had been the loading bays, the sense of it came to
him. It was like stepping into the last chapter of an
Ellery Queen mystery where all the participants have
been gathered so that the mechanics of the crime
could be explained and the culprit unmasked. Soon
someone—Steve Ordner, most likely—would step out
of the crowd, point at him and scream: *He's the one!
Bart Dawes! He killed the Blue Ribbon!* At which
point he would draw his pistol in order to silence his
nemesis, only to be riddled with police bullets.

The fancy disturbed him. He looked toward the
road to assure himself and felt a sinking-elevator sen-
sation in his belly as he saw Ordner's bottle-green
Delta 88 parked just beyond the yellow barriers, exhaust pluming from the twin tailpipes.

Steve Ordner was looking calmly back at him
through the polarized glass.

At that moment the wrecking ball swung through
its arc with a low, ratcheting scream, and the small
crowd sighed as it struck the brick wall and punched
through with a hollow booming noise like detonating
cannon fire.

By four that afternoon there was nothing left of the
Blue Ribbon but a jumbled pile of brick and glass,
through which protruded the shattered main beams
like the broken skeleton of some exhumed monster.

What he did later he did with no conscious thought
of the future or consequences. He did it in much the
same spirit that he had bought the two guns at Harvey's Gun Shop a month earlier. Only there was no
need to use the circuit breaker because Freddy had
shut up.

He drove to a gas station and filled up the LTD
with hi-test. Clouds had come in over the city during
the day, and the radio was forecasting a storm—six to
ten inches of new snow. He drove back home, parked
the station wagon in the garage, and went down cellar.

Under the stairs there were two large cartons of

returnable soda and beer bottles, the top layer covered with a thick patina of dust. Some of the bottles probably went back five years. Even Mary had forgotten about them in the last year or so and had given up pestering him about taking them back for the refund. Most of the stores didn't even accept returnables now. Use them once, throw them away. What the hell.

He stacked the two cartons one on top of the other and carted them out to the garage. When he went back to the kitchen to get a knife, a funnel, and Mary's floor-washing pail, it had begun to spit snow.

He turned on the garage light and took the green plastic garden hose off its nail, where it had been looped since the third week of September. He cut off the nozzle and it fell to the cement floor with a meaningless clink. He paid out three feet and cut it again. He kicked the rest away and looked at the length of hose thoughtfully for a moment. Then he unscrewed his gas cap and slipped the hose gently in, like a delicate lover.

He had seen gas siphoned before, knew the principle, but had never done it himself. He steeled himself for the taste of gasoline and sucked on the end of the hose-length. For a moment there was nothing but an invisible, glutinous resistance, and then his mouth filled with a liquid so cold and foreign that he had to stifle an impulse to gasp and draw some of it down his throat. He spat it out with a grimace, still tasting it on his tongue like some peculiar death. He tilted the hose over Mary's floor-bucket, and a stream of pinkish gasoline spurted into the bottom. The flow fell away to a trickle and he thought he would have to go through the ritual again. But then the flow strengthened a bit and remained constant. Gas flowed into the bucket with a sound like urination in a public toilet.

He spat on the floor, rinsed the inside of his mouth with saliva, spat again. Better. It came to him that although he had been using gasoline almost every day of his adult life, he had never been on such intimate

terms with it. The only other time he had actually
touched it was when he had filled the small tank of
his Briggs & Stratton lawn mower to the overflow
point. He was suddenly glad that this had happened.
Even the residual taste in his mouth seemed okay.

He went back into the house while the bucket filled
(it was snowing harder now) and got some rags from
Mary's cleaning cupboard under the sink. He took
them back into the garage and tore them into long
strips, which he laid out on the hood of the LTD.

When the floor-bucket was half full, he switched the
hose into the galvanized steel bucket he usually filled
with ashes and clinkers to spread in the driveway
when the going was icy. While it filled, he put twenty
beer and soda bottles in four neat rows and filled each
one three-quarters full, using the funnel. When that
was done, he pulled the hose out of the gas tank and
poured the contents of the steel pail into Mary's
bucket. It filled it almost to the brim.

He stuffed a rag wick into each bottle, plugging the
necks completely. He went back to the house, carrying
the funnel. The snow filled the earth in slanting, wind-
driven lines. The driveway was already white. He put
the funnel into the sink and then got the cover that
fitted over the top of the bucket from Mary's cupboard. He took it back to the garage and snapped it
securely over the gasoline. He opened the LTD's tailgate and put the bucket of gasoline inside. He put his
Molotov cocktails into one of the cartons, fitting them
snugly one against the other so they would stand at
attention like good soldiers. He put the carton on the
passenger seat up front, within hand's reach. Then he
went back into the house, sat down in his chair, and
turned on the Zenith TV with his Space Command
module. The "Tuesday Movie of the Week" was on.
It was a western, starring David Janssen. He thought
David Janssen made a shitty cowboy.

*   *   *

When the movie was over, he watched Marcus Welby treat a disturbed teenager for epilepsy. The disturbed teenager kept falling down in public places. Welby fixed her up. After Marcus came station identification and two ads, one for Miracle Chopper and one for an album containing forty-one spiritual favorites, and then the news. The weather man said it was going to snow all night and most of tomorrow. He urged people to stay home. The roads were treacherous and most snow-removal equipment wouldn't be able to get out until after 2:00 A.M. High winds were causing the snow to drift and generally, the weatherman hinted, things were going to be an all-around bitch-kitty for the next day or so.

After the news, Dick Cavett came on. He watched half an hour of that, and then turned the TV off. So Ordner wanted to get him on something criminal, did he? Well, if he got the LTD stuck after he did it, Ordner would have his wish. Still, he thought his chances were good. The LTD was a heavy car, and there were studded tires on the back wheels.

He put on his coat and hat and gloves in the kitchen entry, and paused for a moment. He went back through the warmly lighted house and looked at it— the kitchen table, the stove, the dining room bureau with the teacups hung from the runner above it, the African violet on the mantel in the living room—he felt a warm surge of love for it, a surge of protectiveness. He thought of the wrecking ball roaring through it, belting the walls down to junk, shattering the windows, vomiting debris over the floors. He wasn't going to let that happen. Charlie had crawled on these floors, had taken his first steps in the living room, had once fallen down the front stairs and scared the piss out of his fumbling parents. Charlie's room was now an upstairs study, but it was in there that his son had first felt the headaches and experienced the double vision and smelled those odd aromas, sometimes like roasting pork, sometimes like burning grass, sometimes like pencil shavings. After Charlie had died, almost a hundred people had come to see them, and Mary had served them cake and pie in the living room.

No, Charlie, he thought. *Not if I can help it.*

He ran the garage door up and saw there was already four inches of snow in the driveway, very powdery and light. He got in the LTD and started it up. He still had over three-quarters of a tank. He let the car warm up, and sitting behind the wheel in the mystic green glow of the dashlights, he fell to thinking about Arnie Walker. Just a length of rubber hose, that wasn't so bad. It would be like going to sleep. He had read somewhere that carbon monoxide poisoning was like that. It even brought the color up in your cheeks so you looked ruddy and healthy, bursting with life and vitality. It—

He began to shiver, the goose walking back and forth across his grave again, and he turned on the heater. When the car was toasty and the shivering had stopped, he slipped the transmission into reverse and backed out into the snow. He could hear the gasoline sloshing in Mary's floor-pail, reminding him that he had forgotten something.

He put the car in park again and went back to the house. There was a carton of paper matches in the bureau drawer, and he filled his coat pockets with perhaps twenty folders. Then he went back out.

The streets were very slippery.

There was patch ice under the new snow in places, and once when he braked for a stoplight at the corner of Crestallen and Garner, the LTD slued around almost sideways. When he brought the skid to a stop, his heart was thudding dully against his ribs. This was a crazy thing to be doing, all right. If he got rear-ended with all that gasoline in the back, they could scrape him up with a spoon and bury him in a dog-food box:

Better than suicide. Suicide's a mortal sin.

Well, that was the Catholics for you. But he didn't think he would get hit. Traffic had thinned almost to the vanishing point, and he didn't even see any cops. Probably they were all parked in alleys, cooping.

He turned cautiously onto Kennedy Promenade, which he supposed he would always think of as Dumont Street, which it had been until a special session of the city council had changed it in January 1964. Dumont/Kennedy Prom ran from Westside all the way downtown, roughly parallel to the 784 construction for almost two miles. He would follow it for a mile, then turn left onto Grand Street. A half mile up, Grand Street became extinct, just like the old Grand Theater itself, might it rest in peace. By next summer Grand Street would be resurrected in the form of an overpass (one of the three he had mentioned to Magliore), but it wouldn't be the same street. Instead of seeing the theater on your right, you would only be able to see six—or was it eight?—lanes of traffic hurrying by down below. He had absorbed a great deal about the extension from radio, TV, and the daily paper, not through any real conscious effort, but almost by osmosis. Perhaps he had stored the material instinctively, the way a squirrel stores nuts. He knew that the construction companies who had contracted the extension were almost through with the actual roadwork for the winter, but he also knew that they expected to complete all the necessary demolitions (*demolitions,* there's a word for you, Fred—but Fred didn't pick up the gauntlet) within the city limits by the end of February. That included Crestallen Street West. In a way it was ironic. If he and Mary had been located a mile farther away, they would not have been liable to demolition until late in the spring—May or early June of 1974. And if wishes were horses, beggars would sit astride golden palominos. He also knew, from per-

sonal *conscious* observation, that most of the road ma-
chinery was left parked below the point where Grand
Street had been murdered.

He turned onto Grand Street now, the rear end of
the car trying to wander out from under him. He
turned with the skid, jockeying the car, cajoling it with
his hands, and it purred on, cutting through snow that
was almost virgin—the tracks of the last car to pass
this way were already fuzzy and indistinct. The sight
of so much fresh snow somehow made him feel better.
It was good to be moving, to be *doing*.

As he moved up Grand at a steady unhurried
twenty-five, his thoughts drifted back to Mary and the
concept of sin, moral and venial. She had been
brought up Catholic, had gone to a parochial grammar
school, and although she had given up most religious
concepts—intellectually, at least—by the time they
met, some of that gut stuff had stuck with her, the
stuff they sneak to you in the clinches. As Mary herself said, the nuns had given her six coats of varnish
and three of wax. After the miscarriage, her mother
had sent a priest to the hospital so that she could
make a good confession, and Mary had wept at the
sight of him. He had been with her when the priest
came in, carrying his pyx, and the sound of his wife's
weeping had torn his heart as only one thing had done
in the time between then and now.

Once, at his request, she had reeled off a whole list
of mortal and venial sins. Although she had learned
them in catechism classes twenty, twenty-five, even
thirty years before, her list seemed (to him at least)
complete and faultless. But there was a matter of in-
terpretation that he couldn't make clear. Sometimes
an act was a mortal sin, sometimes only venial. It
seemed to depend on the perpetrator's frame of mind.
The conscious will to do evil. Was that something she
had said during those long-ago discussions, or had
Freddy whispered it in his ear just now? It puzzled
him, worried him. *The conscious will to do evil.*

In the end, he thought he had isolated the two big-gies, the two hard and fast mortal sins: suicide and murder. But a later conversation—had it been with Ron Stone? yes, he believed it had—had even blurred half of that. Sometimes, according to Ron (they had been drinking in a bar, it seemed, as long as ten years ago) murder itself was only a venial sin. Or maybe not a sin at all. If you cold-bloodedly planned to do away with somebody who had raped your wife, that might just be a venial sin. And if you killed somebody *in a just war*—those were Ron's exact words, he could almost hear him speaking them in some mental tap-room—then it wasn't a sin at all. According to Ron, all the American GI's that had killed Nazis and Japs were going to be okay when the Judgment Trump blew.

That left suicide, that hissing word.

He was coming up to the construction. There were black-and-white barriers with round flashing reflectors on top, and orange signs that glowed briefly and brightly in his headlights. One said:

ROAD ENDS TEMPORARILY

Another said:

DETOUR—FOLLOW SIGNS

Another said:

BLASTING AREA!
TURN OFF 2-WAY RADIOS

He pulled over, put the transmission lever in park, turned on his four-way flashers, and got out of the car. He walked toward the black-and-white barriers. The orange blinkers made the falling snow seem thicker, absurd with color.

He also remembered being confused about absolution. At first he had thought it was fairly simple: If you committed a mortal sin, you were mortally wounded, damned. You could hail Mary until your tongue fell out and you would still go to hell. But Mary said that wasn't always so. There was confession, and atonement, and reconsecration, and so on. It was very confusing. Christ had said there was no eternal life in a murderer, but he had also said whosoever believeth in me shall not perish. *Whosoever*. It seemed that there were as many loopholes in biblical doctrine as there were in a shyster lawyer's purchase agreement. Except for suicide, of course. You couldn't confess suicide or repeat suicide or atone for it because that act cut the silver cord and sent you plunging out into whatever worlds there were. And—

And why was he thinking about it, anyway? He didn't intend to kill anybody and certainly he didn't intend to commit suicide. He never even thought about suicide. At least, not until just lately.

He stared over the black-and-white barriers, feeling cold inside.

The machines were down there, hooded in snow, dominated by the wrecking crane. In its brooding immobility it had gained a dimension of awfulness. With its skeletal gantry rising into the snowy darkness, it reminded him of a praying mantis that had gone into some unknown period of winter contemplation.

He swung one of the barriers out of the way. It was very light. He went back to the car, got in, and pulled the transmission lever down into low. He let the car creep forward over the edge and down the slope, which had been worn into smooth ridges by the comings and goings of the big machines. With dirt underneath, the tendency of the heavy car to slip around was reduced. When he got to the bottom he shifted back into park and turned off all the car's lights. He climbed back up the slope, puffing, and put the barrier back in place. He went back down.

He opened the LTD's tailgate and took out Mary's

bucket. Then he went around to the passenger seat and set the bucket on the floor beneath his carton of firebombs. He took the white lid off the bucket and, humming softly, dipped each wick in gasoline. That done, he carried the bucket of gas over to the crane and climbed up into the unlocked cab, being careful not to slip. He was excited now, his heartbeat hurrying along, his throat tight and close with bitter exultation.

He splashed gas over the seat, over the controls, over the gearbox. He stepped out on the narrow riveted catwalk that skirted the crane's motor hood and poured the rest of the gas into the cowling. Hydrocarbon perfume filled the air. His gloves had soaked through, wetting his hands and turning them numb almost immediately. He jumped down and stripped the gloves off, putting them into his overcoat pockets. The first packet of matches dropped from his fingers, which felt as distant as wood. He held onto the second pack, but the wind snuffed the first two he had scratched. He turned his back to the wind, hunched over the match folder protectively and got one to stay lighted. He touched it to the rest, and they hissed into flame. He tossed the burning matches into the cab.

At first he thought they must have gone out, because there was nothing. Then there was a soft explosive sound—*flump!*—and fire boiled out of the cab in a furious gust, driving him back two steps. He shielded his eyes from the bright orange flower opening up there.

An arm of fire ran out of the cab, reached the engine hood, paused for a moment as if in reflection, and then sniffed inside. This time the explosion was not soft. KA-PLOOM! And suddenly the cowling was in the air, rising almost out of sight, fluttering and turning over. Something whizzed past his head.

It's burning, he thought. *It's really burning!*

He began to do a shuffling dance in the fiery darkness, his face contorted in an ecstasy so great that it seemed his features must shatter and fall in a million smiling pieces. His hands curled into waving fists above his head.

"*Hooray!*" He screamed into the wind, and the wind screamed back at him. "*Hooray goddam it hooray!*"

He dashed around the car and slipped in the snow and fell down and that might have saved his life because that was when the gas tank of the crane blew debris in a forty-foot circle. A hot piece of metal winged through the right window of the LTD, punching a stellated hole in the safety glass and sending out a drunken spiderweb of cracks.

He picked himself up, frosted with snow all the way down his front, and scrambled behind the wheel. He put his gloves back on—fingerprints—but after that, any thought of caution was gone. He started the car with fingers that could barely feel the ignition key and then heavy-footed the accelerator, "dragging out" they had called it when they had been kids and the world was young, the rear end of the station wagon whipping left and right. The crane was burning furiously, better than he ever would have imagined, the cab an inferno, the big windshield gone.

"Hot damn!" he screamed. "Oh Freddy, *hot damn*!"

He skated the LTD in front of the crane, the firelight sketching his face in two-tone Halloween colors. He rammed his right index finger at the dashboard, hitting the cigarette lighter on the third try. The construction machines were on his left now, and he rolled down his window. Mary's floor-bucket rolled back and forth on the floor, and the beer and soda bottles chattered frantically against one another as the wagon jounced across the gouged and frozen earth.

The cigarette lighter popped out and he slammed both feet down on the power brake. The station wagon looped the loop and came to a stop. He pulled the lighter out of its socket, took a bottle from the carton, and pressed the glowing coil against the wick. It flared alight and he threw it. It shattered against the mud-caked tread of a bulldozer and flame splashed gaudily. He pushed the cigarette lighter back in, drove twenty feet farther, and threw three more at the dark hulk of a payloader. One missed, one struck the side and spilled burning gasoline harmlessly into the snow, and the third arced neatly into the cab.

"Fuckinbullseye!" he screamed.

Another bulldozer. A smaller payloader. Then he came to a house trailer up on jacks. A sign over the door said:

> LANE CONSTRUCTION CO.
> *On-Site Office*
> NO HIRING DONE HERE!
> *Please Wipe Your Feet*

He pulled the LTD up at point-blank range and threw four burning bottles at the large window beside the door. They all went through, the first shattering the glass of both window and bottle, dragging a burning drape in after it.

Beyond the trailer a pickup truck was parked. He got out of the LTD, tried the pickup's passenger door, and found it unlocked. He lit the wick of one of his bombs and pitched it inside. Flames leaped hungrily across the bench seat.

He got back into his car and saw there were only four or five bottles left. He drove on, shivering in the cold, snot running from his nose, reeking of gasoline, grinning!

A steam shovel. He pitched the rest of the bottles at it, doing no damage until the last, which blew one of the tractor treads loose from its aft cog.

He probed the box again, remembered it was empty, and looked in the rearview mirror.

"Mother-*fuck*," he cried, "Oh, holy mother-*fuck*, Freddy you cock-knocker!"

Behind him, a line of isolated bonfires stood out in the snow-choked darkness like runway landing lights.

Flames were belching madly from the windows of the office trailer. The pickup was a ball of fire. The cab of the payloader was an orange cauldron. But the crane was really the masterpiece, because the crane was a roaring yellow beacon of light, a sizzling torch in the middle of the roadwork.

"Demofuckinlition!" he screamed.

A semblance of sanity began to return. He dared not go back the way he had come. The police would be on the way soon, maybe already. And the fire department. Could he get out ahead, or was he blocked in?

Heron Place, he might be able to get up to Heron Place. It would be a twenty-five-degree angle up the slope, maybe thirty, and he would have to crash the wagon through a highway department barrier, but the guardrails were gone. He thought maybe he could do it. Yes. He *could* do it. Tonight he could do anything.

He drove the LTD up the unfinished roadbed, skidding and slueing, using only his parking lights. When he saw the streetlights of Heron Place above and to the right, he fed the car more and more gas and watched the speedometer needle climb past thirty as he aimed at the embankment. It was near forty when he hit the incline and shot up. About halfway the rear wheels began to lose traction and he dropped the transmission lever into low. The engine dropped a note and the car hitched forward. He was almost nose over the top when the wheels began to spin again, machine-gunning snow and pebbles and frozen clods of earth out behind him. For a moment the issue was in doubt, and then the simple forward inertia of the LTD—coupled with willpower, perhaps—carried it up onto level ground.

The nose of the car bunted the black-and-white barrier aside; it toppled backward into a snowdrift, making a dreamy sugarpuff. He went down over the curb and was almost shocked to realize that he was on a normal street again, as if nothing at all had happened.

He shifted back to drive and settled down to a sedate thirty.

He was getting ready to turn toward home when he remembered that he was leaving tracks that plows or new snow might not obliterate for two hours or more. Instead of turning up Crestallen Street, he continued out Heron Place to River Street, and then down River to Route 7. Traffic here had been light ever since the snow had begun to come hard, but there had been enough to chew the snow covering the highway into a loose, churned-up mess.

He merged his tail with that of all the other cars that were moving east and inched his speed up to forty.

He followed Route 7 for almost ten miles, then back into the city and drove toward Crestallen Street. A few plows were out now, moving through the night like gigantic orange mastiffs with glaring yellow eyes. Several times he looked toward the 784 construction, but in the blowing snow he could see nothing.

About halfway home he realized that even though all the windows were rolled up and the heater was on full blast, the car was still cold. He looked back and saw the jagged hole in the rear passenger-side window. There was broken glass and snow on the backseat.

Now how did that happen? he asked himself, bewildered. He honestly had no recollection.

He entered his street from the north and drove directly to his house. It was as he had left it, the single light in his kitchen the only light shining on this whole darkened section of street. There were no police cars parked out front, but the garage door was open and that was just plain stupid. You closed the garage door when it snowed, always. That's why you have a garage, to keep the elements off your stuff. His father used to say that. His father had died in a garage, just like Johnny's brother, but Ralph Dawes had not committed suicide. He had had some kind of stroke. A neighbor had found him with his lawn clippers in his stiffening left hand and a small whetstone by his right. A suburban death. Oh Lord, send this white soul to a heaven where there is no crab grass and the niggers always keep their distance.

He parked the station wagon, pulled the garage door down, and went into the house. He was trembling from exhaustion and reaction. It was quarter past three. He hung his coat and hat in the hall closet and was closing the door when he felt a hot jolt of terror, as riveting as a straight knock of scotch whiskey. He fumbled wildly in his overcoat pockets and let out a whistling sigh when he felt his gloves, still soaked with gasoline, each of them crushed into a soggy little ball.

He thought of making coffee and decided against it. He had a queasy, thumping headache, probably caused by gasoline fumes and helped along by his scary drive through the snowy darkness. In his bedroom he took off his clothes and threw them over a chair without bothering to fold them. He thought he would fall asleep as soon as his head touched the pillow, but it was not so. Now that he was home, and presumably safe, staring wakefulness seized him. It brought fear like a handmaiden. They were going to catch him and put him in jail. His picture would be in the papers. People who knew him would shake their heads and talk it over in cafeterias and lunchrooms. Vinnie Mason would tell his wife that he had known Dawes was crazy all along. Mary's folks would maybe fly her to Reno, where she would first pick up residency and then a divorce. Maybe she would find somebody to fuck her. He wouldn't be surprised.

He lay wakeful, telling himself they weren't going to catch him. He had worn his gloves. No fingerprints. He had Mary's bucket and the white cover that went over the top. He had hidden his tracks, had shaken off possible pursuit just as a fugitive will throw off the bloodhounds by walking in a creek. None of these thoughts brought him sleep or comfort. They would catch him. Perhaps someone on Heron Place had seen his car and thought it suspicious that any vehicle should be out so late on such a stormy night. Perhaps someone had jotted down his license plate number and was even now being congratulated by the police. Perhaps they had gotten paint scrapings from the Heron Place construction barrier and were now cajoling his guilty name out of some auto registration computer. Perhaps—

He rolled and thrashed in his bed, waiting for the dancing blue shadows to come in his window, waiting for the heavy knock on his door, waiting for some bodiless, Kafkaesque voice to call: *Okay, open up in there!* And when he finally fell asleep he did it without knowing it, because thought continued without a break, shifting from conscious rumination to the skewed world of dreams with hardly a break, like a car going from drive to low. Even in his dreams he thought he was awake, and in his dreams he committed suicide over and over; burned himself; bludgeoned himself by standing under an anvil and pulling a rope; hanged himself; blew out the stove's pilot lights and then turned on the oven and all four burners; shot himself; defenestrated himself; stepped in front of a speeding Greyhound bus; swallowed pills; swallowed Vanish toilet bowl disinfectant; stuck a can of Glade Pine Fresh aerosol in his mouth, pushed the button, and inhaled until his head floated off into the sky like a child's balloon; committed hara-kari while kneeling in a confessional at St. Dom's, confessing his self-murder to a dumbfounded young priest even as his guts accordioned out onto the bench like beef stew, performing an act of contrition in a fading, bemused voice as he lay in his blood and the steaming sausages of his intestines. But most vividly, over and over, he saw himself behind the wheel of the LTD, racing the engine a little in the closed garage, taking deep breaths and leafing through a copy of *National Geographic*, examining pictures of life in Tahiti and Auckland and the Mardi Gras in

New Orleans, turning the pages ever more slowly, until the sound of the engine faded to a faraway sweet hum and the green waters of the South Pacific inundated him in rocking warmth and took him down to a silver fathom.

December 19, 1973

It was 12:30 in the afternoon when he woke up and got out of bed. He felt as though he had been on a huge bender. His head ached monstrously. His bladder was cramped and full. There was a dead-snake taste in his mouth. Walking made his heart thud like a snare drum. He was not even allowed the luxury of believing (for however short a time) that he had dreamed everything he remembered of the previous night, because the smell of gasoline seemed rubbed into his flesh and it rose, fulsomely fragrant, from the pile of his clothes. The snow was over, the sky was clear, and the bright sunshine made his eyes beg for mercy.

He went into the bathroom, sat on the ring, and a huge diarrhea movement rushed out of him like a mail train highballing through a deserted station. His waste fell into the water with a sickening series of jets and plops that made him groan and clutch his head. He urinated without getting up, the rich and dismaying smell of his digestion's unsavory end product rising thickly around him.

He flushed and went downstairs on his orangewood legs, taking clean clothes with him. He would wait until the godawful smell cleared out of the bathroom and then he would shower, maybe all afternoon.

He gobbled three Excedrin from the green bottle on the shelf over the kitchen sink, then washed them down with two big gulps of Pepto-Bismol. He put on hot water for coffee and smashed his favorite cup by fumbling it off its hook. He swept it up, put out another, dumped instant Maxwell House into it, and then went into the dining room.

He turned on the radio and swept across the dial looking for news, which, like a cop, was never there when you needed it. Pop music. Feed and grain reports. A Golden Nugget 'Cause You Dug It. A call-in talk show. A swapshop program. Paul Harvey selling Banker's Life Insurance. More pop music. No news.

The water for the coffee was boiling. He set the radio to one of the pop stations and brought his coffee back to the table and drank it black. There was an inclination to vomit with the first two mouthfuls, but after that it was better.

The news came on, first national, then local,

> On the city newsfront, a fire was set at the site of the 784 thruway extension construction near Grand Street in the early hours of this morning. Police Lieutenant Henry King said that vandals apparently used gasoline bombs to fire a crane, two payloaders, two bulldozers, a pickup truck, and the on-site office of the Lane Construction Company, which was entirely gutted.

An exultation as bitter and dark as the taste of his unsweetened coffee closed his throat at the words *entirely gutted*.

> Damage done to the payloaders and bulldozers was minor, according to Francis Lane, whose company got a substantial subcontracting bid on the crosstown extension, but the demolition crane, values at $60,000, is expected to be out of service for as long as two weeks.

Two weeks? Was that *all*?

More serious, according to Lane, was the burning of the on-site office, which contained time sheets, work records, and ninety percent of the company's cost accounting records over the last three months. "This is going to be the very devil to straighten out," Lane said. "It may set us back a month or more."

Maybe that was good news. Maybe an extra month of time made it all worthwhile.

According to Lieutenant King, the vandals fled the construction site in a station wagon, possibly a late-model Chevrolet. He appealed for anyone who may have seen the car leaving the construction area by Heron Street to come forward. Francis Lane estimated total damage in the area of $100,000.

In other local news, State Representative Muriel Reston again appealed for . . .

He snapped it off.

Now that he had heard, and had heard in daylight, things seemed a little better. It was possible to look at things rationally. Of course the police didn't have to give out all their leads, but if they really were looking for a Chevy instead of a Ford, and if they were reduced to pleading for eyewitnesses to come forward, then maybe he was safe, at least for the time being. And if there had been an eyewitness, no amount of worrying would change that.

He would throw away Mary's floor-bucket and open the garage to air out the stink of gasoline. Make up a story to explain the broken back window if anyone asked about it. And most important, he would try to prepare himself mentally for a visit from the police. As the last resident of Crestallen Street West, it might be perfectly logical for them to at least check him out. And they wouldn't have to sniff up his back trail very far to find out he had been acting erratically. He had screwed up the plant. His wife had left him. A former co-worker had punched him out in a department store. And of course, he had a station wagon, Chevrolet or not. All bad. But none of it proof.

And if they did dig up proof, he supposed he would go to jail. But there were worse things than jail. Jail wasn't the end of the world. They would give him a job, feed him. He wouldn't have to worry about what was going to happen when the insurance money ran out. Sure, there were a lot of things worse than jail. Suicide, for instance. That was worse. He went upstairs and showered.

Later that afternoon he called Mary. Her mother answered and went to get Mary with a sniff. But when Mary herself answered, she sounded nearly gay.

"Hi Bart. Merry Christmas in advance."

"No, *Mary* Christmas," he responded. It was an old joke that had graduated from humor to tradition.

"Sure," she said. "What is it, Bart?"

"Well, I've got a few presents . . . just little stuff . . . for you and the nieces and nephews. I wondered if we could get together somewhere. I'll give them to you. I didn't wrap the kids' presents—"

"I'd be glad to wrap them. But you shouldn't have. You're not working."

"But I'm working on it," he said.

"Bart, have you . . . have you done anything about what we talked about?"

"The psychiatrist?"

"Yes."

"I called two. One is booked up until almost June. The other guy is going to be in the Bahamas until the end of March. He said he could take me then."

"What were their names?"

"Names? Gee, honey, I'd have to look them up again to tell you. Adams, I think the first guy was. Nicholas Adams—"

"Bart," she said sadly.

"It might have been Aarons," he said wildly.

"Bart," she said again.

"Okay," he said. "Believe what you want. You will anyway."

"Bart, if you'd only—"

"What about the presents? I called about the presents, not the goddam shrink."

She sighed. "Bring them over Friday, why don't you? I can—"

"What, so your mother and father can hire Charles Manson to meet me at the door? Let's just meet on neutral ground, okay?"

"They're not going to be here," she said. "They're going to spend Christmas with Joanna." Joanna was Joanna St. Claire, Jean Calloway's cousin, who lived in Minnesota. They had been close friends in their girlhood (back in that pleasant lull between the War of 1812 and the advent of the Confederacy, he sometimes thought), and Joanna had had a stroke in July. She was still trying to get over it, but Jean had told him and Mary that the doctors said she could go at any time. That must be nice, he thought, having a time bomb built right into your head like that. Hey, bomb, is it today? Please not today. I haven't finished the new Victoria Holt.

"Bart? Are you there?"

"Yes. I was woolgathering."

"Is one o'clock all right?"

"That's fine."

"Was there anything else?"

"No, huh-uh."

"Well . . ."

"Take good care, Mary."

"I will. Bye, Bart."

"Good-bye."

They hung up and he wandered into the kitchen to make himself a drink. The woman he had just talked to on the phone wasn't the same woman that had sat tearfully on the living room couch less than a month ago, pleading for some reason to help explain the tidal wave that had just swept grandly through her ordered life, destroying the work of twenty years and leaving only a few sticks poking out of the mudflats. It was amazing. He shook his head over it the way he would have shaken his head over the news that Jesus had come down from the sky and had taken Richard Nixon up to heaven upon wheels of fire. She has regained herself. More: She had regained a person he hardly knew at all, a girl-woman he barely remembered. Like an archaeologist she had excavated that person, and the person was a little stiff in the joints from its long storage, but still perfectly usable. The joints would ease and the new-old person would be a whole woman, perhaps scarred by this upheaval but not seriously hurt. He knew her perhaps better than she thought, and he had been able to tell, strictly from the tone of her voice, that she was moving ever closer to the idea of divorce, the idea of a clean break with the past . . . a break that would splint well and leave no trace of a limp. She was thirty-eight. Half of her life was ahead of her. There were no children to be casually maimed in the car wreck of this marriage. He would not suggest divorce, but if she did he would agree. He envied her new person and her new beauty. And if she looked back ten years from now on her marriage as a long dark corridor leading into sunlight, he could feel sorry she felt that way, but he couldn't blame her. No, he couldn't blame her.

December 21, 1973

He had given her the presents in Jean Calloway's tick-
ing, ormolu living room, and the conversation that followed had been stilted and awkward. He had never
been in this room alone with her, and he kept feeling
that they should neck. It was a rusty knee-jerk reaction that made him feel like a bad double exposure
of his college self.

"Did you lighten your hair?" he asked.

"Just a shade." She shrugged a little.

"It's nice. Makes you look younger."

"You're getting a little gray around the temples,
Bart. Makes you look distinguished."

"Bullshit, it makes me look ratty."

She laughed—a little too high-pitched—and looked
at the presents on the little side table. He had wrapped
the owl pin, had left the toys and the chess set for her
to do. The dolls looked blankly at the ceiling, waiting
for some little girl's hands to bring them to life.

He looked at Mary. Their eyes caught seriously for
a moment and he thought irrevocable words were
going to spill out of her and he was frightened. Then
the cuckoo jumped out of the clock, announced one-
thirty, and they both jumped and then laughed. The
moment had passed. He got up so it wouldn't come
around again. Saved by a cuckoo bird, he thought.
That fits.

"Got to go," he said.

"An appointment?"

"Job interview."

"Really?" She looked glad, "Where? Who? How
much?"

He laughed and shook his head. "There's a dozen

other applicants with as good a chance as me. I'll tell you when I get it."

"Conceited."

"Sure."

"Bart, what are you doing Christmas?" She looked concerned and solemn, and it suddenly came to him that an invitation to Christmas dinner and not to some new year's divorce court had been the thing on her lips inside. God! He almost sprayed laughter.

"I'm going to eat at home."

"You can come here," she said. "It would be just the two of us."

"No," he said, thoughtfully and then more firmly: "No. Emotions have a way of getting out of hand during the holidays. Another time."

She was nodding, also thoughtfully.

"Will you be eating alone?" he asked.

"I can go to Bob and Janet's. Really, are you sure?"

"Yes."

"Well . . ." But she looked relieved.

They walked to the door and shared a bloodless kiss.

"I'll call you," he said.

"You better."

"And give my best to Bobby."

"I will."

He was halfway down the walk to the car when she called: "Bart! Bart, wait a minute!"

He turned almost fearfully.

"I almost forgot," she said. "Wally Hamner called and invited us to his New Year's party. I accepted for both of us. But if you don't want to—"

"Wally?" He frowned. Walter Hamner was about their only crosstown friend. He worked for a local ad agency. "Doesn't he know we're, you know, separated?"

"He knows, but you know Walt. Things like that don't faze him much."

Indeed they didn't. Just thinking about Walter made him smile. Walter, always threatening to quit advertising in favor of advanced truss design. Composer of obscene limericks and even more obscene parodies of popular tunes. Divorced twice and tagged hard both times. Now impotent, if you believed gossip, and in this case he thought the gossip was probably true. How long had it been since he had seen Walt? Four months? Six? Too long.

"That might be fun," he said, and then a thought struck him.

She scanned it from his face in her old way and said, "There won't be any laundry people there."

"He and Steve Ordner know each other."

"Well, yes, *him*—" She shrugged to show how unlikely she thought it was that *him* would be there, and the shrug turned into an elbow-holding little shiver. It was only about twenty-five degrees.

"Hey, go on in," he said. "You'll freeze, dummy."

"Do you want to go?"

"I don't know. I'll have to think about it." He kissed her again, this time a little more firmly, and she kissed back. At a moment like this, he could regret everything—but the regret was far away, clinical.

"Merry Christmas, Bart," she said, and he saw she was crying a little.

"Next year will be better," he said, the phrase comforting but without any root meaning. "Go inside before you catch pneumonia."

She went in and he drove away, still thinking about Wally Hamner's New Year's Eve party. He thought he would go.

December 24, 1973

He found a small garage in Norton that would replace the broken back window for ninety dollars. When he asked the garage man if he would be working the day before Christmas, the garage man said: "Hell yes, I'll take it any way I can get it."

He stopped on the way at a Norton U-Wash-It and put his clothes in two machines. He automatically rotated the agitators to see what kind of shape the spring drives were in, and then loaded them carefully so each machine would extract (only in the laundromats they called it "spin-dry") without kicking off on the overload. He paused, smiling a little. You can take the boy out of the laundry, Fred, but you can't take the laundry out of the boy. Right, Fred? Fred? Oh fuck yourself.

"That's a hell of a hole," the garage man said, peering at the spiderwebbed glass.

"Kid with a snowball," he said. "Rock in the middle of it."

"It was," he said. "It really was."

When the window was replaced he drove back to the U-Wash-It, put his clothes in the dryer, set it to medium-hot, and put thirty cents in the slot. He sat down and picked up someone's discarded newspaper. The U-Wash-It's only other customer was a tired-looking young woman with wire-rimmed glasses and blond streaks in her long, reddish-brown hair. She had a small girl with her, and the small girl was throwing a tantrum.

"I want my *bottle*!"

"Goddam it, Rachel—"

"BOTTLE!"

"Daddy's going to spank you when we get home," the young woman promised grimly. "And no treats before bed."

"BAWWWWTLE!"

Now why does a young girl like that want to streak her hair? he wondered, and looked at the paper. The headlines said:

SMALL CROWDS IN BETHLEHEM
PILGRIMS FEAR HOLY TERROR

On the bottom of page one, a short news story caught his eye and he read it carefully:

WINTERBURGER SAYS ACTS OF VANDALISM
WILL NOT BE TOLERATED

(Local) Victor Winterburger, Democratic candidate for the seat of the late Donald P. Naish, who was killed in a car crash last month, said yesterday that acts of vandalism such as the one that caused almost a hundred thousand dollars' worth of damage at the Route 784 construction site early last Wednesday cannot be tolerated "in a civilized American city." Winterburger made his remarks at an American Legion dinner, and received a standing ovation.

"We have seen what has happened in other cities," Winterburger said. "The defaced buses and subway cars and buildings in New York, the broken windows and senselessly marred schools of Detroit and San Francisco, the abuse of public facilities, public museums, public galleries. We must not allow the greatest country in the world to be overrun with huns and barbarians."

Police were called to the Grand Street area of the construction when a number of fires and explosions were seen by

(Continued page 5 col. 2)

He folded the paper and put it on top of a tattered pile of magazines. The washer hummed and hummed, a low, soporific sound. Huns. Barbarians. They were the huns. They were the rippers and chewers and choppers, turning people out of their homes, kicking apart lives as a small boy might kick apart an anthill—

The young woman dragged her daughter, still crying for a bottle, out of the U-Wash-It. He closed his eyes and dozed off, waiting for his dryer to finish. A few minutes later he snapped awake, thinking he heard fire bells, but it was only a Salvation Army Santa who had taken up his position on the corner out front. When he left the laundry with his basket of clothes, he threw all his pocket change into Santa's pot.

"God bless you," Santa said.

December 25, 1973

The telephone woke him around ten in the morning. He fumbled the extension off the night table, put it to his ear, and an operator said crisply into his sleep, "Will you accept a collect call from Olivia Brenner?"

He was lost and could only fumble, "What? Who? I'm asleep."

A distant, slightly familiar voice said, "Oh for Chrissake," and he knew.

"Yes," he said. "I'll take it." Had she hung up on him? He got up on one elbow to see. "Olivia? You there?"

"Go ahead, please," the operator overrode him, not willing to vary her psalm.

"Olivia, are you there?"

"I'm here." The voice was crackling and distant.

"I'm glad you called."

"I didn't think you'd take the call."

"I just woke up. Are you there? In Las Vegas?"

"Yes," she said flatly. The word came out with curiously dull authority, like a plank dropped on a cement floor.

"Well, how is it? How are you doing?"

Her sigh was so bitter that it was almost a tearless sob. "Not so good."

"No?"

"I met a guy my second . . . no, third . . . night here. Went to a party and got s-o-o-o fucked up—"

"Dope?" he asked cautiously, very aware that this was long distance and the government was everywhere.

"Dope?" she echoed crossly. "Of course it was dope. Bad shit, full of dex or something . . . I think I got raped."

The last trailed off so badly that he had to ask, "What?"

"Raped!" she screamed, so loudly that the receiver distorted. "That's when some stupid jock playing Friday night hippie plays hide the salami with you while your brains are somewhere behind you, dripping off the wall! Rape, do you know what rape is?"

"I know," he said.

"Bullshit, you know."

"Do you need money?"

"Why ask me that? I can't fuck you over the telephone. I can't even hand-job you."

"I have some money," he said. "I could send it. That's all. That's why." Instinctively he found himself speaking, not soothingly, but softly, so she would have to slow down and listen.

"Yeah, yeah."

"Do you have an address?"

"General Delivery, that's my address."

"You don't have an apartment?"

"Yeah, me and this other sad sack have got a place. The mailboxes are all broken. Never mind. You keep the money. I've got a job. Screw, I think I'm going to quit and come back. Merry Christmas to me."

"What's the job?"

"Pushing hamburgers in this fast-food joint. They got slots in the lobby, and people play them and eat hamburgers all night long, can you *believe* it? The last thing you have to do when your shift is over is to wipe off all the handles of the slot machines. They get all covered with mustard and mayo and catsup. And you should see the *people* here. All of them are fat. They've either got tans or burns. And if they don't want to fuck you, you're just part of the furniture. I've had offers from both sexes. Thank God my roomie's about as sex-oriented as a juniper bush, I . . . oh, Christ, why am I telling you all this? I don't even know why I called you. I'm going to hitch out of here at the end of the week, when I get paid."

He heard himself say: "Give it a month."

"What?"

"Don't go chickenshit. If you leave now you'll always wonder what you went out there for."

"Did you play football in high school? I bet you did."

"I wasn't even the waterboy."

"Then you don't know anything, do you?"

"I'm thinking about killing myself."

"You don't even . . . what did you say?"

"I'm thinking about killing myself." He said it calmly. He was no longer thinking about long distance and the people who might monitor long distance just for the fun of it—Ma Bell, the White House, the CIA, the Effa Bee Eye. "I keep trying things and they keep not working. It's because I'm a little too old for them to work, I think. Something went wrong a few years ago and I knew it was a bad thing but I didn't know it was bad for me. I thought it just happened and then

I was going to get over it. But things keep falling down inside me. I'm sick with it. I keep doing things."

"Have you got cancer?" she whispered.

"I think I do."

"You ought to go to a hospital, get—"

"It's soul cancer."

"You're ego-tripping, man."

"Maybe so," he said. "It doesn't matter. One way or the other, things are set and they'll turn out the way they will. Only one thing that bothers me, and that's a feeling I get from time to time that I'm a character in some bad writer's book and he's already decided how things are going to turn out and why. It's easier to see things that way, even, than to blame it on God—what did He ever do for me, one way or the other? No, it's this bad writer, it's his fault. He cut my son down by writing in a brain tumor. That was chapter one. Suicide or no suicide, that comes just before the epilogue. It's a stupid story."

"Listen," she said, troubled, "if they have one of those Dial Help outfits in your town, maybe you ought to . . ."

"They couldn't do anything for me," he said, "and it doesn't matter. I want to help *you*. For Chrissake look around out there before you go chickenshit. Get off dope, you said you were going to. The next time you look around you'll be forty and your options will mostly be gone."

"No, I can't take this. Some other place—"

"All places are the same unless your mind changes. There's no magic place to get your mind right. If you feel like shit, everything you see looks like shit. I *know* that. Newspaper headlines, even the signs I see, they all say yeah, that's right, Georgie, pull the plug. This eats the bird."

"Listen—"

"No, no, *you* listen. Dig your ears out. Getting old is like driving through snow that just gets deeper and deeper. When you finally get in over your hubcaps,

you just spin and spin. That's *life*. There are no plows
to come and dig you out. Your ship isn't going to
come in, girl. There are no boats for nobody. You're
never going to win a contest. There's no camera following you and people watching you struggle. This is
it. All of it. *Everything*."

"You don't know what it's *like* here!" she cried.

"No, but I know what it's like here."

"You're not in charge of my life."

"I'm going to send you five hundred dollars—Olivia
Brenner, c/o General Delivery, Las Vegas."

"I won't be here. They'll send it back."

"They won't. Because I'm not going to put on a
return address."

"Throw it away, then."

"Use it to get a better job."

"No."

"Then use it for toilet paper," he said shortly, and
hung up. His hands were shaking.

The phone rang five minutes later. The operator
said: "Will you accept—"

"No," he said, and hung up.

The phone rang twice more that day, but it was not
Olivia either time.

Around two in the afternoon Mary called him from
Bob and Janet Preston's house—Bob and Janet, who
always reminded him, like it or not, of Fred and
Wilma Flintstone. How was he? Good. A lie. What
was he doing for Christmas dinner? Going out to Old
Customhouse tonight for turkey with all the trim-
mings. A lie. Would he like to come over here instead? Janet had all kinds of leftovers and would be
happy to get rid of some. No, he really wasn't very
hungry at the minute. The truth. He was pretty well
looped, and on the spur of the moment he told her
he would come to Walter's party. She sounded
pleased. Did he know it was BYOB? When did Wally

Hamner have a party that wasn't? he asked, and she laughed. They hung up and he went back to sit in front of the TV with a drink.

The phone rang again around seven-thirty, and by that time he was nothing as polite as looped—he was pissy-assed drunk.

"Lo?"

"Dawes?"

"Dozz here; whozzere?"

"Magliore, Dawes. Sal Magliore."

He blinked and peered into his glass. He looked at the Zenith color TV, where he had been watching a movie called *Home for the Holidays.* It was about a family that had gathered at their dying patriarch's house on Christmas Eve and somebody was murdering them one by one. Very Christmasy.

"Mr. Magliore," he said, pronouncing carefully. "Merry Christmas, sir! And the best of everything in the new year!"

"Oh, if you only knew how I dread '74," Magliore said dolefully. "That's the year the oil barons are going to take over the country, Dawes. You see if they don't. Look at my sales sheet for December if you don't believe me. I sold a 1971 Chevy Impala the other day, this car is clean as a whistle, and I sold it for a thousand bucks. A *thousand bucks*! Do you believe that? A forty-five-percent knockdown in one year. But I can sell all the '71 Vegas I can get my hands on for fifteen, sixteen hundred bucks. And what are they, I ask you?"

"Little cars?" he asked cautiously.

"They're fucking Maxwell House coffee cans, that's what they are!" Magliore shouted. "Saltine boxes on wheels! Every time you look at the goddam things cross-eyed and say booga-booga at them the engine's outa tune or the exhaust system drops off or the steering linkage is gone. Pintos, Vegas, Gremlins, they're

all the same, little suicide boxes. So I'm selling those
as fast as I can get them and I can't move a nice Chevy
Impala unless I fuckin' give it away. And you say happy
new year. Jesus! Mary! Joseph the carpenter!"

"That's seasonal," he said.

"I didn't call about that anyway," Magliore answered. "I called to say congratulations."

"Congratuwhatchens?" He was honestly bewildered.

"You know. Crackle-crackle boom-boom."

"Oh, you mean—"

"Sssst. Not on the phone. Be cool, Dawes."

"Sure. Crackle-crackle boom-boom. That's good."
He cackled.

"It was you, wasn't it, Dawes?"

"To you I wouldn't admit my middle name."

Magliore roared. "That's good. *You're* good, Dawes.
You're a fruitcake, but you're a *clever* fruitcake. I ad-
mire that."

"Thanks," he said, and cleverly knocked back the
rest of his drink.

"I also wanted to tell you that everything was going
ahead on schedule down there. Rumble and roar."

"What?"

The glass he was holding fell from his fingers and
rolled across the rug.

"They've got seconds on all that stuff, Dawes.
Thirds on most of it. They're paying cash until they
got their bookwork straightened out, but everything is
right-on."

"You're crazy."

"No. I thought you ought to know. I told you,
Dawes. Some things you can't get rid of."

"You're a bastard. You're lying. Why do you want
to call a man up on Christmas night and tell him
lies?"

"I ain't lying. It's your play again, Dawes. In this
game, it's *always* gonna be your play."

"I don't believe you."

"You poor son of a bitch," Magliore said. He sounded honestly sorry and that was the worst part. "I don't think it's gonna be a very happy new year for you either." He hung up.

And that was Christmas.

December 26, 1973

There was a letter from *them* in the mail (he had begun to see the anonymous people downtown that way, the personal pronoun in italics and printed in drippy, ominous letters like the printing on a horror movie poster), as if to confirm what Magliore had said.

He held it in his hand, looking down at the crisp white business envelope, his mind filled with almost all the bad emotions the human mind can feel: Despair, hatred, fear, anger, loss. He almost tore it into small pieces and threw it into the snow beside the house, and then knew he couldn't do that. He opened it, nearly tearing the envelope in half, and realized that what he felt most was cheated. He had been gypped. He had been rooked. He had destroyed their machines and their records, and they had just brought up a few replacements. It was like trying to fight the Chinese Army singlehanded.

It's your play again, Dawes. In this game it's always gonna be your play.

The other letters had been form jobs, sent from the office of the highway department. *Dear Friend, a big crane is going to come to your house sometime soon. Be on the lookout for this exciting event as WE IMPROVE YOUR CITY!*

This was from the city council, and it was personal. It said:

December 20, 1973

Mr. Barton G. Dawes
1241 Crestallen Street West
M——, W——

Dear Mr. Dawes:

It has come to our attention that you are the last resident of Crestallen Street West who has not relocated. We trust that you are experiencing no undue problems in this matter. While we have a 19642-A form on file (acknowledgment of information concerning City Roads Project 6983-426-73-74-HC), we do not yet have your relocation form (6983-426-73-74-HC-9004, blue folder). As you know, we cannot begin processing your check of reimbursement without this form. According to our 1973 tax assessment, the property at 1241 Crestallen Street West has been valued at $63,500, and so we are sure that you must be as aware of the situation's urgency as we are. By law, you must relocate by January 20, 1974, the date that demolitions work is scheduled to begin on Crestallen Street West.

We must also point out again that according to the State Statute of Eminent Domain (S.L. 19452-36), you would be in violation of the law to remain in your present location past midnight of January 19, 1974. We are sure you understand this, but we are pointing it out once more so that the record will be clear.

If you are having some problem with relocation, I hope you will call me during business hours, or better yet, stop by and discuss the situation. I am sure that things can be worked out; you will find us more than eager to cooperate in this matter. In the meantime, may I wish you a

Merry Christmas and a most productive New
Year?

Sincerely,

For the City Council

JTG/tk

"No," he muttered. "You may not wish it. You may
not." He tore the letter to shreds and threw it in the
wastebasket.

That night, sitting in front of the Zenith TV, he found
himself thinking about how he and Mary had found out,
almost forty-two months ago now, that God had decided
to do a little roadwork on their son Charlie's brain.

The doctor's name had been Younger. There was a
string of letters after his name on the framed diplomas
that hung on the warmly paneled walls of his inner office, but all he understood for sure was that Younger
was a neurologist; a fast man with a good brain disease.

He and Mary had gone to see him at Younger's
request on a warm June afternoon nineteen days after
Charlie had been admitted to Doctors Hospital. He
was a good-looking man, maybe halfway through his
forties, physically fit from a lot of golf played with no
electric golf cart. He was tanned a deep cordovan
shade. And the doctor's hands fascinated him. They
were huge hands, clumsy-looking, but they moved
about his desk—now picking up a pen, now riffling
through his appointment book, now playing idly across
the surface of a silver-inlaid paperweight—with a lis-
some grace that was very nearly repulsive.

"Your son has a brain tumor," he said. He spoke
flatly, with little inflection, but his eyes watched them
very carefully, as if he had just armed a temperamen-
tal explosive.

"Tumor," Mary said softly, blankly.

"How bad is it?" he asked Younger.

The symptoms had developed over the space of eight months. First the headaches, infrequent at the beginning, then more common. Then double vision that came and went, particularly after physical exercise. After that, most shameful to Charlie, some incidence of bedwetting. But they had not taken him to the family doctor until a terrifying temporary blindness in the left eye, which had gone as red as a sunset, obscuring Charlie's good blue. The family doctor had had him admitted for tests, and the other symptoms had followed that: Phantom smells of oranges and shaved pencils; occasional numbness in the left hand; occasional lapses into nonsense and childish obscenity.

"It's bad," Younger said. "You must prepare yourself for the worst. It is inoperable."

Inoperable.

The word echoed up the years to him. He had never thought words had taste, but that one did. It tasted bad and yet juicy at the same time, like rotten hamburger cooked rare.

Inoperable.

Somewhere, Younger said, deep in Charlie's brain, was a collection of bad cells roughly the size of a walnut. If you had that collection of bad cells in front of you on the table, you could squash them with one hard hit. But they weren't on the table. They were deep in the meat of Charlie's mind, still smugly growing, filling him with random strangeness.

One day, not long after his admission, he had been visiting his son on his lunch break. They had been talking about baseball, discussing, in fact, whether or not they would be able to go to the American League baseball playoffs if the city's team won.

Charlie had said: "I think if their pitching mmmmm mmmm mmmm pitching staff holds up mmmmm nn mmmm pitching mmmm—"

He had leaned forward. "What, Fred? I'm not tracking you."

Charlie's eyes had rolled wildly outward.

"Fred?" George whispered. "Freddy—?"

"Goddam motherfucking mothersucking nnnnnn fuckhole!" his son screamed from the clean white hospital bed. *"Cuntlicking dinkrubbing asswipe sonofawhoringbitch—"*

"NURSE!" he had screamed, as Charlie passed out. *"OH GOD NURSE!"*

It was the cells, you see, that had made him talk like that. A little bunch of bad cells no bigger, say, than your average-sized walnut. Once, the night nurse said, he had screamed the word *boondoggle* again and again for nearly five minutes. Just bad cells, you know. No bigger than your garden-variety walnut. Making his son rave like an insane dock walloper, making him wet the bed, giving him headaches, making him—during the first hot week of that July—lose all ability to move his left hand.

"Look," Dr. Younger had told them on that bright, just-right-for-golf June day. He had unrolled a long scroll of paper, an ink-tracing of their son's brain waves. He produced a healthy brain wave as a comparison, but he didn't need it. He looked at what had been going on in his son's head and again felt that rotten yet juicy taste in his mouth. The paper showed an irregular series of spiky mountains and valleys, like a series of badly drawn daggers.

Inoperable.

You see if that collection of bad cells, no bigger than a walnut, had decided to grow on the outside of Charlie's brain, minor surgery would have vacuumed it right up. No sweat, no strain, no pain on the brain, as they had said when they were boys. But instead, it had grown down deep inside and was growing larger every day. If they tried the knife, or laser, or cryosurgery, they would be left with a nice, healthy, breathing piece of meat. If they didn't try any of those things, soon they would be bundling their boy into a coffin.

Dr. Younger said all these things in generalities, covering their lack of options in a soothing foam of technical language that would wear away soon enough. Mary kept shaking her head in gentle bewilderment, but he had understood everything exactly and completely. His first thought, bright and clear, never to be forgiven, was: *Thank God it's not me.* And the funny taste came back and he began to grieve for his son.

Today a walnut, tomorrow the world. The creeping unknown. The incredible dying son. What was there to understand?

Charlie died in October. There were no dramatic dying words. He had been in a coma for three weeks.

He sighed and went out to the kitchen and made himself a drink. Dark night pressed evenly on all the windows. The house was so empty now that Mary was gone. He kept stumbling over little pieces of himself everywhere—snapshots, his old sweatsuit in an upstairs closet, an old pair of slippers under the bureau. It was bad, very bad, to keep doing that.

He had never cried over Charlie after Charlie's death; not even at the funeral. Mary had cried a great deal. For weeks, it seemed, Mary had gone around with a perpetual case of pinkeye. But in the end, she had been the one to heal.

Charlie had left scars on her, that was undeniable. Outwardly, she had all the scars. Mary before-and-after. Before, she would not take a drink unless she considered it socially helpful to his future. She would take a weak screwdriver at a party and carry it around all night. A rum toddy before bed when she had a heavy chest cold. That was all. After, she had a cocktail with him in the late afternoon when he came home, and always a drink before bed. Not serious drinking by anyone's yardstick, not sick-and-puking-in-the-bathroom drinking, but more than before. A little of that protective foam. Undoubtedly just what the doctor would have ordered. Before, she rarely cried over little things. After, she cried over them often, always in private. If dinner was burned. If she had a flat. The time water got in the basement and the sump pump froze and the furnace shorted out. Before, she had been something of a folk music buff—white folk and blues, Van Ronk, Gary Davis, Tom Rush, Tom Paxton, Spider John Koemer. After, her interest just faded away. She sang her own blues and laments on some inner circuit. She had stopped talking about their taking a trip to England if he got promoted a step up. She started doing her hair at home, and the sight of her sitting in front of the TV in rollers became a common one. It was she their friends pitied—rightly so, he supposed. He wanted to pity himself, and did, but kept it a secret. She had been able to need, and to use what was given to her because of her need, and eventually that had saved her. It had kept her from the awful contemplation that kept him awake so many nights after her bedtime drink had lulled her off to sleep. And as she slept, he contemplated the fact that in this world a tiny collection of cells no bigger than a walnut could take a son's life and send him away forever.

He had never hated her for healing, or for the deference other women gave her as a right. They looked on her the way a young oilman might look on an old vet whose hand or back or cheek is shiny with puckered pink burn tissue—with the respect the never-hurt always hold for the once-hurt-now-healed. She had done her time in hell over Charlie, and these other women knew it. But she had come out. There had been Before, there had been Hell, there had been After, and there had even been After-After, when she had returned to two of her four social clubs, had taken up macrame (he had a belt she had done a year ago—a beautiful twisted rope creation with a heavy silver buckle monogrammed BGD), had taken up afternoon TV—soap operas and Merv Griffin chatting with the celebrities.

Now what? he wondered, going back to the living room. After-After-After? It seemed so. A new woman, a whole woman, rising out of the old ashes that he had so crudely stirred. The old oilman with skin grafts over the burns, retaining the old savvy but gaining a new look. Beauty only skin deep? No. Beauty was in the eye of the beholder. It could go for miles.

For him, the scars had all been inside. He had examined his hurts one by one on the long nights after Charlie's death, cataloguing them with all the morbid fascination of a man studying his own bowel movements for signs of blood. He had wanted to watch Charlie play ball on a Little League team. He had wanted to get report cards and rant over them. He wanted to tell him, over and over, to pick up his room. He wanted to worry about the girls Charlie saw, the friends he picked, the boy's internal weather. He wanted to see what his son became and if they could still be in love as they had been until the bad cells, no bigger than a walnut, had come between them like some dark and rapacious woman.

Mary had said, *He was yours.*

That was true. The two of them had fitted so well that names were ridiculous, even pronouns a little obscene. So they became George and Fred, a vaudeville sort of combination, two Mortimer Veeblefeezers against the world.

And if a collection of bad cells no bigger than a walnut could destroy all those things, those things that are so personal that they can never be properly articulated, so personal you hardly dared admit their existence to yourself, what did that leave? How could you ever trust life again? How could you see it as anything more meaningful than a Saturday night demolition derby?

All of it was inside him, but he had been honestly unaware that his thoughts were changing him so deeply, so irretrievably. And now it was all out in the open, like some obscene mess vomited onto a coffee table, reeking with stomach juice, filled with undigested lumps, and if the world was only a demo derby, wouldn't one be justified in stepping out of his car? But what after that? Life seemed only a preparation for hell.

He saw that he had drained his drink in the kitchen; he had come into the living room with an empty glass.

December 31, 1973

He was only two blocks from Wally Hamner's house when he put his hand into his overcoat pocket to see if he had any Canada Mints in there. There were no mints, but he came up with a tiny square of aluminum foil that glinted dully in the station wagon's green dash lights. He spared it a puzzled, absent glance and was about to toss it into the ashtray when he remembered what it was.

In his mind Olivia's voice said: *Synthetic mescaline. Product four, they call it. Very heavy stuff.* He had forgotten all about it.

He put the little foil packet back into his coat pocket and turned onto Walter's street. Cars were lined up halfway down the block on both sides. That was Walter, all right—he had never been one to have anything so simple as a party when there might be a group grope in the offing. The Principle of the Pleasure Push, Wally called it. He claimed that someday he would patent the idea and then publish instructional handbooks on how to use it. If you got enough people together, Wally Hamner maintained, you were forced into having a good time—pushed into it. Once when Wally was expounding this theory in a bar, he had mentioned lynch mobs. "There," Walter had said blandly, "Bart has just proved my case."

He wondered what Olivia was doing now. She hadn't tried to call back, although if she had he would probably have weakened and taken the call. Maybe she had stayed in Vegas just long enough to get the money and had then caught a bus for . . . where? Maine? Did anyone leave Las Vegas for Maine in the middle of winter? Surely not.

Product four, they call it. Very heavy stuff.

He snuggled the wagon up to the curb behind a sporty red GTX with a black racing stripe and got out. New Year's Eve was clear but bitterly cold. A frigid rind of moon hung in the sky overhead like a child's paper cutout. Stars were spangled around it in lavish profusion. The mucus in his nose froze to a glaze that crackled when he flared his nostrils. His breath plumed out on the dark air.

Three houses away from Walter's he picked up the bass line from the stereo. They really had it cranked. There was something about Wally's parties, he reflected, Pleasure Principle or no. The most well-intentioned of just-thought-we'd-drop-bys ended up staying and drinking until their heads were full of silver chimes that would turn to leaden church bells the next day. The most dyed-in-the-wool rock-music haters ended up boogying in the living room to the endless golden gassers that Wally trotted out when everybody got blind drunk enough to look back upon the late fifties and early sixties as the plateau of their lives. They drank and boogied, boogied and drank, until they were panting like little yellow dogs on the Fourth of July. There were more kisses in the kitchen by halves of differing wholes, more feel-ups per square inch, more wall-flowers jerked rudely out of the woodwork, more normally sober folk who would wake up on New Year's Day with groaning hangovers and horridly clear memories of prancing around with lampshades on their heads or of finally deciding to tell the boss a few home truths. Wally seemed to inspire these things, not by any conscious effort, but just by being Wally—and of course there was no party like a New Year's Eve party.

He found himself scanning the parked cars for Steve Ordner's bottle-green Delta 88, but didn't see it anywhere.

Closer to the house, the rest of the rock band coalesced around the persistent bass signature, and Mick Jagger screaming:

Ooooh, children—
It's just a kiss away,
Kiss away, kiss away . . .

Every light in the house was blazing—fuck the energy crisis—except, of course in the living room, where rub-your-peepees would be going on during the slow numbers. Even over the heavy drive of the amplified music he could hear a hundred voices raised in fifty different conversations, as if Babel had fallen only seconds ago.

He thought that, had it been summer (or even fall), it would have been more fun to just stand outside, listening to the circus, charting its progress toward its zenith, and then its gradual fall-off. He had a sudden vision—startling, frightening—of himself standing on Wally Hamner's lawn and holding a roll of EEG graph paper in his hands, covered with the irregular spikes and dips of damaged mental function: the monitored record of a gigantic, tumored Party Brain. He shuddered a little and stuck his hands in his overcoat pockets to warm them.

His right hand encountered the small foil packet again and he took it out. Curious, he unfolded it, regardless of the cold that bit his fingertips with dull teeth. There was a small purple pill inside the foil, small enough to lie on the nail of his pinky finger without touching the edges. Much smaller than, say a walnut. Could something as small as that make him clinically insane, cause him to see things that weren't there, think in a way he had never thought? Could it, in short, mime all the conditions of his son's mortal illness?

Casually, almost absently, he put the pill in his mouth. It had no taste. He swallowed it.

"BART!" The woman screamed. *"BART DAWES!"* It was a woman in a black off-the-shoulder evening dress with a martini in one hand. She had dark hair,

put up for the occasion and held with a glittering rope spangled with imitation diamonds.

He had walked in through the kitchen door. The kitchen was choked, clogged with people. It was only eight-thirty; the Tidal Effect hadn't gotten far yet, then. The Tidal Effect was another part of Walter's theory; as a party continued, he contended, people would migrate to the four corners of the house. "The center does not hold," Wally said, blinking wisely. "T. S. Eliot said that." Once, according to Wally, he had found a guy wandering around in the attic eighteen hours after a party ended.

The woman in the black dress kissed him warmly on the lips, her ample breasts pushing against his chest. Some of her martini fell on the floor between them.

"Hi," he said. "Who's you?"

"Tina *Howard*, Bart. Don't you remember the class trip?" She wagged a long, spade-shaped fingernail under his nose. *"NAUGH-ty BOY!"*

"That Tina? By God, you are!" A stunned grin spread his mouth. That was another thing about Walter's parties, people from your past kept turning up like old photographs. Your best friend on the block thirty years ago; the girl you almost laid once in college; some guy you had worked with for a month on a summer job eighteen years ago.

"Except I'm Tina Howard Wallace now," the woman in the black dress said. "My husband's around here . . . somewhere . . ." She looked around vaguely, spilled some more of her drink, and swallowed the rest before it could get away from her. "Isn't it AWFUL, I seem to have lost him."

She looked at him warmly, speculatively, and Bart could barely believe that this woman had given him his first touch of female flesh—the sophomore class trip at Grover Cleveland High School, a hundred and nine years ago. Rubbing her breast through her white cotton sailor blouse beside . . .

"Cotter's Stream," he said aloud.

She blushed and giggled. "You remember, all right."

His eyes dropped in a perfect, involuntary reflex to the front of her dress and she shrieked with laughter. He grinned that helpless grin again. "I guess time goes by faster than we—"

"Bart!" Wally Hamner yelled over the general party babble. "Hey buddy, really glad you could make it!"

He cut across the room to them with the also-to-be-patented Walter Hamner Party Zigzag, a thin man, now mostly bald, wearing an impeccable 1962-vintage pinstriped shirt and horn-rimmed glasses. He shook Walter's outstretched hand, and Walter's grip was as hard as he remembered.

"I see you met Tina Wallace," Walter said.

"Hell, we go way back when," he said, and smiled uncomfortably at Tina.

"Don't you tell my husband that, you naughty boy," Tina giggled. " 'Scuse, please. I'll see you later, Bart?"

"Sure," he said.

She disappeared around a clump of people gathered by a table loaded with chips and dips and went on into the living room. He nodded after her and said, "How do you pick them, Walter? That girl was my first feel. It's like "This Is Your Life.""

Walter shrugged modestly. "All a part of the Pleasure Push, Barton my boy." He nodded at the paper bag tucked under his arm. "What's in the plain brown wrapper?"

"Southern Comfort. You've got ginger ale, don't you?"

"Sure," Walter said, but grimaced. "Are you really going to drink that down-by-de-Swanee-Ribber stuff? I always thought you were a scotch man."

"I was always a private Comfort-and-ginger-ale man. I've come out of the closet."

Walter grinned. "Mary's around here someplace.

She's kinda been keeping an eye out for you. Get yourself a drink and we'll go find her."

"Good enough."

He made his way across the kitchen, saying hi to people he knew vaguely and who looked as if they didn't know him at all, and replying hi, how are you to people he didn't remember who hailed him first. Cigarette smoke rolled majestically through the kitchen. Conversation faded quickly in and out, like stations on late-night AM radio, all of it bright and meaningless.

. . . Freddy and Jim didn't have their time sheets so I

. . . said that his mother died quite recently and he's apt to go on a crying jag if he drinks too much

. . . so when he got the paint scraped off he saw it was really a nice piece, maybe pre-Revolutionary

. . . and this little kike came to the door selling encyclopedias

. . . very messy; he won't give her the divorce because of the kids and he drinks like a

. . . terribly nice dress

. . . so much to drink that when he went to pay the check he barfed all over the hostess

A long Formica-topped table had been set up in front of the stove and the sink, and it was already crowded with opened liquor bottles and glasses in varying sizes and degrees of fullness. Ashtrays already overflowed with filter-tips. Three ice buckets filled with cubes had been crowded into the sink. Over the stove was a large poster which showed Richard Nixon wearing a pair of earphones. The earphone cord disappeared up into the rectum of a donkey standing on the edge of the picture. The caption said:

WE LISTEN BETTER!

To the left, a man in bell-bottomed baggies and a drink in each hand (a water glass filled with what looked to be whiskey and a large stein filled with beer) was entertaining a mixed group with a joke. "This guy comes into this bar, and here's this monkey sitting on the stool next to him. So the guy orders a beer and when the bartender brings it, the guy says, 'Who owns this monkey? Cute little bugger.' And the bartender says, 'Oh, that's the piano player's monkey.' So the guy swings around . . .''

He made himself a drink and looked around for Walt, but he had gone to the door to greet some more guests—a young couple. The man was wearing a huge driving cap, goggles, and an old-time automobile duster. Written on the front of the duster were the words

KEEP ON TRUCKIN'

Several people were laughing uproariously, and Walter was howling. Whatever the joke was, it seemed to go back a long time.

". . . and the guy walks over to the piano player and says, 'Do you know your monkey just pissed in my beer?' And the piano player says, 'No, but hum a few bars and I'll fake it.' '' Calculated burst of laughter. The man in the bell-bottomed baggies sipped his whiskey and then cooled it with a gulp of beer.

He took his drink and strolled into the darkened living room, slipping behind the turned back of Tina Howard Wallace before she could see him and snag him into a long game of Where Are They Now. She looked, he thought, like the kind of person who could cite you chapter and verse from the lives of classmates who had turned out badly—divorce, nervous disorders, and criminal violations would be her stock in trade—and would have made unpersons out of those who had had success.

Someone had put on the inevitable album of 50's rock and roll, and maybe fifteen couples were jitterbugging hilariously and badly. He saw Mary dancing with a tall, slim man that he knew but could not place.

Jack? John? Jason? He shook his head. It wouldn't come. Mary was wearing a party dress he had never seen before. It buttoned up one side, and she had left enough buttons undone to provide a sexy slit to a little above one nyloned knee. He waited for some strong feeling—jealousy or loss, even habitual craving—but none came. He sipped his drink.

She turned her head and saw him. He raised a noncommittal finger in salute: *Go on and finish your dance*—but she broke off and came over, bringing her partner with her.

"I'm so glad you could come, Bart," she said, raising her voice to be heard over the laughter and conversation and stereo. "Do you remember Dick Jackson?"

Bart stuck out his hand and the slim man shook it. "You and your wife lived on our street five . . . no, seven years ago. Is that right?"

Jackson nodded. "We're out in Willowood now."

Housing development, he thought. He had become very sensitive to the city's geography and housing strata.

"Good enough. Are you still working for Piels?"

"No, I've got my own business now. Two trucks. Tri-State Haulers. Say, if that laundry of yours ever needs day-hauling . . . chemicals or any of that stuff . . ."

"I don't work for the laundry anymore," he said, and saw Mary wince slightly, as if someone had knuckled an old bruise.

"No? What are you doing now?"

"Self-employed," he said and grinned. "Were you in on that independent trucker's strike?"

Jackson's face, already dark with alcohol, darkened more. "You're goddam right. And I personally untracked a guy that couldn't see falling into line. Do you know what those miserable Ohio bastards are charging for diesel? 31.9! That takes my profit margin from twelve percent and cuts it right down to nine. And all my truck maintenance has got to come out of that nine. Not to mention the frigging double-nickle speed-limit—"

As he went on about the perils of independent trucking in the country that had suddenly developed a severe case of the energy bends, Bart listened and nodded in the right places and sipped his drink. Mary excused herself and went into the kitchen to get a glass of punch. The man in the automobile duster was doing an exaggerated Charleston to an old Everly Brothers number, and people were laughing and applauding.

Jackson's wife, a busty, muscular-looking girl with carroty red hair, came over and was introduced. She was quite near the stagger point. Her eyes looked like the Tilt signs on a pinball machine. She shook hands with him, smiled glassily, and then said to Dick Jackson: "Hon, I think I'm going to whoopsie. Where's the bathroom?"

Jackson led her away. He skirted the dance floor and sat down in one of the chairs along the side. He finished his drink. Mary was slow coming back. Someone had collared her into a conversation, he supposed.

He reached into an inside pocket and brought out a pack of cigarettes and lit one. He only smoked at parties now. That was quite a victory over a few years ago, when he had been part of the three-packs-a-day cancer brigade.

He was halfway through the cigarette and still watching the kitchen door for Mary when he happened to glance down at his fingers and saw how interesting they were. It was interesting how the first and second fingers of his right hand knew just how to hold the cigarette, as if they had been smoking all their lives.

The thought was so funny he had to smile.

It seemed that he had been examining his fingers for quite a while when he noticed his mouth tasted different. Not bad, just different. The spit in it seemed to have thickened. And his legs . . . his legs felt a little jittery, as if they would like to tap along with the music, as if tapping along with the music would relieve them, make them feel cool and just like legs again—

He felt a little frightened at the way that thought, which had begun so ordinarily, had gone corkscrewing off in a wholly new direction like a man lost in a big house and climbing a tall *crrrrystal* staircase—

There it was again, and it was probably the pill he had taken, Olivia's pill, yes. And wasn't that an interesting way to say crystal? *Crrrrrystal,* gave it a crusty, bangled sound, like a stripper's costume.

He smiled craftily and looked at his cigarette, which seemed amazingly *white,* amazingly *round,* amazingly symbolic of all America's padding and wealth. Only in America were cigarettes so good-tasting. He had a puff. Wonderful. He thought of all the cigarettes in America pouring off the production lines in Winston-Salem, a plethora of cigarettes, an endless clean white cornucopia of them. It was the mescaline, all right. He was starting to trip. And if people knew what he had been thinking about the word *crystal* (a/k/a *crrrystal*), they would nod and tap their heads: *Yes, he's crazy, all right. Nutty as a fruitcake.* Fruitcake, there was another good word. He suddenly wished Sal Magliore was here. Together, he and Sally One-Eye would discuss all the facets of the Organization's business. They would discuss old whores and shootings. In his mind's eye he saw Sally One-Eye and himself eating linguini in a small Italian *ristorante* with dark-toned walls and scarred wooden tables while the strains of *The Godfather* played on the soundtrack. All in luxurious Technicolor that you could fall into, bathe in like a bubble bath.

"Crrrrrystal," he said under his breath, and grinned. It seemed that he had been sitting here and going over one thing and another for a very long time, but no ash had grown on his cigarette at all. He was astounded. He had another puff.

"Bart?"

He looked up. It was Mary, and she had a canapé for him. He smiled at her. "Sit down. Is that for me?"

"Yes." She gave it to him. It was a small triangular sandwich with pink stuff in the middle. It suddenly occurred to him that Mary would be frightened, horrified, if she knew he was on a trip. She might call an emergency squad, the police, God knew who else. He had to act normally. But the thought of acting normal made him feel stranger than ever.

"I'll eat it later," he said, and put the sandwich in his shirt pocket.

"Bart, are you drunk?"

"Just a little," he said. He could see the pores on her face. He could not recall ever having seen them so clearly before. All those little holes, as if God was a cook and she was a pie crust. He giggled and her deepening frown made him say: "Listen, don't tell."

"Tell?" She offered a puzzled frown.

"About the Product four."

"Bart, what in the name of God are you—"

"I've got to go to the bathroom," he said. "I'll be back." He left without looking at her, but he could feel her frown radiating out from her face in waves like heat from a microwave oven. Yet if he didn't look back at her, it was possible she would not guess. In this, the best of all possible worlds, anything was possible, even crrrystal staircases. He smiled fondly. The word had become an old friend.

The trip to the bathroom somehow became an odyssey, a safari. The party noise seemed to have picked up a cyclical beat, IT SEEMED TO fade in and FADE OUT in syllables OF THREE AND even the STEREO faded IN and OUT. He mumbled to people he thought he knew but refused to take up a single thrown conversational gambit; he only pointed to his crotch, smiled, and walked on. He left puzzled faces in his wake. Why is there never a party full of strangers when you need one? he scolded himself.

The bathroom was occupied. He waited outside for

what seemed like hours and when he finally got in he couldn't urinate although he seemed to want to. He looked at the wall above the toilet tank and the wall was bulging in and out in a cyclical, three-beat rhythm. He flushed even though he hadn't gone, in case someone outside might be listening, and watched the water swirl out of the bowl. It had a sinister pink color, as if the last user had passed blood. Unsettling.

He left the bathroom and the party smote him again. Faces came and went like floating balloons. The music was nice, though. Elvis was on. Good old Elvis. Rock on, Elvis, rock on.

Mary's face appeared in front of him and hovered, looking concerned. "Bart, what's wrong with you?"

"Wrong? Nothing wrong." He was astounded, amazed. His words had come out in a visual series of musical notes. "I'm hallucinating." He said it aloud, but it was spoken only for himself.

"Bart, what have you taken?" She looked frightened now.

"Mescaline," he said.

"Oh God, Bart. *Drugs? Why?*"

"Why not?" he responded, not to be flip, but because it was the only response he could think of quickly. The words came out in notes again, and this time some of them had flags.

"Do you want me to take you to a doctor?"

He looked at her, surprised, and went ponderously over her question in his mind to see if it had any hidden connotations; Freudian echoes of the funny farm. He giggled again, and the giggles streamed musically out of his mouth and in front of his eyes, crrrystal notes of lines and spaces, broken by bars and rests.

"Why would I want a doctor?" he said, choosing each word. The question mark was a high quarter-note. "It's just like she said. Not that good, not that bad. But interesting."

"Who?" she demanded. "Who told you? Where did you get it?" Her face was changing, seeming to become hooded and reptilian. Mary as cheap mystery-movie police detective, shining the light in the suspect's eyes—*Come on, McGonigal, whichever way you want it, hard or soft*—and then worse still she began to remind him uneasily of the H. P. Lovecraft stories he had read as a boy, the Cthulu Mythos stories, where perfectly normal human beings changed into fishy, crawling things at the urgings of the Elder Ones. Mary's face began to look scaly, vaguely eel-like.

"Never mind," he said, frightened. "Why can't you leave me alone? Stop fucking me up. I'm not bothering you."

Her face recoiled, became Mary's again, Mary's hurt, mistrustful face, and he was sorry. The party beat and swirled around them. "All right, Bart," she said quietly. "You hurt yourself just any way you like. But please don't embarrass me. Can I ask you that much?"

"Of course you c—"

But she had not waited for his answer. She left him, going quickly into the kitchen without looking back. He felt sorry, but he also felt relieved. But suppose someone else tried to talk with him? They would know too. He couldn't talk to people normally, not like this. Apparently he couldn't even fool people into thinking he was drunk.

"Rrrrreet," he said, ruffling the *r*'s lightly off the roof of his mouth. This time the notes came out in a straight line, all of them hurrying notes with flags. He could make notes all night and be perfectly happy, he didn't mind. But not here, where anybody could come along and accost him. Someplace private, where he could hear himself think. The party made him feel as if he were standing behind a large waterfall. Hard to think against the sound of all that. Better to find some quiet backwater. With perhaps a radio to listen to. He felt that listening to music would aid his thinking, and there was a lot of think about. Reams of things.

Also, he was quite sure that people had began to glance over at him. Mary must have spread the word.

I'm worried. Bart's on mescaline. It would move from group to group. They would go on pretending to dance, pretending to drink and have their conversations, but they would really be observing him from behind their hands, whispering about him. He could tell. It was all crrrystal clear.

A man walked past him, carrying a very tall drink and weaving slightly. He twitched the man's sport jacket and whispered hoarsely: "What are they saying about me?"

The man gave him a disconnected smile and blew a warm breath of scotch in his face. "I'll write that down," he said, and walked on.

He finally got into Walter Hamner's den (he could not have said how much later) and when he closed the door behind him, the sounds of the party became blessedly muted. He was getting scared. The stuff he had taken hadn't topped out yet; it just kept coming on stronger and stronger. He seemed to have crossed from one side of the living room to the other in the course of one blink; through the darkened bedroom where coats had been stored in another blink; down the hall in a third. The chain of normal, waking existence had come unclipped, spilling reality beads every which way. Continuity had broken down. His time sense was el destructo. Suppose he never came down? Suppose he was like this forever? It came to him to curl up and sleep it off, but he didn't know if he could. And if he did, God knew what dreams would come. The light, spur-of-the-moment way he had taken the pill now appalled him. This wasn't like being drunk; there was no small kernel of sobriety winking and blinking down deep in the center of him, that part that never got drunk. He was wacky all the way through.

But it was better in here. Maybe he could get control of it in here, by himself. And at least if he freaked out he wouldn't—

"Hi there."

He jumped, startled, and looked into the corner. A

man was sitting there in a high-backed chair by one of Walter's bookcases. There was an open book on the man's lap, as a matter of fact. Or was it a man? There was a single light on in the room, a lamp on a small round table to the speaker's left. Its light cast long shadows on his face, shadows so long that his eyes were dark caverns, his cheeks etched in sardonic, malefic lines. For a moment he thought he had stumbled on Satan sitting in Wally Hamner's den. Then the figure stood and he saw it was a man, only a man. A tall fellow, maybe sixty, with blue eyes and a nose that had been repeatedly punched in losing bouts with the bottle. But he wasn't holding a drink, nor was there one on the table.

"Another wanderer, I see," the man said, and offered his hand. "Phil Drake."

"Barton Dawes," he said, still dazed from his fright. They shook. Drake's hand was twisted and scarred by some old wound—a burn, perhaps. But he didn't mind shaking it. *Drake.* The name was familiar but he couldn't remember where he had heard it before.

"Are you quite all right?" Drake asked. "You look a little— "

"I'm high," he said. "I took some mescaline and oh boy am I high." He glanced at the bookcases and saw them going in and out and didn't like it. It was too much like the beating of a giant heart. He didn't want to see things like that anymore.

"I see," Drake said. "Sit down. Tell me about it."

He looked at Drake, slightly amazed, and then felt a tremendous surge of relief. He sat down. "You know about mescaline?" he asked.

"Oh, a little. A little. I run a coffeehouse downtown. Kids wander in off the streets, tripping on something . . . is it a good trip?" he asked politely.

"Good and bad," he said. "It's . . . heavy. That's a good word, the way they use it."

"Yes. It is."

"I was getting a little scared." He glanced out the window and saw a long, celestial highway stretching across the black dome of the sky. He looked away casually, but couldn't help licking his lips. "Tell me . . . how long does this usually go on?"

"When did you drop?"

"Drop?" The word dropped out of his mouth in letters, fell to the carpet, and dissolved there.

"When did you take the stuff?"

"Oh . . . about eight-thirty."

"And it's . . ." He consulted his watch. "It's a quarter of ten now—"

"Quarter of *ten*? Is that *all*?"

Drake smiled. "The sense of time turns to rubber, doesn't it? I expect you'll be pretty well down by one-thirty."

"Really?"

"Oh yes. I should think so. You're probably peaking now. Is it very visual mesc?"

"Yes. A little *too* visual."

"More things to be seen than the eye of man was meant to behold," Drake said, and offered a peculiar twisted smile.

"Yes, that's it. That's just it." His sense of relief at being with this man was intense. He felt saved. "What do you do besides talk to middle-aged men who have fallen down the rabbit hole?"

Drake smiled. "That's rather good. Usually people on mesc or acid turn inarticulate, sometimes incoherent. I spend most of my evenings at the Dial Help Center. On weekday afternoons I work at the coffee house I mentioned, a place called Drop Down Mamma. Most of the clientele are street freaks and stewbums. Mornings I just walk the streets and talk to my parishioners, if they're up. And in between, I run errands at the county jail."

"You're a minister?"

"They call me a street priest. Very romantic. Malcolm Boyd, look out. At one time I was a real priest."

"Not any more?"

"I have left the mother church," Drake said. He

said it softly, but there was a kind of dreadful finality
in his words. He could almost hear the clang of iron
doors slammed shut forever.

"Why did you do that?"

Drake shrugged. "It doesn't matter. What about
you? How did you get the mesc?"

"I got it from a girl on her way to Las Vegas. A
nice girl, I think. She called me on Christmas Day."

"For help?"

"I think so."

"Did you help her?"

"I don't know." He smiled craftily. "Father, tell me
about my immortal soul."

Drake twitched. "I'm not your father."

"Never mind, then."

"What do you want to know about your 'soul'?"

He looked down at his fingers. He could make bolts
of light shoot from their tips whenever he wanted to.
It gave him a drunken feeling of power. "I want to
know what will happen to it if I commit suicide."

Drake stirred uneasily. "You don't want to think
about killing yourself while you're tripping. The dope
talks, not you."

"*I* talk," he said. "Answer me."

"I can't. I don't know what will happen to your
'soul' if you commit suicide. I do, however, know what
will happen to your body. It will rot."

Startled by this idea, he looked down at his hands
again. Obligingly, they seemed to crack and molder in
front of his gaze, making him think of that Poe story,
"The Strange Case of M. Valdemar." Quite a night.
Poe and Lovecraft. A. Gordon Pym, anyone? How
about Abdul Allhazred, the Mad Arab? He looked
up, a little disconcerted, but not really daunted.

"What's your body doing?" Drake asked.

"Huh?" He frowned, trying to parse sense from
the question.

"There are two trips," Drake said. "A head trip

and a body trip. Do you feel nauseated? Achey? Sick in any way?"

He consulted his body. "No," he said. "I just feel . . . busy." He laughed a little at the word, and Drake smiled. It was a good word to describe how he felt. His body seemed very active, even still. Rather light, but not ethereal. In fact, he had never felt so *fleshy*, so conscious of the way his mental processes and physical body were webbed together. There was no parting them. You couldn't peel one away from the other. You were stuck with it, baby. Integration. Entropy. The idea burst over him like a quick tropical sunrise. He sat chewing it over in light of his current situation, trying to make out the pattern, if there was one. But—

"But there's the soul," he said aloud.

"What about the soul?" Drake asked pleasantly.

"If you kill the brain, you kill the body," he said slowly. "And vice versa. But what happens to your soul? There's the wild card, Fa . . . Mr. Drake."

Drake said: "In that sleep of death, what dreams may come? *Hamlet*, Mr. Dawes."

"Do you think the soul lives on? Is there survival?"

Drake's eyes grayed. "Yes," he said. "I think there is survival . . . in some form."

"And do you think suicide is a mortal sin that condemns the soul to hell?"

Drake didn't speak for a long time. Then he said: "Suicide is wrong. I believe that with all my heart."

"That doesn't answer my question."

Drake stood up. "I have no intention of answering it. I don't deal in metaphysics anymore. I'm a civilian. Do you want to go back to the party?"

He thought of the noise and confusion, and shook his head.

"Home?"

"I couldn't drive. I'd be scared to drive."

"I'll drive you."

"Would you? How would you get back?"

"Call a cab from your house. New Year's Eve is a very good night for cabs."

"That would be good," he said gratefully. "I'd like to be alone, I think. I'd like to watch TV."

"Are you safe alone?" Drake asked somberly.

"Nobody is," he replied with equal gravity, and they both laughed.

Okay. Do you want to say good-bye to anyone?"

"No. Is there a back door?"

"I think we can find one."

He didn't talk much on the way home. Watching the streetlights go by was almost all the excitement he could stand. When they went by the roadwork, he asked Drake's opinion.

"They're building new roads for energy-sucking behemoths while kids in this city are starving," Drake said shortly. "What do I think? I think it's a bloody crime."

He started to tell Drake about the gasoline bombs, the burning crane, the burning office trailer, and then didn't. Drake might think it was an hallucination. Worse still, he might think it wasn't.

The rest of the evening was not very clear. He directed Drake to his house. Drake commented that everyone on the street must be out partying or to bed early. He didn't comment. Drake called a taxi. They watched TV for a while without talking—Guy Lombardo at the Waldorf-Astoria, making the sweetest music this side of heaven. Guy Lombardo, he thought, was looking decidedly foggy.

The taxi came at quarter to twelve. Drake asked him again if he would be all right.

"Yes, I think I'm coming down." He really was. The hallucinations were draining toward the back of his mind.

Drake opened the front door and pulled up his collar. "Stop thinking about suicide. It's chicken."

He smiled and nodded, but he neither accepted nor

rejected Drake's advice. Like everything else these days, he simply took it under advisement. "Happy New Year," he said.

"Same to you, Mr. Dawes."

The taxi honked impatiently.

Drake went down the walk, and the taxi pulled away, yellow light glowing on the roof.

He went back into the living room and sat down in front of the TV. They had switched from Guy Lombardo to Times Square, where the glowing ball was poised stop the Allis-Chalmers Building, ready to start its descent into 1974. He felt weary, drained, finally sleepy. The ball would come down soon and he would enter the new year tripping his ass off. Somewhere in the country a New Year's baby was pushing its squashed, placenta-covered head out of his mother's womb and into this best of all possible worlds. At Walter Hamner's party, people would be raising their glasses and counting down. New Year's resolutions were about to be tested. Most of them would prove as strong as wet paper towels. He made a resolution of his own on the spur of the moment, and got to his feet in spite of his tiredness. His body ached and his spine felt like glass—some kind of hangover. He went into the kitchen and got his hammer off the kitchen shelf. When he brought it back into the living room, the glowing ball was sinking down the pole. There was a split screen, showing the ball on the right, showing the merry-makers at the Waldorf on the left, chanting: "Eight . . . seven . . . six . . . five . . ." One fat society dame caught a glimpse of herself on a monitor, looked surprised, and then waved to the country.

The turn of the year, he thought. Absurdly, goose bumps broke out on his arms.

The ball reached the bottom, and a sign lit up on the top of the Allis-Chalmers Building. The sign said:

1974

At the same instant he swung the hammer and the

TV screen exploded. Glass belched onto the carpet. There was a fizz of hot wires, but no fire. Just to be sure the TV would not roast him during the night in revenge, he kicked out the plug with his foot.

"Happy New Year," he said softly, and dropped the hammer to the carpet.

He lay on the couch and fell asleep almost immediately. He slept with the lights on and his sleep was dreamless.

Part Three

JANUARY

If I don't get some shelter,
Oh, I'm gonna fade away . . .
—Rolling Stones

January 5, 1974

The thing that happened in the Shop 'n' Save that day was the only thing that had happened to him in his whole life that actually seemed planned and sentient, not random. It was as if an invisible finger had written on a fellow human being, expressly for him to read.

He liked to go shopping. It was very soothing, very sane. He enjoyed doing sane things very much after his bout with the mescaline. He had not awakened on New Year's Day until afternoon, and he had spent the remainder of the day wandering disconnectedly around the house, feeling spaced-out and strange. He had picked things up and looked at them, feeling like Iago examining Yorick's skull. To a lesser degree the feeling had carried over to the next day, and even the day after that. But in another way, the effect had been good. His mind felt dusted and clean, as if it had been turned upside down, scrubbed and polished by some maniacally brisk internal housekeeper. He didn't get drunk and thus did not cry. When Mary had called him, very cautiously, around 7:00 P.M. on the first, he had talked to her calmly and reasonably, and it seemed to him that their positions had not changed very much. They were playing a kind of social statues, each waiting for the other to move first. But she had twitched and mentioned divorce. Just the possibility, the veriest wiggle of a finger, but movement for all that. No, the only thing that really disturbed him in the aftermath of the mescaline was the shattered lens of the Zenith color TV. He could not understand why he had done it. He had wanted such a TV for years, even though his favorite programs were the old ones that had been filmed in black and white. It wasn't even the act that distressed him as much as the lingering evidence of it—the broken glass, the exposed wiring. They seemed to reproach him, to say: *Why did you go and do that? I served you faithfully and you broke me. I never harmed you and you smashed me. I was defenseless.* And it was a terrible reminder of what they wanted to do to his house. At last he got an old quilt and covered the front of it. That made it both better and worse. Better because he couldn't see it, worse because it was like having a shrouded corpse in the house. He threw the hammer away like a murder weapon.

But going to the store was a good thing, like drinking coffee in Benjy's Grill or taking the LTD through the Clean Living Car Wash or stopping at Henry's newsstand downtown for the copy of *Time.* The Shop 'n' Save was very large, lighted with fluorescent bars set into the ceiling, and filled with ladies pushing carts and admonishing children and frowning at tomatoes wrapped in see-through plastic that would not allow a good squeeze. Muzak came down from discreet overhead speaker grilles, flowing evenly into your ears to be almost heard.

On this day, Saturday, the S&S was filled with weekend shoppers, and there were more men than usual, accompanying their wives and annoying them with sophomoric suggestions. He regarded the husbands, the wives, and the issue of their various partnerships with benign eyes. The day was bright and sunshine poured through the store's big front windows, splashing gaudy squares of light by the checkout registers, occasionally catching some woman's hair and turning it into a halo of light. Things did not seem so serious when it was like this, but things were always worse at night.

His cart was filled with the usual selection of a man thrown rudely into solitary housekeeping: spaghetti, meat sauce in a glass jar, fourteen TV dinners, a dozen eggs, butter, and a package of navel oranges to protect against scurvy.

He was on his way down a middle aisle toward the checkouts when God perhaps spoke to him. There was a woman in front of him, wearing powder-blue slacks and a blue cable-stitched sweater of a navy color. She had very yellow hair. She was maybe thirty-five, good looking in an open, alert way. She made a funny gobbling, crowing noise in her throat and staggered. The squeeze bottle of mustard she had been holding in her hand fell to the floor and rolled, showing a red pennant and the word FRENCH'S over and over again.

"Ma'am?" he ventured. "Are you okay?"

The woman fell backward and her left hand, which she had put up to steady herself, swept a score of coffee cans onto the floor. Each can said:

MAXWELL HOUSE
Good To The Very Last Drop.

It happened so fast that he wasn't really scared—not for himself, anyway—but he saw one thing that stuck with him later and came back to haunt his dreams. Her eyes had drifted out into walleyes, just as Charlie's had during his fits.

The woman fell on the floor. She cawed weakly. Her feet, clad in leather boots with a salt rime around the bottoms, drummed on the tiled floor. The woman directly behind him screamed weakly. A clerk who had been putting prices on soup cans ran up the aisle, dropping his stamper. Two of the checkout girls came to the foot of the aisle and stared, their eyes wide.

He heard himself say: "I think she's having an epileptic seizure."

But it wasn't an epileptic seizure. It was some sort of brain hemorrhage and a doctor who had been going around in the store with his wife pronounced her dead. The young doctor looked scared, as if he had just realized that his profession would dog him to his grave, like some vengeful horror monster. By the time he finished his examination, a middling-sized crowd had formed around the young woman lying among the coffee cans which had been the last part of the world over which she had exercised her human prerogative to rearrange. Now she had become part of that other world and would be rearranged by other humans. Her cart was half-filled with provisions for a week's living, and the sight of the cans and boxes and wrapped meats filled him with a sharp, agonized terror.

Looking into the dead woman's cart, he wondered what they would do with the groceries. Put them back on the shelves? Save them beside the manager's office until cash redeemed them, proof that the lady of the house had died in harness?

Someone had gotten a cop and he pushed his way through the knot of people on the checkout side. "Look out, here," the cop was saying self-importantly. "Give her air." As if she could use it.

He turned and bulled his way out of the crowd, butting with his shoulder. His calm of the last five days was shattered, and probably for good. Had there ever been a clearer omen? Surely not. But what did it mean? What?

When he got home he shoved the TV dinners into the freezer and then made himself a strong drink. His heart was thudding in his chest. All the way home from the supermarket he had been trying to remember what they had done with Charlie's clothes.

They had given his toys to the Goodwill Shop in Norton, they had transferred his bank account of a thousand dollars (college money—half of everything Charlie had gotten from relatives at birthdays and Christmas went into that account, over his howls of protest) to their own joint account. They had burned his bedding on Mamma Jean's advice—he himself had been unable to understand that, but didn't have the heart to protest; everything had fallen apart and he

was supposed to argue over saving a mattress and box
springs? But the clothes, that was a different matter.
What had they done with Charlie's clothes?

The question gnawed at him all afternoon, making
him fretful, and once he almost went to the phone to
call Mary and ask her. But that would be the final
straw, wouldn't it? She wouldn't have to just guess
about the state of his sanity after that.

Just before sunset he went up to the small half-attic,
which was reached by crawling through a trapdoor in
the ceiling of the master bedroom closet. He had to
stand on a chair and shinny up in. He hadn't been in
the attic for a long, long time, but the single bare 100-
watt bulb still worked. It was coated with dust and
cobwebs, but it still worked.

He opened a dusty box at random and discovered
all his high school and college yearbooks, laid neatly
away. Embossed on the cover of each high school
yearbook were the words:

THE CENTURION
Bay High School . . .

On the cover of each college yearbook (they were
heavier, more richly bound) were these words:

THE PRISM
Let Us Remember . . .

He opened the high school yearbooks first, flipping
through the signed end pages ("Uptown, downtown,
all around the town/I'm the gal who wrecked your
yearbook/Writing inside down—A.F.A., Connie"),
then the photographs of long-ago teachers, frozen behind their desks and beside their blackboards, smiling
vaguely, then of classmates he barely remembered
with their credits (FHA 1,2; Class Council 2,3,4; Poe
Society, 4) listed beneath, along with their nicknames
and a little slogan. He knew the fates of some (Army,

dead in a car crash, assistant bank manager), but most were gone, their futures hidden from him.

In his senior high yearbook he came across a young George Barton Dawes, looking dreamily toward the future from a retouched photograph that had been taken at Cressey Studios. He was amazed by how little that boy knew of the future and by how much that boy looked like the son this man had come to search out traces of. The boy in the picture had not yet even manufactured the sperm that would become half the boy. Below the picture:

BARTON G. DAWES
"Whizzer"
(Outing Club, 1,2,3,4
Poe Society, 3,4)

Bay High School
Bart, the Klass Klown, helped to lighten our load!

He put the yearbooks back in their box helter-skelter and went on poking. He found drapes that Mary had taken down five years ago. An old easy chair with a broken arm. A clock radio that didn't work. A wedding photograph album that he was scared to look through. Piles of magazines—*ought to get those out,* he told himself. *They're a fire hazard in the summer.* A washing machine motor that he had once brought home from the laundry and tinkered with to no avail. And Charlie's clothes.

They were in three cardboard cartons, each crisp with the smell of mothballs. Charlie's shirts and pants and sweaters, even Charlie's Hanes underwear. He took them out and looked at each item carefully, trying to imagine Charlie wearing these things, moving in them, rearranging minor parts of the world in them. At last it was the smell of the mothballs that drove him out of the attic, shaking and grimacing, needing

a drink. The smell of things that had lain quietly and
uselessly over the years, things which had no purpose
but to hurt. He thought about them for most of the
evening, until the drink blotted out the ability to think.

January 7, 1974

The doorbell rang at quarter past ten and when he
opened the front door, a man in a suit and a topcoat
was standing there, sort of hipshot and slouched and
friendly. He was neatly shaved and barbered, carrying
a slim briefcase, and at first he thought the man was
a salesman with a briefcase full of samples—Amway,
or magazine subscriptions, or possibly even the larcenous Swipe—and he prepared to welcome the man in,
to listen to his pitch carefully, to ask questions, and
maybe even buy something. Except for Olivia, he was
the first person who had come to the house since Mary
left almost five weeks ago.

But the man wasn't a salesman. He was a lawyer.
His name was Philip T. Fenner, and his client was the
city council. These facts he announced with a shy grin
and a hearty handshake.

"Come on in," he said, and sighed. He supposed
that in a half-assed sort of way, this guy *was* a salesman. You might even say he was selling Swipe.

Fenner was talking away, a mile a minute.

"Beautiful house you have here. Just beautiful.
Careful ownership always shows, that's what I say. I
won't take up much of your time, Mr. Dawes, I know
you're a busy man, but Jack Gordon thought I might
as well swing out here since it was on my way and
drop off this relocation form. I imagine you mailed
for one, but the Christmas rush and all, things get lost.

And I'd be glad to answer any questions you might have, of course."

"I have a question," he said, unsmiling.

The jolly exterior of his visitor slipped for a moment and he saw the real Fenner lurking behind it, as cold and mechanized as a Pulsar watch. "What would that be, Mr. Dawes?"

He smiled. "Would you like a cup of coffee?"

Back on with the smiling Fenner, cheerful runner of city council errands. "Gee, that'd be nice, if it's not too much trouble. A trifle nippy out there, only seventeen degrees. I think the winters have been getting colder, don't you?"

"They sure have." The water was still hot from his breakfast coffee. "Hope you don't mind instant. My wife's visiting her folks for a while, and I just sort of muddle along."

Fenner laughed good-naturedly and he saw that Fenner knew exactly what the situation was between him and Mary, and probably what the situation was between him and any other given persons or institutions: Steve Ordner, Vinnie Mason, the corporation, God.

"Not at all, instant's fine. I always drink instant. Can't tell the difference. Okay to put some papers on this table?"

"Go right ahead. Do you take cream?"

"No, just black. Black is fine." Fenner unbuttoned his topcoat but didn't take it off. He swept it under him as he sat down, as a woman will sweep her skirt so she doesn't wrinkle the back. In a man, the gesture was almost jarringly fastidious. He opened his brief-case and took out a stapled form that looked like an income tax return. He poured Fenner a cup of coffee and gave it to him.

"Thanks. Thanks very much. Join me?"

"I think I'll have a drink," he said.

"Uh-huh," Fenner said, and smiled charmingly. He sipped his coffee. "Good, very good. Hits the spot."

He made himself a tall drink and said, "Excuse me for just a minute, Mr. Fenner. I have to make a telephone call."

"Certainly, of course." He sipped his coffee again and smacked his lips over it.

He went to the phone in the hall, leaving the door open. He dialed the Calloway house and Jean answered.

"It's Bart," he said, "Is Mary there, Jean?"

"She's sleeping." Jean's voice was frosty.

"Please wake her up. It's very important."

"I bet it is. I just bet. I told Lester the other night, I said: Lester, it's time we thought about an unlisted phone. And he agreed with me. We both think you've gone off your rocker, Barton Dawes, and that's the plain truth with no shellack on it."

"I'm sorry to hear that. But I really have to—"

The upstairs extension was picked up and Mary said, "Bart?"

"Yes. Mary, has a lawyer named Fenner been out to see you? Kind of slick-talking fellow that tries to act like Jimmy Stewart?"

"No," she said. *Shit, snake-eyes.* Then she added, "He called on the phone." *Jackpot!* Fenner was standing in the doorway now, holding his coffee and sipping it calmly. The half-shy, totally cheerful, aw-shucks expression was gone now. He looked rather pained.

"Mamma, get off the extension," Mary said, and Jean Calloway hung up with a bitter snort.

"Was he asking about me?" he asked.

"Yes."

"He talked to you after the party?"

"Yes, but . . . I didn't tell him anything about that."

"You might have told him more than you know. He comes on like a sleepy tick-hound, but he's the city council's ballcutter." He smiled at Fenner, who thinly smiled back. "You've got an appointment with him?"

"Why . . . yes." She sounded surprised. "But he only wants to talk about the house, Bart—"

"No, that's what he told you. He really wants to talk about me. I think these guys would like to drag me into a competency hearing."

"A . . . what? . . ." She sounded utterly befuddled.

"I haven't taken their money yet, ergo I must be crazy. Mary, do you remember what we talked about at Handy Andy's?"

"Bart, is that Mr. Fenner in the house?"

"Yes."

"The psychiatrist," she said dully. "I mentioned you were going to be seeing a . . . oh, Bart, I'm sorry."

"Don't be," he said softly, and meant it. "This is going to be all right, Mary. I swear. Maybe nothing else, but this is going to be all right."

He hung up and turned to Fenner. "Want me to call Stephan Ordner?" he asked. "Vinnie Mason? I won't bother with Ron Stone or Tom Granger, they'd recognize a cheap prick like you before you even had your briefcase unsnapped. But Vinnie wouldn't and Ordner would welcome you with open arms. He's on the prod for me."

"You needn't," Fenner said. "You've misunderstood me, Mr. Dawes. And you've apparently misunderstood my clients. There is nothing personal in this. No one is out to get you. But there *has* been an awareness for some time that you dislike the 784 extension. You wrote a letter to the paper last August—"

"Last August," he marveled. "You people have a clipping serving, don't you?"

"Of course."

He went into a harried crouch, rolling his eyeballs fearfully. "More clippings! More lawyers! Ron, go out and snow those reporters! We have enemies everywhere, Mavis, bring me my pills!" He straightened up. "Paranoia, anyone? Christ, I thought I was bad."

"We also have a public-relations staff," Fenner said stiffly. "We are not nickle-and-diming here, Mr. Dawes. We are talking about a ten-million-dollar project."

He shook his head, disgusted. "They ought to hold a competency hearing on you road guys, not me."

Fenner said: "I'm going to lay all my cards on the table, Mr. Dawes."

"You know, it's been my experience that when anybody says that they're ready to stop screwing around with the little lies and they're about to tell a real whopper."

Fenner flushed, finally angry. "You wrote the newspaper. You dragged your heels on finding a new plant for the Blue Ribbon Laundry and finally got canned—"

"I didn't. I resigned at least a half an hour before they could pink me."

"—and you've ignored all our communications dealing with this house. The consensus is that you may be planning some public display on the twentieth. Calling the papers and TV stations, getting them all out here. The heroic home owner dragged kicking and screaming from his hearth and home by the city's Gestapo agents."

"That worries you, doesn't it?"

"Of course it worries us! Public opinion is volatile, it swings around like a weathervane—"

"And your clients are elected officials."

Fenner looked at him expressionlessly.

"So what now?" he asked. "Are you going to make me an offer I can't refuse?"

Fenner sighed. "I can't understand what we're arguing about, Mr. Dawes. The city is offering you sixty thousand dollars to—"

"Sixty-three five."

"Yes, very good. They are offering you that amount for the house and the lot. Some people are getting a lot less. And what do you get for that money? You get no hassles, no trouble, no heat. The money is practically tax free because you've already paid Uncle the taxes on the money you spent to buy it. All you owe is taxes on the markup. Or don't you think the valuation is fair?"

"Fair enough," he said, thinking about Charlie. "As far as dollars and cents go, it's fair. Probably more than I could get if I wanted to sell it, with the price of loans what they are."

"So what *are* we arguing about?"

"We're not," he said, and sipped his drink. Yes, he had gotten his salesman, all right. "Do you have a house, Mr. Fenner?"

"Yes I do," Fenner said promptly. "A very fine one in Greenwood. And if you are going to ask me what I would do or how I would feel if our positions were reversed, I'll be very frank. I would twist the city's tit for all I could get and then laugh all the way to the bank."

"Yes, of course you would." He laughed and thought of Don and Ray Tarkington, who would have twisted both tits and rammed the courthouse flagpole up the city's ass for good measure. "Do you folks really think I've lost my marbles, then?"

Judiciously, Fenner said: "We don't know. Your resolution to the laundry relocation problem was hardly a normal one."

"Well, I'll tell you this. I have enough marbles left to know I could get myself a lawyer who doesn't like the eminent domain statute—one who still believes in that quaint old adage that a man's home is his castle. He could get a restraining order and we could tie you up for a month, maybe two. With luck and the right progression of judges, we could hold this thing off until next September."

Fenner looked pleased rather than disconcerted, as he had suspected Fenner would. Finally, Fenner was thinking. Here's the hook, Freddy, are you enjoying this? Yes, George, I have to admit I am.

"What do you want?" Fenner asked.

"How much are you prepared to offer?"

"We'll hike the valuation five thousand dollars. Not a penny more. And nobody will hear about the girl."

Everything stopped. Stopped dead.

"What?" he whispered.

"The *girl*, Mr. Dawes. The one you were banging. You had her here December sixth and seventh."

A number of thoughts spiraled through his mind in a period of seconds, some of them extremely sensible, but most of them overlaid and made untrustworthy with a thin yellow patina of fear. But above both fear and sensible thoughts was a vast red rage that made him want to leap across the table and choke this tick-tock man until clocksprings fell out of his ears. And he must not do that; above all, not that.

"Give me a number," he said.

"Number—?"

"Phone number. I'll call you this afternoon and tell you my decision."

"It would be ever so much better if we could wrap it up right now."

You'd like that, wouldn't you? Referee, let's extend this round thirty seconds. I've got this man on the ropes.

"No, I don't think so. Please get out of my house."

Fenner gave a smooth, expressionless shrug. "Here's my card. The number is on it. I expect to be in between two-thirty and four o'clock."

"I'll call."

Fenner left. He watched him through the window beside the front door as he walked down the path to his dark blue Buick, got in, and cruised away. Then he slammed his fist against the wall, hard.

He mixed himself another drink and sat down at the kitchen table to go over the situation. They knew about Olivia. They were willing to use that knowledge as a lever. As a lever to move him it wasn't very good. They could no doubt end his marriage with it, but his marriage was in serious trouble already. But they had *spied* on him.

The question was, how?

If there had been men watching him, they undoubtedly would have known about the world-famous crackle-crackle-boom-boom. If so, they would have used it on him. Why bother with something paltry like a little extramarital boogie-woogie when you can have the recalcitrant home owner slapped in jail for arson? So they had bugged him. When he thought how close he had come to drunkenly spilling the crime to Magliore over the phone, cold little dots of perspiration broke out on his skin. Thank God Magliore had shut him up. Crackle-crackle-boom-boom was bad enough.

So he was living in a bugged house and the question remained: What to do about Fenner's offer and Fenner's clients' methods?

He put a TV dinner in the oven for his lunch and sat down with another drink to wait for it. They had spied on him, tried to bribe him. The more he thought about it, the angrier it made him.

He took the TV dinner out and ate it. He wandered around the house, looking at things. He began to have an idea.

At three o'clock he called Fenner and told him to send out the form. He would sign it if Fenner took care of the two items they had discussed. Fenner sounded very pleased, even relieved. He said he would be glad to take care of things, and would see he had a form tomorrow. Fenner said he was glad he had decided to be sensible.

"There are a couple of conditions," he said.

"Conditions," Fenner replied, and sounded instantly wary.

"Don't get excited. It's nothing you can't handle."

"Let's hear them," Fenner said. "But I'm warning you, Dawes, you've squeezed us for about all you can."

"You get the form over to the house tomorrow," he said. "I'll bring it to your office on Wednesday. I want you to have a check for sixty-eight thousand five hundred dollars waiting for me. A *cashier's* check. I'll trade you the release form for the check."

"Mr. Dawes, we can't do business that way—"

"Maybe you're not supposed to, but you *can.* The same way you're not supposed to tap my phone and God knows what else. No check, no form. I'll get the lawyer instead."

Fenner paused. He could almost hear Fenner thinking."

"All right. What else?"

"I don't want to be bothered anymore after Wednesday. On the twentieth, it's yours. Until then it's mine."

"Fine," Fenner said instantly, because of course that wasn't a condition at all. The law said the house was his until midnight on the nineteenth, incontrovertibly the city's property a minute later. If he signed the city's release form and took the city's money, he could holler his head off to every newspaper and TV station in town and not get a bit of sympathy.

"That's all," he said.

"Good," Fenner said, sounding extremely happy. "I'm glad we could finally get together on this in a rational way, Mr.—"

"Fuck you," he said, and hung up.

January 8, 1974

He wasn't there when the courier dropped the bulky brown envelope containing form 6983–426–73–74 (blue folder) through his letter slot. He had gone out into darkest Norton to talk to Sal Magliore. Magliore was not overjoyed to see him, but as he talked, Magliore grew more thoughtful.

Lunch was sent in—spaghetti and veal and a bottle of Gallo red. It was a wonderful meal. Magliore held up his hand to stop him when he got to the part about the five-thousand-dollar bribe and Fenner's knowledge of Olivia. He made a telephone call and spoke briefly to the man on the other end. Magliore gave the man on the other end the Crestallen Street address. "Use the van," he said and hung up. He twirled more spaghetti onto his fork and nodded across the table for the story to go on.

When he finished, Magliore said: "You're lucky they weren't tailing you. You'd be in the box right now."

He was full to bursting, unable to eat another mouthful. He had not had such a meal in five years. He complimented Magliore, and Magliore smiled.

"Some of my friends, they don't eat pasta anymore. They got an image to keep up. So they eat at steak houses or places that have French food or Swedish food or something like that. They got the ulcers to prove it. Why ulcers? Because you can't change what you are." He was pouring spaghetti sauce out of the grease-stained cardboard takeout bucket the spaghetti had come in. He began to mop it up with crusts of garlic bread, stopped, looked across the table with those strange, magnified eyes and said: "You're asking me to help you commit a mortal sin."

He looked at Magliore blankly, unable to hide his surprise.

Magliore laughed crossly. "I know what you're thinkin'. A man in my business is the wrong guy to talk about sin. I already told you that I had one guy knocked off. More than one guy, too. But I never killed anyone that didn't deserve to be killed. And I look at it this way: a guy who dies before God planned him to die, it's like a rain-out at the ball park. The sins that guy committed, they don't count. God has got to let 'em in because they didn't have all the time to repent He meant them to have. So killing a guy is really sparing him the pain of hell. So in a way, I done more for those guys than the Pope himself could have done. I think God knows that. But this isn't any of my business. I like you a lot. You got balls. Doing what you did with those gas bombs, that took balls. This, though. This is something different."

"I'm not asking you to do anything. It's my own free will."

Magliore rolled his eyes. "Jesus Mary! Joseph the carpenter! Why can't you just leave me alone?"

"Because you have what I need."

"I wish to God I didn't."

"Are you going to help me?"

"I don't know."

"I've got the money now. Or will have, shortly."

"It ain't a matter of money. It's a matter of principle. I never dealt with a fruitcake like you before. I'll have to think about it. I'll call you."

He decided it would be wrong to press further and left.

He was filling out the relocation form when Magliore's men came. They were driving a white Econoline van with RAY'S TV SALES AND SERVICE written on the side, below a dancing TV with a big grin on its picture tube. There were two men, wearing green fatigues and carrying bulky service cases. The cases contained real TV repair tools and tubes, but they also contained sundry other equipment. They "washed" his house. It took an hour and a half. They found bugs in both phones, one in his bedroom, one in the dining room. None in the garage, which made him feel relieved.

"The bastards," he said, holding the shiny bugs in his hand. He dropped the bugs to the floor and ground them under his heel.

On the way out, one of the men said, not unadmiringly: "Mister, you really beat the shit out of that TV. How many times did you have to hit it?"

"Only once," he said.

When they had driven away into the cold late afternoon sunshine, he swept the bugs into a dustpan and dropped their shattered, twinkling remains into the kitchen wastebasket. Then he made himself a drink.

January 9, 1974

There were only a few people in the bank at 2:30 in the afternoon, and he went directly to one of the tables in the middle of the floor with the city's cashier's check. He tore a deposit ticket out of the back of his checkbook and made it out in the sum of $34,250. He went to a teller's window and presented the ticket and the check.

The teller, a young girl with sin-black hair and a short purple dress, her legs clad in sheer nylon stockings that would have brought the Pope to present arms, looked from the ticket to the check and then back again, puzzled.

"Something wrong with the check?" he asked pleasantly. He had to admit he was enjoying this.

"Nooo, but . . . you want to deposit $34,250 and you want $34,250 in *cash*? Is that it?"

He nodded.

"Just a moment, sir, please."

He smiled and nodded, keeping a close eye on her legs as she went to the manager's desk, which was behind a slatted rail but not glassed in, as if to say this man was as human as you or I . . . or almost, anyway. The manager was a middle-aged man dressed in young clothes. His face was as narrow as the gate of heaven and when he looked at the teller (telleress?) in the purple dress, he arched his eyebrows.

They discussed the check, the deposit slip, its implications for the bank and possibly for the entire Federal Deposit System. The girl bent over the desk, her skirt rode up in back, revealing a mauve-colored slip with lace on the hem. *Love o love o careless love,* he thought. Come home with me and we will diddle even unto the end of the age, or until they rip my house

down, whichever comes first. The thought made him
smile. He had a hard-on . . . well, a semi, anyway. He
looked away from her and glanced around the bank.
There was a guard, probably a retired cop, standing
impassively between the safe and the front doors. An
old lady laboriously signing her blue Social Security
check. And a large poster on the left wall which
showed a picture of the earth as photographed from
outer space, a large blue-green gem set against a field
of black. Over the planet, in large letters, was written:

GO AWAY

Underneath the planet, in slightly smaller letters:

WITH A FIRST BANK VACATION LOAN

The pretty teller came back. "I'll have to give this
to you in five hundreds and hundreds," she said.
"That's fine."
She made out a receipt for his deposit and then
went into the bank vault. When she came out, she had
a small carrying case. She spoke to the guard and he
came over with her. The guard looked at him
suspiciously.
She counted out three stacks of ten thousand dollars, twenty five-hundred-dollar bills in each stack. She
banded each one and then slipped an adding machine
notation between the band and the top bill of each
stack. In each case the adding machine slip said:
$10,000
She counted out forty-two hundreds, riffling the bills
quickly with the pad of her right index finger. On top
of these she laid five ten-dollar bills. She banded the
bundle and slid in another adding machine slip
which said:
$4,250
The four bundles were lined up side by side, and
the three of them eyed them suspiciously for a mo-

ment, enough money to buy a house, or five Cadillacs, or a Piper Cub airplane, or almost a hundred thousand cartons of cigarettes.

Then she said, a little dubiously: "I can give you a zipper bag— "

"No, this is fine." He scooped the bundles up and dropped them into his overcoat pockets. The guard watched this cavalier treatment of his *raison d'être* with impassive contempt; the pretty teller seemed fascinated (her salary for five years was disappearing casually into the pockets of this man's off-the-rack overcoat and it hardly made a bulge); and the manager was looking at him with barely concealed dislike, because a bank was a place where money was supposed to be like God, unseen and reverentially regarded.

"Good 'nough," he said, stuffing his checkbook down on top of the ten-thousand-dollar bundles. "Take it easy."

He left and they all looked after him. Then the old woman shuffled up to the pretty teller and presented her Social Security check, properly signed, for payment. The pretty teller gave her two hundred and thirty-five dollars and sixty-three cents.

When he got home he put the money in a dusty beer stein on the top shelf of the kitchen cabinet. Mary had given the stein to him as a gag present on his birthday, five years ago. He had never particularly cared for it, preferring to drink his beer directly from the bottle. Written on the side of the stein was an emblem showing an Olympic torch and the words:

U.S. DRINKING TEAM

He put the stein back, now filled with a headier brew, and went upstairs to Charlie's room, where his desk was. He rummaged through the bottom drawer and found a small manila envelope. He sat down at the desk, added up the new checkbook balance and saw that it came out to $35,053.49. He addressed the manila envelope to Mary, in care of her folks. He slipped the checkbook inside, sealed the envelope, and rummaged in his desk again. He found a half-full book of stamps, and put five eight-centers on the envelope. He regarded it for a moment, and then, below the address, he wrote:

FIRST CLASS MAIL

He left the envelope standing on his desk and went into the kitchen to make himself a drink.

January 10, 1974

It was late in the evening, snowing, and Magliore hadn't called. He was sitting in the living room with a drink, listening to the stereo because the TV was still *hors de combat*. He had gone out earlier with two ten-dollar bills from the beer stein and had bought four rock and roll albums. One of them was called *Let It Bleed* by the Rolling Stones. They had been playing it at the party, and he liked it better than the others he had bought, which seemed sort of sappy. One of them, an album by a group called Crosby, Stills, Nash and Young, was so sappy that he had broken it over his knee. But *Let It Bleed* was filled with loud, leering, thumping music. It banged and jangled. He liked it a great deal. It reminded him of "Let's Make a Deal," which was MC'ed by Monte Hall. Now Mick Jagger was singing.

> *Well we all need someone to cream on,*
> *And if you want to, you can cream on me.*

He had been thinking about the bank poster, showing the whole earth, various and new, with the legend that invited the viewer to GO AWAY. It made him think about the trip he had taken on New Year's Eve. He had gone away, all right. Far away.

But hadn't he enjoyed it?

The thought brought him up short.

He had been dragging around for the last two months like a dog whose balls had been caught in a swinging door. But hadn't there been compensations along the way?

He had done things he never would have done otherwise. The trips on the turnpike, as mindless and free as migration. The girl and the sex, the touch of her breasts so unlike Mary's. Talking with a man who was a crook. Being accepted finally by that man as a serious person. The illegal exhilaration of throwing the gasoline bombs and the dreamy terror, like drowning, when it seemed the car would not lurch up over the embankment and carry him away. Deep emotions had been excavated from his dry, middle-echelon executive's soul like the relics of a dark religion from an archaeological dig. He knew what it was to be *alive*.

Of course there were bad things. The way he had lost control in Handy Andy's, shouting at Mary. The gnawing loneliness of those first two weeks alone, alone for the first time in twenty years with only the dreadful, mortal beat of his own heart for company. Being punched by Vinnie—Vinnie Mason of all people!—in the department store. The awful fear hangover the morning after he had firebombed the construction. That lingered most of all.

But even those things, as bad as they had been, had been new and somehow exciting, like the thought that he might be insane or going insane. The tracks through the interior landscape he had been strolling (or crawling?) through these last two months were the only tracks. He had explored himself and if what he had been finding was often banal, it was also some-times dreadful and beautiful.

His thoughts reverted to Olivia as he had last seen her, standing on the turnpike ramp with her sign, LAS VEGAS . . . OR BUST! held up defiantly into the cold indifference of things. He thought of the bank poster: GO AWAY. Why not? There was nothing to hold him here but dirty obsession. No wife and only the ghost of a child, no job and a house that would be an un-house in a week and a half. He had cash money and a car he owned free and clear. Why not just get in it and go?

A kind of wild excitement seized him In his mind's eye he saw himself shutting off the lights, getting into the LTD, and driving to Las Vegas with the money in his pocket. Finding Olivia. Saying to her: *Let's GO AWAY.* Driving to California, selling the car, booking passage to the South Seas. From there to Hong Kong, from Hong Kong to Saigon, to Bombay, to Athens, Madrid, Paris, London, New York. Then to—

Here?

The world was round, that was the deadly truth of it. Like Olivia, going to Nevada, resolving to shake the shit loose. Gets stoned and raped the first time around the new track because the new track is just like the old track, in that it *is* the old track, around and around until you've worn it down too deep to climb out and then it's time to close the garage door and turn on the ignition and just wait . . . wait . . .

The evening drew on and his thoughts went around and around, like a cat trying to catch and swallow its own tail. At last he fell asleep on the couch and dreamed of Charlie.

January 11, 1974

Magliore called him at quarter past one in the afternoon.

"Okay," he said. "We'll do business, you and I. It's going to cost you nine thousand dollars. I don't suppose that changes your mind."

"In cash?"

"What do you mean in cash? Do you think I'm gonna take your personal check?"

"Okay. Sorry."

"You be at the Revel Lanes Bowladrome tomorrow night at ten o'clock. You know where that is?"

"Yes, out on Route 7. Just past the Skyview Shopping Mall."

"That's right. There'll be two guys on lane sixteen wearing green shirts with Marlin Avenue Firestone on the back in gold thread. You join them. One of them will explain everything you need to know. That'll be while you're bowling. You bowl two or three strings, then you go outside and drive down the road to the Town Line Tavern. You know where that is?"

"No."

"Just go west on 7. It's about two miles from the bowling alley on the same side. Park in back. My friends will park beside you. They'll be driving a Dodge Custom Cab pickup. Blue. They'll transfer a crate from their truck to your wagon. You give them an envelope. I must be crazy, you know that? Out of my gourd. I'll probably go up for this. Then I'll have a nice long time to wonder why the fuck I did it."

"I'd like to talk to you next week. Personally."

"No. Absolutely not. I ain't your father confessor. I never want to see you again. Not even to talk to

you. To tell you the truth, Dawes, I don't even want
to read about you in the paper."

"It's a simple investment matter."

Magliore paused.

"No," he said finally.

"This is something no one can ever touch you on,"
he told Magliore. "I want to set up a . . . a trust fund
for someone."

"Your wife?"

"No."

"You stop by Tuesday," Magliore said at last.
"Maybe I'll see you. Or maybe I'll have better sense."

He hung up.

Back in the living room, he thought of Olivia and
of living—the two seemed constantly bound up together. He thought of GOING AWAY. He thought of
Charlie, and he could hardly remember Charlie's face
anymore, except in snapshot fashion. How could this
be possibly happening, then?

With sudden resolution he got up, went to the
phone, and turned to TRAVEL in the yellow pages.
He dialed a number. But when a friendly female voice
on the other end said, "Arnold Travel Agency, how
may we help you?" he hung up and stepped quickly
away from the phone, rubbing his hands together.

January 12, 1974

The Revel Lanes Bowladrome was a long, fluorescent-
lit building that resounded with piped-in Muzak, a
jukebox, shouts and conversation, the stuttering bells
of pinball machines, the rattle of the coin-op bumper-
pool game, and above all else, the lumbering concate-
nation of falling pins and the booming, droning roll
of large black bowling balls.

He went to the counter, got a pair of red-and-white bowling shoes (which the clerk sprayed ceremonially with an aerosol foot disinfectant before allowing them to leave his care), and walked down to Lane 16. The two men were there. He saw that the one standing up to roll was the mechanic who had been replacing the muffler on the day of his first trip to Magliore's Used Car Sales. The fellow sitting at the scoring table was one of the fellows who had come to his house in the TV van. He was drinking a beer from a waxed-paper cup. They both looked at him as he approached.

"I'm Bart," he said.

"I'm Ray," the man at the table said. "And that guy"—the mechanic was rolling now—"is Alan."

The bowling ball left Alan's hand and thundered down the alley. Pins exploded everywhere and then Alan made a disgusted noise. He had left the seven-ten split. He tried to hang his second ball over the right gutter and get them both. The ball dropped into the gutter and he made another disgusted noise as the pin-setter knocked them back.

"Go for one," Ray admonished. "Always go for one. Who do you think you are, Billy Welu?"

"I didn't have english on the ball. A little more and *kazam*. Hi, Bart."

"Hello."

They shook hands all around.

"Good to meet you," Alan said. Then, to Ray: "Let's start a new string and let Bart in on it. You got my ass whipped in this one anyhow."

"Sure."

"Go ahead and go first, Bart," Alan said.

He hadn't bowled in maybe five years. He selected a twelve-pound ball that felt right to his fingers and promptly rolled it down the left-hand gutter. He watched it go, feeling like a horse's ass. He was more careful with the next ball but it hooked and he only go three pins. Ray rolled a strike. Alan hit nine and then covered the four pin.

At the end of the five frames the score was Ray 89, Alan 76, Bart 40. But he was enjoying the feeling of sweat on his back and the unaccustomed exertion of certain muscles that were rarely given the chance to show off.

He had gotten into the game enough that for a moment he didn't know what Ray was talking about when he said: "It's called malglinite."

He looked over, frowning a little at the unfamiliar word, and then understood. Alan was out front, holding his ball and looking seriously down at the four-six, all concentration.

"Okay," he said.

"It comes in sticks about four inches long. There are forty sticks. Each one has about sixty times the explosive force of a stick of dynamite."

"Oh," he said, and suddenly felt sick to his stomach. Alan rolled and jumped in the air when he got both pins for his spare.

He rolled, got seven pins, and sat down again. Ray struck out. Alan went to the ball caddy and held the ball under his chin, frowning down the polished lane at the pins. He gave courtesy to the bowler on his right, and then made his four-step approach.

"There's four hundred feet of fuse. It takes an electrical charge to set the stuff off. You can turn a blow-torch on it and it will just melt. It—oh, *good one! Good one, Al!*"

Al had made a Brooklyn hit and knocked them all back.

He got up, threw two gutterballs, and sat down again. Ray spared.

As Alan approached the line, Ray went on: "It takes electricity, a storage battery. You got that?"

"Yes," he said. He looked down at his score. 47. Seven more than his age.

"You can cut lengths of fuse and splice them together and get simultaneous explosion, can you dig it?"

"Yes."

Alan rolled another Brooklyn strike.

When he came back, grinning, Ray said: "You can't trust those Brooklyn hits, boy. Get it over in the right pocket."

"Up your ass, I'm only eight pins down."

He rolled, got six pins, sat down, and Ray struck out again. Ray had 116 at the end of seven.

When he sat down again Ray asked: "Do you have any questions?"

"No. Can we leave at the end of this string?"

"Sure. But you wouldn't be so bad if you worked some of the rust off. You keep twisting your hand when you deliver. That's your problem."

Alan hit the Brooklyn pocket exactly as he had on his two previous strikes, but this time left the seven-ten split and came back scowling. He thought, *this is where I came in.*

"I told you not to trust that whore's pocket," Ray said, grinning.

"Screw," Alan growled. He went for the spare and dropped the ball into the gutter again.

"Some guys," Ray said, laughing. "Honest to God, some guys never learn, you know that? They never do."

The Town Line tavern had a huge red neon sign that knew nothing of the energy crisis. It flicked off and on with mindless, eternal confidence. Underneath the red neon was a white marquee that said:

TONITE
THE FABULOUS OYSTERS
DIRECT FROM BOSTON

There was a plowed parking lot to the right of the tavern, filled with the cars of Saturday night patrons. When he drove in he saw that the parking lot went around to the back in an L. There were several parking slots left back there. He drove in next to an empty one, shut off the car, and got out.

The night was pitilessly cold, the kind of night that doesn't feel that cold until you realize that your ears went as numb as pump handles in the first fifteen seconds you were out. Overhead a million stars glittered in magnified brilliance. Through the tavern's back wall he could hear the Fabulous Oysters playing "After Midnight." J.J. Cale wrote that song, he thought, and wondered where he had picked up that useless piece of information. It was amazing the way the human brain filled up with road litter. He could remember who wrote "After Midnight," but he couldn't remember his dead son's face. That seemed very cruel.

The Custom Cab pickup rolled up next to his station wagon; Ray and Alan got out. They were all business now, both dressed in heavy gloves and Army surplus parkas.

"You got some money for us," Ray said.

He took the envelope out of his coat and handed it over. Ray opened it and riffled the bills inside, estimating rather than counting.

"Okay. Open up your wagon."

He opened the back (which, in the Ford brochures, was called the Magic Doorgate) and the two of them slid a heavy wooden crate out of the pickup and carried it to his wagon.

"Fuse is in the bottom," Ray said, breathing white jets out of his nose. "Remember, you need juice. Otherwise you might just as well use the stuff for birthday candles."

"I'll remember."

"You ought to bowl more. You got a powerful swing."

They got back into their truck and drove away. A few moments later he also drove away, leaving the Fabulous Oysters to their own devices. His ears were cold, and they prickled when the heater warmed them up.

*   *   *

When he got home, he carried the crate into the house and pried it open with a screwdriver. The stuff looked exactly as Ray had said it would, like waxy gray candles. Beneath the sticks and a layer of newspaper were two fat white loops of fuse. The loops of fuse had been secured with white plasic ties that looked identical to the ones with which he secure his Hefty garbage bags.

He put the crate in the living room closet and tried to forget it, but it seemed to give off evil emanations that spread out from the closet to cover the whole house, as though something evil had happened in there years ago, something that had slowly and surely tainted everything.

January 13, 1974

He drove down to the Landing Strip and crawled up and down the streets, looking for Drake's place of business. He saw crowded tenements standing shoulder to shoulder, so exhausted that it seemed that they would collapse if the buildings flanking them were taken away. A forest of TV antennas rose from the top of each one, standing against the sky like frightened hair. Bars, closed until noon. A derelict car in the middle of a side street, tires gone, headlights gone, chrome gone, making it look like a bleached cow skeleton in the middle of Death Valley. Glass twinkled in the gutters. All the pawnshops and liquor stores had accordion grilles across their plate glass windows. He thought: That's what we learned from the race riots eight years ago. How to prevent looting in an emergency. And halfway down Venner Street he saw a small storefront with a sign in Old English letters. The sign said:

DROP DOWN MAMMA COFFEEHOUSE

He parked, locked the car, and went inside. There were only two customers, a young black kid in an oversize pea coat who seemed to be dozing, and an old white boozer who was sipping coffee from a thick white porcelain mug. His hands trembled helplessly each time the mug approached his mouth. The boozer's skin was yellow and when he looked up his eyes were haunted with light, as if the whole man were trapped inside this stinking prison, too deep to get out.

Drake was sitting behind the counter at the rear, next to a two-burner hotplate. One Silex held hot water, the other black coffee. There was a cigar box on the counter with some change in it. There were two signs, crayoned on construction paper. One said:

MENU
Coffee 15¢
Tea 15¢
All soda 25¢
Balogna 30¢
PB&J 25¢
Hot Dog 35¢

The other sign said:

PLEASE WAIT TO BE SERVED!

All Drop In counter help are VOLUNTEERS and when you serve yourself you make them feel useless and stupid. Please wait and remember GOD LOVES YOU!

Drake looked up from his magazine, a tattered copy of *The National Lampoon*. For a moment his eyes

went that peculiar hazy shade of a man snapping his
mental fingers for the right name, and then he said:
"Mr. Dawes, how are you?"

"Good. Can I get a cup of coffee?"

"Sure can." He took one of the thick mugs off the
second layer of the pyramid behind him and poured.
"Milk?"

"Just black." He gave Drake a quarter and Drake
gave him a dime out of the cigar box. "I wanted to
thank you for the other night, and I wanted to make
a contribution."

"Nothing to thank me for."

"Yes there is. That party was what they call a bad
scene."

"Chemicals can do that. Not always, but sometimes.
Some boys brought in a friend of theirs last summer
who had dropped acid in the city park. The kid went
into a screaming fit because he thought the pigeons
were coming after him to eat him. Sounds like a *Reader's Digest* horror story, doesn't it?"

"The girl who gave me the mescaline said she once
plunged a man's hand out of the drain. She didn't
know afterwards if it really happened or not."

"Who was she?"

"I really don't know," he said truthfully. "Anyway,
here." He put a roll of bills on the counter next to the
cigar box. The roll was secured with a rubber band.

Drake frowned at it without touching it.

"Actually it's for this place," he said. He was sure
Drake knew that, but he needed to plug Drake's
silence.

Drake unfastened the rubber band, holding the bills
with his left, manipulating with that oddly scarred right.
He put the rubber band aside and counted slowly.

"This is five thousand dollars," he said.

"Yes."

"Would you be offended if I asked you where—"

"I got it? No, I wouldn't be offended. From the sale

of my house to this city. They are going to put a road through there."

"Your wife agrees?"

"My wife has no say in the matter. We are separated. Soon to be divorced. She has her half of the sale to do with as she sees fit."

"I see."

Behind them, the old boozer began to hum. It was not a tune; just humming.

Drake poked moodily at the bills with his right forefinger. The corners of the bills were curled up from being rolled. "I can't take this," he said finally.

"Why not?"

Drake said: "Don't you remember what we talked about?"

He did. "I've no plans that way."

"I think you do. A man with his feet planted in this world does not give money away on a whim."

"This is not a whim," he said firmly.

Drake looked at him sharply. "What would you call it? A chance acquaintance?"

"Hell, I've given money away to people I've never seen. Cancer researchers. A Save-the-Child Foundation. A muscular dystrophy hospital in Boston. I've never been *in* Boston."

"Sums this large?"

"No."

"And cash money, Mr. Dawes. A man who still has a use for money never wants to see it. He cashes checks, signs papers. Even playing nickle-ante poker he uses chips. It makes it symbolic. And in our society a man with no use for money hasn't much use for living, either."

"That's a pretty goddamned materialistic attitude for—"

"A priest? But I'm not that anymore. Not since this happened." He held up the scarred, wounded hand. "Shall I tell you how I get the money to keep this place on its feet? We came too late for the window-

dressing charities like the United Fund or the City
Appeal Fund. The people who work here are all retired, old people who don't understand the kids who
come in here, but want to be something besides just
a face leaning out of a third-story window watching
the street. I've got some kids on probation that scout
up bands to play for free on Friday and Saturday
night, bands that are just starting up and need the
exposure. We pass the hat. But mostly the grease
comes from rich people, the upper crust. I do tours. I
speak at ladies' teas. I tell them about the kids on
bummers and the Sterno freaks that sleep under the
viaducts and make newspaper fires to keep from freezing in the winter. I tell them about the fifteen-year-
old girl who'd been on the road since 1971 and came
in here with big white lice crawling all over her head
and her pubic hair. I tell them about all the VD in
Norton. I tell them about the fishermen, guys that
hang out in the bus terminals looking for boys on the
run, offering them jobs as male whores. I tell them
about how these young boys end up blowing some guy
in a theater men's room for ten dollars, fifteen if he
promises to swallow the come. Fifty percent for him
and fifty percent for his pimp. And these women, their
eyes go all shocked and then sort of melty and tender,
and probably their thighs get all wet and sloppy, but
they pony up and that's the important thing. Sometimes you can latch onto one and get more than a
ten-buck contribution. She takes you to her house in
Crescent for dinner, introduces you to the family, and
gets you to say grace after the maid brings the first
course. And you say it, no matter how bad the words
taste in your mouth and you rumple the kid's hair—
there's always one, Dawes, just the one, not like the
nasty rabbits down in this part of town that breed a
whole tenementful of them—and you say what a fine
young man you've got here, or what a pretty girl, and
if you're very lucky the lady will have invited some of
her bridge buddies or country club buddies to see this

sideshow-freak priest, who's probably a radical and running guns to the Panthers or the Algerian Freedom League, and you do the old Father Brown bit, add a trace of the auld Blarney, and smile until your face hurts. All this is known as shaking the money tree, and it's all done in the most elegant of surroundings, but going home it feels just like you were down on your knees and eating some AC/DC businessman's cock in one of the stalls at Cinema 41. But what the hell, that's my game, part of my 'penance' if you'll pardon the word, but my penance doesn't include necrophilia. And that, Mr. Dawes, is what I feel you are offering me. And that's why I have to say no."

"Penance for what?"

"That," said Drake with a twisted smile, "is between me and God."

"Then why pick this method of finance, if it's so personally repugnant to you? Why don't you just—"

"I do it this way because it's the only way. I'm locked in."

With a sudden, horrible sinking of despair, he realized that Drake had just explained why he had come here, why he had done everything.

"Are you all right, Mr. Dawes? You look—"

"I'm fine. I want to wish you the best of luck. Even if you're not getting anywhere."

"I have no illusions," Drake said, and smiled. "You ought to reconsider . . . anything drastic. There are alternatives."

"Are there?" He smiled back. "Close this place now. Walk out with me and we'll go into business together. I am making a serious proposal."

"You're making sport of me."

"No," he said. "Maybe somebody is making sport of both of us." He turned away, rolling the bills into a short, tight cylinder again. The kid was still sleeping. The old man had put his cup down half empty on the table and was looking at it vacuously. He was still humming. On his way by, he stuffed the roll of bills

into the old man's cup, splashing muddy coffee onto
the table. He left quickly and unlocked his car at the
curb, expecting Drake to follow him out and remon-
strate, perhaps save him. But Drake did not, perhaps
expecting him to come back in and save himself.

Instead, he got into his car and drove away.

January 14, 1974

He went downtown to the Sears store and bought an
automobile battery and a pair of jumper cables. Written on the side of the battery were these words,
printed in raised plastic:

DIE-HARD

He went home and put them in the front closet with
the wooden crate. He thought of what would happen
if the police came here with a search warrant. Guns
in the garage, explosives in the living room, a large
amount of cash in the kitchen. B. G. Dawes, desperate
revolutionary. Secret Agent X-9, in the pay of a foreign cartel too hideous to be mentioned. He had a
subscription to *Reader's Digest,* which was filled with
such spy stories, along with an endless series of crusades, anti-smoking, anti-pornography, anti-crime. It
was always more frightening when the purported spy
was a suburban WASP, one of *us.* KGB agents in
Willamette or Des Moines, passing microdots in the
drugstore lending library, plotting violent overthrow of
the republic at drive-in movies, eating Big Macs with
one tooth hollowed out so as to contain prussic acid.

Yes, a search warrant and they would crucify him.
But he was not really afraid anymore. Things seemed
to have progressed beyond that point.

January 15, 1974

"Tell me what you want," Magliore said wearily.

It was sleeting outside; the afternoon was gray and sad, a day when any city bus lurching out of the gray, membranous weather, spewing up slush in all directions with its huge tires, would seem like a figment of a manic-depressive's fantasies, when the very act of living seemed slightly psycho.

"My house? My car? My wife? Anything, Dawes. Just leave me alone in my declining years."

"Look," he said, embarrassed, "I know I'm being a pest."

"He knows he's being a pest," Magliore told the walls. He raised his hands and then let them fall back to his meaty thighs. "Then why in the name of Christ don't you *stop*?"

"This is the last thing."

Magliore rolled his eyes. "This ought to be beautiful," he told the walls. "What is it?"

He pulled out some bills and said, "There's eighteen thousand dollars here. Three thousand would be for you. A finder's fee."

"Who do you want found?"

"A girl in Las Vegas."

"The fifteen's for her?"

"Yes. I'd like you to take it and invest it in whatever operations you run that are good to invest in. And pay her dividends."

"Legitimate operations?"

"Whatever will pay the best dividends. I trust your judgment."

"He trusts my judgment," Magliore informed the walls. "Vegas is a big town, Mr. Dawes. A transient town."

"Don't you have connections there?"

"As a matter of fact I do. But if we're talking about some half-baked hippie girl who may have already cut out for San Francisco or Denver—"

"She goes by the name of Olivia Brenner. And I think she's still in Las Vegas. She was last working in a fast-food restaurant—"

"Of which there are at least two million in Vegas," Magliore said. "Jesus! Mary! Joseph the carpenter!"

"She has an apartment with another girl, or at least she did when I talked to her the last time. I don't know where. She's about five-eight, darkish hair, green eyes. Good figure. Twenty-one years old. Or so she says."

"And suppose I can't locate this marvelous piece of ass?"

"Invest the money and keep the dividends yourself. Call it nuisance pay."

"How do you know I won't do that anyway?"

He stood up, leaving the bills on Magliore's desk. "I guess I don't. But you have an honest face."

"Listen," Magliore said. "I don't mean to bite your ass. You're a man who's already getting his ass bitten. But I don't like this. It's like you're making me executor to your fucking last will and testament."

"Say no if you have to."

"No, no, no, you don't get it. If she's still in Vegas and going under this Olivia Brenner name I think I can find her and three grand is more than fair. It doesn't hurt me one way or the other. But you spook me, Dawes. You're really locked on course."

"Yes."

Magliore frowned down at the pictures of himself, his wife, and his children under the glass top of his desk.

"All right," Magliore said. "This one last time, all right. But no more, Dawes. Absolutely not. If I ever see you again or hear you on the phone, you can forget it. I mean that. I got enough problems of my own without diddling around in yours."

"I agree to that condition."

He stuck out his hand, not sure that Magliore would shake it, but Magliore did.

"You make no sense to me," Magliore said. "Why should I like a guy who makes no sense to me?"

"It's a senseless world," he said. "If you doubt it, just think about Mr. Piazzi's dog."

"I think about her a lot," Magliore said.

January 16, 1974

He took the manila envelope containing the checkbook down to the post office box on the corner and mailed it. That evening he went to see a movie called *The Exorcist* because Max von Sydow was in it and he had always admired Max von Sydow a great deal. In one scene of the movie a little girl puked in a Catholic priest's face. Some people in the back row cheered.

January 17, 1974

Mary called on the phone. She sounded absurdly relieved, gay, and that made everything much easier.

"You sold the house," she said.

"That's right."

"But you're still there."

"Only until Saturday. I've rented a big farmhouse

in the country. I'm going to try and get my act back together."

"Oh, Bart. That's so wonderful. I'm so glad." He realized why it was being so easy. She was being phony. She wasn't glad or not glad. She had given up. "About the checkbook . . ."

"Yes."

"You split the money right down the middle, didn't you?"

"Yes, I did. If you want to check, you can call Mr. Fenner."

"No. Oh, I didn't mean *that.*" And he could almost see her making pushing-away gestures with her hands. "What I meant was . . . you separating the money like that . . . does it mean . . ."

She trailed off artfully and he thought: *Ow, you bitch, you got me. Bull's eye.*

"Yes, I guess it does," he said. "Divorce."

"Have you thought about it?" she asked earnestly, phonily. "Have you *really*—"

"I've thought about it a lot."

"So have I. It seems like the only thing left to do. But I don't hold anything against you, Bart. I'm not mad at you."

My God, she's been reading all those paperback novels. Next she'll tell me she's going back to school. He was surprised at his bitterness. He thought he had gotten past that part.

"What will you do?"

"I'm going back to school," she said, and now there was no phoniness in her voice, now it was excited, shining. "I dug out my old transcript, it was still up in Mamma's attic with all my old clothes, and do you know I only need twenty-four credits to graduate? Bart, that's hardly more than a year!"

He saw Mary crawling through her mother's attic and the image blended with one of himself sitting bewildered in a pile of Charlie's clothes. He shut it out.

"Bart? Are you still there?"

"Yes. I'm glad being single again is going to fulfill you so nicely."

"Bart," she said reproachfully.

But there was no need to snap at her now, to tease her or make her feel bad. Things had gone beyond that. Mr. Piazzi's dog, having bitten, moves on. That struck him funny and he giggled.

"Bart, are you crying?" She sounded tender. Phony, but tender.

"No," he said bravely.

"Bart, is there anything I can do? If there is, I want to."

"No. I think I'm going to be fine. And I'm glad you're going back to school. Listen, this divorce—who gets it? You or me?"

"I think it would look better if I did," she said timidly.

"Okay. Fine."

There was a pause between them and suddenly she blurted into it, as if the words had escaped without her knowledge or approval: "Have you slept with anyone since I left?"

He thought the question over, and ways of answering: the truth, a lie, an evasion that might keep her awake tonight.

"No," he said carefully, and added: "Have you?"

"Of course not," she said, managing to sound shocked and pleased at the same time. "I wouldn't."

"You will eventually."

"Bart, let's not talk about sex."

"All right," he said placidly enough, although it was she who had brought the subject up. He kept searching for something nice to say to her, something that she would remember. He couldn't think of a thing, and furthermore didn't know why he would want her to remember him at all, at least at this stage of things. They had had good years before. He was sure they must have been good because he couldn't remember much of what had happened in them, except maybe the crazy TV bet.

He heard himself say: "Do you remember when we took Charlie to nursery school the first time?"

"Yes. He cried and you wanted to take him back with us. You didn't want to let him go, Bart."

"And you did."

She was saying something disclaiming in a slightly wounded tone, but he was remembering the scene. The lady who kept the nursery school was Mrs. Ricker. She had a certificate from the state, and she gave all the children a nice hot lunch before sending them home at one o'clock. School was kept downstairs in a made-over basement and as they led Charlie down between them, he felt like a traitor; like a farmer petting a cow and saying Soo, Bess on the way to the slaughterhouse. He had been a beautiful boy, his Charlie. Blond hair that had darkened later, blue, watchful eyes, hands that had been clever even as a toddler. And he had stood between them at the bottom of the stairs, stock-still, watching the other children who were whooping and running and coloring and cutting colored paper with blunt-nosed scissors, so *many* of them, and Charlie had never looked so vulnerable as he did in that instant, just watching the other children. There was no joy or fear in his eyes, only the watchfulness, a kind of *outsiderness,* and he had never felt so much his son's father as then, never so close to the actual run of his thoughts. And Mrs. Ricker came over, smiling like a barracuda and she said: *We'll have such fun, Chuck,* making him want to cry out: *That's not his name!* And when she put out her hand Charlie did not take it but only watched it so she stole his hand and began to pull him a little toward the others, and he went willingly two steps and then stopped, looked back at them, and Mrs. Young said very quietly: *Go right along, he'll be fine.* And Mary finally had to poke him and say *Come ON, Bart* because he was frozen looking at his son, his son's eyes saying, *Are you going to let them do this to me, George?* and his own eyes saying back, *Yes, I guess I am, Freddy* and he and Mary started up the stairs, showing Charlie their backs, the most dreadful thing a little child can see, and Charlie began to wail. But Mary's footsteps never faltered because a woman's love is strange and cruel and nearly always clear-sighted, love that sees is always horrible love, and she knew walking away was right and so she walked, dismissing the cries as only another part of the boy's development, like smiles from gas or scraped knees. And he had felt a pain in his chest so sharp, so physical, that he had wondered if he was having a heart attack, and then the pain had just passed, leaving him shaken and unable to interpret it, but now he thought that the pain had been plain old prosaic good-bye. Parents' backs aren't the most dreadful thing. The most dreadful thing of all is the speed with which children dismiss those same backs and turn to their own affairs—to the game, the puzzle, the new friend, and eventually to death. Those were the awful things he had come to know now. Charlie had begun dying long before he got sick, and there was no putting a stop to it.

"Bart?" she was saying. "Are you still there, Bart?"

"I'm here."

"What good are you doing yourself thinking about Charlie all the time? It's eating you up. You're his prisoner."

"But you're free," he said. "Yes."

"Shall I see the lawyer next week?"

"Okay. Fine."

"It doesn't have to be nasty, does it, Bart?"

"No. It will be very civilized."

"You won't change your mind and contest it?"

"No."

"I'll . . . I'll be talking to you, then."

"You knew it was time to leave him and so you did. I wish to God I could be that instinctive."

"What?"

"Nothing. Good-bye, Mary. I love you." He realized he had said it after he hung up. He had said it automatically, with no feeling—verbal punctuation. But it wasn't such a bad ending. Not at all.

January 18, 1974

The secretary's voice said: "Who shall I say is calling?"

"Bart Dawes."

"Will you hold for a moment?"

"Sure."

She put him in limbo and he held the blank receiver to his ear, tapping his foot and looking out the window at the ghost town of Crestallen Street West. It was a bright day but very cold, temperature about 10 above with a chill factor making it 10 below. The wind blew skirls of snow across the street to where the Hobarts' house stood broodingly silent, just a shell waiting for the wrecking ball. They had even taken their shutters.

There was a click and Steve Ordner's voice said: "Bart, how are you?"

"Fine."

"What can I do for you?"

"I called about the laundry," he said. "I wondered what the corporation had decided to do about relocation."

Ordner sighed and then said with good-humored reserve: "A little late for that, isn't it?"

"I didn't call to be beaten with it, Steve."

"Why not? You've surely beaten everyone else with it. Well, never mind. The board has decided to get out of the industrial laundry business, Bart. The laundromats will stay; they're all doing well. We're going to change the chain name, though. To Handi-Wash. How does that sound?"

"Terrible," he said remotely. "Why don't you sack Vinnie Mason?"

"Vinnie?" Ordner sounded surprised. "Vinnie's doing a great job for us. Turning into quite the mogul. I must say I didn't expect such bitterness—"

"Come on, Steve. That job's got no more future than a tenement airshaft. Give him something worthwhile or let him out."

"I hardly think that's your business, Bart."

"You've got a dead chicken tied around his neck and he doesn't know it yet because it hasn't started to rot. He still thinks it's dinner."

"I understand he punched you up a little before Christmas."

"I told him the truth and he didn't like it."

"Truth's a slippery word, Bart. I would think you'd understand that better than anyone, after all the lies you told me."

"That still bugs you, doesn't it?"

"When you discover that a man you thought was a good man is full of shit, it does tend to bug one, yes."

"Bug one," he repeated. "Do you know something, Steve? You're the only person I've ever known in my life that would say that. Bug one. It sounds like something that comes in a fucking aerosol can."

"Was there anything else, Bart?"

"No, not really. I wish you'd stop beating Vinnie, that's all. He's a good man. You're wasting him. And you know goddam well you're wasting him."

"I repeat: why would I want to 'beat' Vinnie?"

"Because you can't get to me."

"You're getting paranoid, Bart. I've got no desire to do anything to you but forget you."

"Is that why you were checking to see if I ever had personal laundry done free? Or took kickbacks from the motels? I understand you even took the petty cash vouchers for the last five years or so."

"Who told you that?" Ordner barked. He sounded startled, off balance.

"Somebody in your organization," he lied joyfully. "Someone who doesn't like you much. Someone who thought I might be able to get the ball rolling a little in time for the next director's meeting."

"Who?"

"Good-bye, Steve. You think about Vinnie Mason, and I'll think about who I might or might not talk to."

"Don't you hang up on me! Don't you—"

He hung up, grinning. Even Steve Ordner had the proverbial feet of clay. Who was it Steve reminded him of? Ball bearings. Strawberry ice cream stolen from the food locker. Herman Wouk. Captain Queeg, that was it. Humphrey Bogart had played him in the movie. He laughed aloud and sang:

"We all need someone to Queeg on,
  And if you want to, why don'tcha Queeg all over me?"

I'm crazy all right, he thought, still laughing. But it does seem there are certain advantages. It came to him that one of the surest signs of insanity was a man all alone, laughing in the middle of silence, on an empty street filled with empty houses. But the thought could not still his humor and he laughed louder, standing by the telephone and shaking his head and grinning.

January 19, 1974

After dark he went out to the garage and brought in the guns. He loaded the Magnum carefully, according to the directions in the instruction pamphlet, after dry-firing it several times. The Rolling Stones were on the stereo, singing about the Midnight Rambler. He couldn't get over what a fine album that was. He thought about himself as Barton George Dawes, Midnight Rambler, Visits by Appointment Only.

The .460 Weatherbee took eight shells. They looked big enough to fit a medium howitzer. When the rifle was loaded he looked at it curiously, wondering if it was as powerful as Dirty Harry Swinnerton had claimed. He decided to take it out behind the house and fire it. Who was there on Crestallen Street West to report gunshots?

He put on his jacket and started out the back door through the kitchen, then went back to the living room and got one of the small pillows that lay on the couch. Then he went outside, pausing to flick on the 200-watt yard light that he and Mary had used in the summer for backyard barbecues. Back here, the snow was as he had pictured it in his mind a little more than a week ago—untouched, unmarred, totally virgin. No one had foot-fucked this snow. In past years Don Upslinger's boy Kenny sometimes used the backyard express to get up to his friend Ronnie's house. Or Mary used the line he had strung kitty-corner between the house and garage to hang a few things (usually unmentionables) on days when it was too warm for them to freeze. But he himself always went to the garage by the breezeway and now it struck him as sort of marvelous—no one had been in his backyard since snow first fell, in late November. Not even a dog, by the look of it.

He had a sudden crazy urge to stride out into the middle, about where he set the hibachi every summer, and make a snow angel.

Instead he tucked the pillow up against his right shoulder, held it for a moment with his chin, and then pressed the butt plate of the Weatherbee against it. He glared down the sight with his left eye shut, and tried to remember the advice the actors always gave each other just before the gyrenes hit the beaches in the late-night war movies. Usually it was some seasoned veteran like Richard Widmark talking to some green private—Martin Milner, perhaps: *Don't jerk that trigger, son—SQUEEZE it.*

Okay, Fred. Let's see if I can hit my own garage.

He squeezed the trigger.

The rifle did not make a report. It made an explosion. At first he was afraid it had blown up in his hands. He knew he was alive when the recoil knocked him back against the kitchen storm door. The report traveled off in all directions with a curious rolling sound, like jet exhaust. The pillow fell in the snow. His shoulder throbbed.

"Jesus, Fred!" he gasped.

He looked at his garage and was hardly able to believe it. There was a splintered hole in the siding big enough to fit a teacup through.

He leaned the gun against the kitchen storm door and walked through the snow, never minding the fact that he had his low shoes on. He examined the hole for a minute, bemusedly prying up loose splinters with his forefinger, and then he went around and inside.

The exit hole was bigger. He looked at his station wagon. There was a bullet hole in the driver's side door, and the paint had been seared off to show bare metal around the concave hole, which was big enough for him to stick the tips of two fingers in. He opened the door and looked across the seat at the passenger door. Yes, the bullet had gone through there too, just below the door handle.

He walked around to the passenger side and saw where the bullet had exited, leaving another big hole, this time with tines of metal sticking balefully out. He turned and looked at the garage wall opposite where the bullet had entered. It had gone through that too. For all he knew, it was still going.

He heard Harry the gun shop proprietor saying: *So your cousin gut-shoots . . . this baby will spread his insides over twenty feet.* And what would it do to a man? Probably the same. It made him feel ill.

He walked back to the kitchen door, stooped to pick up his pillow, and went back into the house, pausing automatically to stamp his feet so he wouldn't track across Mary's kitchen. In the living room he took off his shirt. There was a red welt in the shape of the rifle's butt plate on his shoulder in spite of the pillow.

He went into the kitchen with his shirt still off and fixed a pot of coffee and a TV dinner. When he finished his meal he went into the living room and laid down on the couch and began to cry, and the crying rose to a jagged, breaking hysteria which he heard and feared but could not control. At last it began to trail off and he fell heavily asleep, breathing harshly. In his sleep he looked old and some of the stubble on his cheeks was white.

January 20, 1974

He woke with a guilty start, afraid it was morning and too late. His sleep had been as sodden and dark as old coffee, the kind of sleep he always woke from feeling stupid and cottonheaded. He looked at his watch and saw it was quarter past two. The rifle was where he had left it, leaning nonchalantly in the easy chair. The Magnum was on the end table.

He got up, went into the kitchen, and splashed cold water on his face. He went upstairs and put on a fresh shirt. He went back downstairs tucking it in. He locked all the downstairs doors, and for reasons he did not wish to examine too closely, his heart felt a tiny bit lighter as each tumbler clicked. He began to feel like himself again for the first time since that damnable woman had collapsed in front of him in the supermarket. He put the Weatherbee on the floor by the living room picture window and stacked the shells beside it, opening each box as he set it down. He dragged the easy chair over and set it on its side.

He went into the kitchen and locked the windows. He took one of the dining room chairs and propped it under the kitchen doorknob. He poured himself a cup of cold coffee, sipped it absently, grimaced, and dashed it into the sink. He made himself a drink.

He went back into the living room and brought out the automobile storage battery. He put it behind the overturned easy chair, then got the jumper cables and coiled them beside the battery.

He carried the case of explosive upstairs, grunting and puffing. When he got to the landing he set it down with a thump and blew out his breath. He was getting too old for this sort of bullshit, even though a lot of the laundry muscle from the days when he and his partner had lifted four-hundred-pound lots of ironed sheets onto the delivery trucks was still there. But muscle or no muscle, when a man got to be forty, some things were tempting fate. By forty it was attack time.

He went from room to room upstairs, turning on all the lights. The guest bedroom, the guest bathroom, master bedroom, the study that had once been Charlie's room. He put a chair under the attic trapdoor and went up there, turning on the dusty bulb. Then he went down to the kitchen and got a roll of electrician's tape, a pair of scissors, and a sharp steak knife.

He took two sticks of explosive from the crate (it was soft, and if you pressed it, you left fingerprints) and took them up to the attic. He cut two lengths of fuse and peeled the white insulation back from the copper core with the steak knife. Then he pressed each bare wire into one of the candles. In the closet, standing below the trapdoor now, he peeled the insulation from the other ends of the fuses and carefully attached two more sticks, taping the fuse firmly to each so that the peeled wire wouldn't pull free.

Humming now, he strung more fuse from the attic

into the master bedroom and left a stick on each of the twin beds. He strung more fuse from there down the hall and left a stick in the guest bathroom, two more in the guest bedroom. He turned off the lights as he left. In Charlie's old room he left four sticks, taped together in a cluster. He trailed fuse out the door and dropped a coil of it over the stairway railing. Then he went downstairs.

Four sticks on the kitchen counter, beside his bottle of Southern Comfort. Four sticks in the living room. Four in the dining room. Four in the hall.

He trailed fuse back into the living room, a little out of breath from going up and down stairs. But there was one more trip to make. He went back up and got the crate, which was considerably lighter now. There were only eleven sticks of explosive left inside it. The crate, he saw, had once contained oranges. Written on the side, in faded letters, was this word:

POMONA

Beside the word was a picture of an orange with one leaf clinging to the stem.

He took the crate out to the garage, using the breezeway this time, and put the box on the back seat of his car. He wired each stick of malglinite with a short fuse, then joined all eleven to a long length with electrician's tape and strung the long fuse back into the house, being careful to slip the fuse into the crack beneath the side door that opened onto the breezeway and then relocking it.

In the living room he joined the house master fuse with the one that came from the garage. Working carefully, still humming, he cut another length and joined it to the other two with electrician's tape. He payed this final fuse over to the battery and peeled the insulation from the end with the steak knife.

He separated the copper core wires and twisted each bunch into a little pigtail. He took the jumper cables and attached a black alligator clip to one pigtail, a red alligator clip to the other. He went to the storage battery and attached the other black alligator clip to the terminal marked:

POS

He left the red clip unhooked, lying beside the post marked

NEG

Then he went to the stereo, turned it on, and listened to the Rolling Stones. It was five minutes past four. He went to the kitchen, made himself another drink, and went back to the living room with it, suddenly at loose ends. There was a copy of *Good Housekeeping* on the coffee table. There was an article in it about the Kennedy family and their problems. He read the article. After that he read an article titled "Women and Breast Cancer." It was by a woman doctor.

They came at a little past ten, just after the bells of the Congregational Church five blocks over had rung in the hour, calling people to matins, or whatever in hell the Congregationalists called them.

There was a green sedan and a black-and-white police car. They pulled up at the curb and three men got out of the green sedan. One of them was Fenner. He didn't know who the other two were. Each of them had a briefcase.

Two policemen got out of the black-and-white and leaned against it. It was obvious from their attitudes that they expected no trouble; they were discussing something as they leaned against the hood of the black-and-white, and their words came out of their mouths in visible white puffs.

Things stopped.

Stoptime,
January 20, 1974

Well fred this is it i guess put up or shut up time oh
i know in one sense it's too late to shut up i've got
explosives strung all over the house like birthday dec-
orations a gun in my hand and another one in my belt
like fucking john dillinger well what do you say this
is the last decision like climbing a tree i pick this fork
then i pick that fork now this now that

(the men frozen in tableau outside in the hallway
between seconds fenner in a green suit one foot six
inches off the pavement as it steps forward good shoes
clad in low fashionable rubbers if there is such a thing
as fashionable rubbers his green topcoat flapping open
like a crusading attorney in a tv lead-in his head is
slightly turned slightly cocked the man in back of him
has made some comment and fenner is cocking his
head to catch it the man who has spoken has a white
plume half out of his mouth this second man is wearing a blue blazer and dark brown pants his topcoat is
also open and the wind has caught it stoptime has
caught his topcoat in midflap and the third man is just
turning from the car and the cops are leaning against
their black-and-white with their heads turned to one
another they could be discussing anything marriage or
a tough case or the shitty season the musties had or
the state of their balls and the sun has come through
the scud overhead just enough to make a single twin-
kle on a single shell of one policeman's assigned
equipment said shell pushed through one of many little leather loops on said policeman's belt the other
cop is wearing shades and the sun has pricked out a
compass point on the right lens and his lips are thick

sensual caught at the beginning of a smile: this is the photograph)

i'm going ahead freddy my boy do you have anything you'd care to say at this auspicious moment at this point in the proceedings yes says fred you're going to hold out for the newspeople aren't you i sure am says george the words the pictures the newsreels demolition i know has only the point of visibility but freddy does it strike you how lonely this is how all over this city and the world people are eating and shitting and fucking and scratching their eczema all the things they write books about while we have to do this alone yes i've considered that george in fact i tried to tell you something about it if you'll recall and if it's any consolation to you this seems right right now it seems okay because when you can't move you can give them their roadwork but please george don't kill anybody no not on purpose fred but you see the position i am in yes i see i understand by george i'm scared now i'm so scared no don't be scared i'm going to handle this and i'm in perfect control myself

roll it

January 20, 1974

"Roll it," he said aloud, and everything began to move.

He put the rifle to his shoulder, sighted on the right front wheel of the police cruiser, and pulled the trigger.

The gun kicked crushingly against his shoulder and the muzzle jerked upward after the bullet had been fired. The large living room window burst outward, leaving only jagged hunks protruding from the molding like impressionistic glass arrows. The cruiser's front tire did not flatten; it exploded with a loud bang, and the whole car shuddered on its springs like a dog that had been kicked while asleep. The hubcap flew off and rattled aimlessly on the frozen composition surface of Crestallen Street West.

Fenner stopped and looked unbelievingly at the house. His face was raw with shock. The fellow in the blue blazer dropped his briefcase. The other fellow had better reflexes, or perhaps a more developed sense of self-preservation. He wheeled and ran around the green sedan, crouched low, and disappeared from sight.

The policemen moved right and left, behind their own cruiser. A moment later the one wearing sunglasses bounced up from behind the hood, his service revolver held in both hands, and fired three times. The gun made an innocuous popping sound after the Weatherbee's massive crack. He fell behind his chair and heard the bullets pass overhead—you really could hear them, and the noise they made in the air was zzizzz!—and bury themselves in the plaster above the couch. The sound they made entering the plaster reminded him of the sound fists made hitting the heavy bag in a gymnasium. He thought: that's what they'd sound like going into me.

The cop wearing sunglasses was shouting at Fenner and the man in the blue blazer. "Get down! Goddammit, get down! He's got a fucking howitzer in there!"

He raised his head a little more to see better and the cop in the sunglasses saw him do it and fired twice more. The bullets thudded into the wall and this time Mary's favorite picture, "Lobstermen" by Winslow Homer, fell off the wall, hit the couch, and then went to the floor. The glass facing on the picture shattered.

He raised his head again because he had to see what was happening (why hadn't he thought to get a kid's periscope?), he had to see if they were trying to flank him which was how Richard Widmark and Marty Milner always took the Jap pillboxes on the late movies, and if they were trying to do that he would have to try to shoot one, but the cops were still behind their cruiser and Fenner and the guy in the blue blazer were dashing behind the green car. Blue Blazer's briefcase lay on the sidewalk like a small dead animal. He aimed at it, wincing at the recoil of the big rifle even before it came, and fired.

CRRRACKK! and the briefcase exploded into two pieces and jumped savagely into the air, flapping, disgorging a flutter of papers for the wind to stir an invisible finger through.

He fired again, this time at the right front wheel of the green sedan, and the tire blew. One of the men behind the car screamed in soprano terror.

He looked over at the police car and the driver's side door was open. The cop with the sunglasses was lying half in on the seat, using his radio. Soon all the partygoers would be here. They were going to give him away, a little piece of anyone who wanted one, and it would not be personal anymore. He felt a relief that was as bitter as aloes. Whatever it had been, whatever mournful sickness that had brought him to this, the last crotch of a tall tree, it was not his alone anymore, whispering and crying in secret. He had joined the mainstream of lunacy, he had come out of the closet. Soon they could reduce him to safe headline—SHAKY CEASE-FIRE HOLDS ON CRESTALLEN STREET.

He put the rifle down and scrambled across the living room floor on his hands and knees, being careful not to cut himself on the glass from the shattered picture frame. He got the small pillow and then scrambled back. The cop was not in the car anymore.

He picked up the Magnum and put two shots across their bow. The pistol bucked heavily in his hand, but the recoil was manageable. His shoulder throbbed like a rotted tooth.

One of the cops, the one without sunglasses, popped up behind the cruiser's trunk to return his fire and he sent two bullets into the cruiser's back window, blow-

ing it inward in a twisted craze of cracks. The cop
ducked back down without firing.

"Hold it!" Fenner bawled. "Let me talk to him!"

"Go ahead," one of the cops said.

"Dawes!" Fenner yelled toughly, sounding like a
detective in the last reel of a Jimmy Cagney movie.
(The police spotlights are crawling relentlessly back
and forth over the front of the sleazy slum tenement
where "Mad Dog" Dawes has gone to ground with a
smoking .45 automatic in each hand. "Mad Dog" is
crouched behind an overturned easy chair, wearing a
strappy T-shirt and snarling.) *"Dawes, can you hear
me in there!"*

(And "Mad Dog," his face twisted with defiance—
although his brow is greased with sweat—screams
out:)

"Come and get me, ya dirty coppers!" He bounced
up over the easy chair and emptied the Magnum into
the green sedan, leaving a ragged row of holes.

"Jesus!" somebody screamed. "Oh Jesus he's nuts!"

"Dawes!" Fenner yelled.

"You'll never take me alive!" he yelled, delirious
with joy. "You're the dirty rats who shot my kid
brother! I'll see some of ya in *hell* before ya get me!"
He reloaded the Magnum with trembling fingers and
then put enough shells into the Weatherbee to fill its
magazine.

"Dawes!" Fenner yelled again. *"How about a
deal?"*

"How about some hot lead, ya dirty screw!" he
screamed at Fenner, but he was looking at the police
car and when the cop wearing sunglasses put his head
stealthily over the hood, he sent him diving with two
shots. One of them went through the picture window
of the Quinns' home across the street.

"Dawes!" Fenner yelled importantly.

One of the cops said: "Oh shut the fuck up. You're
just encouraging him."

There was an embarrassed silence and in it the

sound of sirens, still distant, began to rise. He put the Magnum down and picked up the rifle. The joyous delirium had left him feeling tired and achey and needing to shit.

Please let them be quick from the TV stations, he prayed. Quick with their movie cameras.

When the first police car screamed around the corner in a calculated racing drift like something out of *The French Connection* he was ready. He had fired two of the howitzer shells over the parked cruiser to make them stay down, and he drew a careful bead on the grille of the charging cruiser and squeezed the trigger like a seasoned Richard Widmark-type veteran and the whole grille seemed to explode and the hood flew up. The cruiser roared straight over the curb about forty yards up the street and hit a tree. The doors flew open and four cops spilled out with their guns drawn, looking dazed. Two of them walked into each other. Then the cops behind the first cruiser (*his* cops, he thought of them with a trace of propriety) opened fire and he submarined behind the chair while the bullets whizzed above him. It was seventeen minutes of eleven. He thought that now they would try to flank him.

He stuck his head up because he had to and a bullet droned past his right ear. Two more cruisers were coming up Crestallen Street from the other direction, sirens whooping, blue lights flashing. Two of the cops from the crashed cruiser were trying to climb the stake fence between the sidewalk and the Upslingers' backyard and he fired the rifle at them three times, not firing to hit or miss but only to make them go back to their car. They did. Wood from Wilbur Upslinger's fence (ivy climbed on it in the spring and summer) sprayed everywhere, and part of it actually fell over into the snow.

The two new cruisers had pulled up in a V that blocked the road in front of Jack Hobart's house. Police crouched in the apex of the V. One of them was talking to the police in the crash cruiser on a walkie-talkie. A moment later the newest arrivals began laying down a heavy pattern of covering fire, making him duck again. Bullets struck the front door, the front of the house, and all around the picture window. The mirror in the front hall exploded into jumbled diamonds. A bullet punched through the quilt covering the Zenith TV, and the quilt danced briefly.

He scrambled across the living room on his hands and knees and stood up by the small window behind the TV. From here he could look directly into the Upslingers' backyard. Two policemen were trying the flanking movement again. One of them had a nosebleed.

Freddy, I may have to kill one of them to make them stop.

Don't do that, George. Please. Don't do that.

He smashed the window with the butt of the Magnum, cutting his hand. They looked around at the noise, saw him, and began to shoot. He returned their fire and saw two of his bullets punch holes in Wilbur's new aluminum siding (had the city recompensed him for that?). He heard bullets punching into his own house just below the window and on both sides of it. One whined off the frame and splinters flew in his face. He expected a bullet to rip off the top of his head at any moment. It was hard to tell how long the exchange went on. Suddenly one of the cops grabbed his forearm and cried out. The cop dropped his pistol like a child that has grown tired of a stupid game. He ran in a small circle. His partner grabbed him and they began to run back toward their crashed cruiser, the unhurt one with his arm around his partner's waist.

He dropped to his hands and knees and crawled back to the overturned chair and peeked out. Two more cruisers on the street now, one coming from each end. They parked on the Quinns' side of the street and eight policemen got out and ran behind the cruiser with the flat tire and the green sedan.

He put his head down again and crawled into the hall. The house was taking very heavy fire now. He knew he should take the rifle and go upstairs, he would have a better angle on them from up there, could maybe drive them back from their car to cover in the houses across the street. But he didn't dare go that far from the master fuse and the storage battery. The TV people might come at any time.

The front door was full of bullet holes, the dark brown varnish splintered back to show the raw wood underneath. He crawled into the kitchen. All the windows were broken in here and broken glass littered the linoleum. A chance shot had knocked the coffee-pot from the stove and it lay overturned in a puddle of brown goo. He crouched below the window for a moment, then bounced up and emptied the Magnum into the V-parked cars. Immediately fire intensified on the kitchen. Two bullet holes appeared in the white enamel of the refrigerator and another struck the Southern Comfort bottle on the counter. It exploded, spraying glass and southern hospitality everywhere.

Crawling back to the living room he felt something like a bee sting in the fleshy part of his right thigh just below the buttocks, and when he clapped his hand to it, his fingers came away bloody.

He lay behind the chair and reloaded the Magnum. Reloaded the Weatherbee. Poked his head up and ducked back down, wincing, at the ferocity of fire that came at him, bullets striking the couch and the wall and the TV, making the quilt shimmy. Poked his head up again and fired at the police cars parked across the street. Blew in one window. And saw—

At the top of the street, a white station wagon and a white Ford van. Written in blue letters on the sides of both was:

WHLM NEWSBEAT
CHANNEL 9

Panting, he crawled back to the window that looked out on the Upslingers' side yard. The news vehicles were crawling slowly and dubiously down Crestallen Street. Suddenly a new police car shot around them and blocked them off, tires smoking. An arm dressed in blue shot out of the cruiser's back window and began waving the newsmobiles off.

A bullet struck the windowsill and jumped into the room at an angle.

He crawled back to the easy chair, holding the Magnum in his bloody right hand and screamed: *"Fenner!"*

The fire slackened a little.

"Fenner!" he screamed again.

"Hold on!" Fenner yelled. *"Stop! Stop a minute!"*

There were a few isolated pops, then nothing.

"What do you want?" Fenner called.

"The news people! Down behind those cars on the other side of the street! I want to talk to them!"

There was a long, contemplative pause.

"No!" Fenner yelled.

"I'll stop shooting if I can talk to them!" That much was true, he thought, looking at the battery.

"No!" Fenner yelled again.

Bastard, he thought helplessly. Is it that important to you? You and Ordner and the rest of you bureaucratic bastards?

The firing began again, tentatively at first, then gaining strength. Then, incredibly, a man in a plaid shirt and blue jeans was running down the sidewalk, holding a pistol-grip camera in one hand.

"I heard that!" the man in the plaid shirt yelled. "I heard every word! I'll get your name, fella! He offered to stop shooting and you—"

A policeman hit him with a waist-high flying tackle and the man in the plaid shirt crunched to the sidewalk. His movie camera flew into the gutter and a moment later three bullets shattered it into winking pieces. A clockspring of unexposed film unwound lazily from the remains. Then the fire flagged again, uncertainly.

"Fenner, let them set up!" he hollered. His throat felt raw and badly used, like the rest of him. His hand hurt and a deep, throbbing ache had begun to emanate outward from his thigh.

"Come out first!" Fenner yelled back. *"We'll let you tell your side of it!"*

Rage washed over him in a red wave at this barefaced lie. *"GODDAMMIT, I'VE GOT A BIG GUN HERE AND I'LL START SHOOTING AT GAS TANKS YOU SHITBIRD AND THERE'LL BE A FUCKING BARBECUE WHEN I GET DONE!"*

Shocked silence.

Then, cautiously, Fenner said: "What do you want?"

"Send that guy you tackled in here! Let the camera crew set up!"

"Absolutely not! We're not giving you a hostage to play games with all day!"

A cop ran over to the listing green sedan bent low and disappeared behind it. There was a consultation.

A new voice yelled: *"There's thirty men behind your house, guy! They've got shotguns! Come out or I'll send them in!"* Time to play his one ratty trump. *"You better not! The whole house is wired with explosive. Look at this!"*

He held the red alligator clip up in the window.

"Can you see it?"

"You're bluffing!" the voice called back confidently.

"If I hook this up to the car battery beside me on the floor, everything goes!"

Silence. More consultation.

"Hey!" someone yelled. "Hey, get that guy!" He poked his head up to look and here came the man in the plaid shirt and jeans, right out into the street, no protection, either heroically sure of his own profession or crazy. He had long black hair that fell almost to his collar and a thin dark moustache.

Two cops started to charge around the V-parked cruisers and thought better of it when he put a shot over their heads.

"Jesus Christ what a snafu!" somebody cried out in shrill disgust.

The man in the plaid shirt was on his lawn now, kicking up snow-bursts. Something buzzed by his ear, followed by a report, and he realized he was still looking over the chair. He heard the front door being tried, and then the man in the plaid shirt was hammering on it.

He scrambled across the floor, which was now spotted with grit and plaster that had been knocked out of the walls. His right leg hurt like a bastard and when he looked down he saw his pants leg was bloody from thigh to knee. He turned the lock in the chewed-up door and released the bolt from its catch.

"Okay!" he said, and the man in the plaid shirt burst in.

Up close he didn't look scared although he was panting hard. There was a scrape on his cheek from where the policeman had tackled him, and the left arm of his shirt was ripped. When the man in the plaid shirt was inside he scrambled back into the living room, picked up the rifle, and fired twice blindly over the top of the chair. Then he turned around. The man in the plaid shirt was standing in the doorway, looking incredibly calm. He had taken a large notebook out of his back pocket.

"All right, man," he said. "What shit goes down?"

"What's your name?"

"Dave Albert."

"Has that white van got more film equipment in it?"

"Yes."

"Go to the window. Tell the police to let a camera crew set up on the Quinns' lawn. That's the house across the street. Tell them if it isn't done in five minutes, you got trouble."

"Do I?"

"Sure."

Albert laughed. "You don't look like you could kill time, fella."

"Tell them."

Albert walked to the shattered living room window and stood framed there for a second, obviously relishing the moment.

"He says for my camera crew to set up across the street!" he yelled. *"He says he's going to kill me if you don't let them!"*

"No!" Fenner yelled back furiously. *"No, no, n—"*

Somebody muzzled him. Silence for a beat.

"All right!" This was the voice that had accused him of bluffing about the explosive. *"Will you let two of our men go up and get them?"*

He thought it over and nodded at the reporter.

"Yes!" Albert called.

There was a pause, and then two uniformed policemen trotted self-consciously up toward where the news van waited, its engine smugly idling. In the meantime two more cruisers had pulled up, and by leaning far to the right he could see that the downhill end of Crestallen Street West had been blocked off. A large crowd of people was standing behind the yellow crash barriers.

"Okay," Albert said, sitting down. "We got a minute. What do you want? A plane?"

"Plane?" he echoed stupidly.

Albert flapped his arms, still holding his notebook. "Fly away, man. Just flyyyyy away."

"Oh." He nodded to show that he understood. "No, I don't want a plane."

"Then what do you want?"

"I want," he said carefully, "to be just twenty with a lot of decisions to make over again." He saw the look in Albert's eyes and said, "I know I can't. I'm not that crazy."

"You're shot."

"Yes."

"Is that what you said it is?" He was pointing at the master fuse and the battery.

"Yes. The main fuse goes to all the rooms in the house. Also the garage."

"Where did you get the explosive?" Albert's voice was amiable but his eyes were alert.

"Found it in my Christmas stocking."

He laughed. "Say, that's not bad. I'm going to use that in my story."

"Fine. When you go back out, tell all the policemen that they better move away."

"Are you going to blow yourself up?" Albert asked. He looked interested, nothing more.

"I am contemplating it."

"You know what, fellow? You've seen too many movies."

"I don't go to the movies much anymore. I did see *The Exorcist,* thought. I wish I hadn't. How are your movie guys coming out there?"

Albert peered out the window. "Pretty good. We've got another minute. Your name is Dawes?"

"Did they tell you that?"

Albert laughed contemptuously. "They wouldn't tell me if I had cancer. I read it on the doorbell. Would you mind telling me why you're doing all this?"

"Not at all. It's roadwork."

"The extension?" Albert's eyes glowed brighter. He began to scribble in his book.

"Yes, that's right."

"They took your house?"

"They tried. I'm going to take it."

Albert wrote it down, then snapped his book closed and stuffed it into his back pocket again. "That's pretty stupid, Mr. Dawes. Do you mind my saying that? Why don't you just come out of here with me?"

"You've got an exclusive," he said tiredly. "What are you trying for, the Pulitzer Prize?"

"I'd take it if they offered it." He smiled brightly

and then sobered. "Come on, Mr. Dawes. Come on out. I'll see that your side gets told. I'll see—"

"There is no side."

Albert frowned. "What was that?"

"I have no side. That's why I'm doing this." He peered over the chair and looked into a telephoto lens, mounted on a tripod that was sunk into the snow of the Quinns' lawn. "Go on now. Tell them to go away."

"Are you really going to pull the string?"

"I really don't know."

Albert walked to the living room door and then turned around. "Do I know you from somewhere? Why do I keep feeling like I know you?"

He shook his head. He thought he had never seen Albert before in his life.

Watching the newsman walk back across his lawn, slightly at an angle so the camera across the street would get his good side, he wondered what Olivia was doing at that precise second.

He waited fifteen minutes. Their fire had intensified, but no one charged at the back of the house. The main purpose of the fire seemed to be to cover their retreat into the houses across the street. The camera crew remained where it was for a while, grinding impassively away, and then the white Econoline van drove up onto the Quinns' side lawn and the man behind the camera folded the tripod, took it behind the truck, and began to film again.

Something black and tubular whizzed through the air, landed on his lawn about midway between the house and the sidewalk, and began to spurt gas. The wind caught it and carried it off down the street in tattered rifts. A second shell landed short, and then he heard one clunk on the roof. He caught a whiff of that one as it fell into the snow covering Mary's begonias. His nose and eyes filled with crocodile tears.

He scurried across the living room on his hands and knees again, hoping to God he had said nothing to that newsman, Albert, that could be misconstrued as profound. There was no good place to make your stand in the world. Look at Johnny Walker, dying in a meaningless intersection smashup. What had he died for, so that the sheets could go through? Or that woman in the supermarket. The fucking you got was never worth the screwing you took.

He turned on the stereo and the stereo still worked. The Rolling Stones album was still on the turntable and he put on the last cut, missing the right groove the first time when a bullet smacked into the quilt covering the Zenith TV with a thud.

When he had it right, the last bars of "Monkey Man" fading into nothingness, he scurried back to the overturned chair and threw the rifle out the window. He picked up the Magnum and threw that out after it. Good-bye, Nick Adams.

"You can't always get what you want," the stereo sang, and he knew that to be a fact. But that didn't stop you from wanting it. A tear gas canister arched through the window, struck the wall over the couch, and exploded in white smoke.

"But if you try sometimes, you might find,
You get what you need."

Well, let's just see, Fred. He grasped the red alligator clip in his hand. Let's see if I get what I need.

"Okay," he muttered, and jammed the red clip on the negative pole of the battery.

He closed his eyes and his last thought was that the world was not exploding around him but inside him, and while the explosion was cataclysmic, it was not larger than, say, a good-sized walnut.

Then white.

Epilogue

The WHLM newsteam won a Pulitzer Prize for their coverage of what they called "Dawes' Last Stand" on the evening news, and for a half-hour documentary presented three weeks later. The documentary was called "Roadwork" and it examined the necessity—or lack of it—for the 784 extension. The documentary pointed out that one reason the road was being built had nothing to do with traffic patterns or commuter convenience or anything else of such a practical sort. The municipality had to build so many miles of road per year or begin losing federal money on all inter-state construction. And so the city had chosen to build. The documentary also pointed out that the city was quietly beginning a litigation against the widow of Barton George Dawes to recover as much of their money as was recoverable. In the wake of the outcry the city dropped its suit.

Still photographs of the wreckage ran on the AP wire and most of the newspapers in the country carried them. In Las Vegas, a young girl who had only recently enrolled in a business school saw the photographs while on her lunch hour and fainted.

Despite the pictures and the words, the extension went ahead and was completed eighteen months later, ahead of schedule. By that time most of the people in the city had forgotten the "Roadwork" documentary, and the city's news force, including Pulitzer winner David Albert, had gone on to other stories and crusades. But few people who had been watching the original newsclip broadcast on the evening news ever forgot that; they remembered even after the facts surrounding it grew blurry in their minds.

That news clip showed a plain white suburban house,

sort of a ranch house with an asphalt driveway to the
right leading to a one-car garage. A nice-looking house,
but totally ordinary. Not a house you'd crane to look
at if you happened to be on a Sunday drive. But in
the news footage the picture window is shattered. Two
guns, a rifle and a pistol, come flying out of it to lie
in the snow. For one second you see the hand that
has flung them, the fingers held limply up like the
hand of a drowning man. You see white smoke blowing around the house, Mace or teargas or something.
And then there is a huge belch of orange flame and
all the walls of the house seem to bulge out in an
impossible cartoon convexity and there is a huge deto-
nation and the camera shakes a little, as if in horror.
Peripherally the viewer is aware that the garage has
been destroyed in a single ripping blast. For a second
it seems (and slow motion replays prove that the eye's
split-second impression is correct) that the roof of the
house has lifted off its eaves like a Saturn rocket. Then
the entire house blows outward and upward, shingles
flying, hunks of wood lofted into the air and then re-
turning to earth, something that looks like a quilt
twisting lazily in the air like a magic carpet as debris
rattle to the ground in a thudding, contrapuntal
drum roll.

There is stillness.

Then the shocked, tear-streaming face of Mary
Dawes fills the screen; she is looking with drugged and
horrified bewilderment at the forest of microphones
being thrust into her face, and we have been brought
safely back to human things once more.